The Last KuT.

Graham Banks

Acknowledgements.

My thanks to Jane and Ian Baker for the inspiration, to my wife for her patience and to my family and friends who are consciously or unconsciously always influencing the direction of my thoughts.

Additional thanks go to Don and Phil Everly, John Lennon and Paul McCartney, The Poni Tails, Roy Orbison, Sir Edward Elgar, Claude Debussy, Neil Diamond, Bobby Vee, Joni Mitchell, Paolo Conti, Bob Dylan, Gilbert Bécaud, Lesley Gore, Jimmy Hendrix, Maurice Ravel, Leonard Cohen, Luciano Pavarotti, Marie Leforêt, Daft Punk, Chakra Bleu and Edith Piaf for providing the 'soundtrack.'

Last but not least thanks to Tim Hunt for his brilliant cover design.

To George.

Hoping that he and his generation will restore our country's sanity.

Prologue

I love all things, not because they are passionate or sweet-smelling but because, I don't know, because this ocean is yours, and mine: these buttons and wheels and little forgotten treasures, fans upon whose feathers love has scattered its blossoms, glasses, knives and scissors - all bear the trace of someone's fingers on their handle or surface, the trace of a distant hand lost in the depths of forgetfulness.

Pablo Neruda

1969 - *Normandy*

She was alone in the house. The boy was at school. The kitchen window overlooking the flower garden was open, the pink Albertine roses still reflecting the patina of early morning spring dew, the pungent smell of blue irises mingling with the heady scent of the red geraniums. On the radio a Mozart piano concerto. The recipe for the *madeleines* was propped up against the bread bin. Since moving to Normandy, she had tried hard to keep up with her reading and longed to forget what might have been if she had finished her degree course on early 20th century French literature. She was on her third reading of Proust's *'In Search of Lost Time.'* She still could not get her head around the long sentences but the hyper-sensitivity of Charles Swann and his literary awakenings in Combray resonated with her own discoveries of rural Norman life, childhood, beauty, love, life and death. At heart she considered herself nostalgic not for times remembered but rather for times she had never known. She looked at her face in the mirror and smiled, not too displeased with what she saw. Few wrinkles to speak of and only a few traces of greying hair. She reckoned that her eyes could still sparkle and her lips still full enough to imagine wanting to be kissed. As for the rest of her body she was happy that the mirror was too small to show her spreading figure. Hadn't her mother always told her to watch her weight, weight gain was in the family genes but at least her breasts looked good and with the right bra she was still happy with her cleavage.

What might have been and what should have been were questions she was always asking herself. Today she had loaded her old Renault van with the flowers and plants for the afternoon market. It gave her immense satisfaction to see the results of her work in the garden. Since buying the cottage she had managed to cultivate a sizeable plot which kept her fully occupied from February to November with seasonal harvesting of spring daffodils and tulips to summer geraniums, peonies and gladioli. For one hectic week at the end of October it was the ubiquitous Autumn French chrysanthemums which proved popular as the French spent a small fortune on decorating the family tombs on All Souls' Day replacing the plastic artificial bouquets with which the dead were honoured for the other 11 months of the year. She reasoned that growing and selling flowers and plants on a market stall 4 days a week was not a bad way of making a living and probably preferable to teaching French literature to sullen French students in a *lycée* in a Parisian '*quartier chaud.'* The choice was hypothetical of course. Giving birth at 19 had put a stop to any academic ambitions. Since being widowed and quitting Paris 10 years ago she had turned her hand to English teaching, French teaching, embroidery classes for ex-pats and flower arranging. Her husband had been a junior partner in an Anglo-French Architecture business in Paris. He seemed to be doing well but his choice of friends was a little bizarre. Since the heady days of May '68 he'd maintained his links with the communists. He was fond of telling her that it wasn't the Russian brand of communism rather a sort of communitarianism – more in the socialist sense of caring for the community, but she remained unconvinced. The rot had set in when quite by chance she had discovered he was leading a double life. His partners in the business saw him as the slightly eccentric Englishman, passionate rugby player, committed hard-left socialist with a penchant for left bank intellectuals meeting in smoke filled Parisian basements discussing Sartre and listening to Memphis Slim and Little Joe Turner. What most of them didn't know was that when he'd finished in the office he donned a blond wig, a three-piece tweed suit, heels and went under the name of Collette.

She wondered if you could ever really get to know someone even after living with them for several years. The cynic in her believed everyone had something to hide. In the run up to the '68 *évènements* he'd been a full-blooded young political activist. He had been involved in several skirmishes with the forces of law and order. He had come home face splattered in blood after demonstrating on the *Boulevard St Germain*. He had left the house the same morning carrying a 'jemmy' hidden under his jacket apparently an expert in prising up Parisian cobbles to use as projectiles against the police. She had begged him to see reason and to stay clear of trouble. 'You're an Englishman, this isn't your problem.' She had even considered fleeing back to England with their son but financial considerations and her love of the French way of life made that a difficult decision. She had been doing some deep cleaning of the apartment when she found the blond wig under the mattress. Initially she thought that it had been left behind by a previous tenant. She had confronted him later that day and after blustering ignorance for a while he unconvincingly said that it was a prop from one of his Rugby club parties. Pushing him further he grew angry and told her not to make such a fuss about something so inconsequential. Not willing to leave it at that he had pushed her aside and charged out of the apartment. He did not come back home that evening. It wasn't the first time that he had stayed away but this time she wondered whether something serious might have happened. She called some of his friends without success and then the next morning whilst she was feeding her son breakfast he reappeared. He seemed preoccupied and she thought it better to avoid the subject of the wig. Later in the day, when she looked, the wig had gone.

Over the following weeks his behaviour became increasingly aggressive. The blond wig wasn't mentioned. He seemed touchy about everything; from how she cared for their son to the radio stations she tuned in to and the music she played. He criticised her for being a bad mother and objected to her friends whom he claimed were indoctrinating her with bourgeois ideas and that she had no idea of what life was all about. Arriving home drunk one night he slapped her face for wearing too much makeup, threw her copy of Proust into the garbage can and emptied the contents of her sewing box onto the floor saying that she should go out and get a job instead of wasting her time on sentimental literature and making 'twee' copies of French children's' clothes. He started pushing her towards the wall. She had little answer to his brute force. She made a grab for anything within her reach and flung it in his direction. Casserole lid, flower vase, mixing bowl all weaponised. This only exacerbated his anger. He growled and grunted like a front row forward engaging the scrum. In desperation she picked up the scissors and aimed them dartlike in his direction. The scissors struck home. He rubbed his shoulder and in a moment of absolute horror she noticed a trickle of blood running down his back. He turned to her with a look of surprise and hatred. Slamming the door she heard him leaping down the stairs two at a time and then silence. The drops of blood were slowly spreading over the tiled floor. The boy was standing behind her, shaking and wet eyed. He clutched his ragged teddy and wrapped his little arms around her legs. She slumped to the floor.

He failed to return to the house. She had cleaned up the apartment, wiped the dried blood from the floor, carefully rearranged the contents of her embroidery box and pushed it away in a cupboard already full of broken toys, discarded household tools and other miscellaneous items. She made a mental note to take the boxes to the next *brocante* sale.

The days passed and still no sign of him. Her anger, fury and pride stopped her from contacting his friends and no one rang her. No sign either of his friend Gregoire whose visits to the house had become a regular feature during the street troubles.

A few days later she was sewing one afternoon, the boy was at the nursery when the doorbell rang. Opening the door, she was met by the concierge accompanied by a uniformed gendarme. She had been expecting the worst, but nothing could have prepared her for the reality. Since the incident with the scissors she had wondered where he had stormed off to. Had he gone to casualty for treatment or had her attack on him proved worse than she imagined and he had collapsed in some back alley or fallen into the cold fast flowing Seine? The gendarme asked to enter and closing the door he politely thanked the concierge who was hanging about hoping for some titbit of gossip.

✂

His body, or what was left of it was found under a metro train at *Trocadéro*. It had been early evening, a Saturday, Parisians were on their way to dinner parties, restaurants and concert halls or on their way home from shopping. The train driver on *ligne 6* applied the brakes when he saw a figure falling to the track, but too late, half of the train had entered the platform before the brakes took hold. Passengers absorbed in *'Match'* or *'Paris Soir'* initially oblivious of what was unfolding fell against one another as the train came to an abrupt halt. The station was closed. Shocking and distressing as it was most passengers considered it as one of those things that occasionally happened on the Paris Metro. They left the station more concerned as to how they could complete the rest of the journey on time. It took the authorities several hours to clear the line. The body was unidentifiable but the *'carte de séjour'* stated that it was an Englishman working at The Sorbonne. An Englishman wearing a blond wig and tweed suit. At first it was considered suicide, but later eye-witness reports made it clear that he'd been pushed by an unidentified male companion. A brown-haired man probably in his 40's wearing a trench coat and carrying a leather briefcase.

There was a brief single paragraph tucked away in the weekend 'news' section in Monday's *'Figaro.'* Accidents such as this were not uncommon on the city's metro system and despite the horrific events most people dismissed the story as relatively banal and moved on. The article contained a couple of eye-witness accounts from fellow travellers at the *Trocadéro* station. A young couple reported having seen a blonde woman fall in front of the train. An older man had told the police that he had seen someone rush forward and push the victim on to the tracks. The platform had been crowded on an early Saturday evening but the authorities had quickly cleared the station and a forensic team had immediately started the gruesome task of identification. The *médicin légiste* inevitably took some time to ascertain the cause of death but eventually reported that it was probable that the victim had been pushed to his death by person or persons unknown. A later news report stated that a 47-year-old academic was being held in police custody. He was named as Gregoire St. Marc a bachelor with no criminal record.

Chapter One

July 1944 - North of England

Eunice was sitting on the bed surrounded by a dress pattern and pieces of flower-print cotton fabric. In front of the window was a treadle sewing machine. From outside the summer sun streamed into the room. She could hear the steam locomotive making its regular late afternoon journey to the glass factory. A few cars passed by making their way in the direction of Liverpool and the coalman's shire horse and cart could be heard clip clopping along the road. She was in a happy contemplative mood this afternoon. The war was ending. The Allied invasion of Normandy a month ago had been a success and the less reported fall of Rome a couple of days earlier. Thousands of troops were heading towards Paris and best of all she was getting married at the end of September.

She picked up the letter from the bedside table. Smudge the cat jumped onto the bed and stretched out on the dress material. The letter was from her older brother. Eric was a corporal in the West Kent Regiment based in Italy. She had read the letter several times trying to capture the real essence of front-line Army life, but it was difficult what with the censor's strict editing and the need for brevity. It had been several weeks since the letter had arrived, and she was aching for more news from the Italian Front. She unfolded the flimsy air-mail paper and started reading aloud. Smudge yawned, licked his paws and fell asleep.

Sun. June 18ᵗʰ.
(CMF) Combined Mediterranean Force, Italy.

To all at home,

I think I can echo your sentiments regarding the invasion. I don't think anyone in England could have had their ears glued any closer to the loudspeaker than us on that eventful morning. The first announcements were quoting the German radio as having put over the news of the paratroop landings but we have been caught before and it took the official BBC news to convince us. In the Eighth Army News a reporter said that he'd just got out a super story on the fall of Rome ("I was there" sort of thing) and when the other news broke his story became back page news.

It seems to take the BBC all their time to mention Italy in their news- bulletins these days.

Last night I was listening to the German news in English and they announced, in between slandering "Churchill and his Jewish gang" gave us a terrifically frightening account of their secret weapons. He said London was in flames and the whole of the South Coast was being bombarded by pilotless planes. Why doesn't someone enlighten him about the real news?

For about the past ten days we have been having sweltering weather here, something like N. Africa and it was so hot you could hardly move around. Today, however it's broken and we're having a rare old thunderstorm and I'm now sitting in my bivouac after just checking up whether or not it's been leaking. It's clearing up a bit now but I think there's more to come.

The countryside here is very beautiful after the rain and with a bit of imagination I could well imagine myself in England. The harvest seems to be going quite well and apparently the Germans in their hasty retreat haven't bothered to do anything about it. Their trucks don't seem able to move an inch during daylight and the ditches are crammed with shot-up German vehicles – the Air Force certainly have them taped.

Am glad to hear you got the photographs OK and that you liked them. I'm afraid the handbag must have gone astray as it's quite a long time now since I sent it. It seems that's Cairo's chief trade – selling souvenirs to troops.

Well, that's about all for the present, let's hope they get moving pretty quickly in France, we're getting fed up with the war. Rather good

news the bombing of Japan. What we need is
more of it.

So long for the present.
Love to all at home.
Eric.

She folded the letter and carefully placed it back in the blue envelope. She knew little about the war overseas, hard news was difficult to come by. The fall of Rome was overshadowed by the invasion of France but even that had been surrounded by propaganda and lack of detail. She and her parents and her other brother Alan had listened religiously to the BBC news bulletins on the valve radio reported by Richard Dimbleby and John Snagge. Prime Minister Churchill had made a rousing speech in The Commons on the 6th June. Back home she had felt the direct menace of bombardment when Hitler had thrown his Luftwaffe fire power on to Liverpool and its docks. At that time, she and her family and neighbours had spent night after night in the air raid shelter down the road playing endless card games and listening to the relentless thud of aerial bombardment.

She smiled as she recalled Eric's comments about the leather handbag. He had bought it whilst on leave in Cairo before he landed on the Italian beaches at Salerno. She still held out hope that one day it would arrive. Perhaps I'll have it in time for the wedding she thought to herself. A perfect addition to the 'going-away' honeymoon outfit. The church had been booked and it would be just a small family affair plus a couple of close friends. Pity that Eric would not be back for the wedding. He was hardly going to get leave for his sister's wedding when the 8th Army was advancing up the spine of Italy. From what she had learned from the press and radio it was likely that he had been involved in the battles and eventual capture of Monte Cassino. From there the troops had advanced on Rome which was liberated on the 4th June. She wondered whether her brother had made it to the 'Eternal City.'

She had followed Eric's progress from his call-up in 1942 to his initial training in Scotland, his last home-leave before heading across the Mediterranean to Oman in Algeria and then on to neighbouring Tunisia. After the success of the North African campaign his regiment set off to Southern Italy where they landed on the perilous beaches of Salerno. Now they had defeated the Germans in their once mighty stronghold of Monte Cassino and were pushing northwards. It was clear that victory was in sight.

She had met Bill through work. He was an engineer, a reserved occupation during the war and she was doing secretarial work in the same company. Bill lived on the opposite side of town in a traditional mining area. A small back-to-back Victorian terrace which until recently he had shared with his mother and two unmarried sisters. A far from ideal situation from which he was eager to break away. Then quite unexpectedly two weeks ago his mother died of a severe stroke. It was a cruel blow to Bill who had also lost his father prematurely a couple of years earlier. They decided to go ahead with the wedding. All was organised. The local church booked, the banns due to be read and best of all they had booked their honeymoon in a Blackpool hotel on the seafront with a view of the tower and the 'Golden Mile.' The war had brought much misery to some and moments of happiness to others. You took your chances where you could and prayed for a brighter future.

The honeymoon dress was still in the planning stage. She had managed to save enough rationing coupons to buy the length of cotton fabric and she'd found the pattern in the same fabric shop. She loved the flowery design of the material and considered it a great antidote to the austerity of the past four years.

She 'shooed' Smudge away from the already cut-out front of the dress. Jumping off the bed he knocked the scissors to the floor. She bent down to pick them up knowing well some of the superstitions about dropped scissors and unfaithful love and death. She wasn't superstitious. Superstition was for the old and poorly educated. Her mother always told her that if scissors were dropped you had to ask someone else to pick them up. Worse still if the fallen scissors should stick in the floor heaven only knew what gloom and doom would descend on the unlucky seamstress. Anyway, there was no one near to pick up the scissors. She stroked the scissor handles gently. Her mother had passed the scissors on to her and she took a pride in admiring the delicately engraved initials of her parents on the blades. 'K' and 'T.' Kate and Thomas. The entwined snake design intrigued her, and she wondered about the history of the scissors. Her mother had told her about Signora Louise, an Italian couturier and neighbour. It was Louise who had made her wedding dress. Eunice wished she had known Signora Louise. An Italian couturier who had lived and worked in France would have made an interesting friend.

Her thoughts returned to Eric fighting in Italy. What did she really know about her eldest brother? Intelligent and well educated. Keen cyclist. Smoker and occasional beer drinker. Amateur accordionist. It was always difficult to be the youngest sister with two older brothers. She rarely shared in their social life. She didn't know whether he had a girlfriend. Imagine going off to war without leaving behind a romantic attachment? Perhaps she had missed something. He never mentioned girls in any of his letters home and she doubted the lurid stories propagated by the popular press of British and American army personnel frequenting the numerous brothels of Naples. Her geography wasn't too hot, and she wondered how far away Cassino was from Naples. She would dig out Alan's old atlas of Europe later and look it up. Anyway, she secretly envied the fact that despite the war he was seeing something of the world. Scotland, Algeria, Tunisia and Italy. Places that she could never imagine herself visiting. Well, a honeymoon in Blackpool would be more than most could have expected in 1944 she reasoned.

Now for the back. She knew she would have to be exact in her measuring and cutting. Picking up the scissors she started to cut around the already marked out back section of the dress. The scissors cut well. She carefully followed the chalk marks. Dress making always gave her a great feeling of satisfaction and she took pride in knowing that the result was usually a success. It was Friday and she and Bill were going to The Hippodrome to see the latest Billy Wilder film *'Double Indemnity'* starring Barbara Stanwyck and she was sure he would be asking about the progress of the dress. She enjoyed the cinema and the escape it gave from the daily drudge of war. She loved the darkness, the larger-than-life screen idols, Jimmy Stewart, Bogart, Trevor Howard and Celia Johnston. They'd share a packet of 'Players' and a tub of vanilla ice-cream. She looked forward to the end of the supporting film when the lights would temporarily go up and the usherette would appear with her tray and beaming smile. They'd finish the ice-cream whilst watching the adverts and settle comfortably into their red plush seats awaiting the start of the main feature. They avoided the back row seats where her mother had frequently warned her, 'you never know what the men get up to in the dark.' She and Bill would hold hands whilst watching the film but that was as far as they would go. A short goodbye kiss at the bus stop would keep her happy until the honeymoon. She was less certain of Bill holding out that long. The proximity of others and the mutual complicity of air-raid shelter life had begun to nibble away at pre-war sexual mores but marrying a virgin still counted for much. They had both known several couples who had been forced into early marriage and in spite of the family shame and gossip who could blame them when war promised little happiness for tomorrow. Happiness was where you found it whether in the dark recesses of the shelter or against the wall in the back alley.

Smudge yawned and stretched out his fore paws on a late afternoon sunbeam. Above the nearly threadbare grey carpet dust motes floated like landlocked plankton. A distant motorbike put-putted its way from the direction of town. The 22-trolley bus stopped on the opposite side of the road setting down an elderly couple laden down with shopping bags. As the cream and red bus moved silently away the sound of the motorbike grew louder. Downstairs she could hear her mother raking out the fire. Despite the warm July day the sombre living room was cold in the evening and a fire was always lit winter or summer, the kettle filled at the ready. The radio was tuned to The BBC Home Service for the afternoon transmission of 'Music while you Work.' The familiar strains of Eric Coate's *'Calling all Workers'* always made her smile with its optimistic innocence. Outside in the street the noise of the motor bike was getting louder as it approached from town. Her father would be arriving home from work at the local glass factory later and the first thing he would do would be to take a briar pipe from the pipe rack at the side of the fireplace, pack it with a wad of Dunhill light flake, always Dunhill, light it, puff three or four times until it took hold and then sit in his favourite armchair and wait for the cup of tea to be poured.

She stretched up to put her elbows on the window ledge as she realised that the motorbike she had heard coming up the road had eventually stopped in front of her house. She just managed to catch a view of a uniformed man closing the metal latch on the small front gate. There was a knock on the front door; her mother could be heard unlocking the door. A few words followed and then silence. Moments later the motor bike spluttered back into life and disappeared back down the road towards town. The radio had been turned off. Smudge pricked up his ears and mewed loudly. She stood up and for the second time that afternoon the scissors fell to the floor unnoticed. She stood at the top of the flight of stairs and listened. Slowly she descended the linoleum covered stairs until she reached the curtained off square that separated the small hall from the living room. She parted the heavy velvet curtain calling out 'Mum are you alright?' The room was now in semi-darkness with just a faint glow from the fireplace illuminating the polished surface of the oak dining table. The clock was ticking loudly. Her mum was sitting on the sofa her head in her hands clutching a light brown telegram.

Chapter Two

October 1950

I was sitting on the wooden front-gate my short-trousered legs dangling freely into the space below. I was watching the small, black locomotive that steamed by every afternoon at the same hour on its way between the glass factory and the good's yard. Its rhythmical movements and puffs of white smoke comforting and dependable. It reminded me of my favourite book, *'Thomas the Tank Engine.'*

'Thomas was a cheeky little engine,' I chuckled. Grandfather, affectionately known as Pop said nothing. He clamped his unlit pipe firmly between his teeth and gazed up the road. His tall stature, his balding head and black waistcoat gave him an air of some importance that instilled a sense of awe in my young self. I had just spent the last 15 minutes listening to the humming valve radio. *'Listen With Mother'* was one of my favourites with Fauré's evocative piano music followed by the soothing voice of Daphne Oxenford. 'Are you sitting comfortably? Then I'll begin.' I was disappointed that there was no train story today. It had been a story of a tugboat lost in fog, but I preferred trains. I put my hand in my pocket to touch the shiny shilling that my uncle had given me earlier on in the day. Next door I could see the window of the sweet shop and if I looked hard enough I could make out the rows of jars on the shelves full of the delights that my shilling could buy. Liquorice all sorts, gob stoppers, aniseed balls, sherbet dips, dolly mixtures – all so hard to resist but my mum had made me promise not to spend the shilling until we took the bus and train back home but that was still 3 long days away and I wasn't sure I could wait that long.

'Will they be here soon?' I half-turned and looked up into the face of Pop who was gripping me tightly under the arms.

'In a couple of minutes or so if the match finishes on time.' He strained his head to look up the road. 'First ones are coming now; they'll have left before final whistle to avoid rush.'

I watched anxiously as the first group of men, for they were only men, walked past the gate. Dressed in shabby overcoats and without exception flat caps of uniform colours of grey and black. Cigarettes clamped between their lips. Their demeanour glum. Some nodded in Pop's direction with a half-hearted 'How do, Tom.' More a statement than a question of personal welfare.

'Looks like they've lost again.'

The groups of men soon joined up into a continuous stream. I had never seen so many people in one place in my young life. Where were they going? The crowd seemed oblivious to the two of us at the gate. Pop called out to no one in particular, 'Lost again 'ave they?'

A voice from a group nearest to the gate looked our way.

'Aye 7-9' Wigan again. A lucky Mather try I'll tell ya.'

As a child of 4½ years I had no reason to know that this Saturday was the St Helens versus Wigan Rugby League 'Derby.' The crunch match – the semi-final of the Lancashire Cup. Two of the oldest clubs and founding members of the Rugby Football League locked in 'mortal' combat. Forget cricket's Ashes, Liston against Ali, McEnroe versus Connors, football's England v Scotland this was in these parts the sporting match that really mattered. The 'Derby' matches had been going for 55 years and the rivalry was as intense as ever.

The hordes kept coming. 'Looks like a good crowd today,' Pop said to no one in particular. 'Got to be thirty thousand.'

'Is that a big or a very big number?' I asked.

Pop smiled and just said, 'enough. Let's go and see how them tomato plants are doing in greenhouse. The late ones will need picking before winter sets in.'

He put me down onto the concrete path and paused to relight his pipe. I ran on ahead to the back of the house where the small garden was surrounded by a high brick wall and beyond that row upon row of industrial terrace houses separated by the occasional 'back entry' or 'alley' – a narrow passageway giving access to the backs of the houses. Plumes of coal smoke drifted from soot-stained chimney stacks. Lines of washing fluttered in the breeze.

Although my grandfather has been dead for nearly fifty years, I only have to brush against a tomato plant and release the heady fruity scent to be transported back to the small garden greenhouse in the 30's semi-detached house of my maternal grandparents. Today Pop was explaining to me his 5-year-old grandson the intricacies of cross pollination (using a rabbit's tail on the end of a wooden stick, of course) and how many trusses one plant can support. Feeling bored I ran back into the house where my grandma' was sewing. Nan was sitting in front of the black kitchen range, a grand sombre affair with a pile of freshly cut kindling sticks set to one side and a kettle coming to the boil on the other. Old, grey Smudge the cat asleep on the fireside rug.

'When will mum and dad be back?' My parents had gone visiting my dad's sister. An antisocial 5-year-old I had pleaded to be left behind. I hated the old miner's cottage with its dark rooms and unseen dogs barking out the back. My aunt was kind but over fussy and insisted on taking me to visit all the neighbours which I hated. I should have gone I know. Young children rarely see the pleasure that they can bring to others.

'They'll be back soon I expect. They'll smell the tea brewing.'

Nan was prematurely grey and slightly deaf. When she was happy she sang whilst preparing the Sunday roast. Her favourite was *'I Dreamed I Dwelt in Marble Halls.'* She always cooked kippers for Friday lunch. Every morning the same ritual. The chamber pot covered in a tea towel brought down-stairs and taken to the outside 'lav' to be emptied.

Listening to Radio Luxembourg with big earphones in the evening. No television back then. Today she was sewing. She was using a strange pair of scissors. They fascinated me. The handles were in the form of elaborately carved serpents. On the blades were the letters 'K' 'T'.

'Why are there letters on those scissors?' I asked and then noticing the coiled serpents, grimaced and blurted out, 'I don't like snakes.'

'Oh, there's nothing wrong with snakes. They frighten some people and there's others who have the 'gift' of seeing them but you needn't bother yourself with that.'

'I don't want to see a snake Nan.'

'Not to worry there's none around here. Anyway, the letters on the scissors – can't you guess? They're mine and Pop's names. 'K' for Kate and 'T' for Thomas. When we were planning to get married I asked a dressmaker to make my wedding dress. Her name was Louise Ceccaroli. Her husband Ely carved the initials. I think they were Italian. It was a beautiful dress made of organza and lace. Cost a fortune. Took all my dad's savings.'

Louise was the name of the couturier. She and her husband Elio Ceccaroli (he quickly took on the northern soubriquet of Ely) had come from Northern Italy to find work. They had spent several years in the Champagne Ardennes region of Northeast France where the cutlery factory in Nogent needed skilled workers. Their son Alessandro and daughter Marie Claire were both born in Nogent, but they found the town claustrophobic and unwelcoming to foreigners, so they packed their bags once more and headed for England. Her husband found work in the cutlery industry of Sheffield but when foreign competition began to bite they crossed the Pennines to Manchester where her husband took on labouring jobs in the building trade and did some part-time metal engraving. Louise ran a successful small dress-making business from home specialising in work overalls, but occasionally more lucrative business came her way in the form of wedding dresses or ball gowns for those who had the money or were thrifty enough to save.

With her long dark hair and black eyes, Louise still maintained the vestiges of a once beautiful young girl although the long months of travelling across Europe and the harsh conditions of early 20th century industrial Lancashire took their toll. Weakened she succumbed to the 1918 flu pandemic aged 42 but not before making my grandmother's wedding dress and handing over her precious 'snake' embroidery scissors as a wedding 'present' but insisting that my grandparents gave her a penny in return. Traditional Italian superstition still held sway in her family. Never give scissors away at risk of cutting the friendship. A simple financial transaction would ensure good blood. A week later her husband Elio also died. Officially be too had fallen victim to the Spanish flu, but local talk said that it was due to a broken heart.

Elio who had originally made the scissors had engraved my grandparents' initials on the blades – 'K' 'T'. After his premature death, their two children now aged 12 and 10 were orphans. The neighbours clubbed together to raise enough money to send the children back to their hometown in Maniago, Italy where they were taken in by a cousin of their mother.

I asked if I could hold the scissors for a moment. Nan placed the scissors on the table. 'You must never put scissors into other hands. Always place them on the table first or you will bring bad luck. My dressmaker told me a lot about Italian superstitions. They're very sharp, be careful. They were sharpened only last week by the knife grinder.'

I guessed that superstition was something vaguely bad but I was lost when it came to the knife grinder.

I tentatively picked up the scissors from the table and holding them carefully between my fingers I hesitatingly stroked the snake patterned handles. I shuddered involuntarily. I most certainly did not like snakes. I ran my index finger around the engraved initials. 'What is a knife grinder, Nan?' I asked.

'He's a man on a bicycle who comes round the streets every so often to sharpen knifes and scissors and such like. He has a stone wheel that he turns with his pedals and runs the knife blade along the cutting edge. You can hear him coming because he whistles. He's a lovely man but he's getting old and he finds the pedalling more and more difficult.'

'I wish I could whistle. My dad can whistle.'

I ran to the window and looked out. 'Will he be coming again today; perhaps he can teach me how to whistle.'

'No, love. He won't be around for a few months now.' I'll tell him next time that you want to learn how to whistle.'

I tried to carefully hand the scissors back to Nan forgetting what I had earlier been told.

'No, you must always place them on the table first remember.' Nan snapped. 'You must always be careful with scissors. Scissors and snakes are quite magical.' I was about to ask what was magical about scissors and snakes but before I could open my mouth I heard the front gate open and the sound of my parents' footsteps on the path. I ran to meet them.

Mum and dad came through from the kitchen. 'Well, you were missed this afternoon. Aunty had prepared some nice cakes for you. She was disappointed.' Dad said half-heartedly knowing full well my feelings for the dank, dark house slowly subsiding into the hidden mine workings below. 'What have you been up to then? Hope you haven't spent that shilling that uncle gave you.'

I explained about the football crowd, the steam engine and Pop's tomatoes. 'I've been using Nan's special magical snake scissors,' I continued. 'They're very sharp because a man on a bike whistles and makes them sharp again.'

Mum looked bemused. 'Oh, you mean the dress making scissors. Yes, they are very special. If scissors could talk they'd tell a good tale.'

'What do you mean a good tail? The cat has a tail. Why do scissors have a tail?'

'No not that sort of tail. A tale is a sort of story.'

'Like *'Thomas the Tank Engine'* you mean?'

'Well sort of,' laughed my mum.

I failed to follow the gist of the conversation but before I could ask more Nan began to pour the hot water into the teapot. I wanted to ask if I could play with the accordion that mum had told me had once belonged to her brother Eric but the moment was lost. I wanted to know more about Eric who wasn't around anymore but I would have to wait.

'Now, how about a nice cup of tea? Go and call Pop in from the greenhouse will you, tell him his tea is ready.' Old Smudge the cat rolled over and stretched contentedly in front of the fire.

Chapter Three

68 years later - Carcassonne, France

The shop wasn't difficult to find. Some clever arty type on the local council had strung hundreds of coloured parasols from the roofs overhanging the narrow streets. Great idea when the sun shines he wondered but what will happen when the *tramontane* the cold, dry northwest wind funnelled by the Pyrenees and Massif Central blows in? Today the sky was blue, and the gentle breeze barely moved the suspended parasols or were they coloured umbrellas – was there a difference he mused? It wasn't Bob Martin's first visit to Carcassonne. He had visited the *faux medieval cité* as he liked to call it with his son Jim as a child and they had spent their time exploring the tatty souvenir shops and eating in the *pizzerias* and *creperies*. The *cité* was fun in a 'trippy' fashion but he avoided falling in with the culture snobs who seemed to despise anything that was remotely popular with 'the masses.' The medieval city had been reconstructed by Viollet le Duc in the 19th century. He used his extensive knowledge of medieval architecture to reconstruct and romantically embellish the site. It worked and was a huge success and Carcassonne was firmly established on the tourist trail.

Now he was in the lower town. He'd located the flower shop on his smartphone's satnav app. He turned right off the *Place*

Carnot and entered a narrow street lined with derelict boarded up shops. The old quarter of the town was hardly looking prosperous. He spotted *Fleurs de Alice* almost at once. A couple of trellis tables filled with pots overflowing with hibiscus, agapanthus, geraniums and fuchsia. By the door, a sandwich board carved in the shape of Louis Carrol's Alice holding a large sunflower. He paused by the open door taking in the heady delights of fresh blooms and recently watered plants. He noticed a large '*A Vendre*' notice. So she's selling up he thought to himself. Near the door a greying, older man was precariously balancing on a step ladder watering the hanging baskets with a long-spouted watering can.

'*Regardez le sol, c'est un peu glissant.*' He stepped down and placed the watering can on the counter.

Bob Martin tentatively walked in not sure of what he was going to say. The old man smiled and wiped his palms on his green apron.

'*Puis-je vous aider – un bouquet d'automne peut-être ou une orchidée ?*'

'No, no actually I was wondering if I could speak to Alice. It is Alice Woods who owns the shop, Alice the English lady?'

Slipping easily into English he replied, 'Probably, you mean Alice Clopé. I'm afraid that Madam Alice has just slipped out for a few moments but she should be back soon if you'd care to wait.'

✂

He had first met Alice when they were teenagers. There was a party one winter's evening. He first noticed her standing alone by the door. A petite brunette with a great figure. Attractive but in an unconventional way. He wondered whether she was arriving or leaving. He had tried to strike up a conversation but she feigned disinterest and walked away. Later they bumped into each other in the kitchen. He thought she looked lonely. He touched her arm and asked for a dance. She refused his advances with a cold unsmiling shrug. He told himself to forget it, there were other fish in the sea. Try as he might the rejection had stung more than he cared to admit. A couple of months later he was at a regular Friday youth club dance when he saw her dancing with another girl. He tried to avoid eye contact. To his surprise she came across and asked if he wanted to dance. A local band was playing a poor cover version of The Beatles' 'I Wanna Hold Your Hand.' She grabbed his arm and pulled him onto the dance floor. Later, he walked her home. They held hands and kissed. It was the beginning of his first serious love affair and the first time he had ever wondered what made girls 'click.' For Bob she broke all the rules of what his immature brain considered beautiful. Looking back, he considered that her face had been constructed to some long-lost plan, an architect of the bizarre had been at work. Eyes too far apart, nose too long, mouth too wide and hair disobeying all the rules of the stylist's handbook, breasts perhaps too heavy for one so young, but she was as close as you can get to being stunning in Bob's eyes. Alice no enigmatic Da Vinci smile more a cubism period Picasso. A scramble of body parts but like a Picasso painting a real work of art.

It was a pivotal moment in Bob's young life. The following weekend he spent with his parents rambling over the Malvern Hills. Amazed by life's unfathomable coincidences he recalled how Alice had told him on their first date how her dad loved Elgar's 'Enigma Variations' and how he loved the first variation dedicated to his dear wife Alice. Bob knew little about the life of the great English composer but he had recently seen a TV documentary of the young Elgar riding his bike over the hills and the music had stuck in his mind. Having a wife called Alice was surely a portent.

In the pub after the long walk, downing a pint to the juke box accompaniment of the great Roy Orbison singing *'It's Over.'* He remembered the shocked look on his dad's face as he ordered a pint of 'Double Diamond' but nothing, not even his father's disapproval was going to shake young Bob from the delicious discovery of romantic love. Henceforth Edward and Roy would always transport him back to that wonderful April day when romanticism was first etched into his DNA. That it would prove to be a double-edged sword was in the future. On returning home he spent a month's pocket money on Edward and Roy. The smell of newly pressed vinyl. What an evocative memory! 'Mercury,' 'Parlophone,' 'Colombia,' 'London', 'RCA', 'EMI.' Years later he would argue that he could still smell the vinyl pressings and no he insisted it wasn't a simple trick of memory.

He wandered round the shop pretending to look at the assorted vases of roses, lilies and giant sunflowers. What was it about French florists that made them so special? Everyone loves flowers he supposed although he did recall an ex-girlfriend who detested them. Said they reminded her of death. The relationship unsurprisingly hadn't lasted. He was still thinking about that first kiss when he brushed against a large vase of pungent orange Asiatic lilies when a heavily accented voice from behind said,

'*Attention, monsieur le pollen peut vous salir.*' He turned to see a short, stout woman probably in her 60's. Her ample breasts displayed prominently in a not unappealing *décolletage.*

'*Oui madame*, I know.' He struggled for the right words in French but in the end blurted out in English. 'I've lost count of the number of white shirts I've sent to the dry cleaners after a brush with a bouquet of these beauties.'

'Ah, an Englishman seeking flowers for his wife or mistress perhaps?' She smiled questioningly tilting her head uncertainly to one side. 'I'm Alice. Can I help?'

Suddenly confronted by someone he hadn't seen for 50 years Bob was lost in shock, no idea of what to say or do. The brown eyes still sparkled with mischief, the once chestnut hair now tinted streaky blonde, the freckled nose at the centre of a round full face and the full lips still seductive but what to say? What was the protocol for such occasions? Fling his arms around her? Offer an outstretched hand and a polite 'let me introduce myself?' Before he could decide Alice took a couple of steps forward, turned to deadhead a yellow dwarf potted rhododendron, placed her hands on her hips and admonished Bob.

'For Christ's sake Bob, what took you so long to get here?' Unselfconsciously she stepped forward and gave him a warm hug. He couldn't believe what he was hearing, he was struggling to control an idiotic grin that he felt was spreading over his face. His arms were paralysed. As for words he was completely lost.

It was Alice who mastered the situation. 'Well, well, Hervé come and meet my very first boy-friend, Teacher Bob.' The older man in the green apron put aside a pair of secateurs and came over to shake hands. 'Hervé this is Bob Martin. Bob this is my tried, trusted and much-loved polyvalent assistant, Hervé.' She smiled and winked a complicit smile in Hervé's direction. 'You know what Hervé, I used to squeeze his blackheads.'

Bob pulled himself together trying not to squirm too much at the thought of his adolescent acne. 'How did you know? It's been such a long time. We were just kids. Look I need to sit down and have a glass of something strong. Can we......?'

'Hervé, nous irons dans le Café Sarrazin. Tu peux garder le magasin ?

'Bien sûre, Alice. A bientôt.'

They sat at a terrace table overlooking *Place Carnot*. The afternoon sun was blisteringly hot but Bob failed to notice. He couldn't believe what he was doing here sharing a table in Carcassonne with a woman he hadn't seen for over 50 years. He felt slightly tipsy even before the waiter arrived with their gin and tonics. It was Alice who spoke first.

'So just what are you doing here Bob? Don't tell me you're just chasing after a teenage heart throb who walked in and out of your life for 18 months two generations ago. You can't have been checking me out on social media – don't believe in all that crap. Recapturing your lost youth? We're all guilty of that, simple curiosity of revisiting the lost days of adolescence. Don't think I've never thought of you. You were my first serious boyfriend and one never forgets that first rush of sexual adrenaline. That's what it was wasn't it? The sex. Forget the supposed romance, of listening to Buddy, John, Paul, Don and Phil, holding hands in the dark. It was pure lust. I do have fond memories of those days believe me. You were a sweet guy but we had to move on. Remember that Lesley Gore song '*You don't Own Me.*' I used to sing it to you or at least hum it every time we were together. You pretended not to understand.'

'Yes, I suppose you're right.' Bob smiled and took out a cigar. Lighting up he deliberately nudged her elbow. 'But you're a cynic and I always took you for a true romantic. Let me tell you something it's quite funny really.' He looked her in the eyes and paused for effect. 'For more years than I can remember I've been seeing you everywhere.

......'

She smiled and sipped her G &T.

'Ah c'mon. Where for example?'

'Barcelona Ring Road....'

She paused a moment. 'Possible.'

'Wearing flip-flops and walking the Grand Canyon.......'

'Never wear flip-flops – they hurt my feet. Why would anyone wear flip flops walking the ....?'

'Blue Mosque Istanbul.................'

She sneered. 'Not religious.'

'Trevi Fountain........................'

'Non Parlo italiano.'

'Galeries Lafayette, Paris..........'

'Wow! Quite likely.'

'Headingly Cricket Ground...............'

'Hm. Don't like cricket.'

'Harrod's Food Hall................'

'Most certainly.'

'Café de Commerce, Nantes.....................'

'Now you've got me there – been to Nantes but can't remember the cafés.'

'Freddy Mercury statue in Montreux.'

'Who's Freddy Mercury?'

'Meadowhall Sheffield.'

'Watch your language.'

'Now the killer. Sunderland Public Library..............'

'Stop Bob! enough is enough. You know we see what we want to see.'

Meaning?

'Conspiracy theory for lovers. We want to believe what isn't possible. The object of our desire is going to pop up unexpectedly as if by divine intervention. Remind me to tell you my *'doppelganger'* story.'

'And the last time we saw each other?'

'The bus stop on Hull Road. You were sitting smoking on the bench opposite. You were with Colin. You both laughed when I got on the bus. It hurt. I guess you were making fun of me.'

'You've certainly got a good memory. I can't remember the laughter, probably one of Colin's dirty jokes but it hurt.'

'What do you mean it hurt. What hurt?'

'Seeing you getting on the bus all tarted up probably for a date. I missed you. No matter now it's all in the past.' Bob shrugged and smiled. 'Next question.'

'No matter it was a long, long time ago. I think I missed you too but we were very young. So, Bob, what are you up to now apart from chasing ex-girl-friends half-way across France? I guess from the gold band on your finger that you're married. Kids, grandchildren?'

Bob shrugged and smiled. 'Yes, into my third marriage I regret to say. Never learned my lesson. Charming and beautiful widow from Avignon. Gisèle. An extended family of 3 children and 3 grandchildren. Moved from Normandy to the Dordogne a couple of years back bought a country house near to Sarlat. We're very happy.'

'Why do you regret your third marriage? You said you were happy so why the regrets?'

'No, it's not exactly the right word. It's just I always have the thought in the back of my mind that maybe I've been searching for the unattainable. I suspect I've never really grown up and can't come to face the practicalities of adult life. Of course, it's all your fault.' Bob said smiling. 'You set the benchmark too high.'

'Well, that's a back-handed complement if I ever heard one.' Alice guffawed. 'I don't think I want to hear anymore.'

'Hm, you know what I mean. Never forgetting your first love and all that Mills and Boon romantic stuff. Anyhow there's something I want to show you that indirectly is connected.'

Bob reached down into the zipped pocket of his back-back and slapped an old brown padded envelope on the table.

'What's this then? Bob, you're too generous. A present for me and in such lovely wrapping paper.'

'You might call it a souvenir of times passed. Sorry about the brown paper. Go on look inside.'

'Un *petit coup de theatre* perhaps? Will I be surprised, shocked embarrassed even?'

Alice delved inside and tore open the envelope. She paused momentarily before opening her mouth and screamed. The scissors fell to the floor. The people on the neighbouring tables stopped talking and stared. She put her hands to her face in horror and turned away. Bob expected to see blood seeping from her fingers. But when he looked at her hand there was nothing. Her face was pale and her shoulders were shaking.

'Bob, why are you doing this to me?'

Shaken by Alice's sudden and unexpected reaction he could only blurt out, 'I thought you'd be amused to see the scissors again after all this time. What on earth is the matter? Are you hurt?'

She wiped away a tear and looked long and hard at Bob. 'Not in the way you think. I never wanted to see those wretched scissors ever again and now you turn up and decide they'll give me some sort of pleasure in remembering happy times.' Tears of rage, anger or sadness were streaking her cheeks, Bob wasn't sure which. 'Please Bob put those scissors out of sight, bury them down the deepest mine shaft, drop them in the Mariana Trench, dissolve them in a bowl of sulphuric acid, give them to a scrap dealer but just don't let them cross my line of sight ever again. Understood?'

Bob picked up the scissors and hastily threw them and the padded envelope back into his backpack. He scrunched a 20 euro note under the ashtray.

For several moments they walked in silence back in the direction of the florist shop. It was hardly a mirror image of their first walk together. Bob had no idea what to say. It was Alice who eventually broke the silence.

'I'm sorry Bob. You weren't to know. I owe you an explanation. Look can we meet for dinner later and I'll try to explain? There's a nice reasonably priced restaurant just inside the main gateway to the old city. I think it's called 'La Bastide.' Meet you there at 8.' She kissed her fingers and then pressed them against his lips. She disappeared around a corner leaving Bob feeling distraught and mystified not knowing what secrets and emotions he had unleashed.

He ambled slowly through the streets of the lower town his head buzzing from the events of the last hour. It was great to see Alice again after all these years. She'd changed of course she'd changed. She was now an ageing woman far away in years from the pretty teenage girl he had once known. She still had the charm and sparkle he'd been besotted with at 18 but why should such an innocuous object as a pair of scissors cause such a storm of emotion? Bob crossed the *Pont Vieux* and paused for a moment to watch a couple of local anglers in green waders fighting against the current of the Aude River. He remembered the afternoon when the scissors had been loaned to her. It was a hot Sunday June afternoon. The house had been empty. His parents were out visiting relatives in Liverpool. They wouldn't be back until late. Alice was nonchalantly walking around the bedroom wearing nothing but matching white bra and knickers. She kept humming that infernal Lesley Gore song *'You Don't Own Me.'* Bob failed to see the charm or the point of the song. She'd noticed the scissors on his bookshelf and picked them up marvelling at the snake shaped handles and the letters 'K' and 'T' inscribed on the blades. He'd explained how they'd once belonged to his grandmother; a wedding present from an Italian couturier who'd made her wedding dress. She'd asked to borrow them for a dress making project she was involved with at school. Bob had reluctantly said yes only after she'd kissed him full on the lips and promised to return them at the end of term. He wasn't to see the scissors again for nearly 50 years. They both were soon to go their separate ways and lead quite different lives.

Bob continued up the *Rue Trivalle* hardly noticing the ramparts and turrets of the fine old city. His mind was elsewhere. He turned right into the *Rue de la Gaffe* where he had booked a couple of nights in a small family run hotel. He quite liked spending the odd night alone in a hotel. He enjoyed the freedom and relaxation. Normally the only negative was he didn't enjoy eating alone in the evenings. No problem tonight. He was eager but not a little apprehensive about what Alice might tell him. Before showering and changing he telephoned Gisèle and updated her on the meeting with Alice. Gisèle knew most of the story. She thought him mad but was too wise to say so. She knew well her husband's obsession with the scissors and she also knew her husband's determination to see the issue through to the end – wherever or whenever that may be. He dug out a clean polo shirt and pair of jeans. He shaved and splashed a liberal dose of *Eau Sauvage* over his body.

✄

He arrived a few minutes early at 'La Bastide.' He'd entered the old city by the Narbonne Gate watching the children on the roundabout shrieking with joy as the multi-coloured carousel traced its melodious circles. He wondered why it was that continental children always seemed to enjoy life's simpler pleasures whilst many English children yearned for the sophisticated pleasures of adulthood before they had a chance of experiencing the innocence of childhood. Was it possible that a rotating wooden horse stuck on a pole could compete with a video game? Inside the gate he pushed his way through the early evening crowds heading for the pizza parlours and outdoor terraces. The restaurant was built into the ramparts down a small-cobbled side alley away from the crowds. A blackboard attached to the stone wall announced that tonight's speciality was *civet de sanglier* followed by *crème brûlée*. He wanted to try the local *cassoulet* but before he could dwell on his choice any further there was a tap on his shoulder and there she was.

'Hi Teacher Bob.' She grinned broadly. 'Pleased to see that you turned up after my performance this afternoon.' Alice was wearing a voluminous flowery patterned shift dress. Bob was impressed. She still looked good.

'Did you ever doubt it,' replied Bob. 'You obviously have a story to tell and I can't wait to hear it!'

They took a corner table inside. Bob proposed a bottle of champagne but Alice declared that to be too extravagant so they settled for two glasses of iced *pastis*.

'So, you came all this way to Carcassonne to show me a pair of abominable scissors that I'd long ago discarded in the hope that I'd never see them again.'

'Of course, the scissors gave me a good excuse to see you. After all these years of wondering what you were up to I was more than a little curious.'

Alice pouted and sniffed. 'Oh, you mean you wanted to see if I had grown old, ugly and fat so that you could reconcile the loss of your first love to the ravages of time and happy that you never did chase her to the ends of the earth.'

'No far from it,' replied Bob. 'As the jean manufacturer likes to say, style never goes out of fashion.'

'Oh, you smooth talking card. You would have never considered saying that to me when you were 18. It was so long ago we were just kids. What did we know of life at such a tender age?'

Bob knew she was right. They'd both travelled long and far to arrive at this point in their lives. He raised his eyes in tacit agreement but before he could add further to the conversation the waiter slid the red covered menus on to the table. Alice muttered a jocular 'Hey ho! *C'est la vie*,' and flicked open the menu. Bob was left reflecting whether even after all the years he knew much about life. He was stopped from further reflection by Alice who evidently had decided she had a lot on her mind and not just food.

Look, how about you checkout the menu and I'll tell you my *doppelganger* story. Not exactly a *doppelganger* but the sobriquet will do.'

'Bought a car a long time ago. A coupé. Quite a swish job really. Could shift on the autoroute believe me. On the first weekend I owned the car I went to a concert. As I was parking up I noticed a couple of about my age getting out of an identical car, same model, same colour on the opposite side of the street. They went to the same concert as me and sat just in front. The guy had a sort of goatee beard and his wife was quite plump (no physical resemblance I can assure you,' she laughed). 'Anyway, over the next 4 years I 'bumped' into the same couple numerous times at concerts and whilst out and about. At one concert they sat exactly opposite me – it was a concert in the round and it was difficult to avoid eye contact. We never had the opportunity to speak or maybe I was just a little scared of confronting them in case they vanished into thin air which in fact is just what did happen. I sold the car years later. From that day on I've never seen the couple again despite attending numerous other concerts and events in the same area. An example of what we see what we desire to see or don't see something we don't want to see – or something like that if you catch my drift. I'm not making myself very clear am I?'

'Perfectly clear. Wasn't seeing your *doppelganger* supposed to be a harbinger of death and anyway without wishing to spoil a good story wasn't it all a great example of mysterious coincidence?'

They were interrupted by the waiter arriving to take their orders.

Bob still thinking about *doppelgangers* and lost loves apologised to the waiter and asked him to come back in a couple of minutes.

'Think I'll go for the *cassoulet*.' Bob asserted. 'I'll give the starters a miss. I like the idea of a dish that was invented to keep the French alive whilst the Black Prince and the English hordes battered the city walls of Castelnaudary just down the road from here. I guess the English will never learn. A Medieval Brexit in reverse. The Brits demanding entry and being turned away but let's not go down that pot-hole filled road of malfunctioning UK foreign policy over the years.'

Alice groaned. 'I prefer to think of my stomach rather than politics although the Brexit result guaranteed several bouts of the worst kind of indigestion I'd rather not think about. The Arabs knew a thing or two about cooking and some historians believe that the *cassoulet* had its origins in the Moorish invasion but either way it's what you might call the signature dish of these parts. But having said all that I'm going to have the *magret de canard* and one of those *crème brulée* desserts they do so well here.' Alice called the waiter over to take their order.

'May I suggest a local *Cabardés* wine. The *Chateau de Pennautier* is particularly good,' advised the young waiter who hardly looked old enough to know about such things, but he made all the right moves with his left hand behind his back and an obsequiousness that was charming without being annoying.

'I'll go along with that,' enthused Bob always ready to widen his oenological repertoire. 'So, what has seeing the object of our desires got to do with your *doppelganger* story. I don't see the connection.'

'Simple really.' Alice replied. 'In this case it's the opposite. I couldn't stand the thought that somebody else might have the same car and worse still someone who wasn't at all like me, so I guess that my subconscious was working overtime to confront me with my rather snobbish taste in cars. How dare someone else drive the same car as me?'

'What complicated creatures we are,' reflected Bob. 'Have you ever considered that some techno whiz kid might at some time in the future invent a mobile app that notifies us when someone thinks of us? It would have to be limited to our list of stored contacts otherwise it would get out of hand but it might prove interesting. On the contrary no hits might prove devastating.'

'Um, I see you've still got that crazy imagination of yours. An intriguing idea that would certainly cause devastating relationship problems if the wrong person checked the contact list. Anyway, how would your i-phone know that you were thinking of someone? There would have to be some contact with the brain and I don't see technology solving that one any time soon.'

'Yes, I guess you're right and you would never know whether the person who was thinking of you had negative or positive thoughts. It would give a new dimension to hate mail or stalking. I'd have to be careful on the Barcelona ring road. My in-box would be blocked.'

Before Bob could elaborate further the waiter arrived with the wine. He made great play of showing Bob the label and Bob always enjoying playing the 'show-off' nodded in a way that he thought might indicate appreciation even though the wine was new to him. The bottle was uncorked. It was Alice who offered to do the tasting. She sniffed and slurped for a moment before smiling at the waiter and saying *'C'est bien.'* Bob was about to say something along the lines of 'bull-shit' but thought better of it. He had to accept that Alice's knowledge of French culture was certainly superior to his own.

How do waiters always manage to uncork the wine so efficiently at the table wondered Bob? He was thinking of the numerous occasions at dinner parties when he'd left half the cork in the neck of the bottle and had to disappear into the kitchen to gouge out the recalcitrant remains with an old screwdriver. Worse still Bob privately recalled when he'd elected to taste a white wine at some 'posh do' and then having given the waiter the nod discovered to his horror that everyone else considered the wine to be 'corked.'

'So, you think my *doppelganger* story was an example of pure coincidence?' Alice took a sip of the wine and cooed appreciation.

'Well yes,' replied Bob, 'you can't be implying that some mystic force was at work were you? I've got a story of my own anyway. I was on a passenger ferry from Cherbourg to Southampton. Although it was the tail end of August the English Channel was at its capricious worst. A Force seven had blown up. Ron Bailey an old friend and I were on the road from Bayeux. We'd taken the opportunity of having a bachelor weekend in the Normandy tapestry town. You know the sort thing. A couple of nights in a 3-star hotel, a bit of sightseeing, a lot of drinking and just a smidgeon of womanising. Anyway, the crossing was very rough. We started on the cognac as soon as we'd passed through the harbour entrance in anticipation of something to settle our stomachs. Today the cross-channel ships are well stabilised and you can always bunk down in one of their comfortable cabins but back in the 80's you were lucky if you found a seat on some of the busier summer crossings and on this occasion we ended up sitting on the floor. Conversation between us was limited and most other passengers were flat out or gazing into their sickbags. We must have been about 2 hours out of Cherbourg and those who had found their sea-legs were making their way to the restaurant when there came an announcement over the loudspeaker. 'Would Mr Martin and Mr Bailey come to the restaurant on C-deck. Their table is ready.' I looked at Ron, he looked at me. We both had the same thought. Something to the effect of you steaming idiot what the hell were you thinking of booking lunch on a day like this?'

More out of curiosity than hunger we stumbled over the green-faced passengers and tried to find our balance as the ship rose and fell to the regular clang of the ship's bow crashing into another wave. Unsurprisingly there were few diners. Just two people in front of us. A couple of bearded fellows with the look of seasoned travellers. An elderly weather worn Eric Tabarly type in a beige roll- neck sweater and navy-blue blazer accompanied by a younger man in a tweed jacket sporting a flat cap and an unlit briar pipe clenched between his teeth. They moved forward to the reception and the older of the two announced that they had a table reservation. The waiter smiled and asked their names.' Bob paused for dramatic effect. 'Martin and Bailey.'

'*Très bien*, messieurs. Table Six. *Bon appétit.*'

Alice put her hand to her mouth and laughed. 'Are you telling me that there were two other guys on the same ship travelling together with the same surnames as you and your friend. But that's incredible. Could you have misheard?'

'No, that was our first thought. We checked the waiter's reservation list and sure enough it confirmed that there were two other people called Martin and Bailey. Just coincidence like your *doppelganger*. Several years later I was reminded of the incident when I came across an article about a book written by an American writer, Morgan Robertson. *The Wreck of the Titan* pre-dated the *Titanic* disaster by 14 years and yet the coincidences between the work of fiction and the real event were staggering. Robertson wrote of the sinking of a huge ship, struck by an iceberg and the lack of sufficient lifeboats for the passengers and even the naming of the ship 'The Titan' closely paralleling the ship sunk in the catastrophe of 1912. Bizarre, no?'

'Are you suggesting that coincidence is more than just coincidence? Do we have some hidden capacity to mentally change how we think and see the world?' Alice was intrigued.

'No, I don't think so although it's a riveting thought. Albert Einstein said that coincidence is God's way of staying anonymous. I like that but I prefer to think that it's all about mathematical probability.'

'Explain.' Alice interrupted.

'Not that difficult,' retorted Bob. 'After reading about 'The Titan' coincidence I recalled the restaurant on the cross-channel ferry. It had been about 15 years since the incident and by then I had access to a computer at work. In an idle moment one lunchtime I stuck the names of Martin and Bailey into the search engine just to see how many times those surnames cropped up on the internet.'

Alice chewed the idea over for a few seconds before adding, 'I guess you're going to tell me that those two names are quite common.'

Bob laughed. 'Quite common. I should say so. In fact, at that time there were half a million Baileys recorded and 2.5 million Martins. You probably know that the name 'Martin' has French origins and is a very common surname both in

France and England so a cross-channel ferry is a good place to find a 'Martin.' With those sorts of numbers there must be a high probability that at some moment in their existence at least two of them are going to find themselves in the same place at the same time. In the vast majority of cases you're never going to know of their existence but every now and then circumstances come together as happened on the ferry. If Ron and I had just ignored the announcement or not happened to hear we would have been none the wiser.'

'Yes, but the probability of two couples with the same surnames turning up for lunch on a cross-channel ferry in the middle of a storm is even more unlikely.'

'How often have you been reading with the radio on in the background when out of nowhere the word you're reading comes on the radio at the very same moment as you read it? It happens. Circumstances don't invalidate the theory. In the infinity of time some things are going to come together if you wait long enough. It's a bit like you and I and a pair of scissors coming together again after 50 years! You've just got to wait long enough and visit enough car-boot sales.' Bob smiled wryly at the thought.

'Back to those bloody scissors again.' Alice pulled her face and rolled her eyes. Their mathematical machinations interrupted by the waiter arriving with their meal.

'Look Bob I think we should really enjoy our meal before I start telling you about those infernal scissors. The food here has an excellent reputation and I don't know about you but I'm hungry and the duck breast is one of my favourites. Anyway, this has to be a special occasion. Do you realise that this is the first time we've ever sat at a table together for a meal? When we were kids back in the 60's we never considered going out for a meal even if we could have afforded to so let's enjoy it.' She raised her glass to Bob's with a hearty *'tchin tchin.'*

The meal passed in increasingly garbled fashion as Bob ordered a second bottle of the excellent *Pennautier*. Alice earnestly explained to him the origins of the *cassoulet* he was now eating with gusto insisting that the Carcassonne recipe was the best even though the inhabitants of Castelnaudry and Toulouse would beg to differ. 'The Black Prince had pillaged the town of Castelnaudry in the Hundred Years War but not before the townsfolk had put up fierce resistance, surviving on their meagre stocks of beans, pork and duck which they cooked together in a stew. That's the legend which the locals like to preserve,' continued Alice, 'but here in Carcassonne they like their cassoulet with mutton and nobody here would dare argue with that.'

Bob nodded in agreement and carefully wiping his mouth with the napkin started to give a potted history of everything he'd done over the last 60 or so years. 'You know it was a great trauma for me when we split up. You had been my first serious girlfriend and although I accepted that we would eventually go our own separate ways it was still hard. One day we were sharing the closest intimacies the next you barely acknowledged me when I saw you at the bus stop. For the next two or three years you were the yardstick by which I measured other girls but by the time I eventually met the girl who I would eventually marry my ideas had changed, I thought I'd grown up and put past loves, regrets and nostalgia behind me but as we all come to realise eventually you never forget your first love. A sort of page-marker in the book of life.'

Alice smiled at him but said nothing. Bob went on to describe in mocking terms what he called his journeyman route through the 'Great British Educational System.'

'I always believed that I was an integral cog in one of the world's greatest social and educational institutions. A world leader in innovative pedagogy. Equality of opportunity regardless of your creed, colour or class. Education seen as a game changer leading to a future society where everyone no matter their background could leave their mark on the world. Sadly, that was all torn apart by competing ideologues of both left and right. Fanciful notions of how children learn came and went. Policies were being changed as often as I changed my socks. All to no avail. Just look at what we've got now. A society riven in two. The rich still getting richer, the poor still poor, Higher culture? Higher culture my arse. You're still frowned on if you don't wear black tie for the opera and wo betide anyone who doesn't understand the dress code for a Buckingham Palace Garden party. Even if you have the correct dress you still need the money. The Labour party's John Prescott who famously metamorphosed from a ship's steward to Deputy Prime Minister, once proclaimed 'we're all middle class now.' Maybe but you can be sure that the Eton, Oxbridge brigade still guard their privileges assiduously.'

'Bravo, Bob. Spoken like a true socialist. I would have never believed it of you.'

'Me neither, but I'm not sure. They do say that with age our politics shift further to the right. Not me. Since living in France I've drifted towards the centre ground. I don't like the hatred seemingly displayed by the far French right and left and as for the corruption enough said. Must say though that going to the opera or ballet in jeans and sweatshirt gives me a class warrior thrill even if I still willingly get a kick out of the fifteen-euro glass of *Veuve Clicquot* in the intermission.'

'Talking of the French and their culture, from what I remember you were pretty hopeless at French in school. What happened to change all that?'

'Thanks for reminding me. Your knowledge of the language always put me to shame. I was well into my forties when I first bought my home in Normandy and as you can imagine it was a bit of a culture shock at first. I had some French neighbours who ran a small village restaurant and I got into the habit of eating regular Sunday lunches there. We got by with a couple of dictionaries and plenty of *calvados*. One day Brigitte, the owner's wife asked about my family and the kids. I had a couple of photos with me and suggested I would show them to her after lunch. Embarrassingly I mixed up my verbs confusing *'montre'* with *'monter'* and said that I would mount her after we had eaten. I was saved from further humiliation by Brigitte's husband who slapped me on the shoulder saying it would be no problem for him.'

'Well, they do say that we learn from our mistakes. Happily, contrary to what the Francophobes think the French do have a sense of humour.'

Bob wanted to move the conversation on to Alice's story. They took their coffee outside onto the terrace. The sun was setting over the ramparts, but the heat of the day still lingered. The narrow streets of the old city buzzed with late evening visitors and the souvenir shops were still full.

'As I remember you were a bright young thing. I imagine you made it into a top University?'

'You probably wouldn't be surprised to know that I had a baby two years after we last saw each other. That buggered up a career in the short term. I decided I'd marry the father.'

'And who was the father?'

'Don't you know? It was your smoking buddy Colin.'

'Colin! Macho Socialist Colin Hardy.' Bob nearly choked on his espresso. 'So that explains his disappearance off my radar. Once we'd all gone our separate ways I lost touch. He wasn't exactly what you'd call a close friend. I didn't share his political views but somehow we muddled along.'

'Well, he's certainly off all our radars now. Did you know he died 45 years ago?'

For the second time in as many minutes Bob absorbed a shock. 'Oh, Alice I'm so very sorry. That must have been awful for you.'

'Forget the sympathy. He was a right bastard.'

'I remember that Colin could be a difficult character but …what happened……. And your child?'

'Stephen. He's now coming up to 50.'

'So where do the scissors come in?'

'You'll have to be patient, let me tell you first about Colin.'

Chapter Four

Alice's Story (1)

'Colin was never on my list of potential lovers let alone husbands. After you and I went our separate ways, I had a succession of largely undesirable boyfriends. You know the 'bad boy' syndrome. Why do the nicest girls always fall for 'Mr Bad Guy?' Well, I still can't explain it. Competition with other girls, adventure, rebellion, hormones – who knows? Anyway, thanks to you I'd found my feet as a woman. I got a place at Durham reading 19th century French Literature. It was a dream come true. The prospect of spending three years studying Hugo, Flaubert and Stendhal and the 'romantics' filled me with joyous optimism for the future. I met Colin on the train coming home for Christmas. As you remember we were all part of the same social circle so at least we had something in common. I remember meeting him for the first time when we were going out together, but he'd made no impression at the time. He came up to me on the train and reintroduced himself. He told me he was studying architecture also at Durham. We got talking and as always one thing led to another. We went out for dinner together at the beginning of January. I remember it well. There had been a heavy fall of snow, the buses had stopped running and we had to walk the two miles to and from the restaurant. I wanted to take a taxi, but Colin was having none of that bourgeois luxury. I should have realised then, but I did find him amusing if provocative company. He'd joined the communist party in his first semester, forged links with like-minded students at Paris Sorbonne and was being touted as a future student leader. Remember how back in the 60's we'd all been climbing on one band wagon or other, whether it was anti-Vietnam, 'Ban the Bomb,' racial equality, Dylan and Baez, Sartre and Beauvoir, Stones and Beatles, Luther-King and Malcolm X? You want a cause – we'll find you one made to measure. Plus, and it was a big plus Colin was Vice Captain of the University Rugby XV. I'm not a great rugby fan but I did enjoy the socialising and the after-match bar was always entertaining. We travelled the length and breadth of the country during winter weekends and the Easter tours to Toulouse, Bordeaux and yes even here to Carcassonne were a bonus for a couple of Francophiles.'

'At the end of our first year we decided to spend the long vacation on a grand tour of France. Colin wanted to visit the great Gothic Cathedrals – Chartres, Amiens, Bourges, Rouen, Reims – that suited me fine. I did most of the planning and organisation and could slip into the agenda visits to Flaubert's Rouen and Hugo's Parisian house. We spent two weeks in the *Marais* district of Paris where we were introduced to loads of chic-romantic intellectuals who passed their evenings drinking illegal absinthe and smoking 'delicious' Galois in sleazy subterranean bars and clubs whilst listening to Juliette Greco and Miles Davies. Colin became absorbed in the novelists' views of Paris and lost himself in the works of Hemingway, Fitzgerald and Wilde. Although he didn't like me using the word *'Bohemian'* to describe his friends it was certainly true that amongst those with whom we mixed there was little concern over sexual preferences or lifestyle. Nobody seemed to care much. The use of the word *'gay'* was yet to come into day-to-day language but there was liberal use of the French *'pédé'* but it was seen as a joke rather than a prejudice. Anyway, Colin seemed to get on fine with them and I just strung along for the ride. They loved his English accent and his macho posturing although most realised that this was a pose. After all, didn't the Parisians think that all English men were homosexual? He'd inherited his mother's sensitivity and creativity, but his dominant father had ensured that superficially at least he could act the alpha male. Colin's streak of creativity ran strong and his talents were warmly received by his colleagues.'

'We'd been in France for about six weeks. We were in Bourges when I realised my period was late. I'd been on the pill back in the UK but had been neglectful of contraception on the other side of the channel where the pill was not yet available to unmarried women. I blamed Colin for not being attentive. After all, why should I take the responsibility? We had an awful row in the nave of Chartres cathedral. I stormed off for the rest of the day. Back in Paris I looked up a local GP who was hardly sympathetic and lectured me on following liberal ideas and the dangers of promiscuity. He gave me a pregnancy test kit. Three days later I had the result – positive! Abortion was out of the question even had it been legal. I'd seen too many 60's 'kitchen sink' dramas where back street abortions were apparently carried out with the help of a bottle of gin and a knitting needle to follow that route. I can still remember that scene from *'Saturday Night and Sunday Morning'* where Albert Finney takes his married girlfriend played by Rachel Roberts to his aunt for a 'cut price' illegal operation. No, I didn't fancy that one bit. I'd come from a family of three children as you know, two younger brothers with not too big an age gap so we got along well. I grew to like the idea of becoming a mother so at the start of September we said *'au revoir'* Paris and *'bonjour'* bedsit land. Obviously I wasn't going to be able to continue with my studies. After much hand wringing, we agreed that marriage was the best solution. My parents reluctantly agreed and although they couldn't do much to help us out financially they at least tried to give us some moral support which was more than could be said for Colin's parents who couldn't have cared less although his mother did squeeze my hand after the Register Office wedding and said something along the lines of, 'it'll be alright, pet.'

'We shared a terraced bedsit in a rather rundown quarter of Durham. Colin continued his studies and I found a part-time job in the university library. Stephen was born the following April and then two weeks later Colin announced that we were going back to Paris. He'd been awarded a prestigious scholarship to study architecture at *Le Sorbonne.* It sounded almost too good to be true. Back to Paris and this time for a whole year but with a small baby it wasn't going to be easy.'

'We left for Paris in September '67. With the help of one of Colin's 'bohemian' contacts we managed to find an attic in a street just off the *Boulevard St Germain.* Climbing three flights of stairs with a small baby and push chair was no joke but there was a kindly *concierge* on hand when I struggled. The tomato-coloured tiled steps must have been witness to countless battles since the revolution. The apartment door had a triple locking mechanism although it would have taken an incredibly determined intruder to even get this far. The interior was small with just enough space for a folding sofa bed, a travel cot for Stephen and a small toilet cubicle. The shower room was outside down one flight of stairs. Cooking was done on an old gas cooker fuelled by large and heavy cylinders which when empty had to be lugged downstairs, taken across the road to the *quincaillerie*, exchanged for an even heavier full cylinder which was then hauled back up to the attic. I was grateful for Colin's front row forward muscle strength. I could never have done it myself. Not that Colin was often available for the domestic chores. His studies at the *fac* took up much of his time and he often wouldn't return until late in the evening. I filled my days taking Stephen on walks around the *quartier* and on finer days we even made it to the *Luxembourg Gardens* and *Les Tuileries*.'

'As Autumn turned to winter and the weather curtailed my push chair excursions I decided to take up again one of my long-neglected school-girl passions. Back in High School Wednesday afternoons were always given over to what in those days was known as D.S. Domestic Science was mainly concerned with cooking and sewing. Skills which it was thought would fully equip a future generation of women for marital life in the last quarter of the 20th century. Along the way educational policy makers had forgotten to check out the changing role of women. Increasingly young women were deferring marriage whilst they established careers for themselves and changing social attitudes to contraception and abortion were bringing a new dimension into their lives. Home cooking was being downgraded in importance with the growth of fast-food outlets. TV and popular culture left little time for sewing, cooking or even reading. Nevertheless, from my point of view I had always enjoyed dress making. I liked the concentration that it demanded and as a solitary creative activity it suited my mood at the time and gave me a respite from maternal demands. I'd remembered to bring my sewing box which I'd hardly opened since leaving school. I'd looked enviously in the windows of the expensive Parisian baby shops on the *Rue St Honoré* and reckoned the Parisians knew a thing or two about baby *chic* and reasoning that this wasn't just the domain of the *'Bourgeoisie'* I set about looking for some patterns that I could use for making Stephen something warm for the winter. I'd seen a cute little coat in the window of *'Maman et Bébé* that would be a good starter project. I came across a pattern for a similar style matinee coat in the *mercerie* close by so one wet Saturday afternoon whilst Colin was at a rugby match I dug out my sewing box, dusted it off and lifted the metal catch of what one of my school friends had called 'Alice's box of treasures.' I'd even sewn some pink roses on to the lid. Opening the box, I wasn't surprised to find the contents predictably disorganised, but I always knew where to find what I was looking for. Underneath the assorted packets of needles and pins were several small drawers with delicate ribbon handles containing a multitude of rainbow-coloured silks and cottons. And there at the very bottom I touched what I was looking for, the scissors with the snake-shaped handles and the initials 'K' and 'T' on the blades. I felt a pang of guilt when I remembered where and when I'd first seen the scissors. They had been on your bookshelf that hot summer's afternoon when we had frolicked half-naked in your bedroom. Remember how I'd asked if I could borrow them for a school dressmaking project and I persuaded you with a long kiss? You'd told me that they'd belonged to your grandmother. I solemnly promised you I'd return them at the end of term. The end of term came and the summer vacation began. We went our separate ways and heigh ho I got to keep the scissors. Not that they would do me any good. Remember the old superstition that scissors should always be sold and never lent? I should have given you a penny instead of the kiss.'

'Colin was at home infrequently. He'd take Stephen for the occasional walk, but his mind always seemed to be elsewhere. He'd often go on weekend jaunts to Marseille or Nantes for architectural conferences. He was becoming increasingly fascinated by the works of *'Le Corbusier'* and on one occasion he had been a specially invited guest to visit the *Cité Radieuse,* Corbusier's masterpiece of contemporary living in Marseille which had been inaugurated 10 years earlier with much critical acclaim. When at home Colin was getting more involved with the politics of some of his academic friends. He came home one evening full of smiles to tell me that he'd been to a meeting with a guy called George Marchais who apparently was a big shot in the Communist Party. Marchais had asked if Colin would like to sit on the local committee and oversee relations with British and American comrades. Of course Colin jumped at the idea and after a few months he was even boasting that he was on nodding terms with Jean-Paul Sartre. Most of this heady political stuff left me cold and I devoted most of my time to the needs of a growing child and in my few spare hours working on my embroidery. I gradually got to know some of the other young mothers in the area and thanks to Colin's political connections I managed to get Stephen into a local private nursery a couple of days a week.'

'As the year turned I sensed a mood of agitation rising amidst the damp winter mists of the Seine. Colin had always reckoned that France was the conscience of the world. Fate had dealt the country a promising hand. One of the most beautiful countries on the planet with a diversity of scenery to die for. From the rugged coves of Brittany to the majestic glacial peaks of The Alps, from the golden Norman beaches to the flesh pots of the Mediterranean, from the extinct Auvergnat volcanoes to the rolling hillside vineyards of Burgundy. Arguably the best food and wines and some of the greatest architecture, but as Colin, an unshakeable atheist had to concede if God exists, or should it be Satan then he or she certainly held the winning hand by placing 60 million people in this earthly 'paradise' the majority of whom seemed unable to appreciate what was in front of their own eyes. A people to whom the idea of contentment was an alien concept, a people whose collective malaise was the tin-can standard of human existence. If the Paris bourse ever traded in happiness bonds the French would be bankrupt. You can guarantee that if a group of French people decide to go to a restaurant they will all choose a different one and if they do eventually reach an agreement will change table at least twice and then having eaten and paid the bill each one will claim that the other restaurants would have been better or cheaper. The birthplace of institutionalised rebellion, abolish the monarchy then restore the monarchy, Napoleon and the civil code – a promising idea at first but then use it to tie the country in administrative knots, Charles de Gaul resistance hero turned into hated 'monarch,' Vote a President into power on a platform of change and then take to the streets when things change.'

Tables were cleared and the staff were hanging around waiting to go home. Bob realised that they were the last ones in the restaurant.

'I think I'd better settle the bill and continue with your story elsewhere. There must be some late-night bars around here. Do you have any ideas?'

Alice rummaged in her bag and found her cell phone. 'I'll give Hervé a call. He'll come and pick us up and we can go back to my place for a couple of cognacs, what do you think?'

'It's a bit late to call out Hervé don't you think. Better take a taxi.'

'No not to worry Hervé is quite used to ferrying me about town. It's part of his job,' she giggled.

Bob looked at her in surprise. 'Well, you've certainly got your shop assistant well trained – what's your secret?'

'No secret. Herve's no ordinary assistant – he's my husband! I'm Madame Alice Clopé.'

Chapter Five

Alice's Story (2)

'Your husband but.......'

'Yes, I know what you're thinking. He's quite a bit older than me. No problem, he's a charming man who looks after me well and he does know his flowers.'

'Well, what a surprising woman you've turned out to be. Doesn't he mind you spending your evening with another man?'

'Not at all and before you ask, yes, he does know about my history and about you. No worries there.'

They were standing by the Narbonne Gate as a grey 60's Citroen DS saloon pulled up. Hervé waved cheerfully as the car drew to a halt. Bob greeted Hervé with a hearty handshake.

'Good to see you again Hervé and may I congratulate you on your exquisite taste in women.' Hervé looked towards Alice with a quizzical smile before they both laughed and Alice took Hervé by the arm and kissed him on the cheek,

'Yes, Hervé can certainly tell his peonies from his primulas.'

They drove the short distance down the hill from the *Cité* and into the lower town. Crossing the bridge over the River Aude, the multi-coloured flood lights highlighting the turreted towers cutting the enveloping dusk and giving the city a fairy tale look, Bob couldn't help but admire the majesty and romance of it all. It certainly was an impressive sight.

'I bet you're happy living in such a wonderful place,' said Bob. 'All the history, tradition and culture. Normandy is great, but this place certainly takes some beating.'

'It certainly does, but it won't be long before we're moving on.'

Before Bob could ask the obvious question, they arrived in front of the flower shop and Hervé unlocked a side door leading to a flight of stone steps joining their apartment above the shop.

The air was heavy with the scent of the flowers from the shop below. In one corner of the living room was a huge vase filled with yellow and red gladioli. The apartment had clearly been decorated with taste and Bob wondered whether it was Alice's or Hervé's influence. The minimalist decor emphasised primary colours. In the middle of the polished woodblock floor was a simple square glass topped table with a Jeff Koons balloon dog lamp in bright metallic red and a single yellow sunflower in a tall white vase. Diego Rivera's *'The Flower Seller'* was the only interruption to a white painted expanse of wall whilst Banksy's *'Draw the Raised*

Bridge' hung above an unlit state of the art semi-cylindrical stainless steel wood burner on the opposite side of the room.

'The Banksy was a birthday present from Hervé. You do remember the original I hope.'

Bob relieved to show that he wasn't a complete ass when it came to art recalled that the original was first 'discovered' on a swing bridge in Hull a couple of years ago.

'Bravo Bob! You remembered. I'm impressed. Now for your reward Hervé will serve us all up one of his special cognac cocktails. Go easy on the Vermouth *cherie* we don't want Bob falling into the *Aude* on his way home.'

The two of them flopped on the white leather sofa whilst Hervé disappeared into the kitchen to mix the drinks. Bob was eager to get back to the story of Colin.

'So, you were talking about Colin's involvement in French politics. His dabbling in the French communist party where did that lead?'

'Well of course we're now talking about May '68. You'll doubtless be familiar with the picture. The French back in 'Revolution Mode.' Six thousand students and fifteen hundred gendarmes on the streets of Paris. Within days ten million workers were on strike. Piles of rubbish festering on street corners, shortages of essential foods in the shops and remember at this time many workers were still putting in sixty-hour weeks. It's all part of history now of course. The seeds of unrest had been silently germinating in the nascent political minds of the student body for some time. Reform was desperately needed. More people were beginning to question whether their 'providential saviour' De Gaulle was still up to it. As the year wore on it became clear that he wasn't.'

Hervé arrived with the drinks. Setting them on the table he turned to Bob saying, 'you must excuse me, Bob but I have to be up early tomorrow to go to the wholesale flower market in Toulouse and I must have what you English charmingly call my beauty sleep.' He bent forward to kiss Alice and then shook Bob's hand.

'Bon nuit, cherie, sleep well.' Alice replied raising her glass in the direction of her husband as he closed the kitchen door. 'Now, where was I?'

'You were talking about the events of '68. What was Colin's role in all of this?'

'Well, at first it seemed that Colin was content to take a back seat. He sided with the ideology of the students and workers but that seemed to be as far as he went. Later when the authorities ordered the closure of the university things began to change. One evening, without any warning he arrived home with a guest for dinner. His name was Gregoire. A fellow communist party member and academic chair holder in *Paris Sorbonne.* He reckoned that he was a relative of one of Napoleon's Generals. Most Frenchmen seem to have connections with the 'little general' so no surprise there. He was somewhat older than Colin, quite tall for a Frenchman, smartly dressed in a charcoal grey suit and blue silk cravat. His brown hair reached down to his shoulders and as I took his trench-coat I noticed the not unpleasant smell of strong tobacco mingled with some expensively smelling aftershave. He spoke impeccable English and with a somewhat over courteous manner took off his black leather gloves and proffered his hand. The limp handshake was a little off-putting but otherwise he exuded typical gallic insouciance. He was the antithesis of Colin. Colin had never been what you might call elegant. He was *Capstan Old Spice* to Gregoire's *Gitane Jean-Paul Gautier*.'

Bob laughed when he remembered Colin's early 60's attachment to brown chords and baggy sweater windswept look.

'I'd scrambled together a quick '*Spag Bol.*' Gregoire had brought a bottle of red which partly redeemed him in my eyes. Back then even in Paris we only managed cheap 'plonk' with the luxury of decent wine reserved only for rare special occasions. Money was tight. He thanked me over profusely for the dinner – he was probably feeling guilty that I'd not been warned of his coming. Later he and Colin disappeared to the bar on the opposite side of the street.'

'Anyway, Gregoire's visits started to take on a regular pattern. Once or twice a week he would arrive for dinner always accompanied by a bottle of something expensive or a bouquet of flowers. After dinner they usually disappeared to the bar. Was it architecture, politics or the tight-jeaned barmaid that occupied them? I was never sure. Colin seemed happy and I never interfered. I'd grown used to his political enthusiasm and his friendship with Gregoire appeared to be based on mutual interests. His intelligence, humour and charm became a regular part of our lives and even baby Stephen, now having passed his first birthday would clap his hands in glee when Gregoire arrived. *'Bonjour Tonton*

Gregoire' had now been firmly implanted in his growing Anglo-French repertoire.'

Bob smiled as he tried to recall his own reactions to the '68 *evenéments* and other pivotal events of that year. Assassination of Martin Luther King and Bob Kennedy, war in Vietnam, the Mexico Olympics, Winston Smith and 'Black Power.' He'd been into his second year of teaching and there seemed to be far more important things to worry about than events on the other side of the channel let alone the other side of the world. He was engaged to the girl who would become his first wife, buying their first house, romantic evenings in country pubs, listening to 'The Beatles,' The Bee Gees and Cream, watching 'The Graduate,' '2001 Space Odyssey' and 'Rosemary's Baby.'

'Who was it said if you remember the 60's you probably weren't there?'

Alice chuckled mischievously before saying 'I don't remember.' They touched glasses and laughed. 'Hervé' can certainly make the best brandy cocktail in Carcassonne. She paused, took a drink and held up the glass to the light. Squinting she turned to Bob. 'Well, are you going to tell me how you got hold of those damned scissors?'

Chapter Six

Bob's Story

Bob drained the cocktail glass, twirled the stem between his fingers before placing it carefully on the table. 'Well, I've always been fascinated by the French love of *brocante* sales. Far more interesting than a plain old car boot sale. It was last August. I noticed a flyer in the local *boulangerie* announcing a *brocante* in a nearby town. From experience I'd always been drawn to these events despite many of the rather 'tacky' stalls selling old clothes, children's' broken toys and empty gas cylinders. There was always some interesting stuff to be found if you were prepared to search hard enough. Old vinyl LP's, DVD's, even picked up a bargain Bowie *'Diamond Dogs'* album. Plus, there was always stacks of old *'Paris Match'* magazines, *'La Poste'* calendars and fireplace accoutrements like the cast iron decorated fireback I'd picked up for a song a couple of years ago. On this occasion I was looking for a pair of firedogs to complement the fireback when I came across a cardboard box filled with what looked like a pile of old junk, broken toys, empty cigar boxes, school rulers, rusty garden tools and so on when I saw a pair of tarnished scissors.'

Alice sat up in the chair and unconsciously clutched Bob's arm her eyes registering stunned surprise.

'Anyhow, I picked them out of the box and noticed something vaguely familiar. A pair of scissors with snake handles. What a coincidence I thought as I recalled the scissors I'd picked out of a drawer when my grandparent's house was being cleared. I scratched the dirty flat blades with my thumb nail revealing the initials 'K' 'T.' Surely there could never have been two identical pairs of scissors with the same design and initials? I stroked the snake handles just as I remembered doing as a small child in my grandparent's parlour on a breezy afternoon light years ago. But how could the scissors end up here, 400 miles from where I'd last laid eyes on them. Visions of you suddenly came flooding back. That afternoon when you'd asked to borrow them for your embroidery project.'

'The old French woman behind the trellis table noticed my curiosity and said that they'd probably clean up again and the blades could be re-sharpened. She suggested 50 euros, I offered 20 and after a lot of huffing and puffing we agreed on 30. I tried to feign coolness but had to ask the woman where she'd come across the scissors. She told me about a neighbour, an English woman who was clearing her house prior to moving south. She couldn't remember the woman's name but she'd passed on the box of 'miscellaneous items' knowing that her neighbour frequented the local *brocantes*. She thought that the English woman had a flower stall on the market at St Pierre-en-Auge. I had visited the market regularly and had a vague memory of seeing the flower seller who had a stall next to the big wooden doors and in the summer months always wore a straw hat with a big yellow sunflower stuck in the cleavage of her green overalls. I'd never taken any further notice. I had my own flower garden and didn't need to buy at the market, so I never had any contact with the flower seller.'

Bob paused desperately trying to conjure up a past memory.

'I took a table on the terrace of the nearest café. I ordered a cold beer, lit up a cigar and placing the scissors on the table contemplated my find. Surely this was too much of a coincidence. It was practically impossible that they were the same scissors passed to my grandmother all those years ago on her wedding day and yet the more I looked at the initials and the weird serpentine handles the more I knew that these were indeed the very same scissors. But could this English flower seller be the same person I'd known and fallen in love with, the young girl whom I'd exchanged the scissors for one very long passionate kiss on a hot July Sunday afternoon? I cursed myself for never stopping to buy her flowers.'

Bob stopped to clear his throat whether as the result of too much alcohol or simple emotion. 'Do you mind if I ask for a glass of water? I shouldn't have ordered that second bottle of the *'Pannautier'* This is all getting a bit too much. Sorry Alice.'

'Don't worry. This is fascinating.' Alice got up and moments later returned from the kitchen with a glass of iced lemon water. 'Please go on.'

Bob took a long drink of the water before breathing deeply and continuing his story. Alice sat upright her left hand covering her mouth. Bob wasn't sure whether she was about to laugh or cry.

'At that stage I had no idea whom you had married. I searched for Alice Woods in the local 'phone book but to no avail. I Googled local flower sellers without success. I went to St Pierre on the next market day and noticed that the flower stall by the door had been replaced by a young Algerian guy selling cell phone cases. He had no idea who had owned the flower stall. The farmer's wife selling eggs out of a straw basket said that she knew the flower seller's name had been Alicia and she was English but other than the first name she knew no more. She suggested I visit the Town Hall and talk to the secretary responsible for licencing market traders.'

'Alice, Alicia – why not the same person? Sure enough at the town hall the secretary after wading through numerous numbered and coded files came up with the answer I was looking for. She told me that the name was Alice Hardy, obviously you'd still kept your married name, and that you'd had the flower concession at the market for 5 years but you'd not paid your dues for the current financial year and your option on the stall had lapsed. Of course, I'd only known you by your maiden name of Woods. As far as the secretary knew she thought that you had upped sticks and gone off to Carcassonne or Castres or some such place down south but that was as much as she could tell me. An internet search for *Alice, flowers, fleurist, Castres, Carcassonne* soon brought me here.'

'The biggest shock was the realisation that we must have been neighbours for several years without ever knowing. I may even have walked past you on the street oblivious to your existence.'

✂

Alice had been smiling for several minutes listening to Bob's story, now she started to giggle stopping Bob in full flow. Bob was relieved to see that she wasn't going to give a repeat performance of the drama on the café terrace earlier that day but her laughter left him bemused.

'Why are you laughing at my story? I would have thought that the revelation that we had been unknowingly neighbours for years would have come as a bit of a shock for you also. It knocked me about a bit I can tell you.' Bob put on a hurt face and shook his head in disbelief.

Alice sipped her cocktail, spluttered and putting the glass slowly on the table said,

'No in fact I'm not shocked or surprised. You see I knew we were living close to each other. I lived in St Pierre and you were living out a cheesy existence in Livarot 20 kilometres away.'

'I don't believe what I'm hearing. But how did you know? C'mon you're pulling my leg.'

'No believe me, every word is true. You used to come to the market regularly on Monday mornings. You were usually accompanied by your wife, son, partner, girlfriend whoever.'

'But how on earth did you recognise me? We've both – well I've aged a little bit. My hair is practically white, well speckled with streaks of wisdom as I heard someone say the other day and much shorter. My paunch.' Bob slapped his stomach and mockingly groaned. 'I'm fatter, well just a little and I think my wardrobe has benefitted from age and experience. I'm not sure that even I would have recognised myself after all these years!'

'Well, as you've already realised, I was the little flower girl.' Alice stood up and leaning over plucked the sunflower from the white vase and plunged it into the neckline of her shift dress. *'Voila!'*

'Oh my god! I feel so ashamed and embarrassed,' exclaimed Bob. 'I can picture you there now and never once did I make the connection. But why didn't you say something?'

'At first I wasn't really sure that it was you. It had been a long time since we'd last seen each other. After you and I finished and went our separate ways I embarked on what in those days would have been considered a promiscuous lifestyle. I lost count of the number of lovers between you and when I met Colin.'

'So, you weren't sure whether I was number one or number one hundred, was that it?'

For more years than he cared to remember Bob had cherished the thought that their relationship had been somehow special and after they had finished he had hoped that Alice would find herself a kind, understanding and sensitive soul who would treat her with love and respect. He never imagined that their paths would cross again but he'd always harboured some sentiment for her in the corner of his heart and had wished her well.

'No, it wasn't that. Don't be stupid. You were the first if that's what you really want to know. Anyway, you never once stopped to even look let alone buy any of my flowers,' Alice continued. 'I remember that you once made a rude remark about my tulips and you had turned to your partner and said something about your spring tulips being much better. Your crummy French accent gave you away and I'd recognise that Adam's Apple anywhere.'

Bob swallowed hard. Momentarily he was too shocked to speak. He sniffed and rubbed his neck self-consciously.

'You didn't come to the market regularly but when you came, I was practically sure to see you. It was always mid-morning, never later than midday. Selling flowers at one of the main entrances to *Les Halles* meant I saw most people passing and to be honest with you there were days when business was slack and all I could do was 'people watch' or arrange the flowers. Sometimes it became like a game. I tried to piece together my memories of you, your walk, hairstyle, clothes, did you still smoke, all the little things that I remembered and above all how any person is transformed by age and the passing years. When you see people regularly you hardly notice the little changes but when there's a gap of 50 years, adolescence to senior citizen masks everything apart from maybe those little mannerisms or tics that we all have and which stay with us all our lives. One day you stopped to hitch up your trousers and that was when I was certain. You always hitched up your jeans with a rather subtle thumb lift and twist and I always found it amusing and somewhat charming.'

'And you still said nothing.'

'No, it was always a game,' continued Alice. 'I didn't want to break the spell and perhaps subconsciously I didn't want to find that I might be completely mistaken. It was a period of transition for me. I'd been living in Normandy for over 20 years. I'd established myself, made contacts, some I might have called friends except that as one grows older good friends are hard to find. I set up the flower business; for a while it worked quite well but there was always a hole inside of me that was growing with the passage of time and I was clueless as to how to fill it. After Colin died I couldn't bear the ghosts of Paris so with Stephen I upped sticks and went to Normandy. I'd always yearned for a small place in the country and at that time house prices were cheap and it was easy to find a small half-timbered, low maintenance cottage. I'd come into a small amount of money from a joint insurance policy which we'd been wise enough to take out when we married and with that I set up a small market gardening company. Stephen went to the local schools, grew up with French his first language and eventually got his literary baccalaureate with distinction and went off to the university in Caen to study French literature. Imagine that Bob, after all those years my only son fulfils my own ambition – how often do you hear of that happening? He was only at the *fac* during the week so we could still have weekends together and as he shared my love of gardening he was able to do some of the harder chores for me. Eventually, however, he completed his studies and landed an editorial position with a publishing house down in Aix-en-Provence. Although he visited from time to time and we often holidayed together I was largely on my own for the first time in years. The flower business wasn't making me a fortune and the winter months were particularly difficult so I decided to turn some of my land over to a tree nursery and I began to sell trees and shrubs in the autumn and spring. At that time in the early 90's, as you doubtless remember, there was the growing influx of our compatriot 'Brits' deserting the 'good ship Brittania' after realising that selling their three up two down detached could release enough capital to buy something considerably more substantial in Normandy. We were all Europeans then in those halcyon pre-BREXIT days. Many made their priority the creation of England's green and pleasant land on this side of the channel. You'd be amazed at some of the garden projects they thought up. *'Perfidious Albion'* had truly created a nation of gardeners and believe me many of them were putting the French to shame with their rectilinear plots, gravel paths and a Romano-Greek fountain or two to say nothing of their Wimbledon sward, snooker table flat, green manicured lawns.'

Bob nodded in agreement as he pictured the mathematical precision of the French gardens he had visited in the grand royal chateaux of the Loire valley. Chambord, Blois and Amboise may have been magnificent but in Bob's opinion they couldn't hold a candle to Chatsworth, Kew or Blenheim. The great landscape architect Lancelot 'Capability' Brown had set the gold standard in gardens and anyway the French didn't have the advantage of the capricious British weather which at its best or maybe its worst could thrust up great oaks, sycamores and beeches plus colouring the countryside in myriad shades of green.

'So, what eventually brought you down here to Carcassonne? Surely not following in the literary footsteps of Kate Mosse or Julian Barnes who incidentally had a character in one of his books who claimed that he had had the best sex of his life in Carcassonne. No need to dwell on that but were you trying to beat them all to it by writing the definitive Carcassonne novel? The weather here is better than in Normandy but it can still be evil when the wind blows in from the Pyrenees.'

'Well, actually no, nothing to do with the climate and sadly despite my ambitions I'm no writer. Anyway, I'm not a fan of historical novels and as for Julian Barnes got fed up with him when he started banging on all the time about Gustave Flaubert. No, it's more to do with those subtle twists of fate which so often mesmerise and unconsciously push us in a certain direction. I'd always fancied having my own *fleurist*. Working on the market was great but I didn't see myself doing that for the rest of my life and then one day I came across an advert in the local paper from someone wanting to go into partnership in the flower business. It was Hervé. We agreed to meet and the chemistry was there straight away. Before he retired he had a career in the wine trade with an amateur interest in horticulture so a move into the flower and plant business was a logical step. He has an amazing knowledge and feel for flowers and plants plus his gallic charm was irresistible. I poured all my savings into the business. I wondered if I had done the right thing. Hervé said that the best way of ensuring my security was to become more than just business partners so after a year setting up the shop here in Carcassonne we sealed the knot. I never felt that I was taking a risk. That was five years ago and I've never looked back. The shop has been a great success but as I hinted earlier the time has come for us to move on.'

'Move on to what?' Bob asked. 'Why on earth give up a successful business?'

'I suppose you could say it's to do with ambition. Stephen, my son, and Hervé hit it off well together and they persuaded me that perhaps we should expand our horizons to cater for modern tastes. You know the sort of thing. The farm shop concept – selling locally sourced products, buying a bit of land and growing our own fruit and veg, we've even got a couple of hectares of vines- all very eco-friendly stuff.'

Alice yawned and stretched. 'Look Bob I'm done in. Too much emotion for one day. How about a stroll in the countryside tomorrow if you've nothing better to do? What do you say if I pick you up at your hotel around 11 and I'll drive you out to *La Montagne Noir* – there's some great walking there and I'll pack us a picnic. We can continue our cutting-edge history over a couple of bottles of cold beer and some delicious Carcassonne *saucisson.*'

'Sounds great to me but are you sure I'm not taking up your time?'

'Not at all. Hervé will be out in Toulouse all morning and the shop is closed on a Thursday and by the way bring those bloody scissors with you.'

'But I thought you didn't want to see the scissors again.'

'I don't and that's why you're going to bring them along in the morning. Call it a ceremony of the last rites.'

Walking back to his hotel as the early morning mist rose over the *Aude*. Bob couldn't help wondering what she meant by 'the last rites' but he reckoned that a bit of mountain walking would do him good plus the added pleasure of a day out with Alice.

Chapter Seven

The next day

'Go on then, do it. Throw those damned things down the well.'

Bob looked to the sky for inspiration. The sun was hot now despite the strong breeze billowing chalky dust into their faces. They'd arrived an hour earlier in a small *Languedocien* village. They'd parked off the main street and walked down the tree-lined avenue pausing to buy a couple of baguettes and taking in the heady delights of this small French community that had yet to lose its soul to tourism. The *River Clamoux* whispered under an ancient stone bridge, a street corner fountain blubbed its soft conversation with itself whilst on the hillside the impressive sight of a renovated windmill, its sails turning in the breeze. They resisted the temptation to stop off at a street-side café – the cold beers could wait awhile. The path took them out of the village and uphill soon narrowing and merging with the vineyards already heavy with ripening grapes. A left turn took them into a new landscape, the *garrigue* with its scrub like terrain dotted with low standing Mediterranean oaks, gorse and wild artichoke and asparagus. The occasional whiff of lavender and wild thyme added to the feeling that this was somewhere special. A worn wooden sign pointed their way towards *'Les Capitelles'* a group of small stone cabins miraculously constructed without cement or wood. On the far side of the path was a stone-walled well.

'It's now or never Bob. Those scissors have never done anyone any good. What about them precipitating the end of our teenage romance? You lent them to me without asking for anything in return, surely a breaking of superstition if there ever was one. Then there was the business with Colin.' Alice hesitated and shook her head. 'But I've said enough for the moment. Get rid now, Bob before they can hurt again.'

Bob moved over to the low wall surrounding the well. He wondered what Alice had meant about the business with Colin but that would be for later. For the moment he looked into the depths but could see no water. He reached into his rucksack pocket for the bubble packed scissors and placed them on the wall. 'I'm not sure I can do this, Alice. Despite their sordid history these scissors have been a family heirloom for 100 years. They are one of the few tangible links that I have with my maternal grandparents.'

He sat on the wall the scissors by his side. Alice looked him in the eye. 'Just do it Bob, now!' Suddenly she was in his arms her lips pressed against his. Momentarily Bob was back in his bedroom on a sunny July afternoon, their semi-naked bodies intertwined. His arm moved towards Alice's back and in doing so knocked the scissors from the wall. The dripping water subdued any echoing splash and anyway Bob was too surprised to do anything except to reciprocate the embrace and groan with pleasure or was it remorse he wasn't sure.

Silence. A faint drip dripping of water into the well. Extricating from one another it was Alice who spoke first.

'Well, there you go Bob. It worked once before so I reckon it was worth a second try. They've gone now, Bob, lost forever. Superstition always sees scissors as the enemy and now the enemy has been vanquished.'

Bob too shocked to speak shook his head as the kiss lingered on his lips and momentarily he was a lovestruck adolescent once more. He looked across to Alice who was smiling and plucking a sprig of honeysuckle hanging down from above the well. She pushed the flower through the top buttonhole of his shirt.

'There, that should bring us good luck from now on. The scissors have gone back to nature. You know the villagers here constructed a very elaborate irrigation system here in the 19th century. Much of it was underground and fed water from a spring up in the hills down into the village. The fountain we saw at the edge of the village was fed by the water as were several other smaller fountains around about. The water was used for the vineyards and small holdings and there were also a couple of drinking troughs for the animals. Eventually the water flows into the *River Clamoux* which in turns feeds the *River Aude* which eventually reaches the Mediterranean just outside Narbonne. This deep well leads directly to the old underground system. So, you see Bob the scissors have now well and truly gone, probably half-way to the sea by now.'

Bob stuck his hands in his pockets and shrugged. He walked over to Alice and kissed her forehead. 'Yes, you're right. Thanks, but don't forget the positive side too. We wouldn't have renewed our friendship if I hadn't found the scissors. We wouldn't be here today.' Still feeling the imprint of her lips on his he touched her hand. 'Let's keep to the friendship bit and not do anything stupid after all we're both happily married aren't we?'

'Who said anything about doing something stupid? A kiss is just a kiss between friends. A means to an end,' she laughed and strutted off up the path. 'C'mon Bob there's a great place for a picnic just round the hill. I'm starving. How about you?'

'Only if you promise me that there won't be any snakes. I'm terrified of the little buggers and you never know on a hot day like today. This is *garrigue* country and noted as a great habitat for reptiles. At least with the scissors gone I need no longer look at those serpentine handles.'

'You've never told me that before. I've spent hours searching for rare plants and flowers in the *garrigue* over the years and never once spotted a snake. Anyway, they are frightened of humans and are only dangerous when surprised. So, when did you first become aware of your snake phobia?'

'Well, I don't actually remember. I seem to have always had a fear of them. I remember sitting with my grandma' watching her sewing one day. I must have been five or six years old. She was cutting the threads with those scissors. I was fascinated by the snake shaped handles but something repulsed me about them also. I told her that I didn't like snakes and she told me not to worry because there were no snakes near their house. Hardly surprising considering that the house was in an urban area a fair distance from any countryside to speak of. She told me that some people had a sort of 'gift' of seeing serpents but that wasn't to bother me.

Every time I picked up the scissors I was reminded of that conversation. It also explains how I quickly identified them at the *brocante* sale.'

'Bravo! So I've done us both a big favour by getting rid of them. Now we can both sleep easy.'

'But it doesn't conclude quite as neatly as all that. You see the 'gift' of seeing serpents that my grandma' spoke of belongs to me.'

Alice turned off the track into a small, shady forest clearing with several large boulders scattered around. She sat down on the largest and unpacked her rucksack. 'How can anyone have a gift for seeing snakes. It's preposterous. More than likely you're just a very observant person who unconsciously is aware of your surrounding environment so you're more likely to spot a snake or maybe other things like wild animals, insects etcetera.'

She passed a knife and a silver foil wrapped *saucisson* to Bob. He unwrapped it and began cutting it into slices whilst Alice opened a pack of sandwiches, snapped a baguette in half and 'popped' a pack of potato crisps.

'Have you heard of 'Snake Detection Theory?' Came across it on the internet a couple of years ago (cynical groans from Alice). Apparently some researchers into human brain evolution reckon that some people are more prone to seeing snakes than others.'

'Surely you know better than to believe everything you read on the web. I thought you were a rational man, Bob. You're not going to be taken in by some pseudo-scientific guff you've come across on your computer?'

'No, believe me this isn't pseudo-science. There's this woman at the University of California College of Biological Sciences, Lynne or maybe Linda Isbell. She's a well published anthropologist who amongst many other things came up with and researched this hypothesis. No pseudo internet conspiracy theories here I can assure you.'

'Ok so you've got me listening. How does this affect you?'

'Well indirectly it seems that humans have evolved their visual systems partly due to the existence of snakes. Isbell thinks that some people are better at detecting the presence of snakes in order to improve their survival chances and that this ability is passed on genetically to their off-spring.'

'So, are you saying that snakes are responsible for the sensitivity of our vision?'

'Yes, in part. It seems that all primates follow this pattern. Snakes have evolved to be difficult to detect and potentially lethal therefore it is essential that the primates including humans have sight which can detect the threat.'

'So presumably what you're saying is that not all humans have developed this faculty to the same extent.'

'Exactly. That's why perhaps I have the 'gift' but I'm not unique because millions of others apparently have also evolved the same faculty. Look at the goose-bumps on my arms, it's always the same when I get on to the subject of snakes.' Bob stopped to rub his arm which felt cold despite the hot September sun. Suddenly a distant memory flashed across his mind, an image that he'd long since forgotten. A hot summer's day in England. A group of friends sitting around smoking in the long grass. Colin arrived laughing maniacally producing from his jacket pocket a grass snake. Everyone jumped up in shock and horror. He recalled the disgust and revulsion on his friend Dick's face. He felt it wiser not to tell Alice. The link between Colin, a snake and the scissors was too much of a coincidence wasn't it?

'This saucisson is delicious. Can you pass me some more bread?'

'I've brought some apples too. Fresh from the market this morning.'

Bob laughed. 'All we're missing is the tree of knowledge and the serpent to make a biblical tableau. What do you make of that Alice or should I call you Eve?'

'Well, it's certainly a paradise here on such a lovely day but I'm hooked on your snake detection hypothesis. Why just snakes? Why not spiders, mice or slugs which many people are equally repulsed by?'

'As I understand things it seems that when researchers, using the latest in MRI technology have shown their trial groups pictures of a range of creatures that usually are responsible for phobias it's always the snakes that create the strongest reaction. Incidentally did you know that *ophidiophobia* is the name given to the snake phobia? Great word isn't it? At first sight it doesn't have any connection to snakes until you discover that *'ophis'* is Greek for serpent.'

'Thanks Teacher Bob, I've always wondered.' She bit into her apple and passed it to Bob. 'Here's to original sin. Anyway, the snake-handled scissors made you conscious of your fear. What happened next? A pair of carved serpents is hardly the stuff of nightmares.'

'My dad had an old book. It was quite large, a sort of single volume encyclopaedia, leather bound, blue cover with gold lettering. It was full of fabulous photos of icebergs, volcanoes and extreme weather events. One day I was flicking through the pages when suddenly I came across a full page black and white photo of a viper. It was such a shock. I remember dropping the book and shuddering. I didn't say anything and for ages afterwards I avoided looking at the book. Even seeing the spine of the book on the bookshelf made me shiver. Eventually I returned to the book – out of curiosity I suppose. I kept looking at the pictures near the beginning or the end of the book, I knew the adder was near the middle but the pages were shiny and my little fingers slithered over the pages and suddenly it was there waiting for me in all its serpentine horror. My curiosity seemed to always get the better of me and whenever I opened the book it always fell open on the same page. The page with the black and white snake picture.'

'Childhood fear. Quite normal no? Can't relate to it myself. You'd probably be surprised to learn that I've never seen a snake apart from in a zoo. Hervé is always telling me to be on the lookout when gathering my wild herbs and flowers but to be honest it's not something I've ever considered.'

'Lucky you. Only wish I could say the same. Remember the story I was telling you last night about the strange coincidence on the Cherbourg ferry? Well Ron Bailey who was the other guy on the trip has a son who at the time made a bit of a name for himself as an amateur naturalist doing talks to schools and occasional TV appearances. He kept a couple of snakes in their airing cupboard at home. I avoided going upstairs to the loo as it would have entailed passing the cupboard. I've always had an over-active imagination you see.'

'But why did the book always fall open on the same page – that old devil coincidence again?'

'Dunno. Perhaps someone else in my family had been looking at the photograph. Perhaps someone else had the same phobia. Funnily enough I never asked. Anyway, that was only the beginning of my revulsion for any member of the reptile family.' Bob fell silent chewing on the remains of his apple. Alice felt a pang of guilt and touching his arm asked him if he was angry with her for throwing the scissors away.

'I'll forgive you. Was for the best I reckon. Anyway I would probably forgive you for anything even splitting from me all those years ago. After we parted I was devastated. I knew it would happen one day but I always secretly hoped otherwise. Remember that bloke who lived on the corner of your street? Dave Jackson, I think he was called? His girlfriend at the time was Sue somebody or other. They started going out at about the same time as us. The last I heard they're still married fifty-five years later would you believe?'

Alice smiled and nodded at the recollection. 'Yes, I remember. A bit of a bore. You wouldn't have wanted that.

Just think what we'd both missed. A life full of divorce, love and loss, intrigue and murder instead of a country cottage with roses around the door, white personalised Audi on the front drive, Saturday night dinner parties and 6 happy kids! Wow!'

Bob wondered where the 'murder' bit came in but dismissed it as a turn of phrase.

'*Quel horreur,*' continued Alice, 'couldn't stomach that. It would drive me crazy. Look at all the 'benefits' of life today whichever side of the water you're on. President Le Pen, Prime Minister Johnson and BREXIT creating havoc everywhere, not forgetting 'The Donald' lurking around waiting for another bite of the cherry. It couldn't get any worse could it? Please tell me that it couldn't get any worse. We're living in unprecedented times, Bob. Future generations will look back on this time with undiluted amusement. I suspect they might also be intrigued by any marriage which has the tenacity to hang on for fifty odd years and furthermore between a man and a woman. Heterosexual marriage! Get that!'

'Now you're really depressing me. More interesting talking about snakes.'

Alice took a bottle of *Perrier* from her rucksack and unscrewing the top passed it to Bob. 'You don't mind sharing do you?' She pulled a comic face of feigned disgust.

'No after you. Give me the secondary tactile pleasure. My reward for the loss of the scissors.'

Alice spluttered 'now look what you've made me do' as she mopped the spilt water from her khaki blouse. There followed a few moments of silence whilst they both took in their surroundings, the walled city of Carcassonne and the distant hazy backdrop of the Pyrenees, a small lake shimmering below a stand of pine trees, the heady scent of mountain thyme and a swallowtail butterfly hovering over the stony ground. It was Alice who spoke first. 'Do you think it was the end of the age of innocence? You know the beginning of the 60's. Wouldn't swap anyone that age of discovery. The music, having a bit of money in our pockets, scary sex, two TV channels, pirate radio, no internet, few drugs to speak of, free education, the list is endless.'

'Yes, I began the decade discovering the female body with my old friend Ken Whitehouse. Would you believe we used to cut out pictures of women's underwear from an old mail order catalogue; bras, knickers, panties, corsets, stockings, suspender belts even saying the words sent us into paroxysms of erotic delight. Inevitably it wasn't long before we moved on to the real thing. It's still hard to forget you in your green gymslip and the flash of white panty when you lay down in the park on the way home from school. I'm not embarrassing you am I?' Alice smiled and gave a non-committal shrug. Bob continued. 'By the close of the decade I was married and holding down a secure job which I was certain would keep me happy until retirement. Funny how things work out or not as the case maybe. Certainly they were interesting times. Perhaps for you and me? Perhaps not everyone would see it like that. Maybe we were the fortunate ones at the time. Do you remember those close buddies of mine Dick and Ralph? Dick was the one who would never leave us alone. *'Agent Provocateur'* in the best sense – he still is! Always turning up when we wanted a quick snog. Ralph the amateur philosopher with a well-honed cynicism and wicked humour verging on the obscene. Ralph eventually went off to Canada to make his way, Ken to The States, not sure if he took the underwear cut-outs with him! Dick and I settled for a life in England. Amazingly we all still meet up every year or so in some smooth hotel with a Michelin star. Not to necessarily reminisce although occasionally the time machine labelled *Chateau Lafitte, Jack Daniels* or *Tetley's* takes us across the frontier into times past, nothing too serious you understand, the scars are still faintly visible after 60 years. Both Dick and Ralph married as happily as one can expect these days. Intelligent, attractive and cultured wives, independent but diligently supportive. They've stuck together through times I can only imagine and I wouldn't dare to pose the question. Broadly successful careers however you interpret that. Dick and Ralph both shared a life-long passion for liquids, beer and oil. Dick would always insist on passing the local oil refinery on the way to the pub and was enthusiastic about D-day memorials. A career working in petroleum provided Ralph with the wherewithal to buy the rounds but no memorials for him. He vehemently opposed any mention of the grim reaper. As for Ken he followed the American Dream or did it become a Trumpian nightmare? Kids, grandchildren, dutiful wife, duplex in a quiet US suburb. Likes to remind me that we're next for the knacker's yard. None of us have made a million but I reckon we've left a few positive marks on each other's lives and would like to imagine on the wider society also although perhaps that's a too arrogant statement of wishful thinking. You'll be familiar with the club of *'Forever 27. Died too Young.'* Hendrix, Joplin, Jones, Morrison, Cobain, Johnson, Winehouse? Died too soon but made an indelible mark. Reverse the digits and Ralph, Dick, Ken and myself make the class of 72 this year – died too old. Not too bad, eh?'

'Colin would have been in the class of 72 also.' Alice looked to the ground and followed a line of ants with her index finger. 'I always felt that you and your friends were practically inseparable and I remember feeling quite jealous at the time but what do you mean by 'scars?' Don't we all carry the traces of emotional or physical upheaval to a lesser or greater extent?'

'Yes, I guess we do but with Ralph and Dick particularly it was great personal loss at a time when life should have been providing stability and firm foundations for the future.' He paused as a brief wave of melancholy passed over him. 'Anyway let's not get too bogged down in that after all I guess that your experiences with Colin have left some deep cuts in your psyche.'

'To a certain extent you're right Bob but my scars have largely healed, thank goodness. Fortunately, I've worked things through in my own way and I think I've come out of the other end of the tunnel in one piece.' She forced a smile and offered Bob the last sandwich.

'Now if you'll excuse me Bob I must go and have a little *pipi* as the French like to say. Back in five minutes. Clean up the picnic and don't see any snakes whilst I've gone.'

Bob once more shuddered involuntarily at the thought and stuffing their sandwich wrappers and half-empty bottle of Perrier into Alice's backpack he turned his mind to other matters. The afternoon sun was still high in the sky and the heat haze had by now completely blocked out the view of the Pyrenees. He was grateful for the shade and noted that the rest of the route was through a pine forest which would give them some protection until they could order a couple of cold beers in the village cafe they'd spotted earlier. The memory of the scissors came back to him and momentarily haunted him like a bad dream. He supposed that Alice was right about getting rid of them. What good had ever come of them? Madame Louise and her husband had died of Spanish flu, his mother seeing them stick into the floor as the telegram announcing Eric's death had arrived, the end of his first romance with Alice as she took them without paying, what other stories could they tell? This was getting too maudlin. It was all pure coincidence, wasn't it? *clumsy / (stole them)*

✂

They managed to find a small table by the fountain under the shade of an ancient plane tree. Bob ordered two beers. The waiter arrived with two chilled glasses and two bottles of *Leffe Light* plus a bowl of salted nuts. She was humming to herself. Bob recognised a Joni Mitchell classic. '*A Case of You.*' He was about to join in and sing a couple of lines but he was interrupted by Alice pushing the bowl of nuts aside with a loud 'yuk!.' The moment was gone.

'You never know how many dozens of customers have placed their grubby fingers in this bowl. Best steer clear.'

Bob laughed and nodded agreement remembering an article he'd read where some scientific group had discovered traces of urine in 90 percent of bar peanuts in London pubs. Not forgetting the urban legend, at least Bob hoped it was a legend, of hotel TV remotes being discovered with an average of 9 different traces of semen. It didn't bear too much reflection.

'Great walk, thanks. Really enjoyable but........' Bob hesitated before going on. He wasn't too sure how far he could push Alice on Colin's death. She'd said the scars had healed but something as traumatic as Colin's early death couldn't easily be swept away. She'd not elaborated but Bob was curious. He'd known Colin in his teenage years but apart from the incident of the grass snake there were few outstanding memories. He thought he'd push his luck.

'You haven't told me much about Colin.' He pressed remembering her description of him as being 'a right bastard.'

'How did he die?'

Alice took a long swig of her beer and not looking directly at Bob she seemed to be focusing on something in the distance.

Still looking afar she pulled a face. 'It's not a pleasant story, Bob. Are you sure you want to hear the gruesome details?'

Bob thought that she was using the word 'gruesome' ironically. After all divorce, separation and death could all be described as 'gruesome' in some way or other depending on the circumstances.

Bob nodded adding, 'only if you want to tell me.'

Alice took a long swig from her beer. She breathed deeply and drummed her fingers on the table.

'We'd had a relatively normal relationship, at least at the beginning. The birth of Stephen was a little unexpected but other couples had children at an early age and I suppose we were lucky, what with Colin getting a bursary to *The Sorbonne* and all that entailed. I suppose with the benefit of hindsight it was the events of '68 that changed him. He'd always been on the left politically but the events in Paris seemed to further shift his stance. He came to know a lot of highly politicised academics, you know what the French are like, and he got involved in what was then described as *'bohemian society.'* You've heard of the *Bo Bo's* I imagine. *Bourgeoise Bohemians.* The old joke about God never finishing off the Parisians. Well, it's probably true. Remember me telling you about Gregoire?'

'You mean the guy who was a regular dinner visitor? Long-haired academic who smoked *'Gauloises'* and had a limp handshake?'

'The self-same. Well, Gregoire was a big wheel in academic circles and influential in the communist party. He was a prof at *Sciences Po*. You know the prestigious university in Paris. Seven recent French presidents are *alumni* so you get the picture.'

Bob nodded as he reflected on the blatant elitism of French politics. At least the best rose to the top which was more than he could say about his own country where mediocrity appeared to have taken over most political parties to say nothing of the parlous state of education and well, journalism for that matter. He didn't dwell on that one preferring that Alice continue her story.

'Well, their friendship seemed relatively normal at the beginning and it was only later, after Colin's death that I discovered they had had a gay relationship.'

'You'd had no idea of Colin's homosexuality? Colin always seemed 'straight' in the days when I knew him. Surely you must have had some idea?'

'Well, I did find a blond wig hidden in the bedroom but he'd always liked playing the fool and dressing up at parties and so on so I thought little of it. It was when Gregoire's trial took place that I discovered the reality.'

'Gregoire's trial? Surely you're not suggesting that Gregoire was in some way responsible for Colin's death?'

Alice paused, breathing deeply. 'You see, Bob, Colin was killed by Gregoire. Gregoire was Colin's murderer.' She paused and stared hard into the fountain. Bob shook his head in disbelief. He called the waiter for a couple more beers. He was beginning to doubt the wisdom of having asked Alice the question. It was too late to retract and his morbid imagination demanded closure. She was in full flow.

'Gregoire pushed Colin into the path of a train on the Paris Metro. Colin's body, what was left of it was wearing women's clothes.' She took a deep breath. 'He'd been leading a double life as male Colin and female Collette. Gregoire had evidently discovered that 'Collette' was having a relationship with another man and the little green-eyed monster had reared its ugly head. It was all too much for Gregoire.'

'So, you and little Stephen had to live through all that? The French popular press must have had a field day.'

'Well not exactly. The trial was reported extensively but remember this was the beginning of 1969 and France was still recovering from *'les evenéments'* of '68. The journalists were occupied with weightier matters.'

'So, what happened to Gregoire? Presumably you were called as a witness.'

'Gregoire tried to claim that it was a *crime passionnel.* A crime of passion. The hearing in the *Cour d'Assisses* was short. As Colin's wife, under French law I wasn't obliged to give evidence. By the end of the third day the jury found him guilty and Gregoire was sentenced to life. The plea of a 'crime of passion' was dismissed on the grounds that Gregoire was not in a formal relationship with Colin.' Alice swallowed hard and looking Bob in the face added, 'Do you want me to go on?'

'You said Colin was leading a double life? Had you any idea of what had been going on? You were his wife after all.'

'Looking back on it now I think that in some ways Paris was the making of Colin. He changed in those first few months from the typical English lad into a fully-fledged political animal. He really had been radicalised. He'd always had a deep interest in left wing politics but once he got in with the academic crowd at the university he was like a butterfly emerging from its chrysalis. He even took on some of the macho French posturing, a role which he seemed to enjoy playing. When he started criticising me for my choice of *'bourgeois'* friends and my preferred reading and musical tastes I saw a side to him that I had no idea existed. I'd fallen for his rough diamond charm, his commitment and determination and sense of humour. You know how humour is very seductive in a guy. Initially we had a good sex-life but it didn't seem a big issue to Colin unlike most of the other guys I'd known. Sorry Bob that wasn't meant to be personal – no offence intended.'

'None taken. I lusted after you mercilessly.'

Alice ignored the comment.

'But Colin's transformation into Collette. You really had no idea?'

'No, none at all. The incident with the wig should have alerted me. He enjoyed playing the fool particularly after a few beers and he once did a bit of cross dressing at a review that he and some colleagues put on at Christmas. I guess the *'Bohemian'* crowd that he got mixed up with must have introduced him to new notions of gender identity. Today these issues are more out in the open but back then most of those ideas were unthinkable and to voice an opinion would have been completely out of the question.'

Alice went quiet looking down into her beer as if deciding whether she should say more.

'I should tell you about the scissors, Bob.'

'Pardon?' Bob felt that he was losing track of the story. Too much sun and beer was addling his brain. 'What the devil have the scissors got to do with Colin's murder? Surely you're not suggesting that............'

'No, they weren't the murder weapon if that's what you're thinking, although they might well have been if I'd been stronger and known more about the human anatomy.'

'Oh, Alice now you're confusing me. Why have we got back to those bloody awful scissors?'

'Yes, bloody being the operative word. You see I attacked Colin one night. He came home worse for the wear. It wasn't the first time but this time he cranked up the anger. He started shouting at me and going on about me wanting to become a *bourgeois* Parisienne. He threw my Proust in the bin and then slapped my face. I started throwing whatever came to hand. It was total panic. I must have blacked out momentarily but when I came to I had the scissors in my hand. Stephen was cowering in the corner, crying. The rest of the contents of my sewing box were scattered on the floor. For a while afterwards I couldn't recall what happened but several days later I had this terrible flashback. I saw that Colin had his back turned and in a rash moment of anger I threw the scissors into his back. The scissors drew some blood but I'd hit his shoulder blade and the injury was minor. The scissors rebounded. He charged out of the door and retrieving the scissors I hurled them with all my force at the door where they hung momentarily before clattering to the ground. It was the last time I saw him alive.'

'You're sure you remember attacking Colin with the scissors? Could you have imagined it?'

'No Bob, not my imagination when seeing the traces of blood on the scissors and it was several days before I wiped them clean and hid them in the cupboard. I couldn't have imagined that.'

Alice brushed a tear from the corner of her eye and breathed deeply. Bob reached across the table and squeezed her hand. For a moment no one spoke. Bob hesitated not really knowing how to respond. It was Alice who broke the silence.

'Apart from Hervé and Stephen you're the first person I've spoken to about this. I never mentioned it to the police at the time and due to the horrific nature of Colin's accident it would have been impossible to detect any trace of the injury in any post-mortem examination. I'd wiped the blood from the blades and put the scissors away out of sight in a box of odds and ends. Later I gave them to a neighbour who frequented all the Normandy *brocante* sales. They stayed there until you rediscovered them on the stall years later. Now perhaps you understand my reaction to the scissors yesterday when you showed them to me in the café.'

Bob suddenly felt an enormous pang of guilt. Ashamed and embarrassed by his cheerful presentation of the bubble wrapped scissors on the terrace of *Café Sarazin* stupidly thinking that she would be pleasantly surprised to see the scissors again. Alice was right the scissors had to go.

'So, did anyone find the identity of Colin's other lover? Another bourgeois academic I suppose.'

'No, not at all. The police weren't interested. The 'mystery' lover never really became known for some time. It was only several months later that I had a visit from a man claiming to have known Colin from his rugby days. He was a part-time barman, Franck Dolzean, from a sleazy joint in the 15th arrondissement where the players used to hang out after matches. He wanted to offer his condolences. There was something about his manner that made me suspicious. He kept asking if Colin had been ill. This was long before AIDS awareness and it was only when I later saw his name in the obituaries under the heading of 'sudden death of Rugby player' did I begin to make a few tenuous connections about a possible relationship between Colin and the Dolzean chap. There was no point in taking it further but I did go and have a full medical examination. There was always talk of 'sexually transmitted diseases' and I just thought you never know better safe than sorry. Colin and I had little sex in the last few months of his life but I reasoned that it was better to be sure.'

'So Gregoire is now festering in *'La Santé'* prison?'

Alice smiled ironically. Bob wondered why considering the circumstances but he remained hooked on her story.

'No. Gregoire is dead. Found dead in his cell one morning with a plastic bag over his head.'

'Oh god!' Exclaimed Bob. 'So now all the protagonists in this sordid affair are dead.' He paused before adding 'except you.'

'Except me.' Alice solemnly sighed.

✂

'So now you know it all,' Alice forced a smile. 'I can't complain. The glass has always been half full for me. I have a life that many others would give their right arm for, an adoring son and a loving husband. I live in a beautiful part of France. The business has been very successful. We've worked very hard establishing clients and contacts in the region. We've put a little money to one side and we're planning another venture. We're doing what we want to do and how many others can say that?'

'So where are you off to?'

Alice recovered her composure and took a deep breath. 'Well, we've decided to invest in a small wine business. Hervé knows the ropes. He worked in the wine business in Bordeaux for many years before he retired. We've bought a small vineyard in Béziers and we're planning to sell direct to the consumer. The farmhouse is old and needs some refurbishment but there's room to build on a small *cave à vin* where we hope to organise tastings and perhaps even put on a few themed events for the tourists in the season. You know the sort of thing. 'Rock in the vineyard' would be straight up the Brits' street or maybe 'Mozart meets Merlot.'' She laughed with genuine pleasure and for the first time in an hour her face lit up with child-like delight. 'Stephen won't be too far away and he'll come over at the weekends and holidays to give us a hand.'

'And what are your plans? Not more teaching I hope!'

'I'm afraid so. Got myself into a partnership in a small enterprise teaching Business English. Quite enjoyable. For the first time in my life I'm effectively my own boss. Gisèle is working at what she does best, running a small kitchen shop and organising some rather exclusive cookery courses. You'd get on well with Gisèle. Perhaps we'll visit one day.'

Alice puffed out her cheeks and shaking her head touched Bob's arm. 'It's been fantastic seeing you, talking with you and all that over the past couple of days but I think we should call it a day at least for the near future. What has passed between us has been nothing less than electric and our story should perhaps end there. Who knows what lies in the future? We'll always have Carcassonne, Bob.'

Alice rummaged around in her purse. She found what she was searching for. 'Here you are Bob. I want you to be the first to have my new business card. Fresh from the printers yesterday.'

As she closed her purse Bob imagined he had caught a glimpse of a ray of sunlight glancing off a pair of scissors. The beer and the heat of the day had clearly gone to his head.

He studied the card. Beneath the address there was a picture of a wine bottle. On the label was a bright yellow sunflower in glorious full bloom.

Chapter Eight

Three years later

Initialled serpentine, silver embroidery scissors.

Italian early 20th Century.

Anonymous loan

A cutlery museum was hardly the place to take a seven-year-old on a hot afternoon in July but Bob was curious and determined that George should have some cultural education on his French holiday. It was the first time away without his parents and his grandparents had decided that a grand tour of France would be in order. Post Brexit Britain under Boris Johnson recently re-elected for a second term was still in chaos and the protracted negotiations with Brussels were still going on years after the disastrous referendum. Scotland was on the verge of independence and Ireland nearly re-united. In the US Trump had miraculously escaped impeachment, lost the election to Biden, survived several civil actions and to no one's surprise was angling to stand again. Even here in France there was no escaping the new world order after the stunning presidential election result which had seen Macron booted out in 2022 and replaced by Le Pen. Not Marine the daughter of Jean-Marie but the charismatic, intelligent blond niece Marion Marechal Le Pen. Apparently less extreme than the rest of her notorious family clan she was politically savvy and had somehow managed to unite a broad swathe of the French right and centre by combining moderate right-wing policies with the 'Trump School' of popularism. Part of the charm of France was its traditional stance against change but even the youngest Le Pen knew that would have to change if the country was to compete with the growing economic might of China. Whether the family fascist tendencies had been subdued was anyone's guess but already the number of illegal immigrants into the country had been drastically reduced and there was talk of changes to France's membership of the European Community.

Bob had lived in France for over thirty years and loved the diversity and charm of the country. A country of incredible paradoxes still fighting off the wave of Anglo-Saxon cultural values. A people who could swing from joyous enthusiasm to being inherently unhappy, argumentative, unpredictable and enormously political. The grand philosophical traditions reigned supreme; French 'exceptionalism' ruled but pragmatism was hard to find. He wanted his young grandson to share the positive side and he considered that now was as good a time as any to introduce him to what he considered to be the civilising effect of continental Europe before it was too late. They'd already visited their favourite Breton and Vendean haunts and much to George's delight done boat trips to several of the islands on the Atlantic coast including Belle Ile, 'Ile d'Yeu and Ile d'Aix. They'd explored the papal city of Avignon, tasted the culinary pleasures of Marseille and Cassis, taken the cable car to the summit of Mont Blanc and now their route since leaving Dijon was heading towards the Vosges mountains. Today's itinerary was due to take them to an amusement park with dinosaurs. That would keep George happy. Bob checked the route looking for a convenient stopping off place for coffee and toilets. The satnav had picked out the small town of Nogent. It seemed as good as anywhere – quite small but big enough to have a café terrace on which they could while away a half hour or so. He vaguely knew something about Nogent being the cradle of the French cutlery industry. He'd never visited before but he was curiously drawn to it. A web search boasted that Trip Advisor had given the museum a score of 4.1 which Bob considered was probably a good recommendation and he was intrigued and not a little curious to read that the museum's scissor collection was 'a must.' He remembered seeing Jean Renoir's film adaptation of Zola's *La Bête Humaine* in which the character Roubeau played by Fernand Ledoux handles a knife saying, *'C'est un beau couteau……mais c'est un Nogent !* Beautiful knives from Nogent. This seemed a wonderful place to stop. George was clearly not so convinced.

'But you said we'd be going to see the dinosaurs in the park.'

'Yes, we will but first we must satisfy Pop's whim. How about an ice cream?' Gisèle shared his lack of enthusiasm and after all they had promised their grandson a trip to the local amusement park.

The museum was in the town's main square in a fine white stone building decked out in geraniums and primulas. They apparently were the only visitors. The pony-tailed receptionist couldn't have been more welcoming even asking young George whether he spoke French and who much to everyone's delight replied *'un petit peu.'* Clearly parents Jim and Charlie had done an excellent job in the language department. Nan and Pop looked on proudly.

The museum had an amazing collection of all things to do with cutlery. Knives, forks and spoons of all designs and shapes, surgical instruments, farming and garden tools as well as scale models of water wheels, forges and industrial machinery. The variety of scissor designs was stunning. Scissors with rabbit handles, hearts, birds of all shapes and sizes, medical scissors, gardening shears, hairdressing scissors, kitchen scissors, sheep shearers and plain ordinary embroidery scissors. On the walls were old photographs of the cutlery workers in the early 20th century, serious faced in their dust encrusted overalls. The curator, Clotilde Estampe, explained carefully in French the history of the industry in Nogent. How it had developed in the 18th century and become the most important cutlery manufacturer in the whole of France. The surrounding area had been rich in iron ore, the forests providing an abundant source of natural fuel, the local streams and rivers providing hydraulic power and the sandstone rock perfect for honing blades. Nogent cutlery had the reputation of being some of the world's finest. The collection we were looking at today belonged for the most part to Jean-Marie Roulot a man whom the guide described as possibly the most passionate scissor collector in the world and who still maintained a workshop where he repaired and renovated old scissors. It was said that when Monsieur Roulot finished a pair of scissors he could hear 'the blades singing.'

George was rapidly losing interest and wandered off to a corner of the room where he leaned against a glass covered display cabinet and yawned. His head hardly reached to the top of the cabinet but he could get a side on view of the objects. Suddenly something unexpected caught his attention and retreating from the cabinet he cried out, 'a snake, look a snake!' The guide laughed and walked over to where George was staring wide-eyed at a pair of scissors.

'I don't like snakes,' he grimaced. 'They're slimy, slippery and slivery and just sooo horrible.'

'Wow! you've certainly mastered alliteration – a budding poet in the making,' laughed Bob nervously intrigued by his grandson's find but something touched a chord and he peered warily into the cabinet. He saw what George had been shocked to see but George's shock was nothing compared to that of Bob's. The scissors had snake handles and intertwined with the snakes were the initials 'K' and 'T.' Bob looked across to his wife and called her over. 'Look it's the scissors. It's like a dream or a nightmare.'

For the second time in his life Bob had rediscovered his scissors. First at the *brocante* sale and now here.

By the side of the exhibit was a note.

Ciseaux à broder avec initiales en serpentine Italien début XXème siècle.

(preté par anonyme)

'The last time I saw those scissors was when they disappeared or I thought they disappeared down a well in Carcassonne. Would you believe it? There can't possibly be another pair of scissors with serpent handles and those same initials.' Bob exclaimed. He shook his head in disbelief and stared intently into the show case. Turning to the curator he asked if she had any idea of the origin of the scissors or who the anonymous donor might have been.

'We received a package sometime last year. It was me who opened the bubble wrapped envelope. The scissors were in poor condition, the tips of the blades blunted as if by repeated hitting against something hard. Inside there was a brief note saying that since the death of the owner they had come into the hands of a close family member who following the wishes of the deceased wanted the scissors to be loaned to a reputable museum. The new owner preferred to rest anonymous but could be contacted at a *Poste restante* in Béziers under the pseudonym of *Asphodel*. No further details. That's all I can tell you. One of our team of volunteer renovators took them down to the cutlery workshop where Monsieur Roulot himself reset the handles and cleaned them up.'

Béziers, thought Bob. Strange coincidence. That was the last place that Alice had chosen to live. He recalled their last conversation sitting by the fountain and how she had produced a new business card from her bag with a picture of a sunflower beneath the address. The owner deceased. Surely not!

Bob turned to Gisèle and clutched her arm. 'Don't you see? Those scissors belonged in my family. They were my grandma's dress making scissors that were passed on through the family eventually ending up in my possession. I used to keep them in my bedside drawer. Don't you remember when I went to visit Alice in Carcassonne a few years ago. It was then that the scissors disappeared or should I say it was then that they disappeared down a well. Well, if the truth be told it was Alice who threw them down a well.' Bob thought it diplomatic not to mention the details of the loss. 'The initials are those of my grandparents – Kate and Tom.'

'Oh, c'mon Bob. Who are you kidding? You're really letting that imagination of yours get the better of you. We drive half-way round France, two thousand kilometres and just by chance in an obscure out of the way French town you discover your grandmother's dressmaking scissors. She was going to say a rural French backwater but thought better of it in front of the curator. Don't you think that's a bit far-fetched? A big chunk of bullshit!'

George was wondering what 'bullshit' was but he was getting bored with all this culture and had other matters on his mind. 'Dinosaurs Pop, dinosaurs come on!' George was getting restless. There were better things to do than looking at an old pair of embroidery scissors but Bob was too absorbed to let the matter drop. He suggested that Gisèle take George for an ice-cream and he would catch up with them shortly.

The curator reluctantly agreed to Bob's request to take the scissors out of the showcase on condition that he wore a pair of white protective gloves. She took a small silver key from her pocket and unlocked the display case. Handling the scissors as if they were likely to crumble into fragments of dust, she placed them on a velvet mat. Carefully he took the scissors in his hands and slowly traced his fingers over the snake handles and the initials 'K' and 'T.' It was over seventy years since he'd first touched the beautifully carved silver handles. What memories they brought back. After a few moments of quiet reflection he tried handing the scissors back only to be admonished by the guide. *'Ne passez jamais les ciseaux de main en main parce que les ciseaux est considérée comme étant l'ennemi.'* He'd forgotten the scissor superstition protocol of never handing scissors directly to another person for scissors are considered the enemy. Annoyed by his *faux pas* and feeling ever so slightly embarrassed he gently placed the scissors back on the mat.

He stood in silence for several moments just staring at the scissors. Clotilde the curator looked on, a puzzled expression on her face. 'Can I be of any further help, *Monsieur*? Bob shook his head and walked to the door where he paused to give the curator his business card. They shook hands and Bob thanked her for her help.

'Please contact me if you have any further information. My address is on the card.' Outside he caught sight of Gisèle and George sitting in the shade licking two giant cornets. As he closed the door he smiled at the curator before concluding, 'got to see a man about a dinosaur, *au revoir et merci beaucoup.'*

'Well, what on earth was all that about?' enquired his wife as he stepped outside into the hot afternoon sunshine. She gave him a lick of her ice-cream. Bob pulled a face. 'You know I prefer pistachio to vanilla.'

'There wasn't any pistachio left besides I didn't know that you were still obsessing over those scissors. Surely you don't believe those old scissors are the ones that once belonged in your family.'

Gisèle remembered that the scissors had been kept in Bob's bedside drawer. His trip to Carcassonne had been shrouded in mystery and she knew better than to ask. She wasn't a jealous wife and assumed that it was a matter between old friends but she did wonder what had really become of the scissors. She recalled them briefly discussing scissor superstitions on their first date when they'd exchanged personal histories. But since then she'd barely given the subject a second thought. Was her husband really suggesting that the scissors they'd just seen in the museum were the self-same ones. The idea was preposterous.

'I think chocolate is best.' George licked his lips and swallowed the last of the cornet. 'Rock, paper, scissors, rock, paper, scissors.' he chimed in. They'd been playing the ubiquitous game over breakfast and much to Bob's chagrin George won most of the time. Bob had some difficulty in remembering whether it was paper that beat rock or vice versa. He was fine with the scissors. Scissors cut.

'Oh, do be quiet,' Bob interrupted. 'I think you were cheating anyway.'

'I wasn't. You're just fed up because I won.'

Bob returned to the real scissors. 'Well, yes actually. I must concede that they're becoming something of an obsession.

Must fill you in with all the details sometime when you have a spare couple of hours.

'OK let's go and find some dinosaurs.' George pumped his fist in delight and ran to the car.

Chapter Nine

Eight months later

Bob had never found it easy to voluntarily close-down certain episodes in his life. Each person or event slotted into his mental filing cabinet from which from time to time he would open the dossier, reflect on the pleasant or unpleasant memories it conjured up and then return to the cabinet for an indeterminate period after which the file might be re-opened. It was a useful strategy particularly in times of stress or difficulty and helped him to rationalise some of his deeper emotions. For longer than he could remember Alice had her own special compartment which he opened with caution. This particular box was a rich treasure trove of sexual fantasy, teenage angst, love and helter-skelter rides around the learning curve of life to the soundtrack of The Beatles or Everly Brothers. Useful? Of course. Depression, frustration, anger? Open the box. Exhilaration, new relationship, new adventure, change of job? Box closed.

This particular box had been closed for some time now, ever since their meeting in Carcassonne. He pretended he didn't care too much about the scissors anymore. Inadvertently they'd led him back to Alice, not to rekindle a lost flame nor to see how life changes our perspectives of human desire or indeed to note the subtle ravages of time but rather to round off some of life's rough edges and in the process answer a few unanswered questions. After all a pair of scissors can destroy as well as create. In medieval times scissors were thought to have the power to ward off evil spirits and witchcraft. Simply opening the blades to make a cross and placing them under the doormat supposedly did the trick. On the other hand dropping a pair of scissors was a warning of an unfaithful lover. Bob's scissors had disappeared down a well or had they? The appearance at the museum left him wondering whether he was going mad or whether the scissors had supernatural properties.

By necessity the scissors had disappeared into Bob's metaphysical filing cabinet. He was in the business of opening new dossiers. A change of life, new marriage, new job, new house. He'd met, fallen in love with and married a French widow from Avignon, they'd bought a house in the Dordogne near Sarlat and they'd both launched themselves into new projects; Bob teaching English to business-people and his wife managing a cookery school. He saw little purpose in letting the scissors become an obsession.

It was a bright, clear Saturday morning in April when Bob decided that the grass cutting season had arrived. He'd been putting it off for some while but something about the weather and his mood today spurred him into action besides he detested the long grass which he always felt might encourage a couple of 'rogue' snakes to venture forth and shatter his bucolic idyll. The estate agent who had first shown them around the property had assured Bob that there was nothing venomous and that they were 'gentil' for hadn't she only that same morning viewed two 'couleuvres' copulating in her very own garden. Even stated in her most charmingly accentuated English Bob was not reassured and was determined to be attentive in the long grass. The thought of two grass snakes copulating on his front lawn was too awful to contemplate. He was reminded of 'snake detection theory' and suspected one of the 'little buggers' would show up one day.

He was pulling the motor mower from the garage and was about to check the oil and fuel when he was interrupted by the sound of the yellow *la poste* van coming up the drive. '*Postier Patrick*' cigarette hanging from his bottom lip shouted a throaty '*bonjour.*' Bob wasn't sure of his real name but '*Patrick*' seemed appropriate. Without opening the van door '*Patrick*' stuck his arm out of the window, gave Bob an obligatory handshake and handed him a brown envelope and without further comment sped off depositing the remains of the cigarette in a yellow tulip head.

Bob looked the envelope over. Official looking with a '*Troyes*' post mark. He couldn't recall having any business contacts in north-eastern France. Probably more publicity for cheap home insulation – he'd lost count of the number of unsolicited telephone calls and letters promising home insulation for €1. Turning the envelope over he noticed a return address again in Troyes and the name *Brunhes & Poitou, Maison de vente aux Enchères.* Why would an auction house be writing to him he wondered? He opened the envelope and found a letter and an accompanying slim brochure detailing a list of fine art objects coming up for auction. The letter in English was headed *Musée de la Coutellerie 52800 Nogent.* He read the letter with growing curiosity and not a little apprehension.

Monsieur Martin,

I hope you will excuse me for writing to you like this but in view of our conversation last year. I thought you might be interested in the forthcoming auction at Brunhes & Poitou. You'd thoughtfully left me your visiting card and happily I'd kept it in the back of our visitors' book. I well remember your visit to the museum and your interest in the scissors which you thought may have once belonged to your family. The horror of your grandson when he noticed the snake handles has long stuck in my mind.

In a nutshell, the pair of Italian scissors which had caught your interest and that of your grandson are coming to auction. You will doubtless remember that the scissors were on loan anonymously. Recently we received a letter from the donor's lawyer asking us if we could give an evaluation of the scissor's worth with a view to selling. A local expert examined the scissors and believed the pair of scissors in our collection was an extremely rare example of Italian craftsmanship and could in fact be one of only two or three originally made in a cutlery factory in Maniago North-East Italy. Certainly, the rarity value of the scissors would push up the price and the expert suggested the figure of around €3000. You may be further interested to know that according to the expert the initials 'T' and 'K' were engraved on to the blades after the original fabrication. In view of this the new owner instructed us through his or her lawyer to either offer an agreed purchase sum or place them in the hands of a local auction house. Naturally we would have liked to have kept the scissors as they represent a fine example of early 20th

century Italian craftsmanship. We offered the owner what we considered a fair price for the scissors but it was rejected. Our small museum isn't endowed with a large sum of money and we rely heavily on donations and loans so we had no choice but to accede to the owner's request.

You will find enclosed details of the sale by auction of various metal artefacts with historic merit at the auction house of Brunhes & Poitou in the city of Troyes at the beginning of May.

If I can be of any further help to you in the matter of this sale or any other related matter please contact me at the museum,

Veuillez agréer, Monsieur, l'assurance de notre parfaite considération.

Clotilde Estampe (Curator)

Bob scanned down the list of sale objects. There were about 50 lots coming up for auction mostly comprising embroidery tools, surgical instruments and cutlery. Item N° 33 caught his attention.

*33.   **Ciseaux à broder avec initiaux en serpentine.** Italien début XXème siècle. Usine de Maniago. Rare. Prix de réserve €2000, $2200, £1700)*

Bob breathed deeply. Too many questions. The grass cutting would have to wait as would the copulating snakes – *quelle horreur!*

Chapter Ten

Three weeks later

Gisèle drove me to Bordeaux St Jean rail station. After kissing her goodbye and dismissing her repeated warnings not to lose my head at the auction I took the early morning train to Paris. One change in the capital and then I should be in Troyes by early afternoon. I indulged myself in a first-class seat and sat back as the TGV sped through the Bordelaise vineyards resplendent in the spring sunshine. I pulled Clotilde Estampe's letter from my jacket pocket and re-read it for the umpteenth time. The letter posed more questions than it answered. Who was the new mystery owner of the scissors and how had they inherited them and why would they want to sell? The previous owner had died. But the scissors really belonged to me, passed down through my family from my grandparents. I couldn't prove anything of course. No certificate of ownership, no personal documentation or photos. The only living people who could possibly identify the scissors were Alice and me. The biggest question of all was how had the scissors really ended up on a beach in Narbonne? Alice had said that the watercourse from the Black Mountains would eventually reach the sea. Did I really believe that? Sealed with a kiss – sod that!

I booked in at a cheap chain hotel. The girl on reception managed to rustle up a map of the town and over a plate of *steak frites* I located the auction house. It was just a short walk from the hotel. I drained the half bottle of local *Irancy* wine and rang my wife to tell her I'd arrived safely. She considered my trip an act of folly but she'd already decided some time ago that most Englishmen were irrational and once they make up their minds about something they stubbornly refuse to change their minds even if they know they are wrong. She wished me well with a cynical laugh and advised me to keep clear of a bidding war and not to raise my eyebrows at the wrong moment. She had no wish that I bankrupt us both for a pair of old scissors. The reserve price was a ridiculous €2000. Did I really want to buy back my own scissors for the price of a week's stay in a luxury hotel overlooking the Med? That certainly seemed like an irrational act. Forget it and go back home and book a week in *Le Negresco*. I idly checked the hotel reservation site on my iPhone. I grimaced and decided that I probably wouldn't be able to afford a single night let alone a week. I'd sleep on it.

I awoke early the next morning to the sound of bins being emptied in the courtyard below. I was no nearer to resolving my dilemma. The breakfast room was practically deserted. The croissants were stale, the fruit was soft and bruised but at least the coffee was hot and strong. What did I expect for €5? Breakfast at *The Negresco* was €30. I returned to my map of the city. The auction house of *Brunhes & Poitou* was off the *Boulevard Gambetta* down a narrow side street in the old town. The sale wasn't until 10.30 so I reckoned I had plenty of time. I would arrive early, have a look at the sale items and get a seat near the front to catch all the action.

The late April morning sunshine reflected off the stained glass of the 13th century gothic cathedral of Saint Pierre-et-Saint Paul as I walked through the narrow streets. I still had to resolve my dilemma – to bid or not to bid. I began to wonder what I was doing here when only a few weeks ago I had been so determined to close the scissor dossier? Perhaps I was obsessed after all.

Commissaires-priseurs Brunhes & Poitou were on the second floor of a *grand hotel particulier* - a sort of private French city centre mansion probably built by rich bankers in the 19th century. A huge solid oak panelled door with several polished brass plaques on either side indicated that its present-day occupants ranged from insurance companies and legal firms to honorary consuls and financial consultants. I searched for the auctioneers and pushed the inset doorbell. A couple of seconds later there was a loud clunk and the door swung open revealing a dark half-timbered entrance hall, toilets and washroom on the left and an old-fashioned grilled elevator to the right. A stooped woman was laboriously mopping the marble floor. She didn't look up as I headed for the elevator. I pressed the button for the second floor. The elevator shook and juddered as if on its last legs. A notice in French, German and English informed all visitors to *Brunhes & Poitou* that they must report to the office.

I presented my passport to an unsmiling secretary in a dark grey suit, black cardigan and a chunky necklace. She spoke excellent English but with an overstated French sophistication, formality and coolness which would bemuse an Anglo-Saxon visitor more familiar with the casual joviality and informality of British or American administration. I showed my passport, signed a register and left an imprint of my bank card just in case I succeeded in any purchases. She handed me a white paddle with the number 8 on and was told to take the lift to the top floor and then follow the signs for the auction room.

The items up for auction were on display in a small ante room just off from the main hall. I picked up a copy of the day's sales catalogue and scanned the items. The lots were described in French and English. A bizarre collection of gruesome surgical instruments whose purpose I could only guess, some ancient farm tools, a diverse collection of cutting implements including assorted knives and scissors. My eyes fell on lot 33 and once again felt a shudder of recognition at the snake handles and the initials of 'K' and 'T.' Should I bid for my own property? Clearly I was not the only one to be interested in lot 33. A smart Oriental type, probably Chinese was talking to an assistant. His immaculately cut suit and coiffured hair reminded me of a tailor's dummy from the days when Burtons was famed for its bespoke suits and all young men of any ambition flocked to their High Street shops to be measured and fitted by a tailor whose tape measure invariably slipped when measuring the inside leg.

The Chinese was holding the scissors and inspecting the handles through an eyeglass. He was caressing the blades as if he'd found a long-lost lover. I felt a twinge of jealousy. I moved closer to get a better look at the prospective buyer. He spoke perfect English and was telling the young assistant that he had come all the way from a rural Chinese province where he had a private collection of 19th and 20th century European cutlery. Clearly the competition was hotting up.

The auction room was already filling up with an assortment of the serious and the curious, the formally dressed and the casual, the rich and the seemingly not so rich. This was my first auction and frankly I had little idea of what to expect. I was reminded of the old French expression '*l'habite ne fait pas le moine*' or literally 'clothing doesn't make the monk.' Certainly the auctioneer himself didn't do the formal. He was dressed in a white open-necked shirt and blue jeans. On the contrary his young female assistant looked as though she'd just come off a Parisian 'catwalk' in a powder blue suit, above the knee straight skirt and ten-centimetre *Louboutin* heels. I wasn't sure whether the bidders would be twitching in the wrong places but the red *Louboutin* soles visible under the table suggested who might be the owner of the richest pair of legs in the room. The relationship between women, power and money still perplexed me.

I managed to find myself a seat in the third row. I took stock of my surroundings. The high ceiling with its carved plaster cornices, an enormous crystal chandelier, the walls bearing numerous paintings of rural French scenes and darkened portraits of long forgotten politicians and businessmen. At the front of the room stood the auctioneer behind a plinth, a white-headed gavel in his hand. Alongside him '*Madame Louboutin*' sat demurely but expressionless in front of an elaborately carved table. Behind them stood two other women seated in front of an array of black telephones. A video screen on the back wall indicated several currency symbols.

The auctioneer banged his gavel on the plinth and a couple of overalled assistants arranged the first lot on the table.

'Lot 1.' Intoned the auctioneer. 'Collection of surgical instruments mostly used between 1970 and 1990. To be sold as complete and as seen. Shall we start at 20 Euros. Do I hear 20?'

I checked the catalogue list. A mesmerising collection of such items as *takahashi* scissors, *Crile* forceps, finger ring cutters and dental chisels. Definitely not for the squeamish. There seemed to be no lack of bidders and in less than two minutes the lot had been sold for 180 Euros. At this rate the auction would be over in little over an hour.

The second lot was less interesting consisting as it did of a hotchpotch collection of pre-Second World War carpentry tools. Hand drills, augers, screw drivers many in poor condition hammers and spirit levels. Again, the lot was knocked down in 2 minutes to a big guy in chunky sweater and cords. The *'Louboutin'* assistant noted his details on her laptop and he left the room smiling, undoubtedly well satisfied with his purchase. I was beginning to have serious doubts as to whether I should bid for the scissors. The bidding process was so fast I wasn't sure I'd be able to follow it all and what if I ended up actually buying the scissors! Heaven forbid. So much for my fantasies. I raised my eyebrows and tugged my ear just in case.

The lots came and went. I began to study the behaviour of the bidders in the room. I'd done a bit of homework on the pitfalls of auction sales. Strategies such as 'early bidders' or 'late bidders,' how to recognise the dealers (you can't), 'plants' placed in the room to drive up the asking price to benefit the seller. I was clearly in danger of being out of my depth here and I had no desire to make a fool of myself in front of a room of complete strangers. As I was contemplating that my gaze fell on an old white-haired guy sitting at the front and to the side of me. His face looked vaguely familiar. He was dressed very smartly in a dark suit and tie – he looked French but Frenchmen are not great tie wearers. The clothes seemed at odds with the face. Who on earth did he remind me of? I'd lost count of the number of times I'd seen 'familiar' faces. I have this thing about categorising similar facial types. This was easier living in a foreign culture – French faces are generally differently proportioned from Anglo-Saxon ones. It was another obsession of mine and sometimes I wondered where I lay on the autistic spectrum. However, this face was definitely very familiar. Occasionally he would turn and speak to a young man at his side.

The lots came and went. To my uncultured eye much of what I saw was rubbish and of little value but certainly to many of the others in the room they were stumbling on hidden treasures. The box of 19th century handcrafted Swiss woodworking tools could have been a work of art and there was an audible gasp in the room when the auctioneer gavelled them at 5000 Euros.

What is it about collectors I wondered? What sort of person would travel the world in search of an object that would more than likely end up in a show cabinet in a fusty attic coming out only to impress impressionable dinner guests? I knew people who had spent their lives collecting toy metal cars whose value was based on them remaining in the original cardboard box. I'd collected stamps. At least it was educational. It was my way of discovering the world.

I could feel the tension rising as the sale approached Lot 33. Despite my earlier apprehension about bidding for my own scissors I was now sensing an adrenaline buzz at the thought. I knew the reserve price to be €2000. What a ridiculous amount of money to pay for a pair of scissors that not only belonged to me but seemed to be cursed in some way. They had never done anyone any good and yet somehow the thought of the scissor's history brought out a bizarre strand of sentimentality in me. Over 100 years old, handmade in Italy, given to my grandparents on their wedding day in England by the Italian couturier who dies along with her husband in the 1918 flu epidemic, witness to the news of my uncle's death in Italy, separation from my first love, witness to Colin's anger, violence and rage in a Parisian attic and the final 'loss' to a passionate embrace next to a well in Carcassonne. The story could hardly get worse. I remember 'Googling' most expensive scissors and finding that a Japanese company *Sasuke* made a pair of *Bonsai* scissors that retailed at $35000 and took 3 months to make and all to cut the branches of miniature trees. I must be crazy. Gisèle was right.

The lots came and went. Mostly rather boring collections of odds and ends but which clearly interested many people judging by the enthusiasm for bidding relatively large sums of money for such obscure items as veterinary implements or 19th century autopsy tools. Surely museum pieces rather than for private collections? 'Come up and see my rather interesting collection of 18th century Arabic circumcision memorabilia,' wouldn't be a chat-up line I was likely to be using anytime soon.

The auctioneer slammed his gavel down to end bidding on Lot 32 and announced the arrival of what I'd been waiting for. An assistant passed in front of the assembled buyers with the scissors on a red velvet cushion. The room fell quiet and clearly the scissors were going to be a highlight of this sale. I almost felt a wave of pride coursing through me except I knew that the scissors were most certainly going to end up in someone else's hands in the next ten minutes or so.

'Lot 33. Early 20th century Italian hand-crafted silver scissors probably originating from the Maniago factory. A rare example of Italian craftsmanship, probably the sole remaining pair of scissors of the type uniquely engraved with unknown initials 'K and 'T.''

I wanted to shout out Kate and Tom. I had the sudden vision of my grandparents on their wedding day. On the morning of the wedding my grandmother had received the engraved scissors as a wedding present from her Italian immigrant couturier the creator of her white wedding dress. Stood next to her I imagined my grandpa' in his grey suit, full hunter pocket watch proudly clasped to his waistcoat. What would they have made of all of this? Over a hundred years later and the gifted scissors about to be auctioned in a provincial French town nearer to their Italian origins than to my relatives' northern industrial home. Damn it all the scissors belonged to me. I clutched paddle N° 8 to my chest. I still hadn't made up my mind what to do when the auctioneer called for a starting bid of €200.

'Do I hear 250, 250 at the back, 300, thank-you sir, 400 anyone 400?'

A nod in the direction of a telephone bidder. The suited Chinese pushed it up to 600.

'600.' I hardly realised I was on my feet waving my paddle. A gasp from a shocked room surprised by the sudden jump in bid price. The auctioneer looked towards his assistant on the telephone '700 to my left, do I hear 800?' The suit raised his paddle 800. 'The gentleman in the grey suit has it at 800 euros.'

I thrust my paddle in the air once more – caution thrown to the wind. 900 euros. By now heads were turning in my direction and I was beginning to enjoy this. Not for long. Out of the corner of my eye I could see the old guy with the familiar face looking in my direction and was that a smile I detected on his face? Suddenly I realised now where I'd seen him before. Involuntarily I lifted the paddle as the bid topped 1000 but the rest of the sale became a blur. I collected my thoughts as the bids topped 2000 but I hadn't the heart or courage to go further. I sat down feeling slightly foolish and tried to look as inconspicuous as possible. By now there were only three people in the bidding war. The Chinese guy and two telephone bidders. The price passed the 3000 barrier and although the suited Chinese struggled on, he eventually pulled out in the face of the anonymous telephone bidders. At 3500 one of the remaining bidders folded and the scissors were knocked down at €3500. As the auctioneer's gavel thumped the table the old guy with the young man at his side hugged one another and leapt in the air fists pumping in delight.

Chapter Eleven

'Hervé, what a surprise,' Bob practically falling over the row of chairs as he reached for the hand of the man he'd last seen in Carcassonne. 'How are you? What brings you here?'

'Bonjour Bob, what a pleasure to see you again. I might have guessed that one day we would meet again. Those scissors have the misfortune to keep reappearing. May I introduce you to Stephen? You may remember that he's the son of Alice.' Bob and Stephen shook hands warmly and one look into his eyes was enough for Bob to see the family resemblance but it was Alice's eyes that shone out and not her father's.

'And how is your mother, Stephen. Not with you today, busy growing sunflowers and treading grapes,' he laughed thinking back to the new enterprise that Alice and Hervé had launched in Béziers.

Hervé and Stephen looked at each other. Stephen turned his head away. It was Hervé who spoke. 'I have to tell you Bob that Alice is dead. Passed away two years ago under somewhat tragic circumstances.'

Stunned, Bob could only gasp for air. He thought it must be a sick joke. Bob wanted to say that people like Alice never die but it sounded too skittish. He stuttered searching for his

words. 'But she was such a wonderful lively woman...........'
He let the words trail off and placed his hands on Stephen
and Hervé's shoulders. 'Can we go somewhere more
private?'

A corner table in the bar of the nearby Hotel St. Jean. For
several moments they just looked at one another each
collecting their own thoughts. Bob was avoiding the question
uppermost in his mind. He needn't have bothered. Hervé
looked across at Stephen questioningly. 'Shall I or do you
want to?' Stephen smoothed his long blond hair, shuffled
uncomfortable and turned to Bob.

'I know a little about you Bob. Mum mentioned you
occasionally and I knew that you had been friends a long
time ago. As for the scissors, well what can I say?'

'What happened Stephen?' Bob could feel a pain strangling
his insides. 'How did she die?'

'I heard about you both meeting in Carcassonne and how you
produced the scissors. It was a big shock for her as you will
remember. When she first told me I was furious with you. I
didn't know how someone could be so insensitive as to place
in front of her the very article that had caused her so much
pain. I learned that you thought they'd been thrown down a
well in the mountains. At the last moment I think Mum

realised that the scissors had meant such a lot to you and for some reason best known to her she wanted another outcome. She wanted the scissors to live on and felt it unfair that the scissors should disappear completely so somehow she retrieved the scissors – how I don't know. It was sometime later that she suggested we loan the damn things to a museum.'

Bob cast his mind back to the hot September day in the Black mountains. How she'd embraced him and how he'd let the scissors fall from his grasp and presumed they'd fallen into the well. He'd not heard a splash and assumed that the well was very deep. He tried to recreate the scene, the picnic under the pines, the discussion about his fear of snakes and yes, he recalled her disappearing for several minutes saying that she needed a *petit pipi* – he was surprised that she'd used the French word. It had made him laugh and at the time he'd caught himself idly wondering about the significance of *wee wee* and *pipi*. How on earth had that come about? Perhaps she'd retrieved the scissors at the same time. Had she known that the scissors had missed the well, was it a spontaneous gesture or was it a well laid plan? Either way she probably knew the effect that the kiss would have on Bob.

Hervé picked up the story. 'So, the scissors once more came into Alice's possession. We moved to Béziers and started the new business. As you know Alice loved flowers and she was particularly fond of wild orchids.' He looked across at Stephen for approval to continue. Stephen gave a slight nod before putting his head in his hands. 'One late spring morning she decided to go and hunt down a rare orchid which one of our neighbours had told us could be found deep in the *garrigue* above the town. It was only a short walk of maybe two or three kilometres. She neglected to take her cell phone.' Hervé breathed deeply and recomposed himself. 'When she didn't return for lunch I was a little concerned but not too much. Alice would often take walks on her own and I respected her independence. If I ever showed too much control she would sing a song, *'You don't Own Me'* I think it was called – not a song I knew but I caught the sense of it.'

Bob closed his eyes and smiled sadly to himself recalling how she'd sung him the same lines when he too had become a over possessive.

'By mid-afternoon I was becoming more concerned. I set off to find her. The *garrigue* as you probably know Bob is a common feature throughout the Mediterranean region. Low scrub and shrubs growing out of the limestone plateaux. Dozens of small pathways but due to the low-level vegetation virtually impossible to get lost, you can always see where you are going. It wasn't unusual for Alice to stay out for a long time but today there was no trace of her. I called out her name several times but no response. I remembered that she had a particularly favourite spot near to an ancient stone *borie*, a sort of old shepherd's hut left over from the days when animals would have grazed the area. It has a great view of the surrounding hills. It wasn't difficult to find. I scrambled around a couple of stunted oaks, scratched my legs on a gorse bush and frightened a rabbit and it was then that I saw her lying in a crumpled heap at the entrance to the *borie,* by her side was her *Nikon*. The scissors were embedded in the ground. In her right hand the remains of a small bunch of *Asphodelus* flowers, Alice loved all flowers but the *Asphodelus* was one of her favourites. She considered it a melancholic flower; I don't know why. She once told me that the Greeks considered it a flower of the underworld associated with the Greek goddess Persephone who was depicted with an *Asphodelus* garland around her head. Alice liked this connection between a flower and the human body. She would sometimes place a sunflower down the front of her dress.'

Hervé overcome by a wave of emotion paused to regain his composure. It was Stephen who took up the story.

'I was out in the vineyard pruning the vines. I'd taken a couple of week's leave from the publishing house in Aix. I wanted to catch up with mum but also find time to help out Hervé with some of the more laborious manual work. My phone had rung and it was Hervé saying that something terrible had happened up at the old *borie*. I dropped everything and ran as fast as I could. I could hear a distant *pompier's* siren coming up the road behind me. By the time help arrived it was already too late.'

'Too late,' repeated Bob. 'You mean that she was dead?'

'The fire-service did their best. They're well trained in medical emergencies here in France, they'd tried a cardio-defibrillator and heart massage to no effect. They had no idea what had happened. Her left arm had taken on a strange blueish tinge. Her heart had stopped probably as a result of a heart attack.' Stephen looked at Hervé, shook his head and put his arm around his shoulder. 'But no, the reality was worse.'

Bob was lost for words. He'd not seen Alice since Carcassonne and before that it had been practically a lifetime since they'd been teenage lovers. 'Please tell me, I know it's hard for you both but please tell me how she died?' In his heart Bob was afraid he already had the answer.

How would you feel if you'd been simultaneously kicked in the groin and beaten about the head, Bob wondered, the intense emotional pain scouring out his insides? The horror and revulsion of what he was thinking. The unbearable conclusion. He waited for Hervé and Stephen to say something but both were lost in the grief of the moment.

After several seconds Stephen delved into his pocket for his iPhone. Flicking through his photographs he found what he was looking for. He passed the phone to Bob. 'This was the last photo that we found on Mum's camera,' he could barely speak the words.

Bob looked at the photo. He saw a purple orchid just coming into bloom and in the background the tall stem of an *asphodel*. It was beautiful. He was about to pass the phone back when Stephen stopped him. 'Enlarge the picture, Bob. Look closer.' Bob carefully spread his thumb and index finger until the orchid nearly filled the frame. 'Now focus on the top left – what can you see?' Bob did as he was told and squinted hard on the top of the orchid. Suddenly he was back looking at the pictures in his dad's old encyclopaedia. There it was. He shuddered involuntarily, nearly dropping the phone. Practically hidden, camouflaged by the bee-shaped purple flowers was the unmistakable scaly head of a snake. A distinctive V shape on the back. A Mediterranean viper.

He closed his eyes and swallowed hard. 'I knew it, I damned well knew it.' He spluttered barely believing the evidence before him. 'It was a..........' He paused. Reflecting a moment unsure of how to frame his words. 'She was killed by a snake wasn't she? A goddam bloody snake.' He didn't know whether to laugh or cry. The abject horror of it all.

Bob sat silently shaking his head and rubbing his arms. He felt the blood draining from his body. The scissors, he must ask about the scissors.

'Why would she have taken the scissors with her when she was out taking photographs and why were they found embedded in the ground?'

Hervé breathed deeply. 'I can only assume that she'd taken the scissors to cut a few herbs and the small bunch of *asphodels*. She nearly always came back from her walks with a sack full of thyme and wild asparagus. She most certainly hadn't seen the viper. She must have spotted the pyramid orchid and decided to photograph it. Judging from the angle of the picture she probably lay on her side to get the best shot and it was then that she surprised the reptile and it struck. The marks from the fangs were on her upper arm. The scissors were stuck into the ground virtually up to the handles. She'd used some force. The gendarme reckoned that she'd tried to kill the snake probably after realising that she'd been bitten. There was no sign of the snake. They are usually susceptible to movement and won't bite unless surprised. It was early spring and having just come out of winter hibernation they would still be lethargic. Normally the bite of a viper needn't be fatal if help arrives quickly but ....'

Stephen looked up with wide eyes and a look of revulsion on his lips. He spoke first. 'How were you to know that Bob? How could anyone guess that outcome?' There was vehemence and bitterness in his voice almost as if he was accusing Bob of her murder.

Hervé touched his elbow but Stephen shook it off and leaning closer to Bob he repeated the question. 'How could you guess? Did you already know? How did you know? You'd read the autopsy report in the local paper – impossible you were hardly going to read such a story in the local Normandy 'rag?''

Bob felt hurt and saddened by Stephen's attitude. He couldn't help wondering whether Stephen's anger was directed towards him or maybe it was the scissors or both? But how could he think that the scissors were implicated in Alice's death unless Stephen had a strong belief in superstition. He remembered that Alice had told him that Stephen knew the circumstances of his father's demise and he wondered how much he knew about the history of the scissors.

'Intuition that's all, intuition. Too long to go into but ever since I first saw the scissors as a young child those snake-shaped handles have instilled a sort of horror into me and although I'm not a superstitious person I have to admit that the scissors have never done anybody any real good and when you told me that she had the scissors with her on the day she died I could only see one possible outcome as horribly frightening as it may sound. Simple coincidence.'

Stephen looked hard at Bob then dropping his eyes spoke softly,

'Sorry Bob didn't mean to suggest – well in case you were wondering Hervé has given me the whole lowdown on the scissors including the circumstances surrounding my father's death. It was mum's idea to lend the scissors to the museum, she felt that it was the best place for something so beautifully crafted and yet at the same time so menacing. Her accident occurred before she could contact the curator. I decided to fulfil her wishes. I'd always thought that the scissors belonged to mum. She'd told me that they'd been given to her by an old friend. I'd no idea that they were originally yours Bob. When I found out that the scissors had an important value, I decided to sell them. I contacted the museum in Nogent. They offered me a price but well below the valuation I'd been given by an expert in Paris so I decided to put them to auction. Believe me I intended to inform you but I had no idea where to find you. I scoured mum's address book without success. I checked the contacts on her cell phone but no trace.'

Bob tried to remember if he had given Alice his contact address but the question of ownership lay heavily on his mind.

'I don't wish to sound unkind or grasping,' Bob tried to choose his words carefully. 'But what are you planning to do with the money you've made from the sale of the scissors? They were knocked down for €3500 this morning. When you've deducted the salesroom's commission of let's say 10 percent you'll still have made nearly 3200. I think I deserve a say in what happens to that money. Of course, I have no proof of ownership so I have no legal claim on the scissors but then neither have you. I was extremely fond of Alice and have no desire to compound the unhappy circumstances that surround your desperately sad loss. I'm not a superstitious person but after all that those scissors have seen I can't help but feel, as stupid as it may sound, that they are cursed in some way and I for one will at last be happy to see them disappear from my life. Yes, I know you're probably wondering why I was at the auction bidding for the darn things? Let's just say that paradoxically the scissors have sentimental value and I have to admit that they are a real work of art.'

It was a mark of Bob's conscious or maybe unconscious attachment to the scissors that had drawn him to the auction. Gisèle thought him mad. She couldn't get her head around the idea that he was going to actually bid for the scissors. Bob knew that he stood no chance of getting them back. He was playing a game, wanting to see for himself the fate of the scissors, participating in the on-going history. He had to follow the scissors no matter where they might lead.

Hervé nodded in agreement. 'I guess Alice would have agreed with your sentiments Bob. I suspect that was her reason for not letting them fall into the well. After much thought Stephen and I have reached a decision which hopefully will satisfy all parties. You must understand that it was never our intention to make capital out of the scissors.'

He turned to Stephen, 'Can you explain to Bob what we've decided.'

'I agree with all that you have just said Bob and I wouldn't want to give the impression that I was consciously cheating you. Therefore, if you agree I would like to donate the money to the centre for research into snake venom in Angers. They have an international reputation for research and if the money can help prevent some of the ten thousand deaths each year worldwide from snakebite it would be money well spent and hopefully close the door on this tragic business. What do you think?'

Bob's head was suddenly full of long hidden memories. Seeing the scissors for the first time sitting in front of the fire at his grandparents' house, Alice's kiss, hearing her ask to borrow the scissors for her sewing project, rediscovering them on a French *brocante* stall, her horror at seeing him place them on the table in the Carcassonne café and the delighted pleasure she showed when he thought the scissors had fallen into the well. The final image of the viper and the orchid was too much to contemplate. It wasn't his memory, he'd seen the photograph, his last impression was a borrowed memory but like the serpent in the encyclopaedia it was always going to haunt him. He felt a wave of guilt over his suspicions of Herve's and Stephen's motives.

'Yes, thank-you. I'm sorry if I seemed to be questioning your motives. It's an excellent idea. I fully approve. Now what about we cheer ourselves up a little and salute the life of an incredibly special woman. *Monsieur. Champagne s'il vous plait!'*

Chapter Twelve

Later the same day

The three of them walked back to the auction room of *Brunhes & Poitou*. Unfinished business. Stephen hoping to collect his sale cheque. Bob had other matters on his mind as he stood by the door while the unsmiling secretary shuffled a pile of documents from one side of the desk to the other. Bob had a question. As the others hung back Bob cleared his throat enough to attract the secretary's attention who was now consigning documents, photocopies of passports, bank accounts, gas bills and other documents so essential to any financial transaction in France to a large grey filing cabinet. If England was a nation of shopkeepers, France was the nation of pen-pushers and jobsworths.

'Monsieur, je peux vous aider ?

'*Oui,* could you possibly give me the name of the successful bidder on lot 33 – the Italian scissors. I seem to remember it was a telephone bid.........' before Bob could finish he could tell by the secretary's body language what the answer would be.

'Non, monsieur that would most certainly not be possible. We are a well-respected auction house and our rules are clear. The anonymity of all our clients is paramount. Giving away personal information might result in an individual's

security being compromised. May I ask why you are demanding this information?'

Bob was beginning to wonder whether his French was up to explaining the intricacies of the scissor's ownership but it was Hervé who came to his rescue.

'Madame, this gentleman is *Monsieur Martin*. Although I am responsible for the sale of lot 33, as the previous, might I say guardian, I must tell you that *Monsieur Martin's* family were the original owners of the scissors and they came into my possession as a sort of gift as you may say from *Monsieur Martin* several years ago. I know it is all a little complicated but perhaps you could find a way of giving me the name of the new owner?'

Madame the secretary squinted hard at Hervé putting on a pair of thick rimmed reading glasses and swivelling around to face the computer screen. 'According to our records the previous owner was a *Monsieur Stephen Woods* domiciled in Béziers. If that information is not correct then I am unable to hand over the proceeds of the sale. You *monsieur* I imagine that you are not Mr Woods?'

It was Stephen's turn to speak up. 'I'm Stephen Woods. The scissors were a gift from *Monsieur Martin* to my mother Alice Woods many years ago. You will see from your records that my deceased mother bequeathed all her possessions to me her only son. Hervé, that is *Monsieur Clopé* is her widower and it was he who put the scissors in the hands of this auction house for sale this morning. Surely we have a right to know the name of the new owners who most certainly would be interested in the history of the article in question.'

Madame Secretaire flashed a frosty 'no go' smile. 'Your request is completely out of the question.' She shut down the computer and reaching for her bag and scarf stood up announcing, *'Monsieur Woods* I will post your cheque on as soon as the necessary paperwork and identification has been completed.' She shot a final steely glance in Bob's direction before adding, 'probably in the next 3 months. Now you must excuse me I have a pressing engagement.' They watched her march through the front door cross the narrow road and enter the hairdressers' shop opposite.

Bob was about to follow and confront her. He wanted to climb on his English 'high horse' and accuse the woman of gross incompetence and suggest that a course in public relations would serve her better than the hairdresser but Hervé tugged on his sleeve. 'You're wasting your breath Bob. Your English charm will get you nowhere with people like this. This is not England you know. Here in France you must learn to play the game of patience and knowing the right people. Perhaps I can suggest another way of finding the information we require.'

✂

Within an hour and a half Hervé had clocked up the 100 or so kilometres to the small town of Nogent.

'Still driving the DS I see Hervé.' Bob recalled the evening in Carcassonne when Hervé had collected Alice and himself from the *Narbonne Gate* and Bob had discovered that Hervé and Alice were *Monsieur et Madame Clopé.*'

'Will certainly outlive me.' Hervé laughed. 'Best French car ever built. Three hundred and fifty thousand on the clock and still going strong.'

'Anyway, Bob I'm still not clear why you turned up for the auction this morning and actually bid for the scissors.' Interrupted Stephen. 'Were you seriously wanting to buy them back?'

'Hard to explain,' Bob replied. 'I knew I had no chance of making a successful bid but I wanted to stay part of the story. It probably sounds crazy to you but I felt I had to be there to see who would buy the damned things. Whoever now owns the scissors has the right to know their history. I owe that to my grandparents, parents, Eric and Alice. Bidding was a kind of bluff to make me feel involved. I guess there was a lot of adrenaline pumping. Dare I say that for me they've become something of a Holy Grail, I feel that their destiny is somehow inextricably linked to mine.'

Hervé pulled to a halt in the town square. Bob remembered his last visit to the town with his wife and grandson George. No ice creams and dinosaurs today but the museum was open.

Clotilde, the curator recognised Bob immediately and after he'd introduced the others they sat down in her office and she ordered coffee all round. The walls were covered with posters advertising various exhibitions throughout France to which the museum had contributed. Although a small museum it clearly had ambitions as Clotilde explained that she'd only just returned from an international conference in the *Louvre* on the future of the museum in the digital age. She explained that they were already planning some new innovations for the museum including a virtual reality tour of a 19th century cutlery manufacturer. Her English was excellent and her manner charming. Her enthusiasm for her work very evident, quite the opposite of the secretary at *Brunhes & Poitou* thought Bob.

'So, at last,' she turned to Stephen. 'I get the chance to meet the mystery owner of the serpentine scissors or perhaps I should say ex-owner as I imagine that since this morning you are no longer the owner, am I right?'

'Well,' Bob interrupted. 'In some ways the three of us were in different ways and at different times owners of the scissors but I'm not going to bore you with the long story now.' He glanced at the trim figure on the other side of the desk. She was wearing a 60's style twin set and pearls, large round glasses, no wedding ring, her chestnut brown hair tied back in a youthful pony-tail. For a moment Bob considered that perhaps she would be an eager listener and scintillating company over dinner and a bottle of *Aloxe Corton* but Bob hastily put the thought out of his mind reminding himself that he was now a happily married man with his adventuring days long in the past. *'Born too Late'* a 1950's song by the American girl trio *The Poni Tails* sprang to mind. Accompanying saxophones wailing and resonating with teenage angst. Funny how musical memories influence both conscious and unconscious thoughts. He hastily and guiltily dismissed the thoughts. Clotilde was asking Stephen and Hervé how the auction had gone.

Hervé switched to French as he explained how the scissors had been knocked down for three thousand five hundred euros. A result hardly expected before the auction.

'Well, that's certainly a good price. As you know the museum would have liked to have kept the scissors but a price like that is beyond our meagre means. So, who was the lucky buyer?'

'Well that's the problem,' replied Bob, 'we don't know, and the secretary at *Brunhes & Poitou* wasn't exactly helpful. She claimed that for professional reasons she wasn't allowed to divulge such information so that's why we thought you might be able to help. There is such a long story attached to the scissors that I'm sure any new buyer would want to know.' Bob flashed his best 'pathetic man' smile at Clotilde hoping that she might take pity on him.

Clotilde turned towards her computer and opened a file. 'Not an impossible task. There are a number of collectors known to the museum who might be able to help. If we can't identify the buyer we might be able to find someone who is connected professionally. Collectors are generally sociable people with carefully organised professional networks. They like to keep an eye on what others are up to and they maintain a lot of pride in their collections. In this case there are only a limited number of specialist cutlery and scissor experts so it may not be too difficult. It would help if we knew the buyer's nationality. You didn't happen to notice what language was being used for the telephone bid?'

'No, the telephones were too far away to hear anything. The bidding was conducted in English so difficult to tell nationalities apart. I assume that it was some distance away or why bother making telephone bids? Could be from anywhere.'

'Well not necessarily. Many collectors prefer to keep their identity private.' Clotilde swung the computer monitor around so that all could see. 'This is a list of collectors with whom the museum has had contact recently. Sometimes they call in personally or more often they send e-mails asking for photos of particular items.'

'Why would they do that?' demanded Stephen. 'Presumably the museum is not often in the business of selling off their treasures.'

'No, that's generally true – your case is happily an exception. We prefer to keep on good terms with our donors. That's not a criticism, you have your own very good reasons for selling. Many collectors and experts in the field like to keep track of certain items, maybe for comparison purposes or simply to see what's new in cutlery history. It may seem banal or even boring to many people but I can assure you that cutlery and scissor history is a cutthroat business if you'll excuse the pun. Think of the passion that people have for collecting stamps, coins or royal family memorabilia from your glorious and noble Queen. Nostalgia is a growing business that attracts not only the very rich speculator but also the ordinary man in the street.'

She clicked on the mouse several times. Several lists appeared on the screen under speciality headings.

'There's a guy here from San Francisco who specialises in First Empire artefacts mainly jewellery, bracelets and necklaces belonging to the Empress Josephine and her entourage. Can't see that he'd be interested in a pair of scissors from a different period.' She scrolled down the list. 'Here's someone from Singapore who's a cutlery collector but he doesn't mention scissors. It seems he mainly specialises in hand-carved table and hunting knives of Japanese or Chinese origin which were often very popular in 19th century France.'

Silence. Hervé, Bob and Stephen looked on expectantly.

'Ah! Now this one sounds quite promising. Can't be certain of course. A cutlery and scissor collector from the Lake Maggiore region of North Italy. He called us last year asking for pictures of decorative hand-made knives and scissors. I'd sent off several photos including the snake handled embroidery cutters – he would probably have been aware of today's auction; the salesrooms have an interest in keeping their past clients well informed.'

The list came to an end. Clotilde untied and retied the barrette fastening her pony-tail. She fingered her pearls and adjusted her glasses. 'Well, what do you think?'

Hervé was first to speak. 'The Italian sounds a likely candidate, what do you two think?'

Stephen nodded in agreement and looked across to Bob.

'Can you give us any further information such as address or maybe his name?'

Clotilde squinted at her computer screen. 'His name is Ceccaroli, first name Ricardo and yes, you're in luck I do have his e-mail address and mobile number.' She scribbled the details on a notepad and passed it to Bob.

Bob looked hard at the name. *Ceccaroli.Ricardo@Ceccaroli-spa.it* – sound like a company address he thought. Turning back to Clotilde he asked. 'You said that he lived in the Lake Maggiore area?' Ceccaroli rang a bell perhaps the name of an Italian footballer or maybe a politician but Bob was fairly sure he recognised the name. He was curious as to know how the curator knew the area where he lived.

She laughed at Bob's question and pulled a face. 'The last message I had from him several months ago was to thank me for the photographs I had sent him. He was very happy to receive them and suggested that next time I should deliver them personally. He said that Lake Maggiore was exceptionally beautiful in the spring so I put two and two together. I think he was trying to – how do you say in English *draguer*?'

'Seduce you,' Hervé quipped, 'or maybe just to chat you up as the English are fond of saying – it sounds more respectable.'

Clotilde looked a little sheepish. 'I'm sure I said nothing to encourage him.'

'Don't worry, you know what the Italians are like. They need little encouragement,' Stephen interrupted.

Bob cast another enquiring glance towards the curator who self-consciously cleared her throat and tried to look serious and professional.

'What do you intend to do now?'

'Well, I'd like to get in touch with him, confirm whether he is the new owner.' replied Bob. 'If he is then perhaps I can arrange a meeting or at least fill him in on the history of the scissors.' Bob was still digging deep into his memory trying to locate the name Ceccaroli. 'Could you possibly give him a call on my behalf and politely inquire as to whether he is the owner and if so suggest that we meet up?' Bob wondered whether he wasn't pushing his luck with Clotilde a little too far but she seemed genuinely interested in the idea and it would be better if it was her who made the initial contact.

'Of course. I'll 'phone him directly and let you know the result. I have to be careful with issues of professional confidentiality but I'll see what I can do.' She seemed enthusiastic. Evidently Bob wasn't the only one caught up in the historical web woven by the scissors.

'Perhaps if he knew about the real history of the scissors he might regret his purchase.' Hervé chipped in.

'In which case the museum might get the scissors back.' Clotilde mused half seriously, standing up smoothing down her skirt. 'Well, I wish you luck. Keep me informed of progress.'

Hervé dropped Bob off back at his hotel in Troyes. Stephen, Hervé and Bob said an emotional goodbye. They'd formed quite a deep bond in a very short time thanks to their shared relationships with Alice and the scissors. He said that he would keep them up to date. They waved their farewells and Bob entering the hotel found a corner seat in the hotel bar and ordered a beer. He checked his text messages and found one from Clotilde.

'Ceccaroli IS the new owner. He speaks English and will be happy to talk to you. Good luck. C.'

Bob was delighted and immediately telephoned his wife.

'Hello darling, good news. I'm on my way home and you'll be pleased to hear that I haven't bought the scissors.'

'Well, that is a relief,' sighed his wife, perhaps now we can afford that holiday in Nice that you've been promising me for months.'

'Holiday perhaps, Nice not this time. Will give you all the details later but make sure that you've cleared your agenda for the next couple of weeks. I'm taking the 6.36 TGV to Paris in the morning so if I can make my connection should be back in Bordeaux by midday. Can you pick me up from the station and we'll grab some lunch together and I'll keep you up to date on what's been going on and oh, if you have a couple of minutes can you check the availability of flights from Bordeaux to Milan Linate for next Thursday. Have you missed me?'

'Missed you?' Haven't stopped since you left and what a pleasure to have the house to myself, so quiet – missed you of course I've missed you, no one to empty the dishwasher, no one to do the hoovering and of course no one to make a mess in the bathroom. What a question. Bordeaux Milan next Thursday? Sounds interesting. Must rush, expecting a couple of cookery clients in half an hour and I've yet to prepare the fish marinade. See you tomorrow *Cherie, bisous. A demain et Bon Voyage!*

He'd got used to Gisèle's impressions of the nagging wife. After all wasn't it a result of that famed fiery temperament of Provençal women? He downed his beer and collecting his key from Reception headed for the lift and an early night.

✀

'Hang on a moment Bob. Why Lake Maggiore?' Bob had just stepped off the train and they were heading for the nearest station buffet. 'I'm sure it's very nice but why all the rush? Can't it wait until the summer? There's so much work to do in the garden and we don't have a hotel booking and what are we doing for transport?'

'Don't worry about the details, *cherie*. I didn't get the scissors so we still have the money I put by. Did you check out the flights? I'll look at the hotels over dinner this evening and fill you in with what happened at the auction. Lake Maggiore will certainly be better than 3 nights at the *Negresco*.'

'*Comment?*' quizzed his wife. She'd always found it difficult to understand her husband's wanderlust but his impulsive plans to visit new places certainly made for an interesting life.

Over lunch Bob related the events of the auction and his meeting with Hervé and Stephen. He was finding the right words difficult to come by but eventually as calmly as possible he announced,

'She's dead. Alice is dead.'

Gisèle clutched her napkin and fingered her wineglass. 'What? Alice is dead?'

She had no personal attachment to Alice and they'd never met but from what Bob had told her she knew that she was a significant person in her husband's life. 'Bob what are you talking about? What happened in Troyes? Tell me the story.'

Bob told her about the auction and his meeting with Stephen and Hervé, the mystery Chinese bidder and the eventual closure of the sale to the profit of a certain Signor Ricardo Ceccaroli a Milanese businessman.

'Alice bitten by a snake!' But Bob that's awful. Surely advances with anti-snake venom have made such incidents virtually impossible.'

'Yes, you're right,' Bob hastily interrupting his wife's shocked reaction. 'If help arrives quickly. The emergency services in France are well trained in the correct procedures but there must be a rapid intervention if a life is to be saved. In Alice's case her body wasn't found for several hours, her arm had turned bright blue, she must have suffered if only she............'

He left the sentence hanging. The thought of Alice suffering at the fangs of a venomous reptile was still too horrific for Bob to contemplate.

From what her husband had told her she'd pieced together an image of Alice as a spirited lively woman who never gave up easily and who had suffered enough trauma in her life as to merit some kind of immortality.

'I'm afraid it's all true. If she'd remembered to take her cell phone on that day things may have turned out very differently. The emergency services could do nothing.'

'It all sounds too incredible to be true. You want me for moral support, is that it? Well, you're in luck. Your little wife has checked out flights. Booked two Economy for Thursday morning, plenty of availability but must be up early. I'll leave you to book a hotel and hire a car.'

'Yes, thanks darling. Some moral support will be welcome. Look on the positive side, it's not every day that you get a chance to meet a rich Italian industrialist and,' he reached out for his wife's hand, 'I'm making plans for a romantic interlude in Tuscany afterwards but I'm keeping the lid on that until I've spoken to Ceccarolli.'

'Ok, Casanova, now you'd better load the dishwasher whilst I wash your shirts and knickers.'

'Gisèle, darling. How many times do I have to tell you that in England women wear knickers and men under-pants?'

Bob headed for his study and dug out his box of European travel guides. He'd been promising himself for some time that he'd have a good clear out and reorganise his rather out of date collection of assorted tourist leaflets and books. After some searching he found his maps of Italy, his *Lonely Planet* guide to Tuscany, the *Michelin Green Guide* to Florence and a precious 1867 edition of *Baedeker's handbook for travellers in Italy*. Over on his bookcase he unearthed his first edition of D.H. Lawrence's *Tuscan Places*. 'He'd never really read it in any detail since picking it up by chance at one of his favourite Normandy *brocante*. The seller probably thought that anything by Lawrence was going to be a little smutty, with naked, black-faced Nottinghamshire coal miners and nubile nymphomaniacs romping through Sherwood Forest. Bob considered that he had grabbed a bargain. Published posthumously in 1932 it was hardly a travel guide more of a short ramble with a friend around Tuscan burial grounds. He packed them at the bottom of his suitcase and turned his attention to the dishwasher.

Chapter Thirteen

One week later

The autostrada from Milan-Linate airport was relatively quiet for the time of the year. The tourists had yet to arrive and the Italians for once were behaving themselves behind the wheel. According to the French the Italians were worse drivers than them but Bob doubted that there was much to separate them. In his experience most Latin drivers showed a cavalier approach to driving and it was just as well to be wary. He was reminded of the old French joke about the difference between English, French and Italian traffic lights. For the English they are an instruction, for the French a suggestion and for the Italians Christmas decorations. Today the road was straight and the early morning sun was glinting off the distant snow-clad alps. It felt good to be on the road. Bob never considered himself a happy flyer preferring the train or better still the motor car. At Gisèle's insistence he'd opted to hire a middle range Peugeot over his personal preference for an Audi. French chauvinism raising its ugly head again. In an hour or so they could look forward to lunch and a good bottle of *Barolo* in some atmospheric backstreet trattoria.

'Well, I suppose it was worth getting out of bed at 4.30 if only for the half-empty economy class and the spectacular views.' She leaned over and brushed his cheek with a kiss. 'I hope that the 'Sherlock Holmes' or should it be the 'Hercule

Poirot' of scissors has booked us into a chic Italian hotel where we can enjoy a second honeymoon perhaps. After all you have saved us some money by not buying those wretched scissors.'

Bob winced at the thought. Had he really wanted to buy back his own scissors or was it really the memory of Alice he wanted to preserve? 'Well actually I think you'll be happy with the hotel. Probably the best in Stresa. Hemingway stayed there briefly whilst writing *A Farewell to Arms* and the receptionist did promise me a room with a lake view. Sadly no windmills or goats.' he said mockingly.

Gisèle chose to ignore for the moment his jocular reminder of their first date. 'You mean to say that you didn't book through a travel web site. My my! Bob you'll be telling me next you made the reservation in Italian! You are getting more adventurous but then that is thanks to your darling cultural *'attaché.'* But of course, you English know that *'Globish'* will always open the right doors. It is we poor continentals who must give up the language of Molière or should I say, on this beautiful Italian morning, the language of Dante? *Parlez-vous Globish Madame?'* or *Parli Globish Signore.* You know someone once called *Globish* 'decaffeinated English.' Good don't you think? A bit like that mysterious theatre language that we French call *'Grommelot.'* It's a sort of imitation language that sounds like gibberish. Strangely I've never found it in any dictionary. Someone once described it as a word without paper.'

'Well that's a new one on me,' exclaimed Bob. 'You're not suggesting that *Globish* falls into the category of gibberish are you?'

'Well, could be. You remember on our first date when I found that 'unspeakable' object on the path? I seem to think that the words that came out of your mouth very nearly fell into that category.

'What on earth are you talking about? What unspeakable object?. All I remember was the kiss.'

✂

They had first met 6 years earlier. Bob had been taking a short 'singles' holiday in the Provençal village of Fontvieille. One evening he'd managed to get a ticket to an open-air piano recital given by the Portuguese virtuoso Maria Joao Pires. Opening the programme she played one of his favourite Mozart concertos. Half-way through the second movement of piano concerto number 9 *'Jeunehomme'* at a particularly quiet moment someone on the front row farted – this no ordinary half-repressed release of trapped wind more a percussive explosion redolent of Shostakovich rather than Wolfgang. The woman next to him impulsively grasped his arm stifling a guffaw and immediately hiding her mouth behind her hand whispered *'Je suis vraiment desolé.'* Bob reckoned that she was apologising for grabbing a stranger's arm rather than admitting her own guilt. Or at least that was what he hoped. At the intermission they arrived together at the champagne bar where again she apologised, 'I hope you didn't think it was me.'

Bob laughed. *'Ne t'inquiétez pas l'humour des toilettes n'est pas ma tasse de thé. Laisse-moi t'acheter un verre de champagne.'* Bob thought that this was a perfect chance to try out his French chat-up' lines but before he could open his mouth further she introduced herself in English. 'That's kind of you. My name is Gisèle Langon and you?'

Bob always felt a little miffed when French people 'sussed' out his Englishness as soon as he opened his mouth but he considered that in the presence of a beautiful woman this wasn't one of those moments to protest his hurt pride.

'Bob, Bob Martin. How do you do? Please accept my apologies for *tutoying* you. My understanding of the mysteries of the French language is not as sophisticated as I would like.' He felt very embarrassed by the slip of the tongue when suggesting that he should offer a drink. He never felt comfortable with the French formal and informal forms – when to use *tu* or *vous*. He recalled once overhearing a conversation where an English colleague asked a French *professeur* if he minded if he *tutoyed* him. The response was a polite but cold refusal with the Frenchman stating that it would make him feel uncomfortable. Bob had tried to remember the language protocol but often he was guilty of an embarrassing oversight.

Gisèle a petite brunette with striking brown eyes, casually dressed in jeans and trainers was eager to talk. 'Oh, for heaven's sake please don't worry about that. *Je vous excuse.* Are you English or American?'

'Doesn't my accent sort of give me away?' Bob replied.

Gisèle Langon nodded and smiled. 'Yes, of course and if you don't mind me saying what a charming accent it is. Of course, the jacket and tie are a give-away. Aren't you hot dressed like that?'

'Well, actually yes I am. Back in England it's always 'the 'done thing' to dress up for a concert. Must confess to preferring the continental way.' He loosened his tie and smiled at her forthrightness. Clearly *Madame* or was it *Mademoiselle* Langon was no ordinary woman.

He tried to explain as best he could the English reluctance to discuss bodily functions particularly with strangers. She laughed and said that she found the English most charming but eccentric and casting her gaze around the crowded bar challenged Bob to pick out the explosive culprit. Bob recalled seeing the Milos Forman film *Amadeus* which pulled no punches when it came to Wolfgang's toilet humour. Perhaps the uninvited flatulence was in homage to the great Austrian composer. Why clap when you can fart like Mozart?

Before he could finish explaining his theory to the charming Gisèle the bell rang for the end of the intermission and they returned to their seats. The second half of the programme was the Franck piano and violin sonata, but Bob hardly noticed. After the second or maybe the third encore the crowds began to drift away towards the exits. After both agreeing on the superb artistry of the soloists, they reached the parking and as they were about to go their separate ways Bob couldn't resist prolonging their conversation. He asked Gisèle where she was heading. 'Avignon' she replied. 'And you?'

'Oh, I'm spending a few days exploring the villages of the *Alpilles*. I expect you know the region well. Do you recommend anywhere in particular? I've still got a couple of days left to fill.'

'I imagine you are familiar with Daudet's windmill – made famous by French writer Alphonse Daudet. All French people know the *Letters from my Windmill*. A favourite of French people everywhere and second only to *Le Petit Prince* in popularity.'

Bob hesitated, uncertain of his answer and conscious of not wanting to show his ignorance. 'Well as a matter of fact it is on my list of places to visit. Maybe tomorrow.' He vaguely remembered seeing a signpost to a *moulin* near his hotel, but his knowledge of French writers precluded Daudet.

'Tell you what,' Gisèle said brightly. 'If you want, I can give you a personalised tour tomorrow, that's if you've got nothing better to do. I presume a man who goes to a concert on his own in a foreign country must be an independent traveller.' Before he could answer she added, 'I think you'll like Daudet. A real Provençal. An imaginative writer with a touch of eccentricity just like the English. You'll like his goat story too. What do you say? And oh, leave your jacket and tie at the hotel.'

Bob was uncertain about the goat but an opportunity to spend a few hours with Gisèle was an opportunity too good to dismiss. What else could he answer? He was smitten. They arranged to meet the next morning in front of Daudet's windmill. Gisèle arrived wearing a pair of tight red slacks and white Provençal blouse with small-embroidered flowers around the open collar. Under her arm she clutched a copy of *Lettres de mon Moulin* – 'Letters from my Windmill' by Alphonse Daudet, which she presented to Bob with great ceremony announcing that a reading of the book would give him a perfect introduction to Provençe and the Provençal culture. They spent the morning exploring the mill and the small museum. They sat on a rock whilst Gisèle told him the melancholic story of 'Mr Seguin's Goat.' Bob was spell bound. They lunched in *Les Beaux de Provençe* on the terrace of a small gastronomic restaurant with breath-taking views over *'Les Alpilles.'* They both laughed at the circumstances of their meeting the previous evening. Bob even suggested that the explosion of flatulence was a deliberate act of homage to the great musician. Maybe even the existence of a secret Mozart society whose objective was to publicly fart at as many Mozart concerts as possible. A theory which Gisèle dismissed as ridiculous and very English, after all didn't the Germanic people and the English share a cultural heritage?

It was the first of many such debates concerning their diverse cultures. As Gisèle later learned it wasn't just language which separated the French and the English.

As the wine began to oil the conversation they moved on to more personal matters. Gisèle was keen to know about Bob's history. She was intrigued to know what a single, middle-aged English man was doing spending summer alone in Provençe. Bob was a willing interviewee and enjoyed talking.

'I suppose I have to admit to two failed marriages. Probably my fault it must be said. One grown-up son, one small grandson. A couple of stepsons and a couple of step grandchildren. Career educator, schools, university. Ambitious, sometimes overly so. Always strangely seemed to get to where I wanted to go even though the route was often convoluted. Lived in Normandy for the past 20 odd years. Left England not because I disliked the English but rather I felt at that time that I wanted to embody the idea of Europeanism. Looking back I knew so little; I was naïve and unadventurous. I wanted to explore new cultures and see if I could transform myself in some way from the suburban, middle class, security conscious person into something a little more worldly. To discover the real me if that doesn't sound corny. I loved the idea that in theory at least I could leave my home in France and continue on dry land all the way to the North China Sea rather than living on an insular island where leaving home necessitated the conscious effort of booking an airline ticket or a ferry boat passage. I suppose I saw myself rather arrogantly as the playboy of the western world.' He laughed at the absurdity. 'Adventurer of sorts but always a little reluctant to push the boat out too far in case I got out of my depth. Happy? Yes, I think so. Maybe also selfish. Romantic? Enormously but it doesn't always show. Heart-broken too many times but the carapace has hardened. Too malleable in the wrong hands.' He broke off aware that perhaps he was giving too much away. 'Now, what about you? If I may say so it's not often you find attractive, single women. I assume you're single – no wedding ring – risking their virtue in old windmills and being plied with *Cote de Rhone* in an expensive restaurant with an English guy you met less than 24 hours ago!'

She smiled wordlessly as if assessing how much she should tell. Still smiling she cast her gaze in the direction of the distant hills. 'I consider myself a reasonably good judge of character and I wouldn't be here now if I thought you a threat. Having said that, I'm sometimes a risk taker. As for my virtue the less said the better. I'm a widow. My husband died 15 years ago. It was an accident before you ask. He worked in *Le Cirque du Soleil*. I imagine you've heard of them. Formed in Montreal, Canada, a circus with a difference, no animals and very artistic. They were doing a winter season in Paris when I first met him – a trapeze artist who'd actually worked with the famous funambulist, Philippe Petit – you must remember him, he was the guy who illegally crossed between the World Trade twin towers in 1974 on a tight rope.' Bob nodded. He had once seen a TV documentary on the eccentric Frenchman who someone had once described as the artistic criminal of the century.

'Anyway, I was a young legal secretary working for a high-flying Parisian firm – no pun intended, when he came into the office one day over some minor legal issue. On his way out he left a couple of complimentary tickets.' Bob listened intently, a million questions swarming into his head. 'I can guess what you're thinking. What was a young Provençal girl doing in Paris and getting mixed up with a guy who earned his crust every day from walking a tight-rope 20 meters off the ground? Like I said, I'm sometimes a risk taker and I'm often attracted to other risk takers. Like you I was young and ambitious, wanting to see the world. Eventually we married. It was quite an open marriage. It had to be. Raymond, my husband, was often away, Dubai, Vegas, Macao, New York, Orlando. I would sometimes fly out to join him when I had some down time and often in the winter he would be at home in Paris for two or three months. We never had time to think about having a family. Raymond was incredibly superstitious and was afraid that too much happiness would somehow jeopardise his life, in some respects he had a great need to feel insecure. He often said that it was his sense of insecurity that kept him from becoming over-confident. Over confidence is not a quality that a funambulist needs if he is to stay alive.'

'It all sounds very complex to me.' Bob mused. 'Tell me about your husband's superstitions.'

'You have to understand that circus folk are extremely superstitious, believing in good and bad luck. Their success comes from their skills of course but even the most skilled of performers know that they will have good and bad days and like everything else in life luck plays a part. He once told me that 10 million rabbit feet were bought every year in the US to ward off bad luck. In today's world of uncertainty is it surprising? Circus artists are facing danger every time they perform. They won't wear anything coloured green as green is regarded as bad luck, green is the colour of nature and therefore symbolises both life and death. Seeing a bird inside the 'Barnum' is a bad omen. Birds are regarded as the souls of dead people coming to take away a living person.'

Raymond was fascinated by all the different superstitions particularly those connected to trapeze and high wire acts.

'So, were there any particular superstitions that he believed in?'

'For a trapeze artist or funambulist their biggest obsession is naturally enough the reliability of their equipment and materials, the security harness, the state and quality of the wire or rope and the stability and strength of the stanchions or supports holding each end of the wire. It's very important that nothing that might weaken their security is left lying around. An obvious example might be wire cutters. You won't believe this but Raymond absolutely forbad that we should have a pair of scissors in the apartment. Sounds ridiculous doesn't it? There wasn't a single pair of scissors in our Paris apartment. Imagine no scissors! Nail cutters and knives aplenty. No secateurs, no garden shears, no wire cutters, especially no wire cutters! Nothing which might resemble a pair of scissors.'

Bob swallowed hard. 'So, I guess there was a tragic accident?'

'Raymond always wanted to push the limits. Higher, further, longer. He nearly always worked with a safety harness but the risk-taking instinct in him was too strong. He had this enormous admiration for Petit's feats. He'd been with him when he'd crossed the Sydney Harbour bridge pylons and he'd been a spectator when he'd crossed from the second floor of the Eiffel Tower to the Trocadero. He wanted to try something similar. He was doing a spectacle in Vegas and on one of his weekends off he'd decided to do the traverse of the Grand Canyon by slackline. I'd planned to join him that weekend. I'd booked a flight from Paris to Phoenix with a connecting flight to Flagstaff. Unfortunately, Charles de Gaulle Roissy was fogbound so my departure was delayed which meant I missed my connection to Flagstaff. By the time I eventually arrived 12 hours later he was already dead. He'd misjudged or maybe not even taken into consideration the swirling air currents rising from the canyon. As I've said he loved taking risks.'

Bob exhaled deeply. 'God I'm so sorry, it must have been horrific for you.'

'Yes and no. Yes in the sense that it's always a terrible shock when you lose someone close but no because when I married him I knew what risks he was taking. We both accepted that and it was always a possibility although we never discussed it. It was a sort of taboo.'

Bob grimaced and let the silence hang. He drained the last of the red wine and took out a cigar.

'Ok if I smoke?'

'No go ahead. Can't stand cigarette smoke but cigars are ok. Why did you react when I mentioned scissors? You're not superstitious also are you?'

'No, not particularly, but evidently scissors cut, they cut paper, string and ………rope! Of course, it's obvious. But it's completely irrational. Did Raymond think someone might try and cut his rope?'

'I don't think so, all superstition is irrational. Think about it. Somebody even claimed that after Petit's walk between the World Trade Centre twin towers in 1974 they left a pair of wire cutters behind. Makes you think......'

Bob considered what Gisèle had just told him. He wondered whether he should tell her about the snake-handled embroidery scissors but decided against it. Now, on a first date was not probably a good moment.

'A lot of superstitions are rational though. After all scissors can do a lot of damage, they also incite religious symbolism by forming a cruciform shape. Good against witchcraft and evil spirits. Good for self-defence.............'

'Hm,' Gisèle smiled. 'For a teacher you seem to be quite an expert on scissors. Don't tell me it was the subject of your PhD. You're obviously quite a man Bob, Mozart lover, Francophile, gourmet, expert on flatulence and now a Doctorate in superstitions. Any more surprises awaiting me?'

Bob found himself blushing. Had the *Côte de Rhone* loosened his tongue too much? Was he in danger of making an idiot of himself or worse still was Gisèle lightly poking fun at him? He sought to retrieve some sense of normality.

'Yes, well me and scissors do have a back story over recent years but let's not spoil a perfect Provençal afternoon by talking about me. What do you say we take a walk?'

✂

'So, what did you do after Raymond's death?'

They were strolling along a narrow stony pathway in the *garrigue*. Bob was keen to learn more about Gisèle's life.

'The media attention was diabolical particularly in the States. Here in France nobody seemed to care. I don't think that the French like eccentrics. I carried on working for the legal firm for a while and then out of the blue came the chance to work in the diplomatic sector. I got a posting to Madrid and then three years later to Rome. I did 8 years in Italy and then decided to call it a day. Raymond had insurance cover when working for *'Soleil'* but wasn't covered for any independent projects so I inherited nothing. Fortunately, I'd saved up enough to buy a small *mas* near to Avignon where with the help of a couple of local chefs I fulfilled a lifelong ambition of running a cookery school and that started a couple of years ago and as you might say I'm a work in progress! And you Bob? You're still working?'

'Yes, a few hours a week of teaching Business English– enjoy it. Great not to have to worry about ambition and the next step up. If it's not too arrogant to say it, I reckon I'm doing some of the best teaching in my life. I'm considering going into partnership in a new language teaching enterprise down in the Dordogne but nothing settled yet. It'll be a big wrench leaving Normandy after all this time.'

'Ah, there you go. What was it you said about risk taking? I don't know you well, Bob but I say go for it, go for it – the next big adventure! Who knows perhaps I'll come and give you a hand with the cookery?' They both laughed at the seeming impossibility of the idea but it set Bob thinking. Moments later Gisèle stopped and stooping picked something from the path.

'Wow! Look at this Bob. Not often you see one of these.'

'What on earth is it?' Bob squinted down at the scaly piece of skin.

'A snakeskin, Bob. That's a really lucky sign. Hope you like serpents Bob?

Bob closed his eyes and tried not to look. He felt the familiar goose bumps on his bare arms, the flashback to the photo in his dad's encyclopaedia and the shot of Alice and the wild orchid and *asphodel*. He must focus his mind on other things. He touched Gisèle on the shoulder and whispered, 'I would like to kiss you.'

✂

And as they say, the rest is history. They were married six months later, a balmy autumn day in the Town Hall of *Villeneuve Lès Avignon*. Bought a place in the Dordogne, Gisèle sold up in Avignon and they set up a small enterprise teaching English and cookery – sometimes both at the same time.

Not many relationships start with a fart! A good 'party piece' when people asked how they met.

Chapter Fourteen

The Borromean islands lie in the northwest corner of the Northern Italian Lake Maggiore. They have been in the hands of the Borromeo family since the 17th century when they started out as rich and influential bankers from the region of Milan. Over the years the family produced cardinals and bishops and even a saint as well as founding banks in Milan, Florence and Venice. Their influence spread to cover most of Northern Italy and their fiefdoms gave them control over local armies up until 1797 when Napoleon Bonaparte invaded Milan and put a stop to the influence of the Borromeo family. All they were left with were their properties and land on the Borromean islands. Today they own three of the five islands. One of the remaining islands was too small to be of any interest to them and in the late 19th century it was bought by the Ceccaroli family at a knockdown price.

Ceccaroli Industries SpA is a powerful economic and political force in Italy. Its board members include several high-profile ex-politicians as well as rich financial 'wheeler-dealers' from The Middle East and Asia. Ricardo Ceccaroli is said to be on first name terms with the Italian President and as a rich and influential catholic he is a frequent visitor to The Vatican. The company was founded in the late 20's by Alessandro Ceccaroli, Ricardo's father who transformed a small engineering workshop into a lucrative light armaments company which later came under the discrete patronage of *Le Duce* - Mussolini himself. Alessandro had learned the skills of the trade working for a small craft cutlery company in Maniago a small town in the province of Pordedone. After World War 2 the Ceccaroli family hastily distanced themselves from fascist Italy and moved into the motor industry providing machine tools and components for the burgeoning car industry. From 1958 and the beginning of the European Union the company began to spread its influence throughout Europe particularly in France and Germany. After the fall of the Berlin Wall in 1989 and the collapse of old Soviet Russia the company forged joint ventures in several of the ex-Soviet Union countries. There has been the occasional whiff of scandal and suspected Mafia links as well as unproven corruption claims in dealings with ex-Prime Minister Berlusconi's media empire.

Alessandro married Carmelita, the daughter of the local *boulanger* in 1946 and it wasn't until 9 years later in 1955 that baby Ricardo came along. Many told her that she was too old to have children but Carmelita persisted ignoring their advice. Tragically she died in a difficult caesarean birth but baby Ricardo survived.

✂

Ricardo Ceccaroli sat on his balcony overlooking the lake. He was breakfasting late this morning after a gruelling business meeting in Turin. As boss of one of the most powerful enterprises in Europe he'd been asked by the General Confederation of Italian Industry *(Confindustria)* to give the keynote speech on the changing relationship between the European Union and 'Big Business.'

He had already had his usual morning swim in the lake. The water had been cold but refreshing. When at home on his island an early morning swim had become a well-practiced ritual for Ceccaroli whether summer or winter. Today as ever he was accompanied by Winston his springer spaniel. Winston stood by the table and vigorously shook himself whilst Ricardo towelled himself dry. This morning was going to be special. He knocked back the glass of freshly squeezed orange juice, ate a couple of dried figs and then shouted down to his housekeeper Rosa to bring him up a cup of coffee. Rosa had been with the Ceccaroli family since his father's time and had once been his lover. Since his father Alessandro's death, Ricardo had kept the baroque mansion on despite its size and the loyal Rosa had become an inseparable part of the household.

Ricardo shuffled in his chair as he watched the small boats skimming the smooth surface of the lake like giant insects. Rosa arrived with his *latte* and silently placed it on the table. A larger boat came into view the sun glinting off its bows. Ricardo immediately recognised it as the mid-morning taxi bus from Stresa bringing the mail. The Italian Postal Service - *Posta Italiane* – he had received an SMS saying to expect his purchase today. He took the gravel path leading down to the small wooden pier, the cicadas were already tuning up and small green lizards were scurrying between the cracks of the low stone wall, a sure sign of a hot sunny day to come. It was moments like these when he felt a selfish, sensual delight in his island seclusion and the knowledge that his riches would see him through to the end of his days. He traced his finger around the sculpted 'Borromean Rings' set into the stone wall by the small wooden pier. The rings a reminder of the glory of the former owners of the island. 'Strength in Unity.'

The taxi bus didn't tie up at the pier. The few early morning tourists on the vessel looked curiously on as *il postino* in his blue polo shirt and baseball cap waved to Ricardo. No tourist landings on his private island. As the pilot slowed the motor and drifted the boat close to the pier the postman shouted across to Ricardo. He took a small package from his leather bag. '*Signore un piccolo pacco a partira dal Francia – la tua firma, per favour.*' Ricardo hastily scribbled his name on the electronic pad and taking the small parcel thanked the official. '*Grazie,* stop by for a small *grappa* next time. Rosa will be delighted to see you.' *Il Postino* laughed, made an exaggerated wave and shouted a cheery *ciao.* It was no secret that Tommaso the postman had designs on Rosa. He was a regular visitor to the island particularly when Ricardo was away and Rosa's trips to the market in Stresa weren't just about buying a kilo of fresh peaches and a chunk of *formaggio pecorino.* Ricardo didn't care – if they were happy so what. The idling motor spluttered back into full life and the taxi headed back out towards the centre of the lake. A couple of American tourists immortalised the scene on their camera phones.

Ricardo checked the package. It was what he was expecting. The postmark the French town of Troyes and on the back the name *Brunhes & Poitou – Commissaire-priseur*. He'd organised the money transfer from his bank as soon as he had been assured that his bid had been successful. He'd waited a long time for this moment. His collection of fine, rare cutlery and scissors would be enhanced by this latest acquisition and what an acquisition it most certainly was. He was reminded of his e-mail exchanges with the attractively sounding Clotilde Estampe at the French scissor museum and regretted that he'd never paid her a personal visit. Still the scissors were the real prize. His feeling towards his collection was akin to erotic joy. He could live happily with his precious cutlery and considered that any romantic connection would only complicate his life.

Rosa was shouting down to him that his coffee was going cold. He glanced up at her on the balcony and waved the package. 'It's here Rosa, what I've been waiting for all these years.' Rosa had heard all this many times before. His father Alessandro had been a collector of beautiful women but his son preferred antique cutlery. What a waste she thought. Ricardo joined her on the balcony. She took the cup of cold *latte* and sizing up the package tutted. 'What is it this time? Another extravagance to be hidden away in the library to be occasionally brought out to impress visiting business-men and politicians?'

'No this is something really special Rosa. Wait.' He carefully slit the sticky tape with his thumb nail. Folding back the triangular carton edges he opened the small box and pulled out a bubble wrapped package. Carefully peeling back the plastic he took the scissors in his hand. 'Just look at these Rosa. Aren't they magnificent?' He held the scissors in the air like the priest holding the host aloft at Sunday mass. The morning sun was glinting off the handles. He brought the scissors to his lips and in a moment of pure ecstasy kissed the handles with extraordinary Italian passion.

Rosa was unimpressed. 'You don't know where those scissors have been. You might have wiped them down first. Just look at them. You don't know who has been touching them. Let me look.'

Ricardo passed the scissors to Rosa who pulled a face as she noted the serpentine handles. 'Who on earth would want a pair of scissors with snake handles? And look here have you seen these initials on the blades? Beautifully carved I'll admit but scissors are strange implements that can bring great joy and happiness to some but misery and disaster to others. Remember what your father used to say about scissors. Never trust them. I'll bet that the original owners were glad to see the back of these.'

'Oh, don't be such a miserable doom monger Rosa. I have the feeling that these scissors have had a very interesting past. Let me tell you something. You know who originally made these scissors.............?' He was interrupted by his phone ringing. Rosa disappeared before he could explain further.

He didn't recognise the number; a French dialling code aroused his curiosity. A heavily accented female French voice had passed the phone to someone called Bob Martin, an Englishman living in France and claiming to be a previous owner of the scissors. Ricardo Ceccaroli remembered last week's call from the charming Clotilde asking if he would agree to a meeting. He had never met the museum curator but was mesmerised by her charming French accent. He considered it unlikely that he could refuse her anything. Bob Martin had told him that he and his wife would be in Stresa the following day. Ricardo was thrilled. He loved a good story and it seemed that Bob Martin might turn out to be a good storyteller. He shouted down to Rosa.

'Two guests for lunch tomorrow. Something to shock the tastebuds of the English.'

Chapter Fifteen

Later the same Day

'Talking of languages,' Bob was still amused with the idea of decaffeinated English. The kilometres were flashing by and Bob felt in fine form. He recalled that it was a Frenchman, Jean-Paul Nerrière who had first coined the name – a portmanteau word of 'Global' and 'English.' 'I don't know an Italian equivalent, 'Globit' sounds a possibility but perhaps a little too vulgar for Italian ears. Anyway, you're the one who speaks Italian and very well if I may say so.'

'I feel uneasy when you flatter me like that. You're after something I can tell. Cut out the English charm and tell me what's on your mind Bob and don't try telling me that we're here for a *Valpolicella* tasting and a second honeymoon.'

 Bob paused looking sheepishly sideways at his wife sat in the passenger seat. 'Not sure about the *Valpolicella*, I prefer a good bottle of *Barolo* but let me tell you more about Ceccaroli, the fella who bought the scissors at the auction.'

'I thought the scissors would soon open their ugly blades again,' groaned Gisèle.

'Well, his full name is Ricardo Ceccaroli. He fought off quite a challenge from a Chinese collector of renown and not forgetting yours truly who did his best but in the end fate decided that it wasn't a good idea to buy back his own scissors and anyway Ceccaroli is certainly a lot richer than me. He'd done his bidding over the phone so I hadn't a chance of speaking to him personally but after a bit of research, which I won't bore you with now, I tracked him down and what do you think I found?'

'Let me guess,' interrupted Gisèle. 'He lives in Stresa.'

'Well not exactly more like on a secluded island in the middle of the lake.'

'In the middle of Lake Maggiore? Bob this story is really getting quite ridiculous. So, you've decided to track him down and once you've found him what then?'

'You know those scissors have had a remarkable history.'

Gisèle was increasingly familiar with her husband's scissor odyssey. The tracking of the scissors from an industrial Lancashire town, crossing the Pennines to Yorkshire, lost and found in Normandy before disappearing down a well in Carcassonne and reappearing in a cutlery museum. The story could have made a great road movie. All the ingredients were there. Romance, jealousy, murder, nostalgia, phobia and not a few coincidences and the journey was continuing.

'I think that the new owner has the right to be informed of the history. If something like these scissors comes into your possession you're always going to be curious as to the previous owners and their story. If you're a serious collector you want to build up a picture of the past. All objects have a story to tell.'

'Even if that story includes tragedy and misfortune?'

'Especially if it includes tragedy and misfortune – that's what makes some objects collectable. Just think about the collector who a couple of years ago paid 15000 euros for a silk slipper once worn by Marie Antoinette. Can you imagine the emotion of touching something that once was in the possession of one of the most famous, beautiful and tragic figures in French history?'

The car entered another of the numerous poorly lit, hazardous tunnels that are a necessary feature of a largely mountainous country. Bob was concentrating on the route ahead and missed Gisèle's scathing comment on French royalty. She was a great admirer of the British royals but made no secret of her loathing for the French bourgeois ambitions for a new Bonaparte. By the time they came out into the daylight Gisèle was off on another track.

'Have you actually contacted Ceccaroli?'

Before he could answer her the traffic in front began to build up and suddenly ground to a halt. Ahead was yet another tunnel, a long one. The sign at the side of the road indicated 2800 metres. Twenty or thirty vehicles lined the right carriageways leading to the tunnel and ominously there were no vehicles coming in the opposite direction.

'Looks like an accident.' Bob declared wearily, his dreams of a good pasta luncheon receding with the morning mist. He checked the satnav which confirmed his fears. 'Hopefully nothing too serious.' He said hesitatingly. 'I read somewhere recently that there are nearly 300 serious accidents a year in

Italian road tunnels. Most of them caused by poor visibility or poor distance judgement.'

Drivers and passengers were now beginning to leave their cars as small groups formed gazing ahead towards the tunnel entrance. Most of the men were lighting up cigarettes and gesticulating wildly.

'Typically Italian.' Laughed Gisèle. 'Give them a small drama and they'll talk and smoke their way through it. It'll doubtless end up as an opera. Culture my dear Bob, culture. None of your English stiff upper lip here. I'll go and investigate.'

Before Bob could stop her, she was out of the car and heading towards the nearest group of blue overalled truck drivers. Bob knew from experience that Gisèle's speciality was extreme curiosity and nothing that he could say would ever change that. There was a lot of pointing and raised voices. One guy was banging his index finger to his head in an exaggerated 'they're all mad' gesture. The others laughed and slapped one another's backs. Gisèle was listening intently whilst a convoy of ambulances and *carabinieri* sped past, lights flashing. Five minutes later she returned to the car with a calm look of quiet acceptance.

'Do you want the bad or the good news, Bob?'

'Stop playing games and just give me the details. How long are we likely to be stuck here?'

'Well, if my understanding of the local Lombardo-Milanese dialect is anything to go by we could be in for a long wait. I didn't understand all, but the regional dialect has evolved from vulgar Latin and as such has similar roots to Provençale which was the language of my mother and therefore it seems..........'

'Yes, yes.' Bob replied impatiently, save the linguistics lesson 'til later. Just tell me will we be in Stresa in time for my *zucchini* fritters and bottle of *Barolo*?'

'You English are always the same. Full of charm and self-deprecating humour until you meet a small crisis and then all you can think about is your stomach and a bottle or two of wine.'

This was a recurring theme between Bob and Gisèle. Neither could really get their heads around how culture, language and personality affected their interpretation of mood and situation. A Latin temperament with its sudden flare ups and equally sudden calms didn't sit well with the Anglo-Saxon 'say what you mean and mean what you say' attitude. Telling someone they're an ignorant oaf attacks the very heart of the Englishman's pride and self-esteem whereas for the Mediterranean types it is all part of an elaborate game of philosophical one-upmanship. All to be resolved with a victory smile, a peck on the cheek and another glass of *pastis*.

'The situation is apparently that there has been a serious accident on the other side of the tunnel. No one is really sure, but these truck drivers still use their CB radios to communicate and some of them have sent messages from the other side of the tunnel.'

'I thought CB radio disappeared years ago. Surely the cell-phone has superseded them.'

'Well yes, but I'm just telling you what I heard. The good news is that we're outside the tunnel. Inside there is a lot of smoke and many drivers have had to abandon their vehicles. At least we're in the fresh air. The bad news is that the truckers think it will take two hours to clear the tunnel. So, Bob, forget your stomach, pay your beautiful wife some attention and concentrate on telling me what you've been getting up to since leaving home.' She fished inside her bag and produced a Paolo Conti disc. Conti the idiosyncratic Italian Jazz and Blues singer. One of Gisèle's favourites. 'Bought this from home – will give us some Italian ambiance and help you forget your *zucchini fritters* or whatever.'

Bob sighed knowing full-well that he could never win these culture wars. He dutifully slipped the disc into the player, lit up a cigar and sat back. Paolo Conti was singing *'Un gelato al limon.'* It was true what they said about the Italian language. Music to the ears. Who wouldn't be seduced by the magical cadences? He'd considered learning Spanish a while back. A major world language and growing in usage. Some estimate that in 100 years-time Spanish will overtake English as the most spoken second language but in Bob's opinion it couldn't hold a candle to the romance of Italian. 'Lemon ice-cream.' 'So sensual,' he muttered to himself. 'Only an Italian could possibly write a song about lemon ice-cream.'

'How many of your women friends tolerate your cigar smoking habit?' Gisèle looked across to Bob. 'I'll bet they weren't all as tolerant as I am.'

'Hey, but you told me when we first met that you liked cigar smoke.' Another ambulance tore past them, siren blaring.

'Yes, but not in the confined space of a car. Wind the window down. So come on, you haven't answered my question. You feel obliged to visit the new owner to tell him what exactly – that the scissors are cursed, that he shouldn't touch them and he should throw them in to the lake *tout de suite*? Have you contacted him and does he know you're coming?'

Bob pulled a face and drew heavily on the cigar. Gisèle's questions were the same ones he had been asking himself ever since the auction room in Troyes. He refused to believe in superstition or curses. He considered himself a rational man. Coincidence? Maybe he could accept. Terrible coincidence was another thing and why did the name Ceccaroli ring a few bells?

'Actually, darling that's where you come in.'

'A ha! Should have seen this one coming. You want me to contact him. That's it isn't it?'

'Oh, just a brief call. Good excuse to dust down your Italian. Suggest that we meet up for a chat – that sort of thing.'

'…And if he refuses what then?'

'Doubt that he'll refuse. If he does we're off on a second honeymoon. Collectors are always fascinated by the history of the objects they collect. Besides Italian men never miss an opportunity to meet a beautiful woman.'

'Who says I'm coming?' Gisèle replied in mock affrontery. I might just decide to spend the day by the pool and find myself a *gigolo*. Ceccaroli hardly sounds my type.' Gisèle said in her best coquettish manner before smiling at her husband. 'You think I would miss the opportunity. You're not the only one with a sense of curiosity. You try and stop me!'

Bob handed his phone over to his wife. 'Ceccaroli's number is in the repertoire. Don't forget to add the Italian International code. It's 39.

Gisèle looked across at Bob with her 'don't take me for a fool' look and scrolled through the numbers. She dialled Ceccaroli's number. He answered almost immediately. She slipped comfortably into Italian.

'Il signor Ceccaroli? Mi chiamo Gisèle Martin. Mio marito è un inglese ed è l'ex proprietario delle forbici che hai comprato la scorsa settimana. Vorrebbe parlarvi, se possibile?' Parli inglese o francese?'

A moment's pause whilst Gisèle listened intently a smile forming on her lips.

'Bene, bene. Parla con mio marito, per favore.'

She passed the phone at the same time mouthing silently to an anxious looking Bob. 'Don't worry he speaks English.'

Five minutes later a relieved and somewhat surprised Bob shut down the phone and announced with undisguised glee that they'd been invited for dinner tomorrow.

'He says he would be very happy to talk about the scissors. We must take the 10.30 ferryboat and tell the captain to drop us off at Ceccaroli's island. He'll be waiting on the pier.'

196

✂

Car doors were slamming, lorry drivers stubbing out their cigarettes and the stream of vehicles began moving slowly in the direction of the tunnel opening.

The tunnel was badly lit as Bob had already explained to Gisèle but this one seemed narrower than most and it was difficult to make accurate judgments about distance and speed. The lanes narrowed even further and had been coned off by the traffic police. On the right they passed the burnt-out wreck of two huge 8-wheeler trucks. The traffic slowed yet again as people *'rubber necked'* to get a better view of what looked like a serious and deadly accident. The whole front of the second truck was horrifically squashed. Driving too close and too fast. It was hardly possible that anyone could have survived such an impact.

'Why on earth do people always slow down when they see horrific accidents?' Alice asked. 'Even the drivers on the opposite carriageway slow down. What is it they want to see? A few dead bodies lying around is that it?'

Bob tried to keep his eyes on the road ahead and the welcoming circle of daylight that marked the tunnel exit. 'I heard someone say recently that there was beauty in horror. How about that? Think of all the paintings down the ages that depict horrible scenes of cruelty, suffering and death. All the famous crucifixion scenes, not forgetting *Caravaggio's* 'The Beheading of John the Baptist' or *Gericault's* 'The Raft of the Medusa.' They all draw and hold our gaze in the same way as people passing a road traffic accident are drawn to look.'

'So, it's our obsession, fear and curiosity about death and destruction that grabs our imagination and practically forces us to look,' added Gisèle. 'Remember those portraits of Anne Boleyn in The National Portrait Gallery. Fascinating to look at when you remember what happened to that head.'

'I think we'll change the subject,' replied Bob. 'This is all getting pretty depressing. We'll soon be in Stresa and hopefully in time to grab some lunch.'

'There you go again,' laughed Gisèle. 'Always thinking about your stomach and a typical English refusal to accept the realities of life and death. Ostrich! Talking of tragedies you've yet to tell me how Hervé and Stephen reacted to Alice's tragic death.'

'How do you expect them to have taken it? Stephen wanted to pin the blame on anything and everybody including me. He found it awfully hard to accept that it was just a tragic accident.'

'Surely he couldn't blame you Bob. You could have done nothing to help. You were hundreds of kilometres away at the time.'

'No, but don't you see it was me who had re-introduced Alice to the scissors. I lent them to her in exchange for a kiss all those years ago. It was me who had re-discovered them at the *brocante* and it was me who took them all the way to Carcassonne. Who can blame Stephen for seeing me somehow responsible? You're probably right. Perhaps I am an ostrich. Sometimes I'm not comfortable with the realities of life and death.' Bob took a deep breath. He ejected Paolo Conti and tried to focus on the road ahead and for a moment the only sound that could be heard was the drumming of the wheels on the autostrada.

'Tell me about Hervé.' Gisèle interrupted the silence. 'It may be easier for me to understand the complex emotional set up of a compatriot. How often does French TV show close-up shots of people amid great turmoil? Looks like he or she's going to shed a tear – camera close-up of watery eyes.'

Bob tried hard to organise his thoughts into something approaching objectivity.

'Hervé was more philosophical about the whole thing. The French cartesian approach to problem solving and all that. Maybe even an acceptance of fate. Does fate sit comfortably in the great French philosophical tradition?'

Gisèle thought for a moment. She recalled reading Voltaire's book, *'Zadig ou la destinée'* which references an old Persian story *The Three Princes of Serendip* to explore the notion of existence being out of human control and in the hands of destiny.

'So, your conclusion would probably be that Hervé saw it as Alice's tragic destiny whereas Stephen would see it as a terrible but avoidable tragedy?'

'Bob, that's too simplistic. You make it sound as though Hervé was able to rationalise the whole drama and move on. You know it's not like that. Hervé's feelings for Alice as a companion and lover must have run deep, perhaps not as deep as a son's feeling for his mother but profound, nevertheless. It's just a different way of seeing the world. If someone is struck down in a terrorist attack or some mega virus kills millions you can't just let it happen and put it down to fate. If that were the case scientific research would cease to exist, no need for security forces and doctors would be largely redundant. There would be no point because everything would be predetermined.'

'A bit like the hand of cards that life deals us?' Bob said with a slight edge of cynicism in his voice.

'Depends on who's doing the dealing.' Gisèle replied.

'Or even if the cards are dealt from the top or bottom of the pack.'

Bob was stopped from further consideration of what a huge can of worms the original scissor maker had unknowingly opened when the satnav burst into life and announced that their destination was imminent.

'Not far now. Don't you think that having a good lunch is one of the realities of life? Keep looking ahead and the lake will soon come into view.'

They brooded in their own thoughts for a few moments. The road began to descend and then suddenly it was there. Lake Maggiore in all its spring tinted splendour.

'*Voila,* Stresa the jewel of Maggiore. Do you realise that we're going to be treading in the footsteps of 'greats' like Stendhal, Dumas, Dickens, Chaplin and Byron? It's even rumoured that Mozart and his missus came here in 1770 when they were in Milan rehearsing a production of *Mithridate.*'

'Impressive. Which website did you get all that from and which Dumas by the way?'

'You mean there was more than one?'

'Père ou fils ?'

Bob chose to ignore the comment. He opened the window and breathed deeply. 'Just breathe in that fresh lakeside air. Can't you just smell that distant whiff of *Chianti* and *spinach Ravioli?* Hey! Wasn't that Hemingway we just passed at that roadside cafe drinking absinthe with Scott and Zelda?'

'You've been watching too many Woody Allen films.' Gisèle interrupted. 'Concentrate on your driving.'

Chapter Sixteen

The next day

Bob woke early. He had a splitting headache. Gisèle was still fast asleep. Through the half open curtains of the hotel room he could see the sun rising over the eastern side of the lake. It was a splendid view. Lake Maggiore was mirror smooth with only a couple of early morning boating enthusiasts disturbing the surface. Dawn clouds clung to the mountains to the north. Late spring snow cladding the peaks over the border in Switzerland. He knew they shouldn't have gone for the second bottle of *Frascati* but after only eating a light lunch they'd decided to binge in the evening in a cosy little *trattoria* in a barely locatable back-alley of Stresa. They were both ravenous and the *Risotto* was too good to be true hence the second bottle. Bob's adrenalin always had the habit of getting the better of him and inevitably caution went out of the window. For Bob adrenaline fed his enthusiasm and excitement. A new place plus a new adventure. They'd got lost walking back through the narrow streets still warm in the late evening. They'd been drawn by the sound of a local rock band doing poor Rolling Stones covers before some officious local dignitary pulled the plug on their amplifiers and told everyone the show was over but at least he could point them in the direction of their hotel. Eventually they dragged themselves back to their room and collapsed into deep slumber.

He took a long hot shower and tried to clear his head. His thoughts turned to *Signore* Ceccaroli. He was looking forward to their lunch together and somewhat relieved to have discovered that he spoke good English. As Clotilde Estamp from the Nogent museum had suggested cutlery collectors were not only a sociable bunch but also curious by nature and let's face it thought Bob it's not every day that you get a lunch invitation to the private island of a top industrialist.

Gisèle had been awakened by Bob's showering. She often wondered why such a routine activity could entail such a noise. It could have been worse, Bob usually sang in his shower, out of tune. She gazed across the still lake wondering what makes the difference between our perceptions of a lake and the sea. She supposed it was smell and sound and maybe the horizon. Most sea views were open unless there happened to be a bay or an island to focus the view.

Bob interrupted her thoughts and came and sat on the side of the bed. He kissed his wife on the lips with something approaching urgent passion but his still aching head put a stop to any other ideas that he may have had.

'Hungover my poor darling? Serves you right for ordering that second bottle and I expect you don't remember the large complementary *limoncello* you downed after paying the bill.'

'*Limoncello*? I don't remember that. Are you quite sure?' Bob frowned as Gisèle ran her fingers through his wet hair. 'Well, when in Rome and all that.'

'But we're in Stresa not Rome and surely you're not suggesting that the Italians drink more heavily than the English?'

'Well, you know what I mean,' retorted Bob. First hangover I've had in years, must have been a bad bottle of *Frascati!'*

'Aye, aye, aye good bottle bad bottle you still drank it. Come off it darling your passion for Italian dining got the better of you. Go on admit it. Anyway, don't forget we have a rendezvous with the ferryman at 10.30. You'll feel better after a good breakfast.'

By the time Bob had downed two cups of coffee and a plate of *Parmesan* and *Culatello* ham he was beginning to feel himself again and rediscovering his culinary tastebuds.

'The waiter told me that the *Culatello* is one of Italy's rarest hams. Apparently, the name means 'Little Ass' if that's any help and the great Michelin starred chef Massimo Bottura says that this ham isn't a meat it's a myth.'

Gisèle shrugged her shoulders. 'A personal friend of yours, is he? Typical of the Brits. Make a friend of the waiter and you think you'll get preferential treatment. Well, if you believe what every Italian waiter tells you about food, you're a fool. It's all about marketing don't you see. Eat up and let's get going. Even I'm beginning to get the scissor bug and lunch with a rich Italian businessman on his private island intrigues me. Remind me to tell you my spoon story sometime.'

Bob wasn't sure that his wife wasn't mocking him with her little story. He ignored the provocation. 'Yes, I'm looking forward to it too. What do you think he'll be serving up for lunch?'

'There you go again. Always thinking of your stomach. And don't forget to go easy on the wine. It'll probably be a tomato *bruschetta* and a bottle of tap-water so don't build up your hopes.'

Bob raised his eyebrows and shrugged. 'Wouldn't be surprised if Ceccaroli serves up an *Osso Bucco*. You know how I detest *Osso Bucco*, nearly as bad in my book as a *cous cous* or bread and butter pudding.'

Gisèle smiled at him charitably and taking his hand they headed for the elevator.

✂

'Do you think I'm suitably dressed for lunch with a rich Italian?' They had bought their tickets and were waiting on the quay with a small group of other people for the boat to arrive. Gisèle, always conscious of her appearance was dithering over whether her *'gamine'* look was appropriate for their meeting with Ceccaroli. Bob knew the routine well. Reassurance was the order of the day.

'Well, if *Signore* Ceccaroli is a big fan of Audrey Hepburn in *'Breakfast at Tiffany's'*, seems to be the right age, you'll be a sensation. Stop worrying he's probably past the age of admiring younger women anyway.'

Without answering she nodded in the direction of Bob's yellow slacks. 'You've obviously learned your French fashion lessons well. Yellow trousers, white shirt and blue silk scarf. Very Alain Delon. You'll do for me.' Before Bob could come up with an appropriate answer the ferry boat blasted its horn announcing its approach.

'Don't forget to tell the pilot that we're going to Ceccaroli's private island. We'll likely be the only people allowed to disembark. Is your Italian up to it?'

Gisèle raised her eyebrow and pursed her lips. 'No more snide remarks today please Bob and don't say that it's just your English sense of humour.' They climbed aboard. Gisèle approached the pilot who was also acting as ticket collector. *'Per favore puoi fermarti al Signor Ceccaroli. Siamo suoi ospiti Sinor e Signorina Martin.'*

The pilot nodded and checked his electronic tablet. *'Sì, certo. Ho un messaggio qui dallo stesso Signore Ceccaroli. Si prega di sedersi ai sedili più vicini all'uscita. Sarete gli unici autorizzati fuori all'isola.*

'What was all that about?' Asked Bob.

'He said that my husband must show his knowledge of the Italian language before he can disembark.' She dug Bob in the ribs before adding, 'no of course not stupid. He said that we must sit in the seats near to the exit as we will be the only ones disembarking at the private jetty.'

'Impressive,' muttered Bob under his breath.

Ten minutes later the boat swung starboard towards a small island. On the borders of the lake was a profusion of citrus, acacias, laurels and several tall cypress trees. Just showing above the vegetation was a 3-story baroque mansion.

The pilot sounded the siren – two long blasts followed by a short one. The motor idled towards an old wooden pier where a tall, well-built, bearded Pavarotti-like type was walking to the lakeside. His hands were in the pockets of a tweed jacket and he sported a pair of rather incongruous looking khaki shorts. On his head a straw boater that wouldn't have looked out of place at a top English public school. At his side a fat black and white springer spaniel barked and enthusiastically wagged its tail. The man waved expansively at the pilot. *'Ciao Alberto. Come stai oggi? Mi hai portato alcuni ospiti?*

'Si una bella donna e suo marito inglese.' Waving his hand in the direction of Gisèle and Rob.

Gisèle nudged Rob. 'You need me to translate darling?'

'Don't bother. A *bella donna* is recognised everywhere as are the ubiquitous *inglese*. Do you doubt he's a fan of Audrey Hepburn or maybe Gina Lollobrigida? He looks old enough to remember them both in their hayday! Probably preferred Hepburn riding a *vespa* with Cary Grant in *'Roman Holiday.'*

Before Gisèle could correct her husband and inform him that the *Vespa* rider was Gregory Peck and not Cary Grant, the boat nudged the wharf and the tall Italian, spaniel at his side extended his hand to help them ashore.

'Riccardo Ceccaroli. Welcome to my island.'

'Hello, pleased to meet you. I'm Bob Martin and this is my wife Gisèle.' Ceccaroli extended his hand to help them both ashore. Winston barked, jumping up and down enthusiastically.

Bob was pleasantly surprised to see that Ceccaroli didn't fit the stereotype of Italian Man. He was tall, dressed like an Englishman on vacation and spoke near perfect English with just a trace of an accent. No *'Globish'* spoken here Bob was professionally relieved to notice. Ceccaroli turned to his dog. 'Winston, say hello to our guests. Winston is my oldest and best friend. More faithful than any woman I've known,' and then smiling at Gisèle added with a laugh 'Well more than any Italian woman I've ever known. But I will make an exception for Rosa my lifelong housekeeper and bearer of all my anxieties and insecurities. Come up and meet her.'

They followed Ceccaroli down an acacia lined path towards the house and up a short flight of stone steps leading to a half-opened oak door and then up a splendid marble staircase. The walls were lined with sombre paintings of long-gone ancestors intermingled with photographs and drawings of old machine parts, cutlery and maps. At the top of the stairs, they turned down a short corridor that led through a double French window onto a large wooden balcony with views through a stand of cypresses to the lake beyond.

A small, slim, greying woman with long cascading grey hair greeted them. She was wearing a mustard-coloured floral dress reaching down to her ankles. From a distance she could have passed for an older version of a *Dali* ex-muse. Taking off a pair of sunglasses and casually parking them on her head she smiled warmly in their direction. Ceccaroli effected the introductions.

'Let me introduce you to Rosa.' Ceccaroli reverted to his native Italian as he presented Bob and Gisèle. *'Signora e mister Martin.* They have come to talk to me about scissors. Isn't that splendid Rosa?'

Rosa smiled and raised her eyebrows. *'Temo di non condividere l'entusiasmo di Ricardo per la sua collezione, anche se li pulisco regolarmente.'*

'She says that she doesn't like my collection but is happy to clean them for me.' He laughed heartily, squeezing Rosa's hand and nodding vigorously. 'She is only joking of course. She loves my collection. She calls them my little trinkets.'

In an effort to show feminine solidarity Gisèle touched Rosa's arm and spoke a few words in Italian. The workshop laughed and nodded agreement in her direction. Ceccaroli felt obliged to translate for Bob. 'Your wife thinks that women should indulge in what you English like to call a man's whims. I trust that your delightful wife indulges your smallest whims *Signore?'*

'All the time,' replied Bob winking at Gisèle. But Bob wanted to move the conversation on to other matters. 'May I complement you on your English, *Signore* Ceccaroli. What is your secret?'

Ceccaroli smiled warmly at his guests and suggested that they stop all pretence of formality and use first names. 'Thank-you very much Bob. So I have always been a great admirer of the British even in spite of those twin jackals Cameron and Johnson and the ill-advised referendum. The departure from the European Union was an act of treachery that future historians will look back on with stupefaction. However, I'm sure you'll agree that that is not a suitable subject of conversation on such a pleasant occasion and on such a beautiful spring morning. My business interests take me all over Europe and with due respect to your charming French wife I find the English one of the more civilised societies. The French have it all but if I may say so Gisèle their obsession with political *macchinazioni* as we Italians like to say has ruined one of the most beautiful and cultivated societies. Our friends the Americans have lost their way and as for Italy I am a great patriot but the less said about that the better. Patriotism in my country doesn't have a great history.'

'No, no *Signore* – Ricardo. I am of the same inclination. We French have lost our way a little but I have confidence in the future. My compatriots will eventually see the folly of their ways. They are always a little slow in making social progress and the election of President Le Pen will result in a serious reality check but do continue your thoughts on the British. I too share a certain love for *Perfidious Albion.'* She leaned towards Bob and planted a kiss on his cheek.

'Evidently,' he laughed. 'You will have noted I hope my modest taste in English clothes.' He unbuttoned his tweed jacket and ran his thumb down the collar. Best quality Harris Tweed. Walter Slater of London. I'm assured it will outlive me and the Hebridean craftsmanship is second to none.'

Bob was about to go off on a geography lesson of the UK and point out that The Hebridean Islands are in fact Scottish; but he thought better of it. Scottish independence had just been won and the Scottish parliament were preparing to rejoin the EU and adopt the Euro. Now wasn't the time for such polemic particularly as the Italians themselves were embroiled with renogiating European treaties after their latest financial crash.

Ricardo continued. 'I have always been impressed by the British character, their resilience and great sense of humour ever since I learned of the history of my family but more of that later.' He turned to Rosa. '*Rosa per favore servire gli aperitivi.* Time for a little drink before lunch. Please take a seat and Bob you can tell us about your passion for collecting scissors.'

Rob was left wondering about what connections Ricardo's family could have had with England when an idea began to form in his mind. The name Ceccaroli stirred something. 'Oh no Ricardo I'm no collector of scissors. You are mistaken. My interest rests with just one pair of scissors which are now I believe in your expert hands. My profession is an English teacher.'

'Ah, a teacher of English,' Ricardo exclaimed with undisguised surprise. So I must be in very revered company and your praise for my usage will really be taken to heart. Bravo English man and thank-you for the complement.'

Rosa arrived with a tray of drinks. '*Grazie Rosa.* I explain. *Aperol* is a well-know Italian aperitif. It is made from best Italian bitter oranges, gentian and rather unusually rhubarb. It is made by the celebrated *Campari* company in which I have a small interest. Just a few *azioni* you understand. How do you say '*azioni*' in English Bob?'

Bob shrugged somewhat embarasingly and demurred to his wife who always delighted to show off her knowledge of Italian and English vocabulary calmly interjected with 'shares.'

'Ah, yes 'shares' *azioni*. I like that. I will commit that to memory. '*Tchin Tchin.*' Now I propose a toast. Please raise your glasses to *le forbici,* the scissors.'

Bob spluttered. Raising a toast to the object that had brought so much misfortune stuck in his craw. He coughed and wordlessly raised what Bob observed to be the very best in Venetian cutglass ware whilst the other three shouted out '*le forbici.*' He hoped he wouldn't drop the glass. Rosa seemed less than certain but went along with Ricardo anyway whilst Gisèle whose involvement with the scissors was more peripheral played along. Bob silently wondered what Alice would have made of all this ceremony.

'You seem to be lacking any great enthusiasm for the scissors, Bob.' Ricardo said perceptively.

'I hoped that you hadn't noticed. I must apologise and perhaps we can have the opportunity to discuss the history of the scissors shortly,'explained Bob.

'Yes, most certainly. I am somewhat intrigued with what you may have to tell me but for the moment let's enjoy our drinks. Rosa will be preparing a very special lunch for us. She makes the finest *Osso Bucco* this side of Milan don't you Rosa. I hope you like our local speciality.'

Gisèle pronounced a very typical, gutteral French *ooh la la!* and surreptitiously kicked her husband's foot under the table. 'You bet we do. It's one of our favourite Italian dishes isn't it *cherie*?'

Bob giggled and squirmed. He returned the kick before hastily moving his foot away. 'It certainly is Ricardo. You couldn't have chosen better. Yum, yum! My wife is a great cook. She is a partner in a French school of cuisine in Sarlat specialising in traditional French dishes but this will be the first time that we will have had the opportunity to taste a real *Osso Bucco* in situ so to speak isn't it darling?'

Gisèle interrupted quickly before her husband could dig a deeper undiplomatic hole for himself. 'Oh my knowledge of Italian cuisine is very much at the experimental stage you understand. I'm sure I can learn a lot from Rosa.' She turned to Rosa. *'Forse potrei venire in vostra cucina e guardare i vostri preparativi. Sono sicuro che potrei imparare molto.'*

Rosa coloured up and beamed. *'Certamente signora mi darà grande piacere di avere qualche aiuto in cucina. Ricardo non è mai interessato alla preparazione solo nel mangiare.'*

Ricardo roared with laughter. 'I am never allowed into the kitchen when Rosa is at work. It's her territory like my collection of cutlery objects is mine. Everyone to their own passion eh Bob? You are a highly honoured guest *madame* to be invited into Rosa's kitchen. I suggest that the ladies prepare lunch whilst Bob and myself get down to the sharp end of our business. You like that Bob? Sharp end!' He roared with laughter at his pun.

Bob nodded in amused agreement, joining in with the laughter and applauding his host's humour whilst knocking back the last dregs of his aperitif.

Rosa and Gisèle departed downstairs to the kitchen chattering away in Italian like old friends. Ricardo led Bob through a heavily pannelled door into a room part library part art gallery. Winston, tail wagging followed dutifully if somewhat sluggishly. A large bay window looked out over the far side of the lake and *Isola San Giovanni.*

'This room, Bob is very special to me. The Americans talk of their family room, the English the living room, the French *salon,* we Italians prefer *il soggiorno.* This is where I like to take an afternoon siesta or to commune with my family and my books or as you perhaps might have noticed practice my English with watching a few of your great American and English TV series. Bob noted the pile of DVD's siting next to the flatscreen – 'The Avengers', 'Dallas', 'Colombo', 'The Prisoner', 'Starskey and Hutch.'

'Yes, certainly those represent a golden age of TV series. Never matched since. Do you have some favourite characters?'

'Huh, what a question Bob. Who can ever forget J.R. Ewing, John Steed or the ubiquitous N° 7? You have discovered one of the secrets of my love of the English language. Some people prefer pornography but I'll settle for an hour with the most charming and sensual Emma Peel.'

Laughing he moved over to the bay window. 'As you can see I have a great view over to the island of *San Giovanni*. This island is still owned today by members of the Borromeo family. They are very discreet and very very rich but I have little to do with them. I prefer the company of my faithful Winston and of course my precious cutlery collection. But more of that later.' In the corner Winston had found a patch of sunlight. He yawned and flopped down.

Bob checked out the stacks of books on the right of the room. Leather bound volumes mostly with Italian titles but some in French and English. On the opposite wall hung a grand collection of paintings, family portraits and photos. In one corner Bob spotted a series of photos obviously taken in an industrial context. A workshop with several craftsmen working at different stages of knife production, handles, blades and in another picture a small anvil situated next to a furnace with a face-shielded workman hammering a piece of white hot metal with an industrial hammer. On the floor beneath the pictures was a sandstone grinder, its worn wheel showing the effects of years of sharpening knives. Bob turned the handle gently and thought back to that day long ago when Nan had told him about the whistling knife grinder.

Bob looked back at the framed photos. 'So this must be an old photograph of your working company? When was it first established?' asked Bob peering intently at the group of workers.

'Yes, you are looking at the second oldest picture I have of my family's enterprise. It was taken sometime in the 1920's when my father, Alessandro was in the process of transforming a small cutlery company into something a little grander. It was situated in the small village of Maniago in the Pordedone province of north east Italy. The town is known as the 'City of the Knife' and has been making cutlery items since the 15th century. The town is fortunate to be at the conjuncture of 2 valleys and it was this availability of water that helped the installation of the knife and other sharp object industry. The workshop you can see was only small but quite profitable and my father was gaining quite a reputation as a skilled craftsman specialising in cutting tools, knives scissors and increasingly agricultural and surgical equipment. Here you can see several of the artisans at work. Now you may be wondering why I said the second oldest photograph, Bob.' He guided Bob by the arm further along the wall. 'I think this one may well surprise you. I should explain that my father Alessandro was the son of Louise and Elio my grandparents. If you look at this, the oldest photograph in my family collection you will see them together. Elio is at the back and my grandmother is sitting at the table with their two children standing on either side of her. Here is the surprise Bob, look closely at the photograph Bob. Look closely and what do you see?'

Bob peered closely at the faded sepia photo. The family were gathered around a table. Elio stood at the back, moustached, suited and a flat cap on his head. He was smoking a briar pipe. His wife Louise, long fair hair tied at the back in a bun, dressed in a high necked white blouse over what looked like a long grey skirt. Under the table you could just see her stockinged feet wearing a pair of buckled leather shoes. The two children stood either side of their mother and in front of their father. Alessandro appeared to be in early adolescence, dressed as a smaller version of his father and also sporting an oversize grey flat cap. His younger sister Marie-Claire maybe 9 or 10 years old in a patterned dress and bonnet her right hand resting on her mother's arm. In keeping with many family group photos of the time their faces were impassive. Behind the group a small crucifix hung on the wall beside a long ornate sideboard with a mantelpiece clock the time partly obscured by Elio's cloth cap. The table in the foreground seemed to be covered with some sort of garment, maybe a woman's dress.

'Looks like a typical family photo of the late 19th or early 20th century. Any idea of when it might have been taken?' Asked Bob.

'Not really,' Ricardo replied. 'Quite possibly a couple of years before my great grandparents ....But before I tell you more look more closely at the picture. Perhaps your eyesight is not too good Bob.' He laughed and going over to a desk by the window he opened a drawer and took out a pearl handled magnifying glass. 'How you say *lente d'ingrandimento* English teacher?'

'I assure you my eyesight's fine but pass me your beautiful **magnifying glass** and I'll take a closer look.'

'How very clever Bob to give me the translation in another sentence. I see that certainly you are an excellent teacher.'

Bob took the glass replying modestly, 'you learn a few tricks after many years in the classroom. Always make sure that your students are attentive to every word and hear the changes in intonation. Now let me look closely at the photo. I suspect I know what I might find.' For a fraction of a second Bob's thoughts were back in front of Alice's last photo and the discovery of her killer. He shuddered involuntarily but he knew with certainty that it wasn't going to be a deadly snake that was nestling in the folds of the half-finished dress.

✂

Back in the kitchen Rosa and Gisèle were busy preparing the *Osso Bucco*, literally bone with a hole. Rosa was browning the calf shanks in butter and olive oil whilst Gisèle was busy dicing the onions and chopping the parsley and celery. Rosa explained that she was making the traditional Milanese *Osso Bucca* made without tomatoes but including *Gremolata* a sort of sauce made from chopped herbs and lemon and orange zest mixed with olive oil. She was happy that she could understand most of what Rosa was saying. Her tenure at the French embassy in Rome several years back had given her a good understanding of Italian and she was grateful that she had done an intensive course with the local *Scuola Leonardo da Vinci*. Rosa was explaining the importance of rolling the veal in flour before brazing it in the frying pan. Gisèle wanted to add a clove or two of garlic but Rosa was shaking her head. 'There are many other flavours here with the celery, parsley and not forgetting the paprika. We don't need the garlic. But we do need the wine. Open the fridge and you will see a bottle of white *Gavi di Gavi* on the rack. The *Cavatappi* is in the drawer.' Gisèle found the chilled white wine and eventually realised that the *Cavatappi* was the cork screw. Rosa continued to stir in the tomatoes and herbs in the large casserole pan. 'Now we need three wine glasses. They are in the cupboard on the left of the refrigerator.' Gisèle was a little puzzled as to why three glasses were required but said nothing. She uncorked the wine and waited for further instructions. 'Now fill the three glasses with the *Gavi di Gavi*. The first glass is for you, the second one for me and the third for the pan. Always remember priorities Gisèle.'

They both laughed and raised a toast to Franco-Italian cooperation. The wine glasses were large and Gisèle soon found the wine going to her head. The steaming *Osso Bucco* also added to the sense of intoxication. Rosa dipped a spoon into the simmering sauce and offered it to Gisèle to taste. Gisèle blew on the sauce to cool it before putting the spoon to her lips. She closed her eyes for a second or two before exclaiming , '*Incroyable!* Rosa, this sauce is fabulous. What a delicious mixture ofa flavours. It's like all the good things of Italy rolled into one. You could bottle the sauce and sell it as a luxury perfume.'

'I don't think that would be such a good idea. It would spoil a great many beautiful clothes.' Gisèle's semi-inebriated humour was lost on Rosa. Gisèle herself thought that a little less slurping of the white wine might be a good idea before she began spouting many more stupid ideas whether humourous or not. 'Culture Gisèle, culture,' she said to herself remembering the number of times that Bob had cautioned her about humour not always crossing international frontiers.

'So now we wait. In one hour the *Osso Bucco* will be ready to be served, certainly our men will be hungry after their long discussions about what? A pair of scissors? What is there to be discussed about a pair of scissors?' Rosa laughed mockingly and muttered something about never understanding men. 'And you Gisèle you share your man's passion for his tools?'

Gisèle was on the verge of making a suggestive comment about her 'man's tools' but after her earlier attempt at humour thought better of it. It would take too long to explain the *double entendre* and her Italian although good wasn't that good. She turned the shanks of veal and gave the simmering sauce a stir. 'For Bob the scissors have never been a passion.' She explained. 'More like a not very popular family member – tolerated but never loved. I'm pleased that they have fallen into Ricardo's hands. Bob should have forgotten about the scissors a long time ago but somehow his fascination with chance and coincidence plus his phobia of snakes and his incurable sense of romance has always meant that the scissors would inevitably be a recurring theme in his life. Some would call it fate or destiny but for Bob it's an umbilical that's never been cut. An umbilical firmly attached to childhood memories and narratives feeding his need for some sort of spiritual dimension.' She wasn't sure she'd explained herself well. She looked across at Rosa and they both took a long slurp of wine. For a moment the only sound that could be heard was the bubbling sauce.

Rosa broke the silence. '*Alora*, why did Bob sell the scissors then?'

'He didn't sell the scissors. He loaned the scissors, handed down by his grandparents, to his teenage girlfriend, Alice many years ago. Through circumstance she kept them. By chance he rediscovered the scissors many years later and they led him back to Alice. When she tragically died the scissors went to her son who not knowing the real owner put them up for sale and that's when Ricardo stepped in. It's a very long story. Not always a happy one. I expect that is what they will be talking about at this moment. How about I give you a hand with preparing the table?'

Bob returned the magnifying glass to the table by the window. He said nothing. His eyes followed the wake of a speedboat on the lake but his thoughts were further away back in the sitting room of his grandparents. A small boy looking at a pair of snake-handled scissors with the initials 'K' and 'T' engraved on the blades. His grandmother boiling the kettle on the open grate, Smudge the cat curled up in front of the fire, the voices of his parents returning from a family visit. A seemingly impossible thought was forming in his head.

'Well Bob, what did you see?' Ricardo smiled, thrusting his hands into his tweed jacket. If he'd been wearing a deer stalker hat he could have doubled for Sherlock Holmes although the shorts seemed a little incongruous. 'You saw the scissors.' It was a statement of fact rather than a question. 'A strange coincidence don't you think? To my knowledge only one pair of silver snake-handled scissors were ever made.'

Bob went back to the photograph and looked again. 'Impossible to see if there are any carved initials.'

'There are no carved initials.' Ricardo hastily replied. 'My grandfather kept a record of all the tools and artefacts that he made. It would be highly unlikely that he made a mistake over something as important as a pair of scissors. To an Italian craftsman pride in realisation is the essence of existence. Posterity is everything.' Ricardo crossed the room and drew a large book from a shelf. He dusted it down and placed it on the table. He had no need to flick through the pages. The right page was already marked. 'The records were always kept in Italian but of course you realise that. Here is the item in question Bob.' Ricardo ran his fingers under a line of faint elaborated italic.

N. 4298. 5 agosto 1909 – Coppia di forbici da ricamo – acciaio rivestito in nichel – maniglie del serpente.

'I don't think you need me to translate, the meaning is clear, I'm sure you agree. Snake handled scissors. They were originally made by my grandfather in Maniago before he left to find work elsewhere. He gave them to my grandmother, Louise, who apparently treasured them. Life was difficult at that time. Making a living in the Italian cutlery business was not easy so my grandparents took the decision to go to France where they heard there was lots of work to be had in the cutlery factory in Nogent. Louise took all her embroidery things with her in her sewing box including her scissors. Life didn't work out too well for them. Living in eastern France was difficult. Integration wasn't easy and immigrant Italian workers were not popular. Their two children Alessandro and Marie-Claire were born there and eventually when the children were a little older they took the long journey to...........'

'England.' Interrupted Bob suddenly. 'I should have realised earlier.' His heart was racing, he took a deep breath before grasping Ricardo's arm. 'It's all falling into place now. I've had this vague notion since I discovered that it was you who had bought the scissors at the auction.'

Ricardo looked with concern into Bob's wide eyes. 'What are you trying to tell me Bob? You look as though you have seen a phantom.'

'I would hazard a guess that the photograph we have just been looking at was taken not in Italy nor France but in a small industrial suburb of Manchester in the North of

England. I'm right aren't I Ricardo? Your grandparents and mine certainly knew one another whether as neighbours or through a business transaction. The initials on the pair of scissors belong to my grandparents. 'T' for Thomas and 'K' for Kate. I have a distant memory of my grandmother, Nan telling me about her wedding dress. How the couturier had carefully cut the organza and lace and how on the wedding day she had presented the scissors as a wedding present. She told me that the dressmaker was Italian. She'd given the dressmaker a penny to avoid the scissors bringing bad luck.'

Ricardo hastily picked up the order of transaction book and quickly flicked through the worn pages. 'There must be a record of the engraving somewhere here. Although working only part-time in the engraving trade Elio was meticulous in his record keeping. Fortunately his record of transaction leger was sent back to Italy after his death with the few personal possessions. When was the date of your grandparents marriage, Bob?'

'I think it was 1911 but I've no knowledge of the month.'

'The month is not important. Most of my grandfather's work at that time was stone engraving under contract to other people. His metal engraving work would have been limited to a few small jobs.' Ricardo flicked over a few pages until he came to the records for 1911. 'Here look Bob, the page we are looking for. You can see that he took very little personal work at this time so it shouldn't be too difficult.............'

Bob was looking eagerly over Ricardo's shoulder and scanning the book entries. Again the entries were all in

Italian script but suddenly a name stood out from the rest. It was the key piece of information he had been hoping to see.

N.4325. 24 ottobre 1911 – incisione delle iniziali K e T su forbici serpente – regalo per Signore Thomas Wright, Eccleston.

Bob could hardly contain his excitement vigourously pumping Ricardo's hand and shaking his head in disbelief. It had been too much to expect but he'd found it, another missing piece of the jigsaw which linked his grandparents to the origin of the scissors. The gift of the scissors to his grandparents on their wedding day.

Ricardo was as bemused as Bob was delighted. 'So your grandparents initials were 'K' and 'T?' Could this have been a coincidence?'

'Impossible. You see my grandfather was Thomas Wright resident of Ecclestone Lancashire. His wife, my grandmother was Kate.'

Ricardo put the book back on the shelf and taking a small key from his pocket beckoned Bob to follow him. A section of the wall was panelled, decorated with painted pastoral scenes of Italian life, mountains, lakes and cherubic nymphs tending sheep on an Alpine pasture. The key was inserted into a practically invisible keyhole in the navel of one of the nymphs. Ricardo turned the key slowly and a door opened into a small dark room. He flicked a switch and Bob could immediately see that this was Ricardo's treasure house. His collection of prized artefacts. Glass cabinets lined one side of the room with just enough space for a person to pass in front.

Ricardo switched on an overhead light revealing two long glass cabinets. 'Welcome to my treasures Bob. What you see here is possibly the grandest private collection of cutlery in Europe if not the world. You can see that it is well hidden. I don't fear intruders on my island but it's always better to be cautious. This has been my lifelong passion. _La coltelleria, Rasori e pettini, lancette e forbici, al mio comando tutto qui sta._ Cutlery, Razors and combs, lancets and scissors are all here at my command.' For a moment Ricardo's eyes lit up with something approaching maniacal passion. 'You see why I never married,' he chuckled. 'I don't need a wife when here I can lust after some of the most amazing pieces of craftmanship known to humanity. Look at these Bob. Three Egyptian bronze spoons. The oldest spoons in my collection. They were discovered in Thebes in the 1920's. Their value is incalculable. Look at the carved handle in the form of a heron on this one, the sungod Ra and the longest one about 25 centimetres with a scaribee beetle forming the ivory handle. The insect represented the god Khepri who symbolised the rennaisance of the sun. And look at this Bob, a pair of scissors in the shape of the Eiffel Tower made for the opening of the Paris exhibition in 1889.'

Bob had the impression that Ricardo had entered a private world of his own as his hands and eyes darted from one object to another.

'Now for the _pezzo de resistenza_ the new star of my collection. Permit me a little Italian drama.' He turned the overhead light off. The room was pitch black. Reaching inside his jacket he took out his smart-phone and pressed a key.

Suddenly there was an introductory blast of orchestral music. Bob recognised *O mio babbino caro,* 'Oh My Beloved Father' with certainly the voice of the incomparable Callas. Then even more dramatically an illuminated glass panel slid silently open on the far wall, the room in partial darkness save for the brightly lit panel containing a pair of scissors. Not just any pair of scissors. Ricardo gave Bob a hearty slap on the back. There in front of him, in all their terrible glory were the snake-handled scissors.

Bob wasn't sure that he wanted to see them again. 'Ok, Ricardo, they look fantastic but I'm not sure that I can bear seeing them anymore after all they've been witness to.' Images of Alice's last photograph of the orchid, the *asphodels* and the terrible viper head, the telegramme on the sofa and Alice's husband leaving home in a rage, blood dripping from his wounded shoulder flashed across his mind. 'If you don't mind Ricardo I think I've seen enough. It's very kind of you to show.....' Ricardo switched the overhead light back on and opened the panelled door. They stepped out into the sunlit library.

'But surely Bob if what you are saying is correct this remarkable link between our grandparents should be celebrated. Why are you so distressed? Are you angry with me for purchasing the scissors at the auction? Do you feel that you are the lawful proprietor? I planned the purchase even before I learned I was the successful bidder. I had the illuminated panel constructed by Stresa's best artisans in readiness. My purchase only arrived yesterday and how appropriate that you should be the first person to view the treasure. I imagined that my only rival at the auction was the esteemed but amateur *Huazhong* collector Wang Lei but I knew I could outbid him at the end. I had no idea of your profound interest in the scissors. You must enlighten me over lunch.'

'I apologise Ricardo. It wasn't my intention to make you feel guilty. The scissors are rightly yours now and I'm more than happy with that. You are the owner and in a strange way I'm pleased that now they are out of my sight. They are hidden away in your personal collection locked away on a private island in the middle of a lake and in the possession of a man whom I believe recognises their true worth as part of his family heritage. Presumably now they can cause no more pain. Personally I never want to see them again.'

Ricardo went quiet. He locked the door before turning to Bob. To Bob's embarrassment Ricardo stepped forward and vigorously embraced him, patting his back and shaking his hand. 'We are brothers Bob. Brothers.'

Before Bob could reply a bell rang above the door. '*Alora* now you'll see the second greatest treasure in my house, Bob. Rosa's *Osso Bucco* is ready to be served. If we are late to the table we shall never be forgiven.'

The four of them sat around the table on the shaded terrace of the villa. Rosa and Gisèle had evidently got on well in the kitchen and Bob wondered how much his wife had had to drink. She certainly seemed to have more than the usual twinkle in her eye. In Bob's view Latin women always seemed to have an extra layer of emotion waiting to be peeled back. None of the tight-lipped phlegmatism of the Anglo-Saxons. Before he could consider this further Gisèle looked at him across the table. 'You look a little shell-shocked *Cherie*. I hope you're not still hungover from last night's excesses.'

Ricardo picked up on this with consternation. 'What are these excesses, Bob? Surely you're not revealing yourself to have the worst habits of some of your compatriots. I could never understand the Englishman's penchant for drinking himself under the cabinet.'

'Oh! you mean under the table. The cabinet would be more difficult. Perhaps the Prime Minister would succeed in that direction.'

Ricardo laughed and slapping the table repeated 'table, cabinet, table, cabinet. Same result!'

'No in fact it's just seeing the scissors again. Brought back a lot of memories some bad some good. I'm fine. Now I'm looking forward to tasting this delicious *Osso Bucco* I've heard so much about.' He winked surreptitiously, or so he hoped, in the direction of his wife who was doing her best to conceal a slightly tipsy smirk.

Ricardo reached across for the corkscrew. 'Now Bob, what finer wine could we drink with the *Osso Bucco* than a good bottle of Piedmont *Barolo*. The 1996 *Bruno Giacosa* is a great choice I'm sure you'll agree. Of course, my choice is not in any way influenced by my little portfolio in the vineyard but......' He chuckled as the cork was withdrawn with ceremony and he religiously sniffed it discretely away from the table. *'Perfetto.'* Some of my American business colleagues prefer a *Zinfandel* – but what do the Americans know about fine wine when all theirs practically tastes the same? There is always a surprise with an Italian. Like the people their wines are invariable good, bad or indifferent but never ordinary. What do you think Bob?'

'Well certainly the *Barolo* is one of my favourites, but I can't claim much expertise in Italian wines. I love the variety of grape types you have over here and as you suggest there are always a few surprises to be had but I'll follow your lead Ricardo. Doubtless by now some of my compatriots would be unscrewing the plastic cap on a German *Riesling.*'

'Oh, Bob,' interrupted Gisèle. 'You exaggerate. Most of our English friends have excellent taste in wine.' Turning to Ricardo and cupping her hand in his direction she stage whispered, 'Bob is such a wine snob, Ricardo. You'd think he was the only Englishman who'd ever lived in Europe.'

'Yes, I did catch that. Just how much wine did you and Rosa drink in the kitchen?' Rob sneered. 'Remember when the recipe says add wine it refers to the food.'

Ricardo laughed heartily and attempted to translate Bob's remarks to Rosa who looked both bemused and confused.

She said nothing but stood up and lifted the casserole lid. In the still early afternoon air the steamy aroma wafted and then lingered over the table. Bob raised his eyebrows and muttered what Gisèle half-suspected was a rather insincere mm! Looks good.'

Five minutes later Bob was waxing lyrical not only over the red wine but also the *Osso Bucco*. 'The sauce is delicious Rosa and just look at that colour. As for the *risotto* what can I say? *Cherie* you must get the recipe from Rosa and do this at home. It's absolutely delicious.'

Gisèle recalled their conversation over breakfast when her husband had pleaded his hatred for *Osso Bucco*. She remembered her embarrassment when Bob had left most of the *cous-cous* untouched on his plate when invited for dinner at a high-ranking Tunisian diplomat's house in Paris and she didn't want a repeat of that. Turning his nose up at his mother's bread and butter pudding was another matter. English hypocrisy strikes again she thought to herself. The food and wine seemed too good to be spoiled by serious chatter even though she knew her husband was itching to tell Ricardo the history of the scissors.

By the time they'd finished off the last of the *Osso Bucco* and the sauce had been well and truly mopped up with chunks of corn bread, Gisèle was wondering how they were going to see off Rosa's dessert. She needn't have worried. Demolish it they did. The raspberry *granita* with balsamic caramel was accompanied by a chilled bottle of *Moscato d'Asti*. The sweet dessert wine highlighting the delicate raspberry flavour. Ricardo raised his glass to the sky. '*Un matrimonio fatto in cielo.*' 'A marriage made in heaven.'

The four of them chinked glasses. Bob was beginning to regret having eaten so much particularly after his over-indulgence of the night before. Fortunately, Ricardo suggested that they take coffee in the easy chairs in the garden beneath a small shady group of pink laurel bushes. Down in the garden the air was cooler, and a light breeze was blowing across the lake from the north. The bougainvillea, camelia and azalea were coming into their magnificent best whilst the blue hydrangeas hugged the more humid shoreline.

'This really is a paradise Ricardo. How on earth do you manage to ever leave here. It would break my heart if it were mine.'

Ricardo was silent for a moment. He nodded his head slowly and looked up to the blue sky. 'Well, Bob, you are right. It is a paradise and I hope I can live long enough to continue enjoying it well into my old age. You know sometimes you must leave a place in order to appreciate it even more when you return. He nodded once more. Bob thought he detected a hint of emotion in Ricardo's voice. A small yellow butterfly alighted on the arm of his chair and the moment was gone.

'So, Ricardo you really want to hear about the history of the scissors? You may want to change your mind about ownership after hearing my story.'

Rosa arrived with a tray of espressos and a plate of *Baratti-pralina Noccialato* chocolates. Rob was a little reticent to ask Ricardo if he had shares in that company also but when the *Limoncellos* followed the coffee it seemed only polite to raise his glass in Ricardo's direction and politely ask *'azione* in this company also?' Ricardo smiled, nodded affirmation and raised his glass. 'To the scissors!' His was the lone voice, Gisèle and Bob pulled mock horror faces whilst Rosa couldn't resist chipping in with a few sardonic comments. She tut tutted and raised her eyes saying 'scissors, scissors. *Avresti pensato che stesse accogliendo il suo amante quando sono arrivati. Li baciò e li accarezzò come un animale nel calore. Dio solo sa quali batteri avrebbero potuto essere nascosti da loro.'*

Ricardo looked on impassively whilst Gisèle whispered a hasty translation. 'Rosa thinks that Ricardo treats those scissors like a lover. She wonders what germs might be lurking on them.' They all laughed including Rosa who began clearing the table whilst casting incredulous glances in Ricardo's direction.

'I'll help Rosa with the table and the washing up whilst you men talk scissors.' Gisèle's offer of help was rejected by a shocked Rosa who after throwing her arms up in the air took Gisèle's arm and guiding her away from the table suggested that they take a turn around the garden. Ricardo shouted over to Rosa to not forget the *eau de vie* and two glasses *'per olia olio conversazione degli uomini.'* To oil the conversation.

In the event the conversation didn't need any 'oiling.' Disappearing for a moment Ricardo returned with a box of Havana cigars and a miniature cutter modelled on a real guillotine. 'You see this Bob. A perfect replica of the machine that parted Louis XVI's head from his body. Perhaps we could deal the same fate to some of our present-day so-called leaders, what do you think? It was given to me by a French nobleman whose family had links with the revolutionaries. Only three were ever made by the *Laguiole* company and I am the owner of two of them. I'm reliably informed that the third example is in the office of the French President who I imagine, if I understand contemporary French politics, will be bringing back the real thing anytime soon.' He laughed as he cut the torpedo from his cigar and passed the machine to Bob. 'Watch your finger Bob.'

Bob tried to look as cool as possible as he cut the cigar. Too short and the cigar won't draw, too long and the leaves unravel. It wasn't every day that he had the chance to smoke a *Havana Cohiba* – legend has it that they were made specially for Castro himself. He satisfied himself that the cut was in the right place and took the lighter from Ricardo.

'I saw recently that *Laguiole* have brought out a new scissor type cigar cutter,' announced Bob hoping that he sounded knowledgeable on the latest in cigar accoutrements.

Ricardo snorted disparagingly. '*Si, Si*. Another marketing ploy. Inferior quality mass-produced shit if you pardon the expression. The Chinese and the Japanese manufacturers have cornered the market. First, they copied Europe's best products and now they've trained their artisans to make better stuff. Certainly, I will purchase the latest *Laguiole* cutter but only to complete my collection. My Grandfather Elio was a craftsman. Just look at the snake scissors, Bob. That's true craftsmanship down to the last detail. The setting and design of the curved handles, the delicate engraving, the weight and the balance. My grandmother was an excellent couturier but with those scissors in her hand she was a magician.'

'Talking of your grandparents.' Bob said slowly wanting to begin telling Ricardo his story. 'When you were showing me the photograph of Elio, Louise and their family you were about to say something about when the photograph had been taken but you stopped. Were you going to tell me that your grandparents died in England in the 1918 influenza epidemic?'

Ricardo's clenched fist rose to cover his mouth. His eyes closed in a moment of pure drama. Surely thought Bob Ricardo could hardly be feeling emotional about an event that happened years before he was born and to two people he'd never met. He waited for the Italian to recover his composure.

After a few silent moments Ricardo opened his eyes and smiled at Bob. 'Doubtless you are wondering why this news should have this effect on me. It has nothing to do with the effect of this excellent *eau de vie* I assure you. You understand Bob that we Italians have always been great sentimentalists and family people. No one living today has ever mentioned my grandparents' deaths. My father Alessandro and my aunt Marie-Claire were quite young at the time but they both remembered their terrible separation from their parents. My father rarely spoke of the tragedy but my aunt told me that her mother was the one to die first. She remembers the terrible trauma of seeing her mother's body lying on the bed and a vivid memory of the black plumed horses leading the funeral cortege away from the house. Her father died suddenly a week later probably more from the grief than any physical illness. Word was sent to my great cousin still living in Maniago. The children were taken in by neighbours and then brought back to Italy. It must have been a terrible time for them. They'd endured the long days of travelling to England, the difficulties of living in a strange culture and learning a new language and then seeing their parents die like that. It is part of my family's history Bob and when I look again at those scissors it brings it all back. My grandfather was a courageous man and took immense pride in his work. Those scissors are his legacy.'

Bob wondered whether he really should tell Ricardo what the scissors had seen from the day when they had been given to his grandparents until they appeared on the auctioneer's dais in Troyes. What purpose would telling the story serve? Apart from Bob himself and grand-father Elio Ceccaroli, Ricardo knew none of the players. He was just a rich collector whose pleasure was in the ownership of something that he considered beautiful and perhaps more importantly had been hand crafted by his own grandfather. On the other-hand Bob felt an obligation to the protagonists in the story whether conscious of their role or not. As for himself he had long pondered the role of fate in the story. If the scissors had never existed would anything have changed? His grandparents were married for over 50 years, the 1918 epidemic killed millions, Eric was lost in a war that had killed hundreds of thousands of others, Colin was a lousy husband with some problematic character traits and Alice loved flowers and the countryside. If Bob had never lent the scissors to Alice that hot July afternoon in his bedroom none of this would be happening and none of the protagonists would be any the wiser. Ignorance really would be bliss Bob reflected. He thought of Alice's last kiss by the well on *la Montagne Noir* and how he believed that he'd seen the scissors for the very last time. In spite of the warm sun he felt a cold shiver ripple up his arms and into his shoulders.

It was Ricardo himself who forced Bob's hand. 'When I showed you the old photograph, it was that look on your face. A look of realisation. The realisation that our grandparents knew each other, were possibly neighbours in a small industrial town in the north of England and that the scissors would somehow play an important role in both our lives. Please tell me your story Bob. You owe me that.'

Ricardo topped up their glasses with the honey-coloured *eau de vie.*

'………………so, there you have it, Ricardo. You outbid the Chinese collector and now the scissors are yours. They've found their spiritual home perhaps.' Ricardo had listened attentively to Bob's story without interruption.

The afternoon sun was slipping down to the west of Lake Maggiore, the cicadas were chirping ever more loudly and Gisèle and Rosa could still be heard chattering away on the far side of the garden. Ricardo said nothing. His face was set. He stood up and walked slowly to the edge of the lake where he stood gazing at a flight of yellow-legged gulls skimming the still surface. After a few moments he turned and looked towards where Bob was seated. Bob got up and walked towards him.

Ricardo spoke first. 'My father Allesandro bought this island in 1932. It was a wedding present for my mother Carmelita. He'd made quite a bit of money in the pre-war years many accusing him of being in the pay of Mussolini and the armaments business but this wasn't true, it was just jealousy by some of his competitors, my father would never have compromised his political ideals for easy money. Come and look at this Bob.' He led Bob over to the low wall by the wooden pier. 'See these three rings. They are The Borromean Rings. Three interlocking rings that cannot be separated except by cutting. 'Strength in Unity.' It is still the *devise* of the Borromeo family and mine by adoption also. My father heard that the Borromeo family were selling the island. It was too small for their needs and the price was reasonable so it was to here that he came with my mother on their honeymoon. It was here several years later that I was born. I was born by caesarean section but tragically my mother died. It was rumoured to be blood poisoning but my father always claimed it was the result of dirty surgical scissors. He continued to live here and I was brought up by Rosa. The island welcomed many of the rich, famous and beautiful in Milanese society. Allesandro had a certain charm and as doubtless Rosa would confirm he had many lovers but no one ever replaced Carmelita. I started collecting knives and cutlery as a young child. I'd visited my father's factory many times and I was fascinated by the smooth, shiny implements, the smell of the furnace and the noise of the hammers and beaters. My father didn't discourage me from my hobby but he always warned me that knives served the dinner table but also in the hands of the wrong people could serve to kill. As for scissors he was as superstitious as he was religious. He felt that scissors never did anyone any good. Perhaps it related to the death of my mother, I don't know. He was always careful to never leave a pair of scissors open and he warned me never to give scissors away without money changing hands. He even kept a pair of scissors under the doormat to drive evil spirits away.' Ricardo looked pale and wan. He stared out over the lake once more. 'After listening to your story, Bob, I'm beginning to think that I have made a bad decision.'

'Superstition, coincidence, bad luck? Who can say, Ricardo? Personally, I'm happy not to be the owner anymore. I'm not particularly superstitious but shall we say I'm not willing to tempt providence.'

'But Bob, you bid for the scissors at the auction. Why? Do you not consider yourself the legal owner?'

'It's a question I've been asking myself for some time. Who is or was the owner? Your grandparents, your parents, Ricardo? My grandparents? Me? Alice? You? They came into my possession by chance after my grandfather passed away. Alice borrowed them for a kiss. The only people who paid money for them were my grandparents - one penny, and you Ricardo at the auction. I guess that I'm a sentimental guy. I suppose that like Alice I couldn't really see myself parted from the infernal things. They were like a malevolent aunt from a Grimm fairy tale where you keep returning to the story to be frightened again. Always wanting to be frightened. The book always opening on the dreaded page. Alice had died with them in her hand. I guess I owed it to her.'

Gisèle and Rosa reappeared still chattering away in Italian. Rosa looked at Ricardo and pulled a face. She'd already heard Gisèle's version of the story which certainly confirmed her worst fears about the scissors. *'Sembri come se hai visto un fantasma, Ricardo.'* Ricardo looked away. 'I haven't seen a ghost Rosa but maybe a warning from my father come back to haunt me. I could never have imagined such a terrible history of a seemingly inoccuous object.'

'I apologise if my story has upset you Ricardo. It was never my intention.'

'No, Bob. You were right to come here and tell your story. Collectors are always fascinated by the history of the objects in their collections. Usually the objects are not directly connected with the owner. My Egyptian spoons were made over three thousand years ago, the Eiffel Tower scissors were made by an unknown French craftsman in 1889 – none of these objects has the slightest connection to me or my family – except for the scissors.' He paused and looked at the other three. 'What should I do with the scissors?'

Rosa shrugged her shoulders. ' *Ti avevo avvertito che le forbici non avrebbero fatto nulla di buono. Serpenti mai portare fortuna.*'

'You're just a superstitious old fool, Rosa,' shot back Ricardo. 'How do you know snakes bring bad luck? The Egyptians worshipped them for goodness sake.'

Gisèle looked across to Bob who pursed his lips and shuffled in his chair. 'In this case a snake did Alice no favours and I detest the damn things. Honestly it's not my decision Ricardo. You do what you think is best. It's better if I have no more to do with them.'

Ricardo stood up. He groaned and rubbed his stomach. 'Too much to eat. I'll never learn.' Winston jumped up and nuzzled his hand doubtless expecting to be taken for a walk. 'Ok Winston. Time for your walk. It's getting late let's get our friends back to their hotel. I've got a private boat moored on the far side of the island. What do you say to a little boat ride my friends?'

'Yes I think it's time to get back. Thanks for your kind offer Ricardo.' Gisèle reached for Ricardo's hand but instead of shaking it he brushed it with his lips. 'I hope that this visit has not proven too onerous for you my dear?'

'On the contrary Ricardo. We've had a fabulous lunch, thanks to Rosa and I've had a great opportunity to polish up my Italian. Your island is magnificent and we feel privileged to have been invited don't we Bob?'

Bob snapped out of his private thoughts and went over to kiss Rosa. 'Before I tasted your delicious cooking Rosa I would never have believed that I would have enjoyed an *Osso Bucco* so much.'

Gisèle translated to Rosa adding, 'Believe me Rosa that's a complement coming from Bob who won't even eat his mother's rice pudding.' They all laughed. The gloom of a few moments before dispersed. They walked to a small quay where a three seater motor cruiser was moored. Winston was first aboard wagging his tail with gusto and perching his front legs on the prow. Gisèle and Bob took the two back seats whilst Ricardo fired the boat into life. Rosa stood waving from the shore as the boat slid away from the island. Bob and Gisèle didn't exchange a word. The noise from the outboard was too great for any conversation something that Bob was more than grateful for.

Ten minutes later they arrived on the quayside in Stresa. The sun was sinking in the west leaving a mystical glow over the lakeside mountains and reflecting off the roofs of Palazzo Borromeo and Isola Bella. The last of the day's tourists were descending the Mottarone Cableway.[1]

'Thanks again; Ricardo, it really has been a superb day.' Rob and Ricardo embraced with a lot of back slapping and nodding of heads. Winston was joining in the farewell jumping round in circles and barking. Ricardo hugged Gisèle and told her how lucky Bob must be to have such a charming and intelligent wife. Bob looked on bemused and blew a kiss in her direction.

---

[1] 14 people were killed when a traction cable snapped in May 2021on the Stresa Mottarone cable car.

'So. What are you two planning to do for the rest of your stay in Italy?' asked Ricardo as he helped them off the boat. 'Something very romantic I hope. Italy is made for lovers. Think 'Romeo and Juliet', *'Parlami d'amore,' 'Il Postino,'* Sophia Loren, Mastroianni, Lollobrigida, Morricone, the great Italian movies, the great Italian operas not forgetting Capri, Roma, Napoli, Sorrento and of course the food and wine Bob. Don't forget the food and wine.'

'Thanks for the advice Ricardo. We've still got a few days before we're due back at work so I guess we'll do some travelling probably down to Tuscany. It's a region I've been wanting to visit for years. Have some business to attend to. Family affair let's call it.' Before Ricardo could reply Bob and Gisèle mounted the stone steps up to the road and casting a final look in Ricardo's direction shouted, 'You'll keep in touch won't you. Let me know your thoughts on the scissors.' Ricardo gave a thumbs up sign and with a theatrical flourish of his other hand turned the boat in the direction of Isola Ceccaroli. *'Arrivederci, ci vediamo presto.'*

Moments later as they crossed the hotel lobby Gisèle turned to her husband and asked him what he meant by a family affair down in Tuscany.

'Oh, you'll find out soon enough. Let's go and grab a slice or two of that delicious Neapolitain pizza thay serve in the bar.'

'There you go. Thinking of your stomach again. I would have thought that after Rosa's *Osso Bucco* you would have eaten enough for a week. Bob you're incorrigible.'

'I know, but charming and adorable with it,' said Bob brushing his lips against her cheek.

✂

The clock on the bedside telephone showed 2.30 a.m. Bob stood alone on the balcony of the hotel room. Through the net curtain he could see Gisèle fast asleep. His head was buzzing with all that had passed with Ricardo yesterday. Sleep wasn't going to come easily. A bout of frantic love making normally worked wonders but tonight Bob still had much on his mind. He looked out across the dark lake. The sky was clear and the quarter moon was just appearing above Isola Ceccaroli. He thought he detected a faint light shining from Ricardo's mansion. Was he imagining things or did he think that maybe Ricardo was also having trouble sleeping? The history of the scissors had clearly affected the Italian and Bob himself was no nearer to resolving the enigma and his role in the whole affair. He tried to turn his mind to other matters. He switched on his mobile satnav and punched in the town of Cortona. Five hundred kilometres, a jot over 5 hours driving, mainly *autostrada*, the weather forecast looked promising, early morning mist then unbroken sunshine. He'd already decided that they could afford to take a few more days holiday. The language school could manage without him and Gisèle had no cookery clients for another 10 days so they were free to do a little Tuscan exploration.

Chapter Seventeen

The Following Day

The sound of an ambulance siren, blue light flashing followed by a police car greeted them on the route to Milan out of Stresa. It brought Bob back to his senses as he had only managed a couple of hours of sleep the night before and Gisèle was doing the driving.

'Not another tunnel accident, I hope.' Gisèle muttered, remembering the long delay coming up from the airport a couple of days ago. It was early Saturday morning and the roads were relatively quiet and Bob was more than happy to pass the keys to his wife who, although Bob wouldn't have admitted it, had more experience than him and understood better the idiosyncrasies of Italian drivers. What passes for the Italian Highway Code is merely a set of suggestions for most people but Bob was more than sufficiently aware of national stereotypes to not let it upset him too much. He'd heard too many 'bar stories' of the Italians, the French, the Spanish, or the Irish being the worst drivers in Europe. He found some of his compatriots annoying when they took the high moral ground by proclaiming that the 'Brits' were the best drivers when the reality lay in the fact that the Northern Europeans are generally more considerate drivers than their Southern European counterparts. It was mostly down to temperament plus driving in England is much safer because the roads are more packed with traffic – small island large population syndrome – ram jam packed motorways restrict speed and therefore the risk of accidents.

'Just look at that guy hugging two lanes. Just what does he think he's doing?' Bob said more in humour than anger as the romantic skyline of Florence appeared. 'And why's the car behind flashing us?'

'Probably because we're only doing 135 kph and for him that's too slow.' Gisèle eased the car over from the outside lane facetiously blowing a kiss in the direction of the Alpha driver overtaking at break-neck speed. 'Just wait until you see how they park in city centres.'

Ninety minutes later they were heading up the *Strada Provinciale 34* into the centre of the charming Tuscan town of Cortona. Gisèle brought the car to a halt in the *Piazza della Republica.*

'No shortage of hotels here. What do you think, Bob?' Bob had been scrolling through the dozen or so hotels that Trip Advisor suggested had vacancies. 'The Etruscan Palace' looks good, not too pricey and breakfast included but no parking. I think I'd prefer somewhere with parking. Don't want to risk paying a hefty bill to the rental company because of someone else's carelessness.' Bob remembered the £400 excess he'd once paid in London just for a minor bump and he had no wish for a repeat. 'This one looks great. 'Hotel Al Duomo.' He scrolled down the web page. 'It's just past the cathedral, breakfast included and underground parking plus sauna and spa. Just up our street. Agreed?'

Gisèle was quite happy to let Bob do the choosing. After all she knew she would have to do her bit at reception unless English was spoken. Even so she always felt a little wary of looking and sounding too much like a common or garden tourist and at least if she spoke Italian they were less likely to be ripped off by some unscrupulous desk clerk. That was her theory anyhow.

Ten minutes later Gisèle had successfully negotiated a 3-night bed and breakfast tariff and apart from Bob's reluctance to hand over the car keys to a very youthful concierge who assured them that the car would be safe in the underground parking, all passed off smoothly. Their room looked out over the San Francesco church, the ochre roofed houses and in the distance the afternoon sun reflected of Lake Trasimeno.

'A bit too ornate and sombre for my liking.' Bob cast his gaze over the bedroom. 'The King-sized bed looks good but not too keen on the heavy drapes. What's the bathroom like?' He pushed open the door revealing an enormous bath along one wall and a shower cubicle at the far end. Gold plated fittings and double washbasins. 'What is it about the Italians and black tiles?'

'It's Italian Classical,' Gisèle replied somewhat uncertainly. She picked up a small leaflet from the desk by the window. 'It says here, *'L'Hotel Al Duomo è orgoglioso di dare ai nostri ospiti un senso del vero patrimonio italiano di vita, l'eleganza storica.'* The Hotel Al Duomo prides itself on giving our guests a sense of the true Italian heritage of living, historical elegance. Whatever that might mean.'

'Marketing speak. They probably paid someone a fortune to come up with guff like that. By the way did you bring the guidebooks up from the car?'

'They're in my shoulder bag. Why don't you do your homework on Cortona whilst I go and freshen up. A good soak in the bath will do me a power of good and then I suggest that we do a small tour of the city. We'll find the Tourist Office and then it will be time for a couple of *Aperos* before finding somewhere to eat.'

'Now who's thinking of their stomach?' laughed Bob flopping on the bed. 'Very comfortable. You'll love the bed darling,' but his comments were drowned by the sound of running bath water.

✂

The receptionist at the hotel had told them that the tourist office was in the *Piazza Signorelli* and had given them a photocopied map with the route highlighted. Bob was in his element nothing he liked better than playing the tourist guide. 'You know I was once taking a group of school kids around an English cathedral, explaining the history, the architecture, what to look out for and so on when a couple of American visitors latched on to our group. They were hanging on to my every word and when we finished the woman came up to me and pressed a pound coin into my hand.'

'She probably felt sorry for you. Maybe thought you needed some financial assistance to care for all those kids. You weren't wearing that old-patched jacket that you do the gardening in were you? English teachers in my experience hardly have the chic, suave *comportment* of their Latin counterparts and as for the tourist guides in Rome with their Armani suits, black umbrellas or rolled up copies of *Corriere della Serra* held aloft for the punters to follow the English just can't compete.'

'I guess you're right,' Bob replied ruefully. 'What is it about you continental Europeans? Fat chance of *Perfidious Albion* absorbing anything to match Italian chic now that they've left the European Union. Bloody idiots! I think we need to take the next left. Direction not politics.'

The steep narrow cobbled street led directly into the magnificent *Piazza Signorelli*. 'The guide-book says that Luca Signorelli was a 15th century Tuscan painter of the Florentine School born and died in Cortona,' explained Bob. 'His most important work was a series of frescoes in the Orvieto cathedral which reputedly inspired Michelangelo's 'Last Judgement.''

'And all that without an Armani suit and Italian newspaper, Bravo Bob. You're learning fast,' laughed Gisèle. 'Would you like I press something warm into the palm of your hand as a reward?' Bob gave a sideways glance to his wife. 'Not now, darling. Perhaps later.'

'It's now or never!' Gisèle retorted. Bob gave her bottom a quick squeeze but before he could say more Gisèle had spotted the *Palazzo Casali* where the city plan said the *Ufficio Turistico* was to be found.

The girl in the tourist office couldn't have been more helpful and ten minutes later Bob and his wife left with an armful of brochures and maps. 'Do you think she was a civil servant?' asked Bob. 'She was first rate and so charming. Not at all like the civil servants it's been my misfortune to meet.'

'Well since when did you find any woman under the age of thirty not charming?' said Gisèle digging him playfully in the ribs. 'Not that the twenty-euro tip had anything to do with it. Seeing as you ask, yes, she most certainly is a civil servant or as the Italians say a *Funzionario*. Back in the 1990's the tourism industry was doing badly. No strategy, no long-term planning and too many people without a specific marketing background. A shakeup was needed, more and better hotels, better qualified people with international experience. Now Italy has regained its place as a top tourist destination and as you can see it's well merited.'

'Absolutely. Your compatriots in France could learn a thing or two. The service in some of the tourist offices back there is dire. You'd think that it was you doing them a service rather than the other way round. So how do you know about the Italian tourist business?' Bob asked, always surprised by his wife's knowledge of all things cultural.

'When I was working for the embassy in Rome one of my briefs was tourism. I did a lot of liaison work with ENIT the Italian National Tourist Board. Most of it was sitting in on rather boring meetings and taking notes but I did acquire a reasonable understanding of the tourist industry here.'

'Evidently. Look, let's go and get a couple of coffees and check out the town map and find where we're going to eat tonight. The girl in the tourist office recommended the *Trattoria Oro*. It's tucked away in small side street off *Via Ghibellina*.' Bob spotted a café on the far side of the square with a free terrace table still catching the last rays of late afternoon sun. They sat down and smiled at each other across the table. 'Not a bad life is it?' Bob said. 'Sunshine, Italy, culture, coffee and a beautiful wife.' Before Gisèle could reply an aging waiter shuffled across, white napkin draped over his arm. *'Buon giorno. Cosa vorresti?*

'Due caffè expresso per favore e un bicchiere d'acqua.'

'Prego Signora.'

Bob gave his wife a stern stare. 'What's all this expresso stuff? With all your experience surely you know that the coffee is espresso with an 's' not an 'x.'"

'Oh listen to the English teacher talking! Bob don't be so pedantic. Why are the English so obsessed with grammatical correctness? You know better than most that the English language is one of the most adaptable and flexible of languages in existence and yet make a simple change to word pronunciation and the language police come calling. Do your research Bob. 'Espresso' is the currently accepted pronunciation but I think you'll find that most dictionaries recognise that 'expresso' is a quirky and yet acceptable alternative for a quick, express coffee.'

The waiter returned to the table with two cups of coffee and a glass of water and Bob was left reflecting not for the first time on the mysteries of culture and language.

'Ok, Ok, I concede.' Bob threw up his arms in mock surrender knowing full well he would never win their cultural disputes.

✂

It took some finding the restaurant. It was hidden away down the narrow streets and alleys. The *trattoria* was at the foot of a rather gloomy flight of stone steps but the small dining area was tastefully lit, stone walls decorated with a series of black and white photographs of Tuscan hill scenes. A beamed ceiling and a dozen or so tables set with delicate apricot-coloured tablecloths and much to Gisèle's delight, genuine linen napkins. The English-speaking girl in the tourist office had recommended it only after some pushing by Bob who had asked her rather presumptuously, thought Gisèle, where she would like to eat if she was going on a first date with a rich handsome stranger. Reluctant at first to commit herself and a little ill at ease with English humour she pushed a photocopied list of tourist restaurants towards them. As usual it was Gisèle herself who saved the day albeit with a half-truth by telling the girl that she was from the French Embassy and they really wanted a genuine Cortona restaurant with genuine local food. Somewhat reluctantly the girl relented and scribbled an address on a yellow sticker and even offered generously to call the restaurant and make the table booking.

'Obviously twenty euros well spent.' Bob said as he caught the waitress's eye. *'Abbiamo una prenotazione? I signore Martin.'* They were shown to a corner table where Gisèle took off her coat and looked at Bob with amazement. 'Where did you learn that?'

'Time well spent whilst you were taking your bath this afternoon. Stock phrases at the back of the guide book, but don't expect anymore, I've exhausted my knowledge of Italian.' They sat down. The waitress brought the menus. 'I also swotted up a bit of local history at the same time. Bet you didn't know that an ancient legend says that Noah of The Ark fame came here after the flood and even more remarkably that Pythagoras the Greek Mathematician visited and died and was buried here. The story unravels then when it seems that Cortona was confused with Crotone in Calabria which was the genuine final resting place of Mr Maths. As for Noah I'll let you arrive at your own conclusions. What is certain is that this is one of the favourite haunts of retired American academics wishing to melt into the magic environment and write novels for people with over-developed curiosities, huge appetites and wanderlust.'

'Well good luck to them. I suppose it's a bit like your compatriot Peter Mayle hiding away in Secret Provençe, writing a few books about his secret and then being surprised when complete strangers arrived for dinner or tourists picnicked in his garden. It beggars belief. Let's check out the menu. I'm feeling hungry. Can't see any *Osso Bucco* here. Hope you're not too disappointed.'

'Don't say that, darling. I really did enjoy Rosa's meal. It was brilliant and yes I have changed my mind about *Osso Bucco*.' Then as an afterthought. 'My god, was that only yesterday? I wonder what Ricardo is thinking today. I hope that he didn't find my story too traumatic. You know how touchy and emotional some of these continentals can be, nothing personal but.....'

'OK Bob. Don't rub it in. At least it's better than being a stuffy anal retentive Englishman who hides all his emotions. Not that I'm suggesting that.............'

'Touché. National stereotypes raising their ugly heads again. Let's just say that some cultures handle emotions in different ways. Anyway, since the Lady Di business in the UK it seems that my countryfolk are beginning to open up a little on that front.'

The waitress took their order in a smilingly efficient manner. 'Well I'm going to have the *taglietelle caserecce and funghi porcini* what about you darling?'

Bob smiled up at the waitress announcing, 'and for me the *Tortelloni di ricotta basilico.* And oh, a bottle of the 2012 *Montegiachi Chianti* and a bottle of *San Benedetto* mineral water *per favore.'*

'Certainly sir, flat or fizzy?' the waitress replied in what Bob considered to be nearly perfect English. Bob never being one to miss an opportunity of flattering a pretty girl, complemented her. Gisèle looked on in bemusement.

'Fizzy please. What a delightful accent you have. Did you learn to speak English here in Italy?'

Gisèle could barely contain her amusement when the girl replied with a not too well hidden smirk. 'Actually I learned it in England. I was born in Sheffield!'

Gisèle liked playing the game of one-upmanship with Bob. He'd never dropped the mantle of 'teacher' and hated being wrong nearly as much as he hated being made to look a fool.

'Well, how was I to know she was English?' he asked somewhat sheepishly.

'Perhaps if you serve the wine you'll feel better. Humour *cherie*, humour.'

'Yes, I guess you're right.' Bob conceded as he poured two glasses. 'Why don't I just learn to keep my big mouth shut?'

'It's not in your nature. Watching you dig an ever deeper hole for yourself in a discussion is one of your greatest charms. What do you think of the wine?'

Bob did a bit of sniffing followed by a bout of slurping before pronouncing the wine, 'um, dry, tasty, full-bodied – a typical *chianti* with some cherry and hazelnut notes.' He swallowed and frowned as he organised his thoughts. 'It might surprise you to know that back in 1950's England very few people drank wine. Those people who did would usually go for a bottle of German white *'Blue Nun'* or wait for it, a *chianti* in a straw basket. And what do you think they did with the bottle when it was finished?' He paused for effect whilst Gisèle rolled her eyes in mock anticipation.

'Go on, Bob, surprise me.'

'They made it into a lamp, a *chianti* basket lamp. No self-respecting middle-class home would have been without one. Then came the craze for Portuguese '*Mateus Rosé*' with an attractively shaped bottle that surprise, surprise they turned into a lamp.'

'You mean to say that 10 years after the end of World War 2 the Brits were drinking German and Italian wine and turning the empty bottles into table lamps! Unbelievable. Never say that the Brits are boring. Didn't the French get a look in?'

'Hardly. None of their bottles could be transformed into a lamp – joking! Apart from the rich practically nobody drank French wine. It wasn't until the 70's that we began to travel more widely and Sunday lunches began to be accompanied by a bottle of white wine, and it was invariably white, improbably named after a bird such as '*Hirondelle*' or '*Coq d'Or.*' If we made it out to the restaurant we'd treat ourselves to an Italian *Lambrusco* a petillant red from the *Emilie-Romagne* region. We could never get enough! It was all rubbish of course but then when the UK joined The Common Market in 1975, we were literally flooded with European wines. Holidays across the channel became common place, Spain, France, Italy and Greece and my fellow Brits were becoming truly European.'

'Hm. Since when have the Brits been truly European? All you ever wanted from Europe was access to their markets. It was all about trade and commerce. How many people were interested in the culture or language of other countries? Holidays were all about sunshine and cheap booze, lounging around a pool or on the beach and invariably with other Brits who shared the same ideas and spoke the same language.

Your lot have never warmed to the idea of Europe and look where that's got you now. BREXIT has cost you millions and now you're becoming an inconsequential island off the northwest coast of the continent hoping that your great buddies in the US will come to your aid once more. History will not judge you kindly.'

'That's a bit harsh,' replied Bob. 'There have been some positives.'

'Such as?'

'Well,' Bob paused. 'How about '*Erasmus?*' Thousands of British students spending a year in another country paid for by the EU learning about language and culture. That must rank as a great achievement.'

'C'mon Bob we're talking here about the educated élite. What about 'the great unwashed' as you like to call them. The millions who never received a good education, who read Europhobe tabloid newspapers and were conned by lying, cheating politicians more concerned about personal ambition than the public they served. Senior politicians promising fictitious millions for the health service. The public who was 'upset' because their bananas and tomatoes weren't the right shape or the threat of thousands of economic migrants taking their jobs and don't get me started on the loss of sovereignty. Britain lost its sovereignty after the war when it sold out to the Americans. Look at your lot now. How many people drive French or German cars, eat in Italian or Spanish restaurants, drink Irish or Belgian beer and buy cheap Swedish furniture? We're all Europeans now, Bob and you know it. Dual nationality, French wife, German car, French home, bilingual – you must be one of the best adverts for the European Union.'

Bob roared with laughter. 'I would hardly put myself on that pedestal. I've been lucky and privately I know that my European identity is based more on a romantic vision than economic or political reality.'

The waitress arrived with their food. Bob smiled weakly in her direction and muttered a very English 'thank-you very much. That looks delicious.'

'You've no need to overdo it, darling. She probably sees you as just an ageing lecher with an eye for a good pair of legs.'

A couple of hours later they tottered out feeling slightly overwhelmed by that potent mixture of Italian food and wine. The cool evening air was welcome. The *piazza* still thronged with a mixture of late evening tourists and locals many just strolling leisurely others hoping even at this late hour to find somewhere to eat.

'That was fantastic!' Bob said with unconcealed joy. 'The *tortellini* and *ricotta* was out of this world – just the right blend of basil in the sauce too. As for the tiramisu and red berries – simply orgasmic!'

'Steady on there Bob. Don't overdo it although I must admit that my pasta at home is good but the chef tonight certainly knew a thing or two about cooking those nice little *taglietelli* strips with the *porcini* mushrooms. Must try that one at home and then maybe let my students lose on it.'

Bob had got used to the strings of drying pasta draped across the kitchen at home looking like washing hanging above a Neapolitan back street. He knew better than to argue with that after all it wasn't many Englishmen who had the fortune to be married to such an excellent cook.

'I made a mistake with the cheesecake dessert though. What on earth made me go for that I'll never know. Heaven knows what the pastry chef was up to. I thought that it would be something out of the ordinary. I should have known better. It was tasteless! No vanilla flavouring and the biscuit base was too hard.'

They walked through the narrow streets of the town. Down *Via Guelfa* and then cut through *Via Sant Agostino* before arriving at the *Piazza Garibaldi* and the belvedere with its spectacular panorama. The night was clear and the view was stunning. Lights twinkled all over the *Val di Chiana* from the *Lake Trasimène* to the south across to Sienna in the west.

Gisèle rested her head on Bob's shoulder and shivered, not from the cold, the night was mild but from the splendour of the vista. 'We should have booked a week here, darling. Three days is not enough. I could happily live here for the rest of my life.' She breathed in the night air and sighed. 'Have you made any plans for tomorrow?'

Bob didn't speak for a moment. He knew that in their remaining two days there was something he had to do but wasn't sure what his wife's reaction would be. 'Well, I suggest that in the morning we have a leisurely breakfast and then,' Bob hesitated. 'Well then a bit of a surprise, actually. You remember me mentioning a little 'family affair' when we returned from Ricardo's Island yesterday?'

'Well, I did wonder what you were talking about but you sounded secretive and mysterious. I guessed that eventually I'd find out. Don't tell me that there's a branch of the Martin family living in Tuscany or you have another ex-wife hidden away in an Italian *castello*?'

'Family, yes. Living in a *castello*, hardly. That reminds me, talking of ex-wives, did I ever tell you the story of an ex-colleague, an Indian guy? He told me one day that he spoke six languages. I was amazed and asked him how he had accomplished such a feat. He told me that he'd been married six times; each wife had a different nationality – English, French, Italian, Spanish, Arabic and Hindi. He swore it was true.'

'I'm not convinced. Must have cost him a fortune in alimony, anyway, stop trying to change the subject, Bob. What's this family affair all about? I'm intrigued.'

'You're just going to have to be patient. I think you'll find it interesting.'

'Ok; I'll be patient. I just hope that it's got nothing to do with scissors or snakes.'

Bob pulled a face. 'I'm not sure that I can guarantee that, *Cherie*. C'mon, admit you're a little curious. The scissors are tucked safely away in Ricardo's private collection. They can't do any more harm now but there's still a couple more pieces of the jigsaw to assemble and then you'll see the big picture. You'll be glad you did.'

'*Merde*, Bob. I thought we'd heard the last of those damned scissors.'

Chapter Eighteen

The Next Morning

Bob was up early. He checked his pocket Italian/English phrase book. He found the phrase he wanted. On the pretext of buying some cigars he left Gisèle doing her make-up and walked up to the *Piazza República* repeating the phrase silently to himself. He took a narrow street to his right where he found a florist's shop. A middle-aged woman was busy arranging pots of flowers and plants on the sidewalk. An older man was following her around diligently watering-can in hand. Bob's thoughts immediately returned to Alice and his meeting with her and Hervé in their *fleuriste* in Carcassonne. A wave of sadness spread over him as he recalled all that had passed since those tumultuous two days. He spotted a pot of sunflowers but today he wasn't in the market for sunflowers.

'Buongiorno. Vorrei due rose rosse per favore.' He hoped he'd got the phrase right. The woman gave him an indulgent smile and headed into the shop returning moments later with a large vase of red roses.

'Due rose rosse, sì.'

'Si, si. Quanto per favore.' He handed the woman a twenty euro note not being really sure of the price she'd quoted. She tut tutted knowing that this early in the morning she had only

a little small change in the till. She handed the note back and Bob dug deep into his jacket pocket to find a handful of coins. He held out his hand and the woman counted out the coins like a teacher working with an infant. How Bob hated these situations. He detested when he was not in full control. His pleasure at remembering the phrase turned to frustration at not knowing his Italian numbers. He smiled weakly and taking the roses headed back to the hotel where he found his wife already having breakfast in the splendid baroque breakfast room.

'Bob, how splendid. So thoughtful of you. What a surprise, are we celebrating something?'

'Well, in a way.' Bob placed one of the two roses on the table and kissing his wife placed the other across her plate. 'Just the one, darling. The other is for later. Now can you start teaching me Italian numbers?'

'More mystery? I knew you had a mistress hidden away in a *castello*. I look forward to meeting her.' She laughed and winked at Bob. 'No more secrets. Now for the Italian numbers. How many croissants do you want?'

✂

The mist was lingering over the *Val di Chiana* and a light drizzle was falling as the hotel concierge pulled the car over to the hotel entrance. Bob had closed his eyes as the hire car appeared coming down at some speed along the narrow street from the hotel garage and the smiling concierge having screeched to a halt tossed the keys over to Bob and shouted a hearty *'Bon Giorno.'*

'Doubtless he'll be expecting a tip,' chuntered Bob. 'Bet his last job was a pit mechanic at Monza.'

'Now don't be so hostile. He probably does this every day and undoubtedly thinks that you're impressed. You can give him a tip when we leave tomorrow.'

Bob wasn't impressed but he wasn't going to engage in yet another cultural argument with his wife. 'Did you remember the other rose?'

'Yes, of course – it's in my bag. Now, do you want me to programme the satnav or will you do it?' Gisèle knew well that Bob preferred to do it himself. He loved gadgets and the dashboard of the Peugeot was a veritable technological playground with hands free telephone, sound system, internet connection and a multitude of front and rear cameras to assist with parking and avoiding collisions with cats, hedgehogs or errant elks.

Bob tapped in the most direct route to their destination, the small town of *Foiano della Chiana* about a 30-minute drive. He took out a USB from his pocket and slotted it into the interface by the CD player. He always liked to carry his music collection around with him. 'You can choose the music, darling. Something that encapsulates the mood of the morning, serious but not too sombre.'

''The Good, The Bad and the Ugly,' 'A Fool such as I,' or 'Bashful Bob?'' Take your pick.'

'No, come on, get serious. How about Fauré's Requiem or a bit of Brahms or Chopin?'

Gisèle eventually settled for Elgar's Cello Concerto. 'Stirring and romantic, especially the Du Pré version.'

'Yes, an excellent choice,' conceded Bob. Sets the scene nicely for our little outing today.'

Gisèle knew better than to ask. They drove without speaking through the Tuscan countryside the notes of Jacqueline Du Pré's cello swelling and diminishing with each turn in the road. The ochre tinted roofs of *Foiano* came into view. Gisèle reached for the guidebook. 'It says here that the *Pallazzo delle Logge* is definitely worth a visit. Apparently it was a Medici hunting lodge.'

'No, our first stop is just outside the town actually. We're looking for *Via del Porto*. Not on the satnav. We'll just have to use our soon to be lost map-reading skills and a bit of instinct and if all that fails my dear wife will hail a local peasant with her perfect Italian. Do you know that many of us have an instinct for finding the North? We all have a built-in biological clock but it's possible that we may also have an internal compass. It's all to do with our ancient ancestors having developed a way to survive in dangerous conditions, you know the sort of thing, encroaching icesheets, wild animals escaping storms, importance of south-facing caves, food sources or fresh water. Laboratory research on rats has come up with some evidence for connecting this instinct to the Earth's magnetic field but although there is evidence of this in animals, they've found nothing in the human brain that corresponds. Look for example at the migration of Monarch butterflies.......'

Gisèle cut Bob off in full teacher mode. 'Sorry to interrupt but isn't that the road you're looking for, *Via del Porto*? Over there on the left.'

Bob squinted through the windscreen. 'Great! It is! How observant. That's exactly the place. You've just got the job as my full-time navigator. Out of the window with the satnav.'

Gisèle wrinkled her nose as Bob slowed to a halt in a roadside layby. 'But there's nothing here, where's the *castello*, where's the neo-classical *Collegiata di San Martino* that the guide- books insists is a 'must visit?' All I can see is a cemetery, a few trees and a laurel hedge.'

'Exactly, *ma cherie* that's why we are here.'

'Bob, why are we visiting a cemetery? Don't tell me that you've got relatives here.'

Bob didn't immediately reply but checked his cell phone. After scrolling down the screen he muttered, 'Chiana War Cemetery 1B5.' He pocketed the phone and turned to look on the back seat. 'Do you have the other red rose that I bought this morning? Remember there were two.'

'Of course, I already told you when we left the hotel.' Gisèle plundered her large black shoulder bag and waved the foil wrapped rose under Bob's nose. 'Is this what you are looking for? Good job that I didn't leave it on the breakfast table.' Exasperated she let out a long sigh and shook her head. 'For goodness sake Bob, will you please tell me what we're doing here.'

'All in good time, my dear, all-in good time. Let's take a closer look.' He jumped out of the car and running around to the passenger side opened the door for his still bemused wife. He grabbed her hand and led her to a low wrought iron gate that led into the cemetery. Opening the gate they walked along a stone path flanked on both sides by immaculately coiffured grass still damp from the morning drizzle. In front was a white marble cross on a tiered pedestal. 'We're looking for grave 1B5.' I'm not sure how the numbering system works. Let's try left.'

'Presumably 'B5' refers to row B grave N°5. Feminine logic Bob.'

'Yes, that sounds feasible.' They walked towards the second row and walked slowly in front of the white headstones. Bob started reading out the names,

Private Percy George Eric Ross   The Queen's Own…
        6th July 1944

Private Robert Crawford Simpson   The Queen's Own…
        6th July 1944

Private Thomas Gillett   The Queen's Own…
        6th July 1944

L.C. Walter Charles Warren   The Queen's Own…
        7th July 1944

He paused in front of the 5th headstone. He gave his wife's hand a long hard squeeze. He breathed deeply before reading the inscription.

6093706 L.Cpl.

E. Wright

The Queen's Own

West Kent Regiment

6th July 1944

Gisèle looked on bewildered as her husband gazed up into the sky and recited quietly. 'Born 1918, Lancashire, England, 2nd son of Thomas and Kate Wright, brother to Eunice and Alan and died 6th July 1944 aged 26. Love to all at Home.'

For a moment Gisèle didn't see the significance. The silence was palpable. Bob took the red rose from his wife and laid it carefully against the headstone before turning to his wife. 'My Uncle Eric, my mother's brother, died one month after D-Day, died 21 months before I was born. The red rose is the emblem of his home county of Lancashire. Do you see it, *Cherie*? Do you see why we had to come here today?'

She looked up to her husband and then back to the inscription. 'Of course, how could I be so stupid? Kate and Thomas. 'K' and 'T' the initials on the scissors. The scissors given to your grandmother on her wedding day, the scissors with the snake handles, the scissors fabricated by Elio

Ceccaroli, father to Allesandro and grandfather of Ricardo Ceccaroli.'

Bob nodded slowly. His wife reached across and squeezed his hand before kissing her index finger and touching the name 'Eric' on the headstone. 'Sorry, it was a bit thoughtless of me to go on a bit about your obsession with the scissors.' Gisèle had known most of the bare outlines of the history of the scissors but Bob had never explained where his Uncle Eric fitted in.

'You see,' said Bob, my mother was sewing her honeymoon dress when the telegramme from The War Office arrived announcing the death of Eric. At that moment as the telegraph boy knocked on the front door the scissors had fallen from her hands, one point sticking in the wooden floorboard.'

'He'd been called up in '42, preliminary training in Scotland before being posted to North Africa. After the Allied successes there he was dispatched here to Italy early in 1944 where he saw action at Cassino, Monte Cassino that is. That must have been bloody hard. Apparently it was the worst winter weather for years. After the victory at Cassino in May, there was the capture of Rome, largely overshadowed by the Allied landings in Normandy and then they pushed northwards.'

'Why did you say 'love to all at home?'' Asked Gisèle. 'Obviously something important you remembered.'

'Yes, Eric nearly always finished his letters in that way.' Bob reached into his jacket pocket and took out a faded airmail envelope. 'This is his last letter. It was written on 18th June, fifteen days after the liberation of Rome and twelve days after D-Day. He wasn't allowed to say too much about the war. Letters home were heavily censored. He talked about having a day in Naples and how sad he was to see the squalor 'on the most beautiful bay in the world overshadowed by the twin peaks of Vesuvius.' He berated the BBC for their lack of reporting on the liberation of Rome and the Italy campaign in general but conceded that the reports of the Normandy landings had him and his fellow soldiers' ears glued to the loud speakers on that eventful morning.' Apart from that he spent sometime discussing the Italian countryside and the 'delicious ice-cream'. His last written words were 'love to all at home'.'

'How banal, trying to recapture the 'normal' life after living through horrendous battles. You said it was his last letter – there was nothing else?'

Bob sighed. 'Regrettably no. Apart from what was written in regimental records I have little knowledge of what happened over the next 3 weeks or so. However, there was an interesting sequel to one of his letters. The previous February Eric had been on leave in Egypt. Whilst there he bought my mum a handbag which he posted to her back home. The bag arrived but only several weeks after Eric's death. It was assumed to have been lost or stolen at the docks – it often happened, it was wartime after all. It arrived about 9 months after it was posted. The intriguing bit is that the handbag was made of snakeskin and inside was - you'll never guess- a small manicure set with a pair of scissors. Coincidence of course.'

They both stood silently in front of the headstone each with their private thoughts. After several moments Bob took Gisèle's hand and walked her away towards the visitor's book which was on display in a nearby service building. 'Look at this,' said Bob tracing his finger over the writing. He read out loud,

'Early in July 1944 there was heavy fighting in the Chiana valley where the Germans made their last stand in front of Arezzo and the river Arno; the burials in the cemetery date for the most part from the first two weeks of that month.............................On 5th July, the Allies encountered resolute resistance in defence of position just south of a line Ancone-Arezzo-Leghorn, and in particular there was a spell of fairly heavy and inconclusive fighting on both sides of the Chiana valley, leading to Arezzo. To this period belong the cemeteries at Foiano della Chiana and Arezzo.' [1]

They went over and sat beneath the memorial cross. For the first time that morning the sun made an appearance.

'So what do the official records say, Bob? Do they throw any light on,' she paused, 'on how he died?'

Bob took out a Michelin map from his jacket pocket and unfolding it pointed to their present position in *Foiano*. 'Well, from what I understand Eric's battalion were making their way north from here. *Foiano* itself had been occupied at the beginning of July and then they moved up towards *Marciano*, which is just here.' Bob fumbled with the map

---

[1] Extract from Visitors' Book Foiano della Chiana cemetery Italy.

wondering why the place names always seemed to be hidden in the fold. 'It was full summer and the crops were ripening. Apparently, the Germans had placed snipers in the corn fields which obviously impeded progress considerably. On the 4th of July, the battalion were given a rest day before heading off to this place.' Bob squinted at the map and after several seconds of searching found *San Pancrazio*. 'Just north of *Mont Savino*, can you see that, it must be only a small place. Well, the countryside around here was steep and heavily wooded so that again would have made their job more difficult. From what I understand they were fighting in darkness and by the next morning the 6th they were pretty-well shattered. Reinforcements came along in the shape of tanks but the bombardment from the enemy was too much. Again, German sniper fire was lethal and around *Poggio al 'Olma,-* can't locate it on the map.' Bob paused holding back his emotion. 'There were numerous casualties, most certainly including Eric.'

Bob straightened his back and looking into the far distance said, 'in fact it was probably the end of the fighting here. The Germans were driven back. If Eric had lived a couple of days longer he would have probably seen it through to the end of the war. Of course, that's pure romantic speculation.'

They walked slowly back to the car. The warm sun was breaking through the morning clouds once more. In the field next to the cemetery an elderly Tuscan farmer was watering the delicate shoots of his tomato plants. Overhead flocks of swallows and house martins screeched noisily swooping and diving. On the verge of the road, almost hidden from sight was a small bright red field poppy. Suddenly Gisèle let go of

Bob's hand and darted off. She returned moments later with the poppy in hand. 'Look, you won't believe it but I've found a red poppy.' Gisèle stuck the lone poppy behind her left ear. 'Do you think it's a sign? Remember the millions of poppies that flowered in the bombed-out trenches at the end of the Battle of the Somme.'

Bob smiled indulgently. 'I doubt it. Just another coincidence but symbolic anyway.' Gisèle unhooked the flower from her ear and opening the guidebook placed it carefully between the open page describing *Foiano della Chiana*.

'Do you believe in life after death, *Cherie*?'

Bob blustered. 'Wow! That's the biggest question of all. If Eric's soul exists, does it know who it is? We're all too obsessed with the material world to consider such a thing. If there is a God did he intend that 256 souls should fly away in a couple of sunny days in July 1944? To say nothing of the millions of others killed in senseless wars.'

'Why 256?'

'Two hundred and fifty-six is the number of soldiers lying here as a result of the battles of the *Chiana* Valley. Sobering isn't it? Let's go and find ourselves a coffee.'

They sat in the car taking a long last look at the white headstones. 'Ok, so you want a couple of more coincidences,' Bob said slowly. Gisèle wondered whether all this wasn't getting too much for her. Did she really want to hear more?

Bob was determined to plough on. After all, hadn't he only said to his wife last night that there was a piece or two of the puzzle to be completed.

'Well here goes. You remember that I did a spell of teaching in Tunis. A group of us used to go on regular visits to the beach at *La Marsa* on the north coast. Good beach and some nice local seafood restaurants. We used to watch the local Arab boys fishing for squid and octopus which when caught would be cooked on a barbecue in front of us. Well, the fish is neither here nor there but the thing is that I discovered a few years later whilst researching Eric's history that his battalion spent some time on rest leave in *La Marsa* in May '43 during the North African campaign. This was a good 9 months before the troops eventually went to Italy. I must have sat on the same beach many times without realising.' Bob paused for theatrical effect. 'It gets better. Eric died in Tuscany. When he was at grammar school all the pupils were allocated a 'house' for sporting competitions. The name of his 'house' was – what do you think?'

Gisèle pulled a puzzled face, after all the concept of schoolhouses didn't normally exist in France so what did she know? 'How about 'Italy' or 'Roman' or maybe 'Caesar' or 'Nero?'

'No, no and thrice no. I'll give you a clue. It begins with the letter 'E.'' Bob loved his little word games but his wife was less competitive.

'*Pas d'idée,* no idea. Go on tell me, I give in.'

'Etruscan.' 'Etruscan' being the old name for Tuscany.'

Even Gisèle had to admit to being shocked by the answer. 'Oh, c'mon Bob, you're making all this up! More evidence of your over fertile imagination.'

'No, it's absolutely true. In one of his letters he recalls nearly winning a school cross-country race for his house – The 'Etruscans.' I swear it!'

Gisèle breathed in deeply, then whistled through her teeth, 'I think I need more than a coffee.'

Chapter Nineteen

Two Days Previously

The house was all quiet. Rosa had gone to bed. The lake was still. Ricardo was going over in his mind for the hundredth time the story that Bob had told him over lunch. By his side Winston lay curled up on the sofa. The evening seemed hotter than usual for the time of the year. Ricardo mobbed his brow and poured himself another large scotch. The history of the scissors had disturbed him more than he cared to admit. He considered himself a rational, objective man not given to flights of fantasy or superstitious beliefs. His catholic upbringing had opened his eyes to some of the historical travesties committed in the name of his religion and were still being committed today. Privately he believed that the church was more concerned with its image than cleaning up corruption. He was a regular at Sunday Mass at *Chiesa di San Vittore* just across the water in Stresa, he had been presented to The Pope at a Vatican reception for business leaders, went to the confessional a couple of times a year and even occasionally entertained the renowned Cardinal Abramo to lunch. He never expressed publicly his religious doubts, he had the reputation as an astute businessman, generous and discrete charity donor and at least in public a strict catholic. He was proud of his image and would never consider letting the mask fall. Behind closed doors however he considered it all hokum. It suited him that way.

He picked up the whisky tumbler and the half-empty bottle of *Glen Moray* and walked hesitantly towards his *soggiorno*. He whistled to Winston who obediently fell into step at his heels. He opened the door and switched on the light. He walked over to the framed sepia photograph of his parents and grandparents and stared long and hard. He still felt hot and was conscious of beads of sweat on his brow. He flung open the window over-looking the lake. A gentle breeze wafted the curtains. He wondered to himself what his ancestors would have thought. After all his grandparents' generation largely accepted superstition and myth as much as they accepted the word of God. His father, Alessandro was a proud man who had been stung by criticism of cowtowing to Mussolini in the 1930's. After all wasn't he a pragmatist who realised on which side his bread was buttered?

Ricardo took the small key from his pocket and inserting it into the nymph's navel opened the door to his collection. Switching on the lights he thought back to his earlier conversation and Bob's reaction to seeing the scissors. He'd clearly been shocked by the drama of it all, the music the sliding doorpanel those 'infernal' scissors picked out by the spotlights.

'If the Vatican can horde its earthly treasures then why can't Ricardo Ceccaroli?' He spoke to Winston who wagged his tail frantically. He switched on the spotlight and the scissors glistened in the dark. He opened the glass cabinet and carefully took out the scissors. He looked closely with the eye of a craftsman. The intricately carved serpents, the raised initials, the balanced feel of the blades. He caressed the handles and once more raised the scissors to his lips. He knew he was embracing history, his family, Bob's family but what good had the scissors ever done? He recalled once more Bob's story of Alice's first husband and her own demise in front of a viper's fangs.

Suddenly a wave of dizziness and nausea came over him, a pain shot down his left arm and he started to shiver violently. He struggled to walk back into the *soggiorno,* scissors still in his hand. He shakily refilled his glass. Perhaps a good shot of whisky would set him straight. He began to sweat heavily once more. He picked up his cell phone and rang Rosa. No answer, she must be asleep by now and had switched off her phone. He tried to get to his feet but fell heavily to the floor. The tumbler shattered, the golden liquid spread across the wooden floor. The scissors fell from his grasp and skidded towards the window.Winston barked, wagged his tail and licked up the remains of the whisky. This is a great new game he thought.

Chapter Twenty

Bob was still in reflective mood at breakfast the next morning. They'd gone on to Sienna after their visit to the war cemetery and whiled away the early afternoon soaking up the delights of the *Piazza del Campo* in an *Osteria* that served the most exquisite wild boar, *ravioli* with mushrooms and *pecorino*. The food had temporarily lifted their spirits although Bob was disappointed that he couldn't finish off the bottle of *chianti* because he was driving and it was left to Gisèle to pronounce the last rites. They'd returned to the hotel where Gisèle had gone for a swim in the rooftop pool followed by a long session in the beauty salon. Meanwhile Bob bagged a sun lounger and caught up on his local history with the Lawrence and Baedeker books he'd brought from home.

Later that evening, having already indulged themselves over lunch in Sienna they decided that a light meal would be best. They found an unprepossessing pizza bar down a sleazy side street that made a passable *Quattro formaggi* washed down with a carafe of local red. They went over the events of the day.

'Do you think that Eric ever saw the irony of being a Tuscan in Tuscany?' Gisèle was thinking aloud knowing full well that her husband had probably posed the same question himself.

Bob took a moment to collect his thoughts. 'I've been through all of the letters that Eric sent home and apart from the reference to the running race there was no other mention of the word. Does anybody think about things like that when you're fighting a war? Self-preservation is uppermost on your mind I imagine.'

'I guess you're right,' replied his wife. 'But the coincidences are remarkable. Tell me more about his letters.'

'As I said this morning, they're practically all rivetingly boring and that's what paradoxically makes them so fascinating to read. He talks about the weather, hot, cold, windy, muddy, scorched and you know that behind all that he's amid a killing field which the censors stop him from talking about. Someone estimated that a soldier's life was 90 percent boring and banal and 10 percent hair-raising action. They smoked a lot, sat around reading three-week old newspapers from back home, the occasional visit from ENSA – that was the Entertainments National Service Association – they put on shows for the troops, and had periodical rest leave. He went to Cairo, visited the Pyramids and had his photograph taken on a camel. His last rest period was near to Bari in Southern Italy where he ate numerous ice-creams and watched American propaganda films. He was at Monte Cassino in one of the worst Italian winters for years, the battle for the German-held stronghold went on for 4 months with 115,000 Allied casualties and was largely ignored by the media as it was overshadowed by the events of D-Day. 'Cassino – the forgotten battle' it is often called.'

'Oh, yes.' Gisèle recalled. 'I remember once reading an article about Arletty, the French movie star who had a long affair with a German officer called Hans Jurgen Soehring. Soehring had been at Cassino on the enemy side. The relationship caused a lot of controversy in France after the war. She was just a high-profile example of so-called collaboration. Have you ever visited Cassino?'

'Sadly no. It's about a five-hour drive from here between Rome and Naples. Not possible this time as we only have one full day left. Will put it on the 'bucket list.''

'The bucket list – what on earth are you talking about? Never heard that one before.'

Bob laughed. 'Thought I'd get you on that one. A highly colourful English colloquialism referring to things that you must do before you die.'

'But why bucket? What has a bucket got to do with dying?'

'Not sure. There are several possible explanations. The most credible being 'suicide.' You see it's possible to hang yourself while standing on a bucket with a rope around your neck. When you're ready you just kick the bucket and well, Goodbye Cruel World.'

'What a morbid lot you English are,' concluded Gisèle. 'No one but the English could come up with an expression like that. Black humour.'

'Whatever,' replied Bob. 'It would give us a good excuse to visit Rome and you could catch up with a few ex-boyfriends and check out if the Coliseum is still standing.'

'I can't believe that it has been over ten years since I last worked in the city. It would be good to go back and visit my old stomping ground.'

'Yes, it would be good but let's put that on the back burner for the time being.'

'Back burner? Now what are you talking about Bob? Another expression designed to confuse me.'

'Not to worry, *Cherie*. I'll explain later. Now, what's on the agenda for tomorrow? How about checking out the cultural bit. According to Lawrence the Etruscan's were quite an intriguing bunch with a bit of an obsession with death and the underworld.'

'Well, I've been looking through the guidebook and apparently we must visit the MAEC – *the Museo dell'Accademia Etrusca* – the Etruscan Museum. It's close to the tourist office that we visited yesterday afternoon in the *Piazza Signorelli*.'

✂

'You remember what you were saying the other day about the local legend that Noah came here after the flood? Well it got me thinking.' Bob and Gisèle were walking out of their hotel and climbing the steep street towards the *Piazza*. 'I've got a little coincidence of my own here, perhaps a little more speculative than yours but interesting nevertheless. When I was a student I did an internship with a legal company down in Bayonne in the French Basque country. It was routine office administration but I did learn quite a bit about the local history and culture. You see over in the Basque country of Northern Spain and Southwest France there has been this idea running for centuries that the Iberian Peninsula was populated by descendants of no less a person than Noah's grandson, a *mec* improbably named Tubal. Tubal is said to have arrived 35 years after the end of the flood. Some experts have suggested that there is a similarity between Basque place names and Armenian place names especially around the area where the ark was supposed to have grounded. Other researchers have even made the staggering claim that the Basques were originally an Etruscan tribe.[2]' She paused for it to sink in before looking at Bob for his reaction, 'Interesting *n'est ce pas*? 'It wouldn't be too far-fetched to suggest that the Etruscans somehow travelled the relatively short distance from the Italian peninsular to Northern Spain. There are even some myth seekers who claim that the Basque language came directly from 'The Tower of Babel' but let's not go along that route!'

'Um, yes, do you think we're onto something here? The guiding hand of coincidence coming back to haunt us or over-active imaginations? Take your pick, *Cherie*. The world is full of people with weird ideas and mad cap theories and by the law of averages some will doubtless be correct or at least not far off the mark. Why wouldn't the Etruscans travel the Mediterranean coastal plain to Spain – feasible without a

---

[2] The Basque myth – the Basque History of the world.
www.Erenow.net (accessed 14/11/2020)

doubt but there's no evidence? Any artefacts, Etruscan-like tombs in Spain?'

'No tangible evidence for sure,' Gisèle replied, 'but there does seems to be a lot of research into the origins of Basque and Armenian placenames and some of it seems pretty convincing.'[3]

'A lot more plausible than the world being run by giant lizards or that the moon landing was faked in a Hollywood studio I suppose. So, what does my darling culture vulture suggest we should see in the museum?'

'Whilst you were pampering yourself in the beauty salon yesterday I managed to get through D.H. Lawrence's short book on his visit to Tuscany in the 1920's. He explored many of the archaeological sites and principally Etruscan burial chambers. He seems to have been quite an *Etruscophile* if that's the right word. He was fascinated by the Etruscan view of death which they saw as 'a journey to renewal,' and, wait for it 'the life-affirming culture which exalted the pleasures of the body.''[4]

'Was that before or after he wrote 'Lady Chatterley?''

'Is that a serious commentary?' asked Bob smiling. 'Do you think that Constance Chatterley was based on a Tuscan? I hardly think so but Lawrence was living in Florence when he wrote parts of the irascible Lady C. He was apparently also

[3] Armenia & The Basques (Spain) 2017www. allinnet.info/antiquities (accessed 15/11/20)
[4] D.H. Lawrence's Etruscan Places and the Etruscan. 2016 www.magiclibrarybomarzo.wordpress.com (accessed 15/11/20)

something of an amateur botanist and gets quite excited by tall *asphodels*. You remember me telling you that Alice was picking the self-same flowers when she succumbed to the snake bite?'

'Yes, the flower of death and the underworld to say nothing of the afterlife. We've got a lot of them in Provence, they like dry chalky soil and are especially fond of the Mediterranean climate. Strangely enough some people believe them to be a cure for snakebite but I think that is something of a myth. Do you think Alice knew about that or is it just another coincidence?' Bob thought long and hard. 'Strange if she didn't. She'd spent years in the flower business and Hervé would most certainly have known. His botanical knowledge is impressive. Anyway, continue what you were saying. You've got me hooked on *asphodels*.'

'Well, their leaves are used for wrapping some varieties of cheese to keep them fresh. Members of the lily family if I'm not mistaken. I'm surprised that you're not familiar with all that. I thought the English were all nature lovers?'

'I must confess to suffering from what some of my compatriots with supposed 'green' credentials like to call *'Nature Deficit.'* Despite what you think teachers don't know everything!' Bob put on his hang dog look and shrugged his shoulders.

Gisèle took a step away from her husband and clasping her hands together announced, 'I feel a song coming on.'

'Je t'ai donné mes bouquets d'asphodèles.'

Bob shrugged and tried not to look too embarrassed as some of the other museum goers looked on in amusement.

'First written and sung by Marie Laforet, the French singer and actress – don't tell me you don't know her!'

'Never heard of her, haven't a clue. I can't be expected to know everything.' He sulked. 'Bet you didn't know about Lawrence's visit here?'

Gisèle pulled a face, stuck out her tongue and ignored Bob whilst she headed for the ticket booth. She paid for two tickets, a couple of audio guides, one in English the other in French and thanked the girl for a leaflet showing one of the museum's star attractions, the Etruscan Chandelier.

'Are we going to stand here all day arguing like small children or are we going in?' She was still humming provocatively and pulling faces at Bob. These little knockabouts were a frequent feature of their life together, a question of who could show their cultural superiority. It was a sort of game that neither of them really took too seriously but secretly Bob liked to come out on top.

Bob was still mulling over the conversations about *asphodels* and was intrigued by the suggestion that they could cure snakebite. In his mind he could still see Alice's poisoned blue hand clutching the flowers. He was firmly brought back to the present by his wife grabbing his hand and pulling him towards the first exhibit.

'C'mon Bob let's make for the chandelier – sounds fascinating.'

✂

''The mysterious Tuscan civilisation.' That was Baedeker's description over a hundred years ago. Are we any nearer to understanding them today?'

It was 90 minutes later and Bob and Gisèle were squinting under the hot sun of the *piazza*. Bob was in his enthusiastic thirst for learning mode, determined to dissect what they'd just seen before the immediacy of the images faded.

'They probably go back as far as 900 years BC. Seems likely that they were heavily influenced by the Greeks with whom they traded, contact with the Celts and possible founders of Ancient Rome. Fiercely independent. Strong belief in an after-life. So, what's your take on all this *Madame* Martin?'

Gisèle thought for a moment, recalling what her husband had said earlier about Lawrence's view of the Etruscans. 'Most ancient civilisations seemed to have been heavily into death, just think of the Egyptians. Much of the archaeological evidence that exists today was gathered from necropolises and tombs. Look at that rather beautiful Egyptian wooden funeral boat we just saw. Imagine the craftmanship that went into that only to bury it in a tomb. There doesn't seem to be much coming from above ground.'

'Presumably because successive civilisations destroyed all existing visible evidence that was above ground except for large constructions such as The Pyramids or city fortifications which could be recycled,' replied Bob. 'The Romans seem to have absorbed either by peaceful or violent means the Tuscan culture as they became the dominant force in the area. As a result the only places left relatively unscathed would have been the burial grounds.'

'Are you suggesting that our view of history is largely based on death rituals?' Gisèle was sceptical. 'Look at what we learned about the Roman civilisation from Pompeii and Herculaneum, baths, brothels and bars.'

'Ah, but you're conveniently forgetting, *Cherie*, that Pompeii was buried almost instantaneously by the ash from Vesuvius and remained hidden from human eyes for centuries. Besides if you're looking for further evidence to refute my theory don't ignore that rather bizarre *'Cortona Tablet'* which most certainly wasn't part of any death ritual.'

Gisèle had been intrigued by the 2nd. Century BC bronze tablet which had been found locally in 1992. It had been cut into seven rectangles and nobody had ever found the missing eighth piece.

'Apparently, if I understand correctly, it has the third longest transcription ever found in the Tuscan language, describing some kind of land sale transaction. Unusual to find a text relic. The guide said that most of what we know of the Etruscans has been through artistic artefacts. Archaeologists minutely checked the location of the find to see if there was anything else but they found nothing, but why was it cut into pieces, not easy to cut metal. Did the Etruscans use metal cutters?'

'Now there's a good question to ask Ricardo or Clotilde. Their knowledge of ancient metal cutting tools would be invaluable here.'

They walked over to a shaded table in a *piazza* café and ordered a couple of beers and sun-dried tomato and ham *bruschetta*. Bob was still chewing over what they'd seen in the Museum of the Etruscan Academy and he couldn't shake from his mind what his wife had said about *asphodel* plants being a cure for snake bite.

'By the way did you notice the Academy's Coat of Arms? It was above the fireplace in the library.'

Gisèle flicked through the pages of the guidebook which she'd bought in the museum shop. 'Yes, here it is. I'm not sure I understand all the symbolism though. A tripod, serpent and a star. It says in the book the tripod was the symbol of Apollo and the serpent, you'll like this Bob, the serpent was the symbol of wisdom.'

'Um, thought as much. I always reckoned that the little buggers were endowed with intelligence. What does the book say about the star?'

'The star symbolises Electra who was Atlas's mythical daughter and bride of Corinth who it says here was the king and founder of Cortona. Now, that's interesting. I always thought that Electra was the daughter of Agamemnon but what do I know?'

'I'm afraid you've lost me. Never was any good with Greek mythology. However, the snake does interest me. Why were these ancient civilisations so fascinated by the serpent? Look at the museum's most famed possession that marvellous Etruscan chandelier in bronze. It had at its centre a gorgon's head surrounded by serpents. The Greeks and Egyptians also seem to have had a bit of an obsession with the wriggly things, not forgetting Cleopatra's untimely death from the Aspe's venom.'

'Probably something to do with the underworld,' retorted Gisèle. 'The original purpose of the chandelier is in doubt, could have been from a place of worship or maybe a tomb. If it were a tomb why bother to make such an intricate object if it were to be hidden from view?'

'Um, yet another problem to resolve. No problems only solutions. By the way, you know you're always going on about chance and coincidences well how about this? Your great literary compatriot Lawrence actually spent some time in the South of France in late 1928 early 1929 writing some of his best loved poetry.'

'So that's not much of a coincidence. Lawrence loved travelling.........'

'For goodness sake let me finish the story. Why must you always interrupt? It may surprise you to know that the hotel he stayed in was in the small seaside resort of Bandol. The hotel was called *Le Beau Rivage* and it was the same hotel where my mother used to work as a *femme de chambre*.'

'Really? Presumably not at the same time,' Bob joked.

'No, stupid. *Maman* was only born in '22. She worked there after the war. So you don't merit that as a coincidence? It's not just you can go banging on about coincidence. Well, finish your beer and let's take a stroll over to the *Fortezza del Girifalco*. So much to see and so little time, don't forget we're back on the road tomorrow.'

Bob felt he ought to be in conciliatory mode.

'Yes, I suppose it does fall into the category of coincidence. So your mum must have made up the bed, plumped the pillows, turned down the covers and made one of those cute but ultimately useless envelope folds on the loo roll. Do you think he might have left some of his scribblings in the garbage can – would be worth a fortune today.'

Gisèle glowered at her husband but chose not to rise to his sardonic bait. They took the road across the town to the 16th century *Fortezza del Girifalco*. The fort was originally built on the foundations of the Etruscan wall which surrounded the town and once again provided a wonderful vista across the Chiana valley and Lake Trasimeno.

Gisèle had conscientiously been doing her homework.

'Bet you didn't know that this place was once a prison and then home to 250 children in the second world war and provided an excellent observation post for German radio operators, that is until it was liberated by The Allies in '44?'

Bob was studying the view. 'It certainly would have made an excellent observation point. I imagine that Uncle Eric must have come up the valley by the lake route on his way to *Arezzo*. Don't suppose he had much time for sightseeing. God, the horror of war!'

They began walking rather aimlessly around the walls. After the museum the fortress seemed not to offer much of any great interest. That was the problem with historical tourism. There comes a time when archaeological overload kicks in and the brain refuses to assimilate anymore. Bob was quiet, seemingly lost in his own private world.

'A centime for your thoughts,' Gisèle interrupted his reverie.

'Oh, I was just turning over that old chestnut of whether we ever learn from history. Who was it who said that those who don't learn from history are doomed to relive it? Wasn't it Churchill?'

'Probably. I get the impression that he had something to say about most things although these days the social media is swamped by quotations falsely attributed to anyone vaguely famous. Anyway, do you think it's true?'

'Not sure. The world seems to be run by so many idiots these days, the majority of whom have probably never studied history. Just look at those French students I taught a couple of years ago. They were doing their Master's degree so presumably they weren't completely stupid and yet few of them knew who the victor at the Battle of Waterloo was or which Frenchman was the first King of England. Amazingly William's castle was five kilometres down the road and most students would pass it every day on their way to the university. Learn from history – forget it! Vietnam, Iraq, The Balkans, Afghanistan plus myriads of 'minor' wars and skirmishes – we've learned nothing. Dictators and tyrants who think that they still live in the Middle Ages and can send their armies like modern day crusaders to inflict new ideologies on largely innocent and sadly ignorant masses. Crusaders with cell phones and the internet and don't get me going on about 'social media.' The modern-day version of the underworld which instead of being inhabited by mysterious monsters with serpent heads is full of right-wing loonies and conspiracy theorists. So there, *terminée*. So now what should we be looking at?'

Gisèle had grown used to her husband's rants and raves over everything from BREXIT to the state of modern French popular music. She knew that his political stance had changed significantly in recent years from being an ardent fan of Margaret Thatcher to a tentative Labour supporter. Not that he'd voted. He couldn't. The idiot Cameron had disenfranchised ex-pats. No referendum vote. Disenfranchised for living too long outside the country of his birth and then finding that Johnson and his acolytes wanted out of the European Union thus robbing him of a chance of voting in his adopted country.

'Well, the guidebook says that while we are at the fortress we should go and look at the *Chiesa di Santa Margherita,* the Saint Margherita's church. It has some wonderful ceilings and the relics of Saint Margherita herself. Sounds a bit gruesome to me but let's take a quick look and then I suggest that we go back to the *Via Nazionale* where apparently there are some great pastry shops, what do you think?'

'Fine by me. Not so sure about the relics but I'm definitely up for the pastries.'

Chapter Twenty-One

Two Days Earlier

Rosa heard Winston barking, a little strange at this time of the night she thought, probably disturbed by something out on the lake. She chose to ignore it and turned over and fell asleep. It wasn't until the sun was just making an appearance over the eastern shore of the lake that she noticed that the lights had been left on in the corridor that led to Ricardo's library. She sat up in bed and looked around and listened. She thought she could hear Winston snuffling around somewhere. She called out his name but nothing. She got out of bed and opened the door of her room shouting the dog's name once more. This time there was a whimper which she guessed came from the direction of the library.

She found Ricardo lying face down on the wooden floor his shattered whisky glass at his feet. The liquid had dried or been lapped up by Winston but had left a sticky imprint which clung to Rosa's bare knees as she knelt beside Ricardo's prone body. She felt for his pulse and checked his breathing. To her relief he was still alive. The cell phone was still resting on the arm of the chair. She punched in 118 for the medical emergency service. The reply was prompt and a lake water ambulance was dispatched immediately. Ricardo was a well-known figure and the local emergency service was proud of its reputation. They wouldn't want to see a botched response for emergency help from such an esteemed personality. Rosa knew that Ricardo was a bit of a drinker but she had never come across him in this state before. No, she thought this must be something more serious. She called to Winston who was sniffing and licking the pale face of his master. Winston wasn't going to move – he had the sixth animal sense of loyalty in the face of adversity. Rosa was about to go back to her room to put on her bath robe and slippers when she noticed something glistening in the early morning sunlight on the far side of the library. She walked towards the light and picked up the snake-handled scissors with the engraved initials. She tut-tutted to herself and muttered in Italian. '*Gli ho sempre detto che nulla di buono sarebbe venuto dal possedere le forbici.*' Hadn't she always said that nothing good would ever come of those damned scissors. In a mixture of annoyance, panic and frustration she threw the scissors across the room where one blade stuck into the wooden floor. At the same moment she heard the water ambulance arriving at the little private jetty. A stifled groan came from the recumbant body. At least he's alive she thought.

Minutes later two paramedics in high visibility jackets mounted the stairs carrying a collapsable stretcher. Rosa rushed them through to the library. 'He's still alive.' She shouted. 'Probably a heart attack.' The two medics strapped Ricardo to the stretcher and attached an oxygen mask. One of the medics said that it didn't look like a cardiac arrest and looking around the room noticed the scissors still sticking into the floor boarding.

'Was he having suicidal thoughts, *Signorina*? Why are the scissors on the floor?'

Rosa, forced a laugh. 'No, he was not suicidal but he had just discarded his favourite lover I think.'

The two men cast a glance at each other and raised their eyes before guiding the stretcher out of the door and down the flight of stairs to the front door. Winston followed closely by, tail wagging. The ambulance men insisted that Rosa as nominal next of kin should accompany them to the hospital in Milan. Winston would have to stay. He would be free to roam the garden and she imagined that she'd be back before the day was out. She found Winston's long leash and attached one end around the base of a jacaranda tree. They climbed aboard the water ambulance and sped off across the lake to Stresa leaving Winston barking and whimpering back on the island.

It would take the ambulance less than an hour to cover the 70 kilometers to the *Milan Ospedal Maggiore*. The roads were mostly clear with just some light early morning traffic and the blue flashing light and wailing siren would help them stay that way.

Chapter Twenty-Two

'Why is the catholic church so obsessed with relics?' It was Bob's first question as he and Gisèle left the sombre interior of Saint Margherita's church. 'I find it all very morbid looking at the body of someone who died over 700 years ago and is venerated by thousands of gawping, rosary counting pilgrims. Remember all those people looking at the supposed skull of Mary Magdalen in that church we visited in Provençe last summer and what about the millions who go to Turin to see the shroud. It all seems quite irrational and even spooky to me.'

'You don't get it do you *Cherie*? You've grown up as a protestant. Thanks to your misogynist King Henry VIII you cut with the catholic church centuries ago so your man could get a divorce. He then set about destroying the churches, executing the priests and running riot through the virgins of Europe. He was the Donald Trump of his time. Egotistical, narcistic and all powerful.'

'Ah c'mon that's a bit harsh on a man whose legacy lay in being in the forefront of the English Reformation, reorganising the navy, the state religion and improving social conditions. He was much loved as a King who gave the English back their pride and sovereignty.'

Gisèle couldn't hold back her amusement. 'You'll be telling me next that he was a great golfer and probably a Brexiteer ahead of his time. Give me the Catholic church and its ancient relics anytime.'

✂

They could smell the pastry sweetness on *Via Nazionale* even before the *Pasticceria* came into view. The swooning aroma of the best in Italian pastries wafted its way along the street on the warm spring breeze.

'Ok, let's indulge ourselves and take a couple or four cakes back to the rooftop pool. What do you say *Cherie?*'

Gisèle hardly needed any prompting. She was a great pastry cook herself even though she preferred the more substantial dessert delights of a good *tiramisu* or chocolate charlotte. Her cherry *clafouti* wasn't bad either even though Bob's penchant was for all things chocolatey. They'd certainly hit pastry paradise here. The range of cakes was stunning and their Italian names gave an added eating dimension. *Panfortadi, Bomboloni, Sfogliatella, Cannoli,* the very names excited the tastebuds. This was pure sensual pleasure of the highest order.

'I can't resist the *Millefoglie.'* Enthused Bob. Those layers of puff pastry and oozing cream. Practically orgasmic.'

'Careful, Bob, mustn't upset the locals. Anyway, I'm going to be a little more adventurous and am going for a slice of *Sfogliatella*. I remember once eating it in Naples where it originated. Seem to remember someone telling me that it was created by nuns who certainly wouldn't have used your colourful adjective to describe the crème patisserie filling with black cherries, although who knows what 17th century nuns got up to in their spare time.'

After carefully placing the pastries in a coloured box somewhat reminiscent of the depiction in a Renaissance painting of the three magi presenting gifts to the Boy Jesus, the rather austere assistant asked, *'Ci sarà qualcos'altro?'* Bob suspected that she was a little suspicious of the culinary idiosynchracies of visiting tourists. Gisèle replied in Italian asking what she might recommend. The assistant immediately warmed to someone troubling to use her native language and her face broke into a beaming smile.

'Consiglio la specialità locale di Siena. La panforta è molto popolare.'

'She recommends the *panforta*. Look over there. It's that pastry with dried fruit and nuts mixed with a honey syrup. Shall we give that a try also?'

'Si, si, molto bene. Delizioso.' Bob wanted to try out some more of his newly found vocabulary. The assistant was impressed and cutting a small slice from the cake offered a taster to a very self-satisfied Bob. *'Grazie, grazie! Fantastico, delizioso, yum, yum.'*

'Ok, *cherie*, don't overdo it. You've made your point.'

They eventually left the *Pasticceria* practically as old friends with *'Signorina Pastry'* wishing them *'Buon appetito'* and Bob practising his Italian pronunciation like a crazy kid on his first foreign holiday. *'Grazie, Grazie,'* he repeated several times over until Gisèle dragged him outside.

'Now, if you've quite finished showing off your English eccentricities I'd like to buy a couple of postcards from the news kiosk.' Giséle announced narrowly avoiding bumping into a fully-laden 3-wheeled *Piaggio Ape* chugging along the street. The driver klaxoned and blew a casual kiss in her direction.

'Can't understand the popularity of those damned things.' Bob chuntered. 'Seem bloody dangerous to me. Unstable and noisy.'

'There you go again,' Gisèle retorted. 'Just because you don't see them on the streets of London doesn't make your criticism valid. Ideal for narrow Italian streets, cheap to run and very functional. They're converted *Vespa* scooters and have been made since the late 1940's. *Vespa* means wasp and *Ape* – bee. Now what about those postcards. I reckon we need four. Two for my brothers and you mustn't forget Jim, Charlie and family plus your sister and husband and perhaps we should buy one more for Ricardo and Rosa. A good opportunity to thank them once more for their generosity the other day. That makes five and mustn't forget the stamps. How about if we choose two each and a shared choice for Ricardo? Fair division of labour don't you think?' Gisèle turned the carousel around a couple of times before choosing a selection of cards depicting a variety of local buildings and *objets d'art*. Bob was more interested in country scenes of

Tuscan hilltops and lonely trees but one card particularly caught his attention. It was a photo of a religious procession. At first sight it showed just a group of men in religious garb processing along a street bearing aloft a statue of a local saint. What grabbed Bob was that the statue was covered in – he lifted his sunglasses for a closer look – covered in snakes, hundreds of them writhing around the hands and legs of the statue and some in the hands of people solemnly walking alongside the procession. Bob shuddered and felt the familiar goosebumps on his arms.

'Hey, look at this! He turned to his wife. 'I've seen some horrible images but this must take the prize for ultimate revulsion.'

She took the card and turned it over. '*Bien sur*, it's the *Festa del Serpari* in *Cocullo*. A very famous religious occasion in Italy in honour of Saint Dominique. It says here that he was the patron saint of protection against snake bite and also rather bizarrely protection against toothache. If I remember correctly it's held each year on the first of May and has ancient links with the Roman Goddess *Angitia* who was renowned for curing snake bites.'

'So you're familiar with this place and you've never told me. Me! Your snake phobic husband or should I say *ophidiophobic* husband. Imagine if we'd stumbled across this place on our travels without knowing. I might have died from the shock.'

'Oh, don't be so dramatic Bob. I'd forgotten all about this festival and anyway it's in a little mountain village in the

Appenines not far from Rome. It's hardly a place we would visit.'

'So, have you been there?'

'Yes, just once. I passed through it but it wasn't at the time of the festival. I heard the locals talking about it. Don't worry the snakes are not poisonous mostly grass or green whip snakes. After the festival they return all the snakes back to the surrounding woods.'

'That's not the point. Poisonous or not I'm crossing *Cocullo* off my bucket list. Not that it was ever on!'

'Yes cherie, I'll certainly remember that. You and your bucket list.' Gisèle gave him one of her glazed looks which she reserved for those things that she found faintly ridiculous. 'Now, can you pass me that copy of *'Le Monde'* up at the top there. It's probably yesterday's edition but no matter I'll catch up with the goings on in *'La Belle France.'* I'll go and pay and then back to the hotel for pastries by the pool I think.'

✂

'Looks as though we'll be using our fingers,' Gisèle licked her lips as her eyes made a 360 degree tour of the cream and cherry filled *sfogliatella*. Looks too good to eat, should be framed and hung on our kitchen wall. What's your *millefoglie* like Bob?'

Bob adjusted the back of the sun-lounger, sat upright and bit into the *millefoglie* showering flakes of pastry over his towel and bare legs. 'Scrumptious is the word I think, absolutely delicious, worth every centime. You can lick the crumbs off my legs if you want. Won't want to eat anything for dinner tonight after this.'

'Well, that certainly will make a change we've done little but eat since we arrived in Italy. Diet for me once we get back home and no I've no intention of licking the crumbs off your body. What would people think? Are you going to have a swim to work off the calories?'

'No, I don't think I'll bother. The water seems a little cold. I want to checkout a couple of things on the internet and just maybe close my eyes for a short *siesta.* What about you?'

'Yes, I'll take a quick dip and then catch up with the French news.'

The pool area was filling up with late afternoon eaters wanting to sleep off their pasta. Most were Italian, a mixture of young *'poseurs'* showing off their finely tuned bodies and a few elderly couples religiously finding the best position for their sunbeds, carefully laying out their towels, smoothing on a layer of sunblock and opening up their Umberto Eco or Elénor Ferrante novels.

'What was the name of that Roman Goddess of snakes you were talking about in the newsagents?' Bob asked his wife. 'I'll look her up, might prove interesting.'

'Her name was *Angitia* but I thought you had a horror of serpents. You'll be having nightmares.'

Bob hesitated. 'Yes, actually but I'm alright as long as there are no pictures.'

'Oh, Bob you're pathetic. I'm off for a swim.'

Bob watched his wife step daintily across the tiles. She looked good in her blue and white bikini, certainly a match for the Italian women twenty years younger on the opposite side of the pool many already showing signs of ageing from too much sun. She dived in gracefully rising seconds later to the surface, she smoothed back her long brown hair and shouted to her husband. 'Come on in Bob, it's lovely and warm.'

Bob smiled acknowledging the question but choosing not to answer. He opened up his phone and Googled *Angitia*. He was happy to see his response appearing as text, he didn't want to have to confront any more photos of reptiles. 'Hm, impressive. 123000 results. That should keep me busy,' he said to himself.

✂

Gisèle returned from her swim. She shook the water from her hair over Bob and grabbed her towel. Her husband was not impressed. 'That water is absolutely freezing and now you've made me lose my link.'

Gisèle crouched down beside him and kissed the nape of his neck. 'Where's my anaconda's sense of humour gone?'

'I don't think calling me an anaconda is particularly endearing. Look there is some very interesting stuff here.' He turned up a picture of a terracotta statue. 'This is a statue of her. *Angitia* seems to have been a 2nd century BC Greek goddess living in the vicinity of Lake Fucine which if I understand the map is east of Rome in the Aquila province. The lake was drained in the 19th century but it was around here that Angitia worked her sorcery as a miraculous healer of snakebite and apparently she was able to kill a snake just by touch.'

'Yes, that's fascinating stuff,' Interrupted Gisèle. 'Don't forget that magic and medicine were very closely connected in ancient history. The serpent played an important role in many cultures just think of the Egyptians or the Minoans. Remember seeing that remarkable statuette of the goddess found at *Knossus* – the one with the arms held out holding a couple of snakes aloft? What about the symbol of the serpent coiled around a rod which is still used in many parts of the world to denote a pharmacist's shop?'

'Oh you mean the *Rod of Asclepius*, it mentions that here. More Greek mythology. *Asclepius* was the god of medicine and healing and the legend says that one day *Mercury* came across two serpents fighting and he threw a stick at them after which the serpents coiled themselves around the stick. Why didn't he just kill them and have done with the vile things?'

'Not very objective of you *Cherie*. I thought that this was a serious investigation. Do you remember the snakeskin I found on our first date? I still have it you know. Stuck it in the bottom of my purse for good luck. In Provençe we've always regarded snakeskins as having special properties.

You see it's all about symbolism, rejuvination. A snake sheds its skin so it can go on living.'

Bob thought about this for a moment before concluding that Gisèle's argument was illogical. 'If what you're saying is true then snakes should be immortal but evidently that isn't true. Like all other living things thay eventually die.'

'Yes agreed but you see it's the symbolism that's crucial. Symbolic renewal and resurrection.'

'I think I need to think about that one for a while.'

Gisèle knew that was Bob's favourite let out clause when he couldn't win an argument.

'Anyway enough about serpents. Don't forget we still have a pastry to eat.' Gisèle pulled the cakebox from under the shade of the sunbed. 'The famous local speciality *panforta*. What do you say to washing it down with a couple of glasses of *prosecco*?'

'Great idea, you took the words out of my mouth. I'll call the waiter over.'

Bob licked his lips and wiped his hands on his towel. 'Mm, not bad but I still prefer the *millefoglie*. I prefer the sweetness and texture of the pastry but I have to say that the *panforta* goes down well with the *prosecco*. Could quite fancy a refill. What about you *cherie*?'

'No, not for me. The *prosecco* is not bad but in my estimation it can't compare with a good French champagne but you go ahead if you want to poison yourself, sorry, I mean have another glass.'

'You're just a French wine snob. I can't tell the difference,' he paused, 'except for the price.'

'Philistine!' shot back Gisèle. 'Now leave me quiet whilst I catch up on the news from home.'

Bob tried to catch the eye of the waiter to re-order but suddenly he had the impression that he'd become invisible. Whenever the waiter approached he avoided Bob's gaze or at least that was what he thought. He wondered whether he should have tipped him after the first order. He shrugged and returned to his snake goddess research. Gisèle caught her husband's frustration with the waiter and without a word had ordered a second *prosecco*. Bob pretended not to notice.

A few minutes later Gisèle sat upright, smoothed the newspaper page and laughed. 'You won't believe this Bob but you know that news presenter on France TF2, the one with the long brown hair that she always cascades over her left shoulder? The one with the pointed nose and slightly twisted mouth.'

Bob looked up from his phone. 'You mean Nathalie somebody or other. Always wears blue and shows off her boobs?'

'Yes, that's the one. Trust you noticing the finer details. Well, you'll never guess but she's 'bagged' a politician. A minor minister in Finance. Recently promoted and seen as a rising star of the right.'

The romances between French female media journalists and male politicians was a constant theme at home particularly after dinner when they'd watched the evening news and caught up with the events of the day. Bob was particularly fascinated by how the journalists 'bagged' their politicians. Gisèle reckoned that it was standard procedure in French media circles. A high level interview, flash your legs and flick back the hair and accept the dinner invitation when the cameras has stopped rolling and the microphones have been switched off.

'Whatever happened to media impartiality?' Bob said with an air of righteous indignation. 'These 'journos' continue to work and still go on interviewing politicians as if nothing has changed. Surely that can't be fair.'

'Who said anything about fairness and impartiality? It goes with the territory. Media people in France have always maintained close relationship with politicians. Most of the time the relationship is professional but everyone knows the reality. Just look at the relationship between Mitterand and the press back in the '80's. Mitterand has a 'love child' who grows up in an environment funded by the State, paid for by the French taxpayers. The press were told to stay silent. They did! It was only near the end of his political life that the truth came out but was there an outcry? Was there heck!' The French seem to like their presidents to be human. They loved Chirac because he symbolised France and its values plus he had a sense of humour. As for Sarkozy they elect him President and then he shows off by inviting his friends to one of the most expensive restos in Paris, takes off on a celebratory cruise aboard a millionaire friend's luxury yacht, ditches his wife and marries an ex-model come singer with 'form' if you get my drift.'

'Oh you mean Clapton, Jagger to name a few,' Bob sniggered. 'What about Holland pictured in his crash helmet on a scooter taking breakfast croissants to his film star lover? At least neither Sarko or Holland got re-elected.'

'No, you're right but once out of the Elysée Palace they gradually take on the role of senior statesmen and before too long people are looking back with regret and nostalgia for the 'glory years.' Look at Macron. Initially popular but eventually he's discovered to be too young and that worst of personality traits for the French, arrogant. People joked about him being married to his mother but they never criticised Trump for being married to a woman nearly 25 years his junior. Personally I liked Macron. He was like a breath of fresh air but the unions and *les gilets jaune* soon laid into him and that put an end to him.'

'Revolution is in your DNA,' Bob suggested. 'Why on earth can't you French people just settle down to a quiet life and enjoy the wine, cheese and splendid countryside. Forget politics and philosophising and concentrate on the things that really matter.'

'As you say, *cherie*, it's in our DNA – always has been and always will be. The land of Montaigne, Rousseau, Descartes, Foucault, Sartre, de Beauvoir. The list could go on - not forgetting the latest crop of media philosophers led by the one and only BHL – Bernard Henry Lévy.'

'Oh, you mean the guy who drinks *Côte de Rhône* with Native Americans? That was a classic.'

'Why shouldn't he drink *Côte de Rhône* with Native Americans? You're being racist Bob.'

'No you've missed the point. He was drinking *Côte de Rhône* with Native Americans on a reservation in Nevada. Where would they get a bottle of *Côte de Rhône* from? They offered it to him not the other way round for goodness sake.'

'They do have supermarkets in Nevada in case you didn't know and Native Americans do have money. Get real Bob! We're in the 21st century!'

Bob slunk back to his phone. The sun had disappeared over the other side of the pool and it was getting a bit chilly. Bob put on a shirt and lay back. He wondered what Uncle Eric would have made of the modern world of luxury Italian hotels, swimming pools, Italian women, cell phones and *Prosecco*. He came here to fight and die for his country for goodness sake. A Tuscan in Tuscany.

'Hey Bob, look at this.' Gisèle jumped up and folding the newspaper into quarters thrust it in front of his eyes. 'Go on read it!' She was adamant. 'Do you want me to translate into English?'

'No, thanks. I need to practice my translation skills. Never know when it might come in useful.' Bob started tentatively reading aloud the French text and translating as he went along. He found the written word reasonably easy to follow, unlike watching a film in French which he found very difficult particularly when several characters were speaking at once. The concentration was immense and he'd lost count of the number of times he'd nodded off before the end. English subtitles were a copout but at least you could make sense of most of the dialogue.

'*Tour d'horizon des nouvelles européennes. Italie. Dernières nouvelles de notre correspondant à Rome.* I reckon that's the easy bit.'

Gisèle looked on anxiously. Bob continued with the short news item.

'*The Milanese industrialist, philanthropist and collector Ricardo Ceccaroli has been taken to a Milan hospital after collapsing at his home on a private island on Lake Maggiore. His femme de menage, sorry, his housekeeper found him unconscious this morning. He is reported to be gravely ill and in the intensive care unit at the city's Ospedal Maggiore. So far no one at the hospital has been available for comment.*'

'Crikey,' Bob puffed out his cheeks and looked across at his wife. He turned towards the top of the page to check out the date.'

'It's Saturday's late edition before you ask.' Gisèle chipped in. 'We left Stresa on Saturday morning and today's Monday so Ricardo's illness must have occurred sometime between us leaving the island on Friday afternoon and Saturday morning. What are you thinking?'

'Not sure. We've only met the guy once so we don't know anything of his medical history. Could be a heart attack or a stroke. He seemed fit enough, wasn't obviously overweight.'

'Yes, but we don't know anything about his day to day life, the stresses and strains of running a business empire. He was certainly a *gourmet* but was he a *gourmand*? Just look how he set about the *Osso Bucco* and he did drink a lot. I doubt that he found much time for exercise. A stroll around his island with Winston would hardly constitute intensive physical activity although I seem to remember Rosa telling me that he went for a regular morning swim in the lake.'

'Why are we talking about him in the past tense?' Bob said. 'Hopefully he's still alive. Do you think Rosa is with him? Pity we don't have a number for her. What about ringing the hospital direct?'

Gisèle thought for a moment. 'No, I've got a better idea. Look, we're leaving here for Milan tomorrow morning. Do you remember the time of our flight? We must return the car to the airport but if we arrive in Milan early enough we can call in at the hospital beforehand. What do you think?'

Bob picked up his phone and swiped through to his agenda. 'Flight scheduled to leave Linate at 19.15. I'll ring through to *Alitalia* and confirm that. It's about five hours from here so if we leave around nine in the morning we should make it there by early afternoon leaving enough time to call in at the hospital, return the car and arrive at checkout well before departure.'

'That sounds fine. Look I'll get back to our room and start packing whilst you confirm the flight. Happy with that? The *Alitalia* desk always speak English so you won't want my help there.' She punched her husband playfully on the arm and grabbing her towel and bag disappeared in the direction of the lift.

Chapter Twenty-Three

Early May - Béziers

'Domaine des Tournesols' lies just off the Departmental 37 going south-east out of the town of Béziers between the Libron river and the Canal du Midi. A small parcel of vines within sight and sound of the rail line to Narbonne, mostly *Grenache* and *Cinsault* grapes growing out of the scrubby, dry, alluvial landscape. An ideal site for taking advantage of the hot dry mediterranean summers and mild winters, close enough to the sea to profit from the cooling fresh southerly winds which extend the period of maturation and ensure high grape sugar content. The Languedoc Oriental region has seen a surge in wine sales, particularly the reds, over the last 20 years. Gone are the days of insipid reds that had to be blended with imported Algerian wine to give colour and flavour. Nowadays with modern wine production techniques and an expansion of the cooperatives the area is seeing a rejuvination and world sales are on the rise. Young ambitious entrepreneurs are coming into the area many of whom 20 or 30 years ago would have turned their nose up at the prospect of becoming *vignerons*. Many graduates in business management from the top *Ecoles de Commerce* in France taking on the anglo-saxons at their own game and winning over their Napa Valley competitors with cheaper, quality wine.

Hervé and Stephen had bought 3 hectares of old vines. Their piece of the local *terroir*, that practically indefinable French word that encapsulates soils, climate, topology – in total everything that is the essence of grape growing. After a season of heavy, back-breaking pruning they were preparing for their first *vendange* and hopefully their first bottling later in the year. They'd become part of a local wine cooperative which was the only feasible way for a small enterprise to set up production. The cooperative provides all the essential equipment and organises the marketing, all that Hervé and Stephen needed to do was grow and sell the grapes – no mean task but Hervés experience gained from many years as a *négotiant* in Bordeaux was invaluable. Most of the heavy work was shared amongst other members of the cooperative and the picking itself would hopefully be taken on by some seasonal labour, students, backpackers, unemployed looking to make a bit of money and the chance to soak up some mediterranean sunshine, evenings spent eating chunks of coarse bread with *Tomme de Chèvre* a local goat's cheese, washed down with something red and hopefully followed by a night of love under the *Hérault* stars.

The poor reputation of cooperative wines has long since diminished, gone are the *Vin de Tables* which languished on the bottom shelves of the supermarkets alongside the wine boxes now replaced with a multitude of wines vinified from a variety of grape types and increasingly bearing the organic appelation. The mass wine drinking community has become more sophisticated and it's not just the connoisseurs who are looking out for that special bottle. The new generation of *vignerons* know what they are doing.

The *mas* that Hervé and Alice had bought several years ago had been renovated and the farm shop had started to do good business selling mostly local wines, honey, olive oil and herbs. It had been Alice's brainchild and it bore her unmistakeable imprint with a tastefully executed décor, provençal paintings on the walls, bowls of dried herbs and vases of wild flowers, *asphodel* in the spring and the ubiquitous sun flowers in late summer. Since Alice's death Hervé had created a subtle shrine with understated and often hidden symbols of her personality – embroidered wild flower tea cloths, small sunflower insignia on everything from till receipts to wrapping paper and ribbons, short, succinct phrases from Proust or Hugo burnished onto beams and door lintels.

After the death of his mother, Stephen had resigned from his job at the Aix Publishing House and joined Hervé in the business. In his spare time he was studying for an MBA in wine and Spirits Marketing at the Montpellier Business School with a view to taking over the winery full-time, conscious as he was that Hervé was finding the physical activity increasingly difficult. They'd agreed that one day, probably after the launch of their first vintage, Hervé would take over the back-office work whilst Stephen ran the day-to-day operations in the vineyard and the necessary collaborative work with the cooperative. For the next year he would be travelling the 55-minute route on the A9 three times a week but he reckoned in the end it would be worth the effort. When the doubts crept in there was always the image of the little girl and the sunflower to spur him on. His mother Alice was constantly in his thoughts; the grieving was over but the sadness that he still felt was more linked to the loss of those remembered happy times that were always playing in the background of his life. Paradoxically the background was in sharper focus than the foreground – the music they'd shared, eating her *Proustian Madelaines*, the dinners with friends, the dreary Normandy February afternoons curled up on the sofa in front of a roaring log fire watching 6-Nations Rugby, the coming of spring and the rejuvenation of the garden, the summer Saturdays on the beach soaking up the Deauville sunshine and the cider and camembert cheese in the brasserie on their way home. Yes, he owed a lot to Alice but Stephen was now into his fifties, by a long stretch the eldest in his class. His colleagues found his age and his Englishness intriguing, particularly helpful for those who shared his table during the twice weekly 'Business English' classes, somewhat onerous to many of the French students. Popular with the young women in his group but no long-term partner in view. Like many men being used to 'pampering' mothers Stephen was always looking for perfection. After all he had spent most of his formative years alone with his mother, first in Paris and later in Normandy. He'd inherited most of his mother's genes, a love of books and plants, a sensitivity towards nature and art. What remained of his father's genes was not discernible except for his passion for *'Top Quatorze'* Rugby and the Toulouse XV - never missing a game when they played at home or when they travelled south to play against the local Montpellier and Béziers teams. He realised that perfection in women did not exist but he'd keep looking. He considered that his greatest mistake was always thinking that others thought like he did, that they saw the world through his eyes and processed everything in the same way. Women were like men but prettier and with different physical bits. His only really meaningful relationship had been with a colleague at the publishers – Laure, an editor of children's books, stunningly beautiful, long brown hair, brown eyes, cultured and passionate about French literature and poetry but unfortunately married with 2 teenage kids. After three torrid and furtive years of stolen afternoons and weekend publishing 'jaunts' in Paris and Marseille she had called it a day. She had told him that her children still came first and that she owed her future to the father of those children. Stephen was heart-broken but deep down knew she was right. At the very end she had dragged up that hoary chestnut of 'It's all my fault, don't blame yourself, it's me not you,' whatever that was supposed to mean. He would never understand women. Perhaps that was their mystery?

✂

Today Hervé and Stephen had completed the final pruning of the vines. They had been a little late this year. The important pruning was normally done in the winter season but some unseasonal Mediterranean rain had put everything behind schedule. Now they were busy training the vines and pinching out new shoots. Incorrect pruning could ruin a whole year's wine production and that was certainly something that neither one of them dared to consider. They already had plans for a grand launching ceremony in the coming Autumn and a tentative guest list had already been drawn up. This was going to be something special even though the first bottle of *'Domaine des Tournesols'* wouldn't be ready for another two years.

Chapter Twenty-Four

The Next Day - Milan

The journey back to Milan started as a somewhat sombre affair. Both Gisèle and Bob had been shocked and saddened by the news of Ricardo's sudden illness, they'd only known him briefly but their shared histories had somehow made their acquaintance seem much longer than their brief sojourn on his island. Additionally, they had left Cortona with a gentle tug on the heart strings. Over the last 3 days they'd discovered a great deal, the final resting place of Bob's Uncle Eric, the 'Tuscan in Tuscany.' The Uncle he'd never known. The intriguing history of the Etruscan civilisation and perhaps above all the warm welcome of the inhabitants of this charming hillside town with its narrow streets, splendid restaurants and romantic café terraces not forgetting the spectacular views over a landscape that had been witness to a history going back ten thousand years.

Conversation was in short supply. Both Bob and Gisèle lost in their own thoughts. The sun shone brightly over the purple tinted *Apennines* to the east. Bob did the driving and once past Florence he shoved in the memory stick music files. He wanted to lighten the atmosphere but before he could programme Dylan, Clapton or Leonard Cohen, Gisèle had beaten him to it and swiped down the screen to Hardy, Birkin and Gainsbourg. Bob did a haughty, nonchalant shrug of the shoulders his usual response to his wife's choice of music.

'I suppose you are going to tell me again your story of bumping into Françoise Hardy at a piano festival.'

'Only if you go on about sitting behind Sean Connery at Wimbledon or Bobby Charlton sharing his Franz Beckenbauer jokes with you.' Gisèle enjoyed the banter of 'one upmanship' and she'd heard most of his best 'celebrity' stories before.

'Go on then give me your list of famous French artists or cultural icons who you have seen in the flesh so to speak and you can't include Jane Birkin because she's English.'

'Well, I could start with Brassens and then go on to Brel or maybe Lavillier but I know that you'll come back with The Stones, Little Richard, Everly Brothers, Dylan, or Baez so it's not worth the effort. You can't make those sorts of comparisons between two different musical traditions with different roots. For me French music is about language, poetry, history and philosophy. We listen to the words you listen to the music; we make political statements whilst you go on about sex, drugs and Rock 'n Roll.'

'I'm not sure that is totally fair,' Bob hit back. 'Just think about the 60's protest songs or the punk movement coming out of the Thatcher years, we've got artists who are *politiquement engagé'* as you say but on the other side we have made some great fun rock - think of Freddy Mercury and Queen; Chuck Berry, The Who or Black Sabbath – all great stadium artists. Not even mentioned Bowie.

'Whatever, *Vive le difference*, as they say. Just think of the great artists we've seen since we got together. Can't be many people who can say that they met in front of the great Portuguese pianist Marie Jao Pires even if she was accompanied by an orchestrated fart but let's not dwell on that one again.'

'Julian Bream.'

'Simon Rattle.'

'Yehudi Menuhin,'

'Maurice Béjart.'

'Borodine Quartet.'

'Lang.'

'Divine Comedy.'

'Capuçon Brothers.'

'Boris Berezovsky.'

'Martha Argerich.'

'not forgetting Jane Birken.'

'I wish we could.'

'Tracey Chapman. Ahh!'

'Good one. What about *'La Tour d'Argent'*?'

'You can't include restaurants.'

'It does have a Michelin Star and the chef is an artist.'

'Sorry not accepted.'

'Derek Jacobi.'

'Gérard Lenorman.'

***??!

For the first time that morning they both laughed at the futility and silliness of their cultural battle. Bob didn't need reminding what a treasure he'd found in Gisèle. What impulse had made him go to the concert the night they met he'd never know. What a lucky guy he was. Beautiful, talented and cultivated. Bob considered the other women in his life and how different his life might have been if he had made a long-term relationship out of any of the others. Denise, sexy and intelligent but she would have sucked him dry in every sense. Carly, witty and skittish but a wanderer, Carole, cute, great sense of humour, insomniac and lover of dour Napoleonic furniture. Strangely he'd always judged his women friends by the shoes that they wore. Susie used to parade naked in her Doc Martens – a real turn off if ever there was! That was about it he reasoned to himself. He occasionally wondered about the ones who 'had got away.' Brenda who eventually married a Spaniard and opened a luxury hotel in Cadiz and not forgetting the sensuous Anne-Sophie – what ever happened to her? He hadn't even considered his 2 ex's – that was another story. Disasters of his own making best forgotten. That just left the one great love of his life. The first love, never forgotten, the standard by which he had judged all the others, cut down by a serpent on a *Langdocienne* hillside. Dear brave Alice. 'The Flower Girl.'

By the time that they had reached the Milanese suburbs the sky had clouded over and a heavy drizzle had begun falling obscuring the distant mountains. Bob disliked driving north for that very reason – the weather nearly always changed. The further away from the Mediterranean the more likely it was to rain. Not always accurate but Bob liked the hypothesis and it suited his mood today. He didn't buy into the notion of climate change particularly the man-made kind. He couldn't really imagine olive groves in Normandy or Scarborough becoming the new *'Cote d'Azur.'* Climate had always changed and no amount of human intervention was going to make much difference.

Like most large cities the suburbs were unappealing particularly in the rain and Milan was no exception with ugly industrial sites giving way to even uglier shopping centres. Mass urbanisation had a lot to answer for and Bob privately wondered what the ancient Etruscans or Romans would have made of it all. Thank-goodness that Gisèle had insisted on buying a place in the country even though that presented problems in the way of access to shops, cinemas or the theatre to say nothing of a 20-kilometre round trip to the doctor and a hospital that was even further away.

Thinking of hospitals Bob checked the satnav making sure that he had programmed the right coordinates for the *Ospedale Maggiore de Milan*. From the digital screen map it appeared on the south of the city and only about a 15-minute drive from the airport much to Gisèle's relief who was paranoid about missing a flight or rail connection.

The *Via Francesco Sforza* stretched out straight in front of them and Gisèle pointed out a large multi-storied building on the right that looked in her opinion to be a typical Italian hospital.

'Plenty of new building going on. A strange mixture of the traditional and modern. Just look at those arched windows, somebody had a romantic imagination. According to my search engine the hospital is the oldest in the city and was designed to join a lot of smaller medical facilities in the area. It was commissioned by Francesco Sforza and he wanted it constructed in the shape of a cross so that separate wings could house different diseases and avoid the risk of contamination. It was bombed in 1943 presumably by your lot.'

Bob ignored the barbed comment about the war and turned left into a pot-holed street with a large panel indicating *parcheggio pubblico*. Public Parking. He drove through a redbrick arch and parked in the half-empty parking facility.

'Well, at least the parking is easy. Not much like the facilities in France or the UK where you drive around for half an hour and then pay an extortionate amount to park up. Any idea where we are going *Cherie*?'

Gisèle pressed the window button and peered around. 'Yes, look over there, there is a sign indicating *Pronto Soccorso* – Emergency Department – that should be helpful.'

The automatic glass doors opened into an airy, spacious modern atrium. It could have been the reception area of any modern hospital anywhere in the world. Computer monitors flickered as blue and white clad medical officials went about their business. A collection of grey plastic seats stacked next to a coffee vending machine, a group of patients some with arms or legs in plaster-casts others in bandages and one or two lying on gurneys waiting for treatment. Some just staring into space others flicking idly through well-thumbed magazines and newspapers.

Bob and Gisèle walked over to the reception window. A middle-aged woman with short dark curly hair smiled and asked if she could be of any help. Before Gisèle could speak there was a flurry of activity by a side door as a team of paramedics rushed in pushing a mobile stretcher bearing a seemingly lifeless body connected to a life support system. Several nurses and other medical teams pushed the patient over to the lift where seconds later the emergency was whisked away.

'Yes, we are here to see if you have any information on the condition of a Signor Ricardo Ceccaroli. He was admitted 2 days ago I think.' Gisèle was thinking hard in Italian and she hoped that the nurse on reception understood.

'Si, si, Signor Ceccaroli – tutti vogliono kora circa le sue condizioni, la stampa la televisione. È in terapia intensiva e non è in grado diavere giocatori. Devi capire che è

terribilmente malato.' She pushed a printed statement under the glass panel.

'What's she saying?' demanded Bob.

'She says that everyone wants to know about Ricardo, the press, the television, everybody. He is gravely ill in intensive care and no visitors are allowed. The receptionist has given me this latest bulletin on his condition.'

Bob and Gisèle scanned the press release. Gisèle translated. ''It says that Ricardo Ceccaroli is still gravely ill in intensive care where he is under sedation. A further bulletin will be issued tomorrow.' Nothing new there. We can do nothing for the moment. Might as well get ourselves over to the airport in time for our flight.'

Behind them the lift doors slid open. Bob and Gisèle were about to leave the building when Gisèle grabbed her husband's arm and pointed towards the lift. 'Isn't that Rosa. I'm certain it's Rosa. It is you know.' Sure enough a small elegant, long-haired woman in a blue coat, grey headscarf and sunglasses left the lift and headed for the main entrance.

'Rosa, Rosa!' They both shouted. Rosa turned and looked blankly in their direction and then a glimmer of recognition slowly kicked in. It had only been 5 days since they had all dined together on the island but for Rosa it must have felt like a lifetime. The discovery of Ricardo's prostrate body, the whimpering dog, the broken whisky tumbler and the scissors embedded in the parquet floor. The arrival of the water ambulance and the speedy journey to Milan. Bob steered the two women towards the waiting area. Gisèle suggested that Bob should get three coffees whilst she grabbed a couple of plastic seats and sat down. Bob noted that the tell tale smile and twinkle in the eyes had gone. She looked tired and her hair was needing a good comb. He passed the plastic coffee beakers and pulled up a chair for himself. Gisèle was already in active conversation with Rosa who clearly was giving a full report in Italian. The concern on her face grew more pronounced as the story unfolded. Several minutes later Gisèle placed her hand in Rosa's and turned to Bob.

Bob was keen to establish the cause of Ricardo's malaise. 'Well, was it a heart-attack, a stroke or maybe just an accident?' He really was grasping at straws. He knew nothing of the circumstances.

Gisèle was keen to stifle her husband's excited speculation. She explained as best she could how Rosa had found Ricardo in the salon, Winston at his side and the pool of liquid and shards of glass. She wisely decided not to mention the scissors embedded in the floor. That detail could wait.

'So, what are the doctors saying? Surely they must have some idea?'

'Well,' Gisèle said slowly. She wanted to choose her words carefully conscious that her translation may overlook some important detail. 'It seems that his condition is serious but thankfully not life threatening. He was conscious when the medics picked him up but now he has been put into an artificial coma. He has a very high fever and severe breathing difficulties somewhat similar to the classic symptoms of *Polmonite,* Pneumonia that is. The specialist says that his immune system is strong and with luck he should pull through but it's going to take time.'

'Have they any idea how he might have contracted this bacteria or virus? I'm no expert in the right terminology.'

'For the moment it's not clear. Rosa has this wild theory that maybe it's connected to the lake water or even his cutlery collection. Ricardo had the habit of taking a regular early morning swim in the lake much to Rosa's disgust who thinks the water is dirty. I get the impression that Rosa has a bit of an obsession with cleanliness. She described his collection as being unclean. *Impuro, impuro* she kept saying.'

'Si, si, impuro, impuro.' Rosa interrupted. *'Impuro.'*

'So she's suggesting that he could have caught something from his knife and scissor collection?'

'Unlikely as that may sound, yes.'

'What's she going to do now? She can't be going back to the island alone.'

Gisèle spoke briefly to Rosa. There was much nodding and touching.

'She says that she has family living in Milan. She will be staying with them until Ricardo's situation changes. They live not far from the hospital.'

'And Winston the dog?'

'Il cane Rosa, il cane? Chi si sta curando di Winston?

'Il Postino?'

'Si, il Postino.'

'The postman will take the dog back to his house in Stresa – no problem!'

Linate airport was a short drive from the hospital. The late afternoon traffic was heavy but manageable. The last thing that Bob wanted was to be stuck in city traffic particularly Italian city traffic with the blaring horns, gesticulating drivers and scooters and *cinquecentos* cutting him up at every turn. As it transpired they dropped the Peugeot off in good time. The rental car girl was ultra efficient checking every square centimeter of the bodywork for signs of scratches and scrapes. Her officiousness annoyed Bob. He knew the car was in perfect condition and he was in no mood to humour a teenage pen pusher determined to find fault. He made a note to use a different rental company next time. As usual it was Gisèle who came to the rescue pushing Bob out of the way and chatting to the girl in her native language. It seemed to do the trick. She smiled warmly at Gisèle and taking the keys walked back to her office. Had the girl something against English men Bob wondered? His in-built English suspicion of foreigners sometimes rose to the surface on occasions such as these.

They arrived in 'Departures' with plenty of time to spare and managed to grab a plate of smoked salmon and a couple of glasses of *Valpollicella* at the salad bar. Bob's mood had not lightened since they'd left Rosa at the hospital, a combination of the change in the weather, the news of Ricardo and that feeling of anti-climax familiar to everyone at the end of a holiday. Their stay in Stresa and Cortona had been stimulating but now the interminable wait in the Departure Lounge surrounded by noisy children and chattering Italians did little for his mood. What he wanted right now was to be back at home, a glass of Armagnac in his hand and feet up by the fire.

✄

It was gone midnight by the time that Gisèle turned the key in the door of their house back in Sarlat. It was dark and cold, a heavy mist rising from The Dordogne. The drizzle that had accompanied them in Milan had now transformed into a steady rainfall back in France. The drive from Bordeaux Merignac had been slow in the rain and the poorly lit country lanes did not exactly help. Bob had prepared paper and kindling in the wood burner before they had left so within minutes of arriving there was a roaring fire. They pulled up a couple of armchairs and Bob poured two stiff Armagnacs.

'Here's to Ricardo and a speedy return to good health, *tchin, tchin*! I hope Rosa will be okay. She looked so frail and lost when we saw her this afternoon. It must have come as a terrible shock to her. Did you remember to give her our landline number so she can keep us up to date?' Bob knew very well that his wife had taken care of that. He hardly ever dared to question her unrivalled efficiency.

'Of course, she has all our numbers, plus e-mail and house address. Really Bob, I sometimes wonder whether I'm your secretary, personal assistant or wife. You really ought to think of some of these details yourself. But of course you're only a man what should I expect.'

Bob pulled a face and his wife stuck out her tongue in repost. 'I did the driving,' replied Bob. 'Well, most of it. Surely that makes for a fair division of labour.'

'That is a typical male answer which doesn't merit further discussion. Now, *Cherie* can you pour me another drink. I think I've deserved it.'

Bob refilled their glasses and switched on the radio to France Musique where a Debussy quartet was playing. He checked out his cell phone quickly realising that he had switched the phone off on boarding the plane and had forgotten to switch it back on again on arriving in Bordeaux. There were a couple of unread messages. The first from Mike his coproprietor at the language school to tell him that they'd got a group of ten Spanish students booked in for a week's intensive the following Monday. That would certainly keep him very busy and get his feet firmly back on the ground again after the Italian sojourn. The second message was from Clotilde at the cutlery museum. She said that she needed to speak to him as soon as possible. Her voice sounded strained.

'Something wrong?' Gisèle was good at picking up her husband's body language. Bob always signalled his emotions as clearly as if he was waving a flag. It showed in his eyes.

'Dunno, it's Clotilde in Nogent. You remember the curator at the cutlery museum. The one with the glasses and pony-tail.'

'Not your type, *Cherie*. Don't get too excited. What did she want?'

'Not sure, she sounded a bit agitated. Probably heard the news about Ricardo and wants to keep me up to date. Too late to ring back now, I'll give her a call in the morning. Now, how about rustling up something to eat. I'm starving. We haven't eaten since that plate of smoked salmon at Milan airport. I could just about manage a *croque monsieur* – nothing too heavy before bed.'

✄

By the time Bob awoke the following morning the sun had appeared and last night's rain had moved away to the north. Gisèle had already left for the village leaving a scribbled note on the kitchen table. 'Gone shopping – back around 12 – don't forget to ring Clotilde. P.S. The grass needs cutting. *Bisous* G.'

Bob plugged in the juicer and searched for the oranges. No oranges, of course. He would have to make do with cereal and coffee. By the time the coffee machine had warmed up and he had poured himself a bowl of cereal he was beginning to feel awake. He took his cup of *Americano* into the garden and took stock. Only a week since he was last here but already the garden had taken on its overgrown spring mantle. The purple and yellow irises were magnificent and Bob caught a whiff of their astringent pungent odour, the oriental poppies were already shedding their vivid red petals and the spiked blue agapanthus flowers were close to blooming. Their English roses were as ever the stars of the garden. The grass had certainly grown and Gisèle was right it did need cutting but it would have to wait, too damp at present, hopefully dry by the afternoon. He wiped down the seat of a garden chair with the sleeve of his bathrobe and took out his cell phone and called Clotilde's Nogent number. She answered almost immediately.

'Bob, hello, how are you? You received my message yesterday?'

'Yes, didn't listen to my messages until we arrived back from Milan late last night. I expect you rang to tell me about Ricardo Ceccaroli's illness? '

'Well, yes. You already know? How did you find out?'

Bob described how they had lunched with Ricardo and Rosa and then travelled down to Tuscany and by chance picked up a newspaper where they had learned about Ricardo being rushed to hospital in Milan and how they'd decided to call in at the hospital before flying back home yesterday.

'But listen Bob, before you say anymore. You don't know about Wang Lei?'

'Wang Lei. Who is Wang Lei? The name lurked hidden somewhere in the depths of his mind. Perhaps it had been Ricardo who had mentioned him the other day over lunch.

'Wang Lei is a Chinese collector. Didn't you see him at the auction house in Troyes? He would have been there to bid for the scissors. The biggest collector of 19th and 20th century European cutlery on the Asian continent.'

Bob suddenly remembered 'The Tailor's Dummy,' the immaculately coiffured guy in the smart suit, inspecting the scissors through an eyeglass. How he'd seen him caressing the handles. He'd pushed Ricardo all the way in the bidding war but had pulled out at the last minute.

'So, what about this Chinese collector?' asked Bob feeling increasingly anxious about the direction their conversation was heading.

'He's dead, Bob. Collapsed whilst attending a meeting of the local communist party in *Hubei province*. Cause of death unknown. He had only just returned home after his stay here in France.'

'Dead! Dead! Bob repeated. Are you sure of your information Clotilde? How on earth did you find out? The French media surely wouldn't have been interested in some obscure Chinese collector.'

'No, not the media but you remember when we were searching the database in my office to find the likely buyer of the scissors? As I explained at the time the museum keeps in contact with many of the leading cutlery collectors, manufacturers and salesrooms. News travels fast in the art world and I came across the news on a feed from an Asian English language collectors' Forum magazine 'Sharp Ends.''

'Strange that he should die around about the same time that Ceccaroli fell ill. Must be coincidence.' Bob felt the word hanging in the air and for several moments neither he nor Clotilde spoke.

Clotilde broke the silence. 'Yes, coincidence, I suppose, there can't be any other explanation can there?'

'Political? You say that he was at a communist party meeting, perhaps he'd made a few enemies in the Party hierarchy, stranger things happen in these places. Rich businessman travels abroad on the pretext of bidding for a pair of scissors at an auction, suspicious behaviour, contact with unknown officials in the French embassy in Beijing. Poison slipped into his coffee. Surreptitious poisoned dart. The imagination can go berserk over such events.'

'Sounds like something from a John Le Carré novel. It could of course have been natural causes,' Clotilde attempted to get the conversation back on a more rational track.

'Yes, I guess you could be right. Strange nevertheless.'

Bob updated Clotilde on their lunch with Ricardo and the bizarre relationship he had seemed to have had with his collection. He told her about the piece of theatre as he had shown him the scissors' new home, the music and the lighting. Clotilde said that she wasn't surprised at this behaviour as it was often the same expression of passion by ardent collectors who frequently had a quasi-religious relationship with their precious objects.

The agreed to keep in touch if either of them had any further news. It was becoming evident that Bob wasn't the only one to be obsessed with the scissors and all those who had any contact with them. He thought it might not be a bad idea to contact Hervé and Stephen and keep them up to date.

By the time Gisèle arrived home Bob had showered and dressed, gone through the mail and dug up a couple of lettuce and a handful of radishes from the veggie patch. He washed the salad poured some olive oil and seasoning into a salad bowl, tossed in a few leaves, thinly sliced some parmesan and finally added the radishes and several black olives. He uncorked a bottle of *Entre deux Mers* and put it into the fridge to chill.

Minutes later Gisèle staggered in through the back door struggling under the weight of the shopping.

'Give me a hand, *Cherie*. Forgot to take any carrier bags. The supermarket doesn't give away any plastic carriers nowadays and I wasn't going to pay three euros for a couple of so-called 'Eco-bags' when we have a cupboard full of them at home. Bloody climate change activists-when are they going to realise that it's not us that's the problem. They'll only be happy when we're all back living in caves. Go and talk to the Chinese and Indians but oh I 've forgotten that's not politically correct – wouldn't do to upset our nice Asian neighbours. Anyway, have you had a good morning? Nothing too strenuous I hope.' She added sarcastically. But then noting the salad bowl on the table and the place settings. 'Ah, how thoughtful of you to prepare lunch. Sorry, a bit flustered this morning – anti-climax after Italy. *Tu es un amour.*' She gave him a hug, opened the fridge door and took out the bottle of wine. 'I hope it's chilled. Have you spoken to Clotilde?'

Bob reached up and took two wine glasses from the shelf. Not fully chilled but it would do. He carefully poured the wine, sniffed the contents and held his glass up to the light at the same time murmuring a sound of approval to himself. 'Sit down and I'll fill you in with the details.'

'So, this Wang Lei guy. ' Gisèle was intrigued and somewhat anxious about the latest turn in events. She had listened to her husband's account of the auction a couple of times and was increasingly interested in the role of the Chinese. 'You met him at the auction. What was he like? Presumably he spoke English or French. Why come all that way to an auction when he could have bid by telephone?'

'Whoa, slow down, too many questions. I didn't actually meet him – well not face to face. I saw him talking to one of the auction room officials, he wanted a close-up look at the scissors. I got the impression he was speaking French. My guess is that he came in person to see the scissors in the flesh so to speak. Very well-dressed – he could have been a top model or a stand-in James Bond; immaculate suit, polished black shoes, everything about him shouted money and class, in fact awfully hard to imagine him as a member of the communist party – where was his little red book and worker's overalls?'

'You are joking I presume. The days of Mao are long since passed. From your description he sounds very cool.'

'Very cool! Come off it Gisèle. What's your definition of cool?'

His wife smiled knowing that she would have Bob on this one. 'French cool is all about style, the clothes you wear, the way you walk even the way you smoke a cigarette or hold a champagne glass. British so-called 'cool' means being covered in tattoos, scraggly bearded men who speak in grunts and women who don't smile and liberally make use of the word 'fuck' in all its wonderous connotations. You know what 'Coco' Channel said, 'Fashions change but style endures.' Only the French seem to understand that!'

Bob gave his wife's comments some serious consideration. Deep down he knew she was right. He'd met too many French people to think otherwise. He sometimes felt that since coming to live in France his existence was like playing a bit part in a movie. One of those films directed by Godard,

Chabrol, Lelouch or Truffaut with deep, hidden relationships, lobster thermidor in smoky Montmartre bistros, comic overtones and sex on the beach in Deauville or St Tropez. He only had a bit part of course but better that way to sit back and watch the major players. Are the French a reflection of their cinema or the cinema a reflection of the French? He was left pondering that riddle when Gisèle got back to the Chinese.

'You know, Bob the Chinese middle classes are growing in importance both financially and culturally, global travel and access to the best in western education is transforming the country. Forget your traditional Chinese stereotypes. But I'm still wondering why travel all this way only to touch a pair of scissors and then not outbid all the others to have ultimate possession?'

'Perhaps he had another motive?'

'Such as?

'No idea.'

'Not helpful, *Cherie*. I thought the English were masters of intrigue, Conan Doyle, Agatha Christie, Dorothy Sayers. You always come up with an answer.'

'I'll settle for Simenon. Inspector Maigret in seedy Parisian nightclubs and bordellos. Don't suppose there were any Chinese characters there, but if there were he or she would certainly not be up to much good and probably not a scissor collector. You don't really think that 'The Suit' had ulterior motives do you?'

'Pour me another glass of the lukewarm wine. Ulterior motives? The cut-throat world of scissor collectors. All this is making me thirsty. 'The Suit' is dead and I don't imagine that the Chinese authorities will be giving us a personal autopsy report on the cause of his demise. More importantly do you think we'll be getting an update on Ricardo's condition today? I'm sure Rosa would have called if there was any news. If we don't hear from her by this evening I'll give her a call.'

Bob served the last of the salad and drained the bottle. Perhaps he would get around to cutting the grass this afternoon he thought to himself. Hopefully the noise of the machine would drive the *couleuvres* away.

✂

By evening there was no news from Rosa. Bob kept saying that no news is good news but Gisèle was less sure. Judging from Rosa's comportment when they had met at the hospital she was clearly in a state of shock and if the worse had happened she would hardly be ringing a relative stranger with the bad news. By 9 O'clock it was getting to them. Bob poured his second double scotch and lit up his third cigar of the evening.

'Supposing he's dead.' Bob said morbidly. His earlier optimism had dissipated along with the cigar smoke. 'One of the most famous collectors of cutlery dead, another falling seriously ill within 2 days of one another both having bid for a pair of scissors at the same auction. Coincidence? Coincidence be damned. There has to be an explanation.'

Gisèle's cell phone rang. *La cucaracha* ring tone wildly out of sync with their mood. She answered. Bob came across and sat on the arm of her chair.

Ciao - '*Si, si, si* Rosa. *Si, si* Rosa.' Silence whilst Gisèle hoped that she was correctly interpreting the conversation. '*Si, si, bene, capisco.*' Another long silence from Gisèle. She was frowning. Frowning from concentration or frowning from concern? Maybe both, Bob wondered. He wished that he understood Italian. After several more minutes of frowning, head nodding and hair ruffling the conversation came to an end.

'*Ok, parleremo di nuovo domani. Arrivederci. Circa 20 ore.*'

'Well, come on , what did she say?'

Gisèle exhaled sharply, her right hand nervously rubbing her left arm. 'I just hope that I've understood correctly. Rosa has been with Ricardo all day. Apparently his condition is stable and the doctors are quietly optimistic but he's still in an induced coma and needs assistance with breathing.'

'Are they any nearer identifying the cause? Something he had eaten or something more sinister?' Bob was fully aware that they'd all shared the same table for Friday lunch and Ricardo was the only one to have fallen ill.

'From what Rosa understands it seems unlikely that his illness was connected with something he had eaten. We had all eaten the *Osso Bucco* and we're okay. She says that he had a strong constitution and was fastidious in his eating habits. They're still doing tests and hopefully they'll know more by tomorrow. I said I would call her about 8 tomorrow evening for further news.'

'How did she sound? I imagine you did not say anything about Wang Lei?'

'You must be joking Bob. Rosa sounded better than yesterday and certainly I wasn't going to further upset her with a strange story about the death of someone she presumably didn't know and who probably has no connection with either her or Ricardo.'

'Or so we think,' considered Bob.

'Now you're getting conspiratorial again, *Cherie*. How about some relaxing music and I think I've earned another drink.'

'You're becoming an alcoholic,'

'Yes, and it's all your fault. Put on some Keith Jarrett, the concert in Budapest is very soothing.'

Chapter Twenty-Five

The Following Day - Milan

Rosa took the taxi from her sister's apartment in the *Porta Venezia* district of the city to the hospital. It was a splendid sunny May morning and the city was beginning to take on its summer atmosphere. The parks were looking splendid and the café terraces were filling up with tourists but Rosa was too occupied with Ricardo's health to even notice. She had been with the Ceccaroli family since she was a young girl. She had been hired by Ricardo's father Alessandro and his sister Marie-Claire. Alessandro and she had become lovers some years after the death of Ricardo's mother in childbirth in 1955. When Alessandro died in 1986 he left most of his estate to his sister, Marie-Claire and his business interests to his only son Ricardo. Marie-Claire continued living on the island until her death at the grand old age of 98. She generously bequeathed a substantial pension to Rosa on condition that she stay on the island and look after Ricardo for the rest of his life. Rosa was happy to go along with this arrangement – it was in her interests to do so. If anything happened to Ricardo she could be left homeless. Alessandro had added a codicil to his will saying that if Ricardo died without issue the island and house would become the legal property of Ceccaroli Industries SpA. Milan. Rosa could face an uncertain future. Alessandro was probably the last in the

Ceccaroli line and unlikely to give up his precious collection and devote the last years of his life to a woman.

As the hospital loomed into view Rosa checked her phone. No new messages. Since she'd called Gisèle the previous evening to update her there had been no news from the hospital. The specialist in infectious diseases, Dr. Cattaneo had sounded cautiously optimistic but until they could find out the cause of Ricardo's illness he had told her she must not raise her hopes too much.

She entered the main entrance to the hospital, smiled a quick greeting at the receptionist and took the elevator up to the 6th floor intensive care unit. She spoke briefly to the duty nurse and opened the door to Ricardo's room. Inside it was eerily silent with just the heart monitor beeping its reassuring life message. Ricardo was hooked up to a multitude of monitors and sensors. An oxygen cylinder lay at the side of the bed and Ricardo's face was largely concealed by the oxygen mask. The lighting was low and Ricardo's eyes unblinkingly shut. Rosa pulled up a chair and focussed on his face. He looked peaceful and his skin seemed to have recovered something of its normal Mediterranean tint, the pale pallor of yesterday had disappeared. As she gazed at the prone figure she couldn't help recalling Ricardo as a small child, how she had shared much of the responsibility for his upbringing with Marie-Claire after the tragic death of his mother, Carmelita. At the beginning Alessandro had abdicated much of his fatherly responsibility, spending much of his time away dealing with the family business. It was rumoured that he spent his free time with a mistress tucked conveniently away in Venice but Alessandro had never spoken of this. Later as Ricardo reached adolescence his father showed more interest in his upbringing. He organised family holidays to Switzerland. Marie-Claire and Rosa invariably accompanied them. Rosa had never considered that Alessandro had any interest in her other than as the unofficial guardian of his son but one evening in Montreux all that changed. Marie-Claire had been feeling unwell and Ricardo had his head in a book on Pharaonic artefacts in Ancient Egypt. Alessandro suggested to Rosa that they have dinner together at the Casino, she ended up having too much to drink and the next thing she found herself in his bed. She couldn't deny that she found him attractive but the suddenness of it all came as a bit of a shock. She tried to step backwards from any further involvement but slowly their clandestine relationship grew and when back on the island she would frequently make the short trip from her bedroom to his when the rest of the house were sleeping. If Marie-Claire was aware of anything untoward she kept her council although most certainly she had some idea about her brother's relationship with women. Since the death of Carmelita, he seemed to increasingly cast himself in the role of a middle-aged lothario with lovers all over northern Italy. Rosa was happy to collude in this arrangement. Looking at the unconscious body of Ricardo she wondered why Alessandro's son had not shared his father's love of women. His obsession with Ancient Egyptian culture had begun at an early age and by the time he had finished working as an apprentice in the small Maniago cutlery workshop he had developed something of a reputation as an expert in cutlery manufacture and even started his own small collection. By 1980 the family company was booming and expanding into the growing European market. Ricardo had a flair for marketing and was always on the look-out for new opportunities. By the end of the 20th century the business was making a hefty profit as they diversified into the motor industry and invested in a lucrative small weapons branch.

Rosa turned as she heard the door to the room click open. It was Dr. Cattaneo. He placed his hand on her shoulder and whispered that they could talk outside.

'So, Signore Doctor, what is the news today? Has there been any progress in identifying the cause of Ricardo's illness?'

'I'm afraid not. The blood and urine samples are still at the laboratory, it may be some days before we have a definitive result. The good news is that his breathing has stabilised, and his heart rate is down. If all goes well in the next 24 hours we should be in a position to begin pulling him out of the artificial coma. Don't build your hopes up too much it will be some time before we can be sure that Signore Ceccaroli will make a complete recovery.'

Rosa felt reassured by the doctor's diagnosis, but she was still worried about the cause of his illness. She refuted any suggestion that it may have been some form of food poisoning and doubted whether any of his business rivals with mafia connections could possibly be involved. Privately she was unhappy with his purchase of the serpent-handled scissors. Hadn't his father Alessandro held strong superstitious beliefs about scissors and wasn't it the Englishman Bob Martin who only the other day had raised some serious concerns over the history of the scissors? She recalled Ricardo's enthusiasm on the day that the package arrived. She had always felt that nothing good would come of his purchase. She caught sight of the crucifix above the door and hastily crossed herself before saying goodbye to the doctor who continued on his daily round. Rosa returned to the bedside and sitting down took Ricardo's left hand in hers and whispered a silent prayer.

Chapter Twenty-Six

The Same Day - Nogent

Clotilde felt sure that there must be a connection between Ricardo's illness and the death of Wang Lei. It would be too much of a coincidence that two men, both well-known in the art world, both ardent cutlery collectors, both recently bidding for the same artefact should fall ill, one dying, at practically the same time from an undiagnosed, mystery illness. Thinking about the scissors and their rather lurid history was a somewhat melancholic occupation but Clotilde was hooked and her professional curiosity as well as a growing personal commitment drew her like a magnet. She did her best to rid herself of any notion of a curse or spell emanating from childhood memories of fairy tales – that would be too ridiculous for a rational mind to contemplate but the thought still would not leave her. She powered up her desk-top computer and started scrolling down the list of contacts that the museum had had over the years.

The museum was proud of its collection of folding knives, scissors, table cutlery, hand-tools, surgical implements and shaving items many of them going back to the 18th century. The museum had long played an important cultural role in the transmission of traditional skills from generation to generation and thus had dealt with collectors and artisans from all over the world as well as the public at large.

Together with a huge database of people whose interest was linked to cutlery the museum also had access to a multitude of trade journals and newsletters from other museums and workshops world-wide and it was with this in mind that Clotilde wondered what she could turn up on the deceased Wang Lei. She remembered how relatively easy it had been for her to find information on Ricardo Ceccaroli and now she wondered whether a search for the Chinese collector would be just as forthcoming.

Ten minutes later and she'd turned up several minor references to Wang Lei. Mostly they were to do with descriptions of various pieces held in Chinese museums and private collections but one longer piece seemed more promising. A collectors' journal written in English describing the Hangzhou Arts and Crafts museum in Hangzhou a large city about 200 kilometres southwest of Shanghai. Wang Lei had authored an article examining the role of swords, knives and cutting implements at the time of the Ming dynasty in the 14th and 15th centuries. She rapidly read through the document noting as she did so the expert understanding shown by Wang of what must have been a very niche area of study. He clearly knew his stuff but what caught her attention was the footnote at the end of the article which gave a brief biography of the writer.

Professor Yong Wang Lei has held the chair of Animal and Veterinary Epidemiology at the Huazhong University of Science and Technology since 2006. He is a senior member of the local branch of The Huazhong Peoples' Communist Party and an expert in the history of Chinese and Asian cold weaponry.

Clearly a man of many talents considered Clotilde. The story was becoming increasingly convoluted. Why would a man of his calibre travel thousands of kilometres to NOT buy a pair of rare scissors? Did he have another reason for being in France and was there any connection between his professional work and his interest in ancient Chinese weaponry?

She thought for a moment, tapped her pencil on the desk several times and reached for the phone.

Bob had just finished the first day of his English course with a new group of Spanish students. The usual hotch-potch. They were all supposed to be beginners but Bob knew from experience that the reality would be different. He'd already marked *faux debutante* next to several names, students whose knowledge of English was more than just 'beginner.' Some did this out of ignorance but most needed to be able to feel in control, to not to be seen to be struggling, to feel that they were better than the others. He'd done it himself when first starting French lessons many years ago. 'Ego Protection' he liked to call it. By the end of the week most of them would have made some progress, after that it would be up to them. Motivation was the key factor, those who really wanted to learn the language would work hard to do so, those who didn't, would fall by the wayside and the best teachers in the world could do little to help those who couldn't help themselves.

His phone rang. It was Clotilde.

'Hi Bob, how are you? Any news?'

'Hello, Clotilde. I'm fine. Just a little weary after a day of teaching. The good news is that Ricardo Ceccaroli is now in a stable condition. He's been brought out of his coma but he's still being kept in intensive care for the time being. Gisèle spoke to Rosa yesterday and she is feeling optimistic but she is a little anxious about a lack of news on the origin of Ricardo's illness. The medics are privileging some kind of virus but they're not prepared to commit themselves until further tests are carried out. What about you? A busy day in the museum?'

'No very quiet. So quiet in fact that I've had some time to do some research of my own. I have discovered something interesting about our deceased Chinese collector, Wang Lei.'

'Really! Go ahead, I'm all ears.'

'Pardon, Bob. You are all what? I didn't catch your last phrase.'

'All ears. It's an English phrase that means I am listening carefully.'

Clotilde laughed self-consciously. 'Sorry Bob, I do wonder if my English will ever become fluent. So many phrases and expressions to learn.'

'Don't worry Clotilde, your English is very good. Just give it time and keep practicing. Anyway do continue.'

'Well, it seems that our friend Wang is more complicated that we first thought. I turned up a document he'd written a couple of years ago about knives in the Ming Dynasty. I won't bore you with the details but the article gave a brief biography and it turns out that our friend 'The Suit' as you like to call him is only a part-time expert in cutting tools. He has another job.'

'Another job? What sort of other job?

'He is no less than an academic professor in a top Chinese University. What do you think his speciality is?'

'Speciality?' Bob considered for a moment. 'Probably a history prof, archaeologist, something like that?'

'No, nothing so obvious. Professor Yong Wang Lei is professor of Epidemiology in the faculty of animal and veterinary research at the University of Huazhong.'

'Professor of Epidemiology? Is there a connection there with scissor collecting? If there is I can't see it?'

'No, of course not. No connection, but could his premature death be linked to his job? You must remember a lot of fuss a couple of years ago about viral epidemics being caused by viruses crossing over from animals to people. Think of those ideas about AIDS originating from monkeys and bird flu infecting humans, to say nothing of your famous 'mad-cow disease.'

'What are you suggesting Clotilde? That our Mr. Wang or should I say Professor Wang was involved in animal experimentation?'

'Well, it's just a thought. More ridiculous things happen. Supposing Wang in spite of strict hygiene measures managed to catch something as a result of his experiments. Innocently he goes about his life, attending meetings and so on and then suddenly he collapses and dies.'

'So,' concluded Bob. 'It was just a coincidence that he happened to be taken ill at a Party meeting. No suggestion of a communist conspiracy to bump off one of its members who for whatever reason incurred the wrath of the powers that be.'

'It's just a thought,' Bob 'but you have to admit that it's all a little strange.'

'.........and Ricardo. Where does he fit in to all this? Can't be possible that Ceccaroli is suffering from the same infection which somehow jumped from China to Italy. Where's the common link?'

Silence on the other end of the line before both Bob and Clotilde uttered the same word at the same moment. 'The scissors!'

He promised Clotilde that he would get back to her when he had further news on Ricardo. After switching off his phone he grabbed a coffee from the machine and pausing to light a cigar he strolled outside and sat down on a bench overlooking the River Dordogne. He thought back to the morning at the auction room in Troyes and tried to conjure up his memory of Wang moments before the start of the auction. He smiled to himself when he recalled thinking that this well-dressed Chinese looked like a Tailor's dummy in an old Burton's bespoke men's wear shop. He had used a small eyeglass to examine the scissors and Bob had wondered what detail he was hoping to see. He seemed to be caressing the blades but he could just have been testing their sharpness. At the time Bob had been more preoccupied with whether he would bid himself for the scissors than to notice too much about a stranger.

Recalling their dinner together at his island home Bob remembered Rosa's comments on how Ricardo treated his objects like lovers and how she warned him of the germs that might be lurking on them. Perhaps it was just Rosa's sense of humour or maybe jealousy? Bob recalled Rosa saying something about scissor superstitions or had that been Ricardo telling Bob about his father's warning about sharp tools? Bob was beginning to feel that it was all part of a very bad dream.

Bob was still feeling in a confused state by the time he arrived home. Gisèle had been busy with one of her cookery classes and the kitchen had been transformed into something resembling a Neapolitan back street with strings of pasta of all shapes, colours and sizes replacing the drying washing strung from balcony to balcony. Fighting his way under and over the green and beige garlands of *capellini, tagliatelle, vermicelli, rigatoni* and *spaghetti* he caught site of his wife sitting in the garden glass of white wine in hand.

'You've arrived at the right moment, *Cherie.* Bring another glass from the cupboard. How has your day gone? Your Spanish students not too demanding I hope.'

Bob pulled up a plastic garden chair, kissed his wife and poured himself a generous glass of *Sauvignon.* 'Not too bad, I suppose for the first day. A lively bunch from Barcelona, couldn't stop them from speaking Spanish all the time. They will insist on translating every word and analysing the grammar in detail instead of listening to context and the entire phrase. Suppose it's only to be expected.'

'You've forgotten that you were probably the same when you started learning French.'

'Yes, I guess you're right. Anyway more to the point I had a fascinating call from Clotilde in Nogent just as I finished my last class. She has dug up some interesting background stuff on the Chinaman. It seems that he is, or should I say was, a high-flying academic in a prestigious university faculty studying epidemiology and animals. Clotilde's proposition is that Wang may have been doing research into viruses that cross the animal human barrier. Supposing that Prof Wang discovered such a link and somehow became infected himself. It's very speculative I know, but it is a theory that could explain a lot don't you think?'

Gisèle looked sceptical. 'You are presumably then going to make a connection between Wang, Ricardo and the scissors?'

'A bit of a long shot I agree but not that outrageous if you consider that both Wang and Ricardo fell ill.................'

Gisèle cut him short. 'Wait a moment. I must tell you something that will most certainly destroy your theory *tout de suite*. I spoke to Rosa at lunchtime. She called me to say that the test results on Ricardo have come through. Apparently, the cause of his malaise was most certainly due to swallowing infected water on his daily swim in the lake. Not only had the Milanese laboratory come to this conclusion but they'd asked another lab in Rome to double check and they reached the same conclusion. Some kind of bacteria often found in lake water. Rosa kept calling it ARI and said that it caused severe breathing problems. I didn't understand everything she was saying but I checked it out on a French medical website. ARI is Acute Respiratory Illness and can be caused by swallowing infected water. In Ricardo's case there is a suspicion that there may be something called *algal toxins* in some fresh water sources which possibly are caused by chemicals used in agricultural sites close to the lake. I wonder if the lake authorities have done any recent tests on the water. There was quite a fuss a few years ago about pollution levels in Italian lakes, suspicions of *e-coli*. I would imagine that Ricardo would have been aware of the risks?'

'Perhaps he thought the risk worth taking. After all he has lived by the lake for most of his life. Anyway, that apart. The conclusion is that there is no connection with Wang?'

'No Chinese connection, Bob. Don't be too disappointed. You weren't really looking for a link to the scissors were you?'

'No, not really but it would have been a neat resolution. It would have provided a fitting end to the imagined curse of the scissors. On the positive side the others who have encountered the scissors since 'The Suit' touched them are not at risk including that abomination of a secretary at the auction house.'

'And who might this so-called abomination be if I may ask?'

Bob chuckled. 'Oh, just an unbelievably bad example of the French Administrative Class. Not worthy of further mention. Anyway, changing the subject how is Ricardo?'

'Rosa said he was now conscious, breathing unaided and due to move out of intensive care tomorrow if all is well. He'd spoken to Rosa and sounded in good spirits.'

'Well, that's something positive. Perhaps life can return to something approaching normality now, although I must confess to having got a bit of a buzz from all the intrigue. I'm sure that Clotilde will be disappointed, I think that she saw herself as a budding Agathe Christie.'

'But there is still one unanswered question which I'm sure hasn't escaped my dear Hercule Poirot's attention.'

'Oh, yes. Why on earth did Wang travel all that way for an auction to not buy the scissors? He could have arranged to bid by telephone or by proxy. Unless, hm, unless he had another reason for being in France?'

'*Voila Cherie!* There's something else for you to ponder in your idle moments.'

'I don't think I'll bother. What do you mean by 'in my idle moments?' I don't have any.'

Bob drained his glass and with a long sigh of satisfaction announced. 'No, now I'm going back to my obsession with sex hungry serpents.'

Gisèle laughed and refilled their glasses. They looked out across the garden in its late spring splendour, clinked glasses and smiled.

'Do you think that now might be a suitable time to cut the grass, Cherie?'

'Um, not sure if I should after two glasses of wine. Drunk in charge of a motor-mower? Might mangle a couple of grass snakes. Yuk! Let's finish the bottle.'

Chapter Twenty-Seven

Three Days Later - Milan

Ricardo Ceccaroli sat up in his bed. He had just been moved out of intensive care and now he was looking out of the window of his private room at the distant silhouette of the *Duomo* of Milan. The Cathedral of the nativity of Saint Mary, one of the largest and most majestic religious edifices in Europe. He'd visited it often and had even received his first communion there as a 12-year-old. The Archbishop of Milan was a family friend yet another member of the local religious hierarchy unaware of Ricardo's hypocritical and often wavering faith.

This morning the sunlit view of the cathedral stirred something strangely new in Ricardo. He felt different. He didn't know how close to death he had been but his memories of the last few days had been hazy. He remembered nothing of his arrival at the hospital. His last memory had been looking at the scissors in his library, talking to Winston and then the sudden pain and blackout. He had sensed Rosa's presence at his bedside but little else. He thought he had heard her praying but it could have been his imagination. He looked at the crucifix on the wall opposite and wondered.

Now he was anticipating a visit from Doctor Cattaneo the specialist in charge of his case. Frank Cattaneo had built up a Europe wide reputation as a fine bacteriologist, but he was also known for his stern views and inflexibility when it came to professional relationships. Ricardo had yet to have a conversation with the great man but the nurses had warned him to let the Doctor talk and not to dispute his advice. Ricardo was used to working with tough business associates and even politicians but then he was sure of his ground. Medicine wasn't on his *curriculum vitae*.

Cattaneo certainly cut an eccentric figure with his shoulder length grey hair and beard. His surgical coat was unbuttoned revealing a white tee shirt emblazoned with the blue, black and white circle logo of the local soccer club 'Inter.' His tall stature and slight frame gave him a slightly comical look, something akin to Jacques Tati's Monsieur Hulot character in the film *Monsieur Hulot's holiday*.

'Buongiorno Signore Ceccaroli. Come ti senti oggi?'

Ricardo tried to sit up a little further in the bed but he ached and a wave of fatigue swept up his body. 'Happy to be alive, Doctor.'

Cattaneo didn't react to his patient's comment. He pulled up a chair and sat at the side of the bed.

'You're approaching your 65th birthday I see from your records. The age when many people will be looking forward to a quiet retirement. If I may say so your company has posted high profits for the last few years. I guess that you're not short of money so why not use it to enjoy the last part of your life. Leave the running of the company to some of those high-flying Business School graduates we hear so much about these days. Perhaps invest in a swimming pool and give up your morning poisoning session in the lake. You could have died you know. Take my advice, it's not too late to change your lifestyle. I gather you're not married. Plenty of attractive fish in the sea looking for the right bait, if you get my meaning.

Ricardo wasn't sure that he liked what he was hearing but he was too weak to argue. Interesting that a physician should be such a keen follower of the financial markets. It was true that Ceccaroli Industries was doing well, profits had risen on average by five percent a year over the last three years and a raft of new contracts had come in from European and Japanese carmakers keen to get into the electric vehicle market. The company had moved on from its days of purely making fine cutlery and small arms, it was thanks to Ricardo that he had foreseen how the business could expand and had poached several young and ambitious marketing and management specialists from Fiat and Pirelli with promises of rapid promotion and high salaries. So far his strategy had proved successful and the shareholders were content. Perhaps now would be a good time to hand over the reins.

As for marriage. It had never really been an option that he had seriously considered. He had been 'married' to the company for all these years and his spare time was taken up with his collection and the search for rarer and more beautiful artefacts. He couldn't imagine finding a wife who would possible share his passion for knives, forks and scissors.

Cattaneo stood up and patted Ricardo's arm. 'Think about what I've said. *Abbiamo solo una vita.* Just one life and stay away from swimming in the lake.'

He must have dozed for a couple of hours. Not fully rested Cattaneo's advice had troubled him. He was still pondering his words when the duty nurse entered the room in somewhat of a fluster announcing that Ricardo had a visitor. He hardly felt like entertaining. Probably someone from the company he thought and Rosa wasn't due until the afternoon. He certainly wasn't expecting a visit from the clergy. Cardinal Abramo strode into the room in a bustle of clerical garb imbued with the distinctive smell of incense.

'Ricardo, my friend. How unfortunate to find yourself in this sorry state. Are they treating you well? Good food? Keeping you away from the bottle? May God bless you my son.'

Ricardo reached for the Cardinal's right hand to kiss the episcopal ring but Abramo withdrew his hand. 'His Holiness has forbidden the kissing of rings. He says that it is better to avoid possible transmission of infections. In your present state, my friend it would be better to follow the Pontiff's advice.'

'Certainly, Your Eminence but I assure you that I am recovering and hopefully will soon find myself back in my home. This is a pleasant surprise. I am very grateful for Your Eminence's concern.'

'The whole of Milan has heard of your unfortunate malady. I could do nothing less in respect of my old friend's health but I am more concerned for your spiritual well-being. When was the last time that you took mass or made the act of confession? Would you like me to hear your confession this morning?'

Ricardo closed his eyes trying to remember the last time that he had been to confession and wondering what on earth he could find to confess to today. He speculated on whether he had been guilty of worshipping false prophets when he had caressed the scissors and if giving your life over to a collection of cutlery could count as selfishness. When he had gone to confession as an adolescent he had found it easy to invent a few transgressions to keep the priest happy, carnal longings for Bianca Derosa or sneak peaks at Cianna Mariani's breasts usually did the trick only eliciting a couple of 'Hail Mary's' but he couldn't fall foul of the system by using the same 'sin' each confession so sometimes he would risk stealing cigarettes from his uncle or copying his homework from his friend Giuseppe. There were real sins which he never dared repeat but then he'd never considered dishonesty a real sin after all didn't everyone tell little white lies from time to time?

This morning he didn't feel in the mood for playing games. Perhaps better to be completely honest and confess his weakened faith and throw himself on His Eminence's merciful presence. However, he was saved from going down that precarious route by Abramo's compassion for his old friend.

'I can see that you're feeling weak, Ricardo. It would be unfair of me to put too much pressure on you at the moment. After all this is not the moment for your last rites.' The Cardinal smiled at his own dark humour. 'We will leave the confession until you are back in good health. Meanwhile reflect on what you will say when you eventually meet your Maker. Remember what Saint Matthew said. *'Do not accumulate for yourselves treasures on earth, where moth and rust destroy and where thieves break in and steal.''* Cardinal Abramo crossed himself and laid his hand on Ricardo's head. '*Che Dio vi benedica figlio mio.* God bless you my son.'

He was left to contemplate the Cardinal's words and the advice of Dr. Cattaneo. What was so wrong with earthly treasures? After all they did make him happy didn't they? As for thieves breaking in and stealing his treasured collection hadn't he only recently installed a state of the art anti-theft system with cameras and movement detectors? The thought made him reach for his cell phone in the bedside cupboard. He switched it on and was greeted by a string of text messages from colleagues and other well-wishers. He would deal with them later but for now he clicked on his security app. The menu consisted of several small camera icons each dedicated to the surveillance of a different part of the island villa. He clicked on the camera installed in his 'treasure room.' Immediately his collection was illuminated. All was in place except, except for the scissors but then he recalled that on his last night at home he had taken the scissors from their cache to examine them more closely. He switched to the *il soggiorno* cam which gave a 360 degree view. He scanned the room, the chairs, the bookcases, the escritoire no sign of the scissors. He felt a growing sense of panic until at last he saw them. There they were, in the corner, one blade embedded in the floorboarding. How had they ended up there, he wondered? His father's words came flooding back to him as he spoke of scissor superstitions. How scissors could create but how they could also kill. Wasn't it once thought that scissors stuck in the floor by their blades foretold a funeral?

From outside he could hear the bells of the *Duomo* tolling midday. Ricardo put down his phone and shuddered.

Chapter Twenty-Eight

Two Months Later - End of July

In the Dordogne the fine late spring weather turned into hot summer. The hottest July for a century claimed the climate statisticians and August was predicted to be even hotter. Bob had always been a bit of a climate change sceptic; he still remembered the dire warnings of a new ice age back in the 70's and what on earth had happened to acid rain which was predicted to destroy all our trees in the 80's? As for the ozone layer the less said the better. However, even Bob the sceptic was beginning to have doubts as the thermometer regularly smashed the 40° barrier. The river level had dropped substantially but that didn't deter the tourists or the kayak concessionaires who profited in equal measures. River tourism was growing in popularity all over France as a viable alternative to a crowded beach, no more so than on the Dordogne one of the most beautiful and accessible of French water ways. In Sarlat Bob wasn't complaining, his English classes finished in mid-July and the grass had stopped growing weeks ago so he could now look forward to spending a few days with Grandson George and his family, a long-awaited trip to Euro Disney followed by a week soaking up the sun on the beaches of Ile de Ré. The rest of his time he could devote to reading and preparing his courses for the *rentrée* in September.

The hot, sultry evenings suited him. Nothing he liked better than sitting outside at midnight, a cold glass of beer to hand, listening to the cicadas, watching the circling bats and smoking a good cigar. He reckoned he did his best thinking at this time of the day. Gisèle preferred the company of the late-night television chat shows, popular in France but not to Bob's liking who found the humour humourless, the music rooted in the past and too derivative, the politics adversarial. Bob found it hard to understand why France seemed to be always in election campaign mode. No sooner had one election finished than the candidates were queuing up to announce their candidacy for the next one. Not that he disliked all television programmes. Some of the documentaries were first rate and the French made excellent films which were often a breath of fresh air compared to their Hollywood counterparts. A lot of romping and bonking normally placed about 20 minutes into the script followed by a round or two of family disputes usually set in a holiday location on the Cote d'Azur, Brittany or Normandy and ending in a motorway service station in the rain where the central character, usually a man, is alone in his Renault 12 searching for a packet of cigarettes. The wipers judder across the windscreen as the credits start to roll. All very existential, all very French!

Down in Béziers Stephen and Hervé's first year as *vignerons* was going well. Proximity to the Mediterranean had cooled the unseasonal heat but that hadn't stopped their anxiety over the grapes ripening too soon and worrying about the correct balance between too much or too little sun. The dry weather had been tempered by the coastal humidity which had helped the growth potential. The developing grapes were a good size and there was no evidence of skin burning which would have been a disaster. Their associates in the cooperative had explained the importance of grape balance and tannin structure and how the *Grenache* grape could produce delicate strawberry and raspberry flavours such as found in many of the *Côte de Rhone* wines like *Chateauneuf-du-Pape* or some of the up-and-coming Australian reds.

Stephen left the technical details to Hervé. Marketing was his responsibility and already he was planning his publicity handouts and web site. The farm shop had had a good season. Since he and Alice had started the enterprise a few years back its reputation had grown but most of the customers were from the local area and both Stephen and Hervé had set their sights on more distant horizons tempting more tourists off the well-beaten tracks and staking a niche in the lucrative mail order market. The launching of their very own wine would hopefully add that important extra touch.

They were both looking somewhat apprehensively at the coming harvest. *Le temps des vendange* was fast approaching. Normally in the south-west the grape picking begins at the end of August and by the beginning of August they needed to be organising their workforce. The cooperative relied on hand-picking which necessitated a committed and strong group of workers. Stephen was also thinking a little further ahead to the launching of their first *recolte*. Their first bottling would take place in September and they would have to wait another year before the first uncorking could take place. They were planning a launch of the appellation *Domaine des Tournesols* in the coming Autumn and this would give Stephen and Hervé their first big marketing opportunity to really get Alice's brainchild off the drawing board and onto the map.

Ricardo Ceccaroli left the *Milan Ospedal Maggiore* 4 weeks after the fateful night in his library. The day was hot and he was looking forward to getting back to the relative freshness of his island home. Dr. Frank Cattaneo had given him the all clear but not before warning him once more of the perils of swimming in the lake. Another mouthful of *Algal Toxins* would do for him. His immune system could hardly be expected to fight off another respiratory virus. Rosa was delighted to get back to the villa. *Il Postino* returned with Winston who seemed to have enjoyed his daily boat ride delivering and collecting mail to and from lake residents. However, he was clearly overjoyed by his return to the familiar sounds, sights and smells of the island and smothered Ricardo in a lavish show of doggy affection. On arriving back home Ricardo's first task was to go to the *soggiorno*. It felt strange being back on the island.

Paradoxically he had felt somewhat normal in the hospital. He had established a daily routine, meals brought to him on a tray three times a day, a regular stream of visitors some welcome others not so, the feeling that others were caring for him and that all responsibility and worry had been taken out of his hands. Now, back at home the atmosphere loomed heavy. Rosa was back with him, a long list of functions to be carried out in order to see that Ricardo continued his recuperation, dietary arrangments, medication, what to eat and what not to eat, no alcohol, no cigars and twice weekly visits from a private nurse charged with checking blood pressure, heart-rate and lung capacity.

The *soggiorno* smelt musty after being closed off for several weeks. Before Ricardo returned Rosa had opened the window to freshen the room up a little. She had cleaned the whisky -stained floor and most importantly prised the scissors from the floorboard where they had stubbornly remained since she had thrown them away in terror and horror the night that Ricardo had been taken ill. She picked them up with a sense of disgust. She placed them on the desk, stood back and looked at them from what she considered to be a safe distance. The snake handles and the engraved initials looked somewhat dulled compared to the last time she had seen them but she was adamant that she wasn't going to touch them ever again. From now on cleaning was to be Ricardo's responsibility.

Winston hesitated before the panelled door and looked up at his master as if asking 'what now?' Ricardo retrieved the scissors from the *escritoire.* He didn't look at them closely but he could feel the shape of the blades and the shallow indentation of the 'K' and 'T.' The key was still where he had left it, in the navel of the cherubic nymph. He entered the 'sanctuary', switched on the overhead light and placed the scissors back into the glass case. He switched off the light, closed the door and turned the key. Putting the key back in his jacket he patted the pocket, looked down at Winston and whispered, *'La vita è un viaggio e solo io tengo la chiave.'* Life is a journey and only I hold the key.'

Chapter Twenty-Nine

Two Weeks Later - August

Predictions of hot August nights had been accurate. Daytime temperatures were regularly in the low 40's and the nights were becoming insufferable. Bob took a cold beer from the fridge and pulled up a sun lounger on the edge of the scorched brown lawn. To the west a milky quarter moon was slowly rising through the evening heat. The sprinkler slowly rotated over the vegetable patch giving the precious tomatoes and aubergines their daily soaking. He was doubtful that the local authorities would allow the use of non-essential sprinklers for too much longer, he had a special concession to take water directly from the Dordogne River itself but rumours of limiting the concession were rife and you didn't need a degree in hydrology to see that the river level was exceptionally low even for the month of August.

He quaffed from the bottle, inserted his ear pods and made the connection with his cell-phone. He ran down the list of music on his streaming service uncertain as to what might suit his mood this evening. Streaming had transformed listening in recent years. The availability of millions of recordings meant that you were spoilt for choice. Gone were the days when you could check out your own collection of treasured 'Rock' or 'Classic' albums sitting on the shelf in vinyl, cassette or CD form. The music was your own or at least it gave the illusion of belonging to you. Now it belonged to the world. He wanted to listen to a new Morricone film collection but then suddenly changed his mind as he scrolled through a playlist of 50 and 60's favourites. A hint of nostalgia on a night like this, Bob thought. A bit of Elvis, Marty or Cliff. Perhaps throw in an assortment of Piaf, Brel, Aznavour or Trenet. My god he thought to himself the list is endless. Why should he feel guilty about feeling nostalgic?

Gisèle was sprawled out on the sofa in front of the TV. Overhead a rotating fan moved the air gently. Both she and Bob had agreed that modern air-conditioning units were not 'eco-friendly' so they had gone for traditional ventilator fans which Bob romantically imagined conjured up images of colonialist India or a scene from a Graham Greene novel. Tonight, she was watching her favourite Saturday night chat show. *'Samedi Soir en direct'* – 2 hours of chat, music, politics and scandal as *'Tele7jours'* magazine liked to bill it, hosted by the ever popular and affable Alain Baleine. Perfect late-night viewing and no need to worry about getting up early tomorrow morning. Most of it was 'popcorn TV' not too demanding on the senses unless you happened to be English in which case it was 'level 3 competence' in everyday French i.e., moderate level of difficulty. The politics slot was generally more instructive and Gisèle was always interested in how the guests squirmed and wormed their way round the questions. Compared to political shows in the US or UK this was fairly tame stuff. Most journalists preferred the light touch and if as often rumoured their jobs could be at risk if the questioning became too menacing they consequently avoided anything too controversial or embarrassing. The cosying up that went on between certain journalists and politicians disturbed Bob. At least that was his opinion, an opinion not shared by his wife who considered the Anglo-Saxon journalists too aggressive and invasive, always looking to trip up their guests. Generally, Gisèle had a great respect for UK television with its eclectic range of drama, comedy and documentary but she loathed the 'reality' shows which everyone seemed obliged to watch and which provided the tabloids with their next day headlines. The English 'herd' instinct as opposed to French individualism.

Tonight's political interview was proving to be interesting. Gisèle sat up from the sofa as she picked up a couple of intriguing phrases coming from a high profile left-leaning investigative journalist.

'Would you consider this to be the unfreezing or paradoxically hardening of Franco-Chinese relations?' asked Baleine. 'Rumours of secret visits to The Elysée Palace by Chinese academics have been rife for some time now. Are the French public being deliberately kept in the dark?'

Gisèle shouted outside to Bob. '*Cherie* come in and listen to this.' Bob was in the middle riff of 'Purple Haze' and Hendrix's playing drowned out his wife's call.' She opened the patio door and yelled 'serpents!' It had the desired effect. Bob jumped up spilling his beer on the deck chair. He knew his wife was winding him up but nevertheless it aroused the usual goose pimples. How could anyone shiver on such a hot evening he wondered.

'What on earth do you want? Interrupting Hendrix is practically a capital crime and the 'S' word is taboo.'

'It's that investigative journalist from *Mediascan*. You know the one you can't stand.'

'Oh, you mean the guy with the Stalin moustache and smirk. What has he unearthed this time?'

Mediascan an on-line independent journal had become a very sharp thorn in the side of successive French governments. It was they who had first broken the Sarkozy-Gaddafi affair when the ex-President had allegedly received millions from the Libyan dictator, money which was channelled into the Sarkozy re-election campaign.

'Sorry about that, but you must come and watch this.' Bob huffed and puffed but eventually sat down next to his wife on the sofa. He detached his ear pods and attempted to get his mind back into French language mode.

'Secret Chinese links to The Elysee.' She whispered by way of explanation as the interview continued. 'Links denied by the government – listen!'

The *Mediascan* journalist, Jacques Le Breton was explaining that a leak from the office of the Foreign Minister had suggested that a high-ranking Chinese politician and academic working in the field of animal epidemiology had come to France on the pretext of meeting similarly minded French researchers. The rumours suggest that he had made an important breakthrough in his animal research which potentially could have military implications and that the Chinese authorities were targeting dissidents in Taiwan and Hong Kong.

Baleine stepped in to ask what was meant by 'military implications.'

'For some time now there has been a suggestion that the Chinese want to find a way of reclaiming control over Taiwan. Overt military intervention might prove to be too dangerous and risk an escalating conflict with the Americans and their allies. Many in the west have been looking for an excuse to confront China over its human rights abuses, increasing commercial control over communications technologies and pouring millions of yuans into Africa. China is increasingly seen as a not too well-hidden threat to western democratic traditions. We have already seen how the people of Hong Kong have been subjected to harsh new laws shutting down free speech and any move to re-democratise the former British Colony. The Chinese may have discovered a more subtle means of control.'

'Meaning what?'

'Meaning using some form of bacteriological warfare. Our inside source suggests that the leading Chinese researcher was experimenting with animal-human crossover viruses. It seems that his research had purely peaceful objectives possibly to counteract future virus mutations that have been linked to diseases such as avian flu. He published the research; the Chinese authorities saw possible uses for the virus perhaps for population control or more devious applications.'

'So why come to France?'

'It seems that our Chinese academic was a bit of a Francophile. He was interested in western culture and in his spare time he liked to collect artefacts that told the story of the development of our culture. As France was the instigator of universal human rights it seemed only natural that he approach the French government first to warn the world of the potential misuse of his discovery.'

'And do we know his name?'

'Unfortunately, no. We have approached the Ministry of Foreign Affairs to find out more. As of this morning the Ministry has denied all knowledge of any such meeting and describes our story as 'fanciful.''

A screenshot of the latest on-line *Mediascan* report with the headlines **'High level cover-up of lethal Chinese bug?'** appears on the studio's giant screen. Applause from the studio audience – cut to next guest, rap celebrity cum actor Joey Starr. Anchor man Baleine on his feet clapping wildly, generic music, whoops and shouts from the studio audience.

Gisèle took the remote control and cut the sound. She looked at her husband, concern and surprise on her face but it was Bob who got in with the first word.

'What are the odds of there being two Chinese academics specialising in animal human virus mutation and collectors of cultural artefacts?'

'Pure speculation,' replied his wife. 'Where is the evidence? Who is responsible for the leak? Why would the Foreign Ministry want to block a story such as this?'

'Dafter things happen. I'm no 'tin hat' conspiracy theorist but aren't we back to our old friend coincidence again? It's a bloody good coincidence I must admit. If it's not coincidence then I'm privy to some very interesting evidence. If this is really Wang Lei does the journalist from *Mediascan* know that he's dead and are they aware of his appearance at the *Brunhes & Poitou* auction house bidding for a pair of scissors that he had no intention of buying?'

'Cover up.'

'What do you mean cover up?'

Gisèle swept her hair from her eyes. 'Supposing that Wang is who we think he is. He comes to France on the pretext of bidding at an auction for a collector's piece. That's the cover up. Presumably the Chinese authorities knew of his interest in Western cultural artefacts and just possibly he had permission to contact researchers in the same medical field perhaps at the Institute Pasteur or some other research lab. All very innocent so far. The next bit is very speculative………'

Bob picked up the thread. 'So, he tips off one of the top guys at 'The Institute' who has high level contacts in the government. He arranges a rendezvous and warns the French government of the Chinese plans. Somebody leaks the details of the meeting to an investigative journalist and bingo!'

'And his death? Suspicious? Killed by his own discovery or murdered by 'The Party' when they discover what he had been up to. A bit far-fetched at first sight perhaps but plausible on reflection– what do you think?'

'Too many ifs and buts. We can't be certain it's the same man. We have no idea of the cause of death. We don't know whether he contacted other medical researchers and we are assuming that there was contact between the top academic researchers and the government, not forgetting the reliability of the journalist himself. Do *Mediascan* have a strong track record?'

'I'm no expert on investigative journalism but if you check out the *Mediascan* web site you'll find that they have exposed quite a few well-known politicians and their acolytes including Sarkozy, Bettencourt, and Cahuzac not forgetting the recent Benalla affair.'

Bob looked at his wife and smiled. 'I'll take your word on that. I think I'd better text Clotilde to see if she's up to date on all this. Probably safely tucked up in bed at this hour I'll bet.'

✂

Clotilde had stayed up late. The thought of going to bed on such a hot night had kept her in front of the television longer than usual. She had taken a cold shower and poured herself a glass of iced Perrier. By the time she received Bob's text message she was already in a bit of a spin. At first she hadn't paid too much attention to the guy from *Mediascan*. With only half an ear on what he was saying she had untied her ponytail and was busy brushing her hair out. It was only when she heard the words 'animal-human cross over virus' that she sat up and began to pay attention. Without any detailed descriptions or actual names there was little to suggest that the man could have been Wang Lei. The journalist had mentioned the field of research and the academic background of the mystery man but in a country with such a large population there were bound to be many people working in similar areas. She wasn't surprised when her phone buzzed an incoming message and saw Bob's name.

'Mediascan investigation reported on Baleine's TV show tonight. Is it our Chinese scissor man? Can you get it on replay and get back to me with your thoughts?'

She rang Bob straight back. 'Hope I've caught you still up.'

'You bet, after watching the show tonight I doubt that I'd be able to sleep anyway – what with the heat as well. Did you catch all of the report?'

'I think so. I understand that *Mediascan* are exploring a leak from the Foreign Ministry and following up on the idea that a 'mystery' Chinese academic has been warning the French government on a possible biological warfare threat against Taiwan and Hong Kong. Sounds like something out of James Bond movie. Don't you think it's a bit far-fetched?'

'Difficult to say. If it is Wang Lei then presumably they are not aware of his death and most certainly don't know of his visit to Troyes and the auction. They have little of real substance to work on unless someone fills in some of the gaps.'

'Are you suggesting Bob that the 'someone' should be us?'

"Um, that's the big question. Should we really get involved with this?' Bob paused for a moment bereft of any ideas. 'Damn those scissors! Why couldn't Ceccaroli's ancestors have stayed in Italy instead of messing about with sewing wedding dresses and carving the initials of my grandparents on to the scissors as a wedding present? If only they had known what chain of events they had set in motion.'

'What does Gisèle think?'

Bob passed the phone to his wife and switched on loudspeaker mode. *'Bonsoir Clotilde. Ça va?* What a story, yes. The scissors are now back in Ricardo's family. Wang Lei is dead, Alice is dead and Eric is dead. Perhaps there is no reason to continue with the story.'

Bob interrupted. 'You forgot to mention that Colin, Alice's first husband is also dead. Don't you think that we owe it to them all to affect closure or are we all blaming the scissors for a series of unrelated events that should be simply put down as chance or coincidence. Aren't we imbibing the scissors with supernatural, superstitious powers that had we lived in the 16th century would probably have sent us to be burned at the stake or drowned on the ducking stool? Aren't we all guilty of irrationality? Let's bide our time. There's absolutely no point in a knee-jerk reaction. Sorry, Clotilde that translates as a *reaction impulsive* or maybe *réflexe inné* Another one for your collection of colourful English expressions.'

Gisèle kicked her husband on the shins. 'Don't you ever stop being the teacher?'

Clotilde just laughed. 'So, Bob are you saying that we do nothing?'

'For the time being, yes. We could go to Mediascan and tell them about the auction but that wouldn't necessarily prove a link to their story. Your research, Clotilde, proved that Wang Lei was a scientist looking into the transmission of diseases between animals and humans and a spare time collector of European cutlery– that's more concrete and could help the investigation.'

'What would you do Clotilde?' Gisèle interrupted .

'C'est très difficile mais....... possibly give *Mediascan* what we already know and leave the rest to their ingenuity. After all they have plenty of experience in the field of cover ups.'

Laughing Bob added, 'yes, they could go and talk to the miserable secretary at *Brunhes & Poitou*. Best of luck to them. Can't see them getting anything out of her if my experience is anything to go by.'

'What on earth did she ever do to you? That's the second time you've mentioned her. She must have made a big impression. Was she attractive?'

'You must be joking! Had the charm of a viper! Oops shouldn't have said that. Forget I spoke. If there is any real substance to *Mediascan's* investigation then presumably knowledge is dangerous. By telling what we know potentially puts us at risk. If Wang Lei is really the Chinese '*lanceur d'alerte*' or 'whistle blower' then we've colluded in putting this whole issue at the feet of the Chinese and possibly creating a major international row.'

'Isn't that a bit of an exaggeration, Bob.' Gisèle always considered that her husband sometimes was given to overdramatising situations. '*Mediascan* would hardly want to involve us. They'd want to keep all the credit for the disclosure to themselves surely.'

Clotilde agreed. Let's just tell *Mediascan* what we know. No danger in that. Tell them about seeing 'the suit' at the auction. How I had quite by chance come across his death notice in an Asian collectors' journal. How you had a vague recollection of his name being mentioned by Ricardo Ceccaroli. All straightforward. We then 'by chance' happen to watch Baleine's chat show and put two and two together.'

'And get 5!' Bob cynically jested. 'Ok, so we spill the beans. Do we tell Hervé and Stephen? What about Ceccaroli?'

'Spill the beans?' laughed Clotilde. 'What are you saying?'

'Sorry Clotilde, another of my husband's colourful phrases. He means, '*faire des révélations,*' '*dévoiler un secret.*' Spill the beans. Should we tell all we know to *Mediascan*?'

'Yes, I think it would be for the best but for the moment let's leave the others out of it. We can tell them later.'

Yes, perhaps. I'm not one hundred percent sure but I'll go along with that. Will you contact *Mediascan*, Clotilde? You'll sound more convincing than me.'

'Yes, that will not be a problem. I'll use the museum as an excuse for giving the details. After all it was me who discovered the Wang Lei link.'

'That would be great,' replied Bob. 'Just be careful and stick to the facts. No need to mention names and by the way don't forget that this year happens to be the Chinese year of the snake!'

Chapter Thirty

One Week Later

Open letter to the Minister of Foreign Affairs. Quai d'Orsay, Paris.

High level cover-up of lethal Chinese bug?

New Revelations.

16th August. Jacques Le Breton - Mediascan

Cher Monsieur le Ministre,

Several new leads have come to light concerning the alleged visit to The French Foreign Ministry of a Chinese researcher working in the field of animal/human cross over viruses. My source who wishes to remain anonymous has indicated that someone fitting this person's profile was believed to have spent some time in the North-eastern French town of Troyes in early May. He was seen at an auction house in the town bidding for a rare pair of Italian embroidery scissors. Apparently, the Chinese researcher in question has an interest in metal artefacts and cutting tools. My source who has a professional interest in the field of European cutlery tells me that when checking the background of the bidder at the Troyes auction he was named as Professor Yong Wang Lei of the University of Huazhong. His specialism is Animal and veterinary Epidemiology.

I contacted the auction house of *Brunhes & Poitou* in Troyes but they were unable or unwilling to disclose the identity of any of their clients. The Institute Pasteur in Paris did, however, reveal that in May they had received a Chinese researcher by the name of Wang Lei who was collaborating on a research project.

Professor Wang has been a senior member of the local branch of The Peoples' Communist Party for several years. The English language professional cutlery collector's Asia magazine, 'Sharp Ends' ran his obituary recently. It seems that he died of heart failure at a local Party meeting sometime between the end of May and middle of June.

So far requests for information from the University of Huazhong have not been met.

The Ministry of Foreign Affairs in Paris have said they know nothing of Professor Wang's existence.

Monsieur le Ministre isn't it time that you told us the full facts behind Wang Lei's visit? What information did he give you and why is there a possible coverup? The French people and the free world have a right to know if the Peoples' Republic of China pose a threat to Taiwan and Hong Kong or indeed the rest of the World.

Our investigations are continuing and we will

keep you up to date with
any further developments.

Gisèle switched off the computer screen. Bob stood up with
a grunt of satisfaction. 'Well, Clotilde seems to have done a
decent job there. Stuck to the facts and remained discrete.
Perhaps a bit over dramatized but that's journalists for you –
always looking to create a buzz. I wonder what *Mediascan's*
next move will be?'

'Your guess is as good as mine. Keep asking questions.
That's their job. Perhaps now would be a suitable time to
send the *Mediascan* web link to Stephen, Hervé and Ricardo.
I don't imagine they've seen it.'

'Yes, of course,' Bob agreed. 'I suspect that none of them
will be thrilled. Stephen and Hervé both want to put this
whole business behind them. The latest developments will
open up a lot of old wounds but nevertheless I think we're
honour bound to keep them up to date. As for Ricardo I
suspect that this news will come as a bit of a blow. He has
always retained a little bit of old-fashioned Catholic
superstition and his father did warn him if you remember.'

'Yes, he said that scissors never did anyone any good. I guess
that this latest news may make him think. Did Ricardo know

Wang Lei? According to Clotilde collectors keep a close eye on one another and follow the sales with great interest.'

'Yes,' Bob replied. 'I vaguely remember Ricardo mentioning his name to me when we were looking at his collection but it didn't really register at the time. He was talking about a Chinese collector who was the only one likely to outbid him at the auction. It was only later when Clotilde told me about his death that I recalled his presence at the auction. He was the man I rather unkindly referred to as 'The Suit.' I don't think that Ricardo and Wang had ever met face to face. I got the impression that most of Ricardo's bidding at auctions was done via the telephone.'

'You know, 'Gisèle ventured. 'I suggest we forget the scissors. That maybe your concern but we're losing sight of the real issue here which is the use or misuse of Chinese soft power that one way or another could lead to a major catastrophe.'

In the middle of an Italian lake someone else's thoughts were far away from forgetting the scissors. Ricardo had received Bob's message and was checking out the *Mediascan* report. Sitting at his desk overlooking the lake he read with growing anxiety. He had never met Wang Lei but his reputation amongst collectors world-wide was second to none, never for a moment had Ricardo considered that there was another professional side to the man, a side that hinted at someone who probably innocently had walked into a trap of his own making and seemingly paid the ultimate price. Ricardo was deeply shocked. His natural superstitious nature led him into wondering whether somehow the scissors were to blame. After all wasn't it his grandfather who had forged the blades and serpent handles in Maniago and wasn't it his grandfather who had carved the initials in the backroom of his house in Northern England and wasn't it he himself who had reclaimed those same scissors a century later?

He considered the recent conversations he'd had since being hospitalised. Rosa's stark reminders of Allesandro's words of warning, her horror at the sight of the scissors and her disgust at his obsession with touching and stroking them. Cardinal Abramo's spiritual lecture on accumulating earthly treasures and Doctor Cattaneo saying it was never too late to change his lifestyle, maybe retire, find a wife. Bob's story of the scissors, the tragic deaths that seemed to follow the scissors as well as his obvious relief in no longer owning them. The story had deeply affected him at the time but he'd dismissed any negative thoughts, after all hadn't he established a valuable collection of artefacts that anyone would be justly proud of? However, wasn't it Rosa who had once asked him with whom he shared his passion? He had thought long and hard about that one and realised hardly anyone. What a waste.

He stood up and walked to the door. Opening the door he shouted downstairs. 'Rosa, Rosa, can you please come up for a moment?' Winston knowingly wagged his tail and barked.

Hervé had just come in after his regular morning inspection of the vines. It was a glorious summer morning with a hot sun shining down from a cloudless sky and a light southerly breeze floating in from the Mediterranean. The grapes were beginning to turn and the *vendange* couldn't be far off. Stephen had gone to Narbonne for a meeting at the printers and to collect the publicity flyers. He would be having lunch later with his new girlfriend before heading home. Hervé made himself a strong espresso and switched on his laptop. He opened his mailbox to find the usual plethora of messages, most of them spam. Hervé had come late into computer technology and although a fast learner he still hankered after the 'snail mail' days when opening the batch of morning mail was a leisurely process starting with a gentle walk to the end of the garden, unlocking the mailbox, finding a couple of handwritten personal letters, or several bills which could wait until the end of the month for payment, and some local publicity which he would bin straight away. Anything marked 'urgent' meant that he had at least an entire day before his reply would make it into the local post office where it would lie for several hours before collection. Now he knew that 90 percent of his e-mails would be trash, unwanted publicity for cheap hotels, dating agencies, retirement homes or thermal underwear. Out of all these a few might demand his immediate attention. This morning most of the mails were from students looking for seasonal work or advertising blurb for wine production equipment but one message caught his eye. It was a message from Bob under the rubric of '*this might interest you!*' He hadn't seen Bob since the day of the auction when they'd driven over to the museum in Nogent. He clicked open the message.

Five minutes later he leaned back in his swivel desk chair, rubbed his eyes and drained the dregs of his espresso. He re-read Bob's message and wondered whether it was a joke – the famed English sense of humour! He didn't think that Bob had a sick sense of humour.

He tried to picture the auction room and recall the Chinese bidder. He'd been sitting near the front and stood out in his immaculate suit and neatly groomed black hair. The bidding war had been intense and he recalled being distracted by the realisation that the guy behind him might be Bob, or someone who certainly closely resembled Bob. Moments later as the bidding was concluded it was Bob himself who came over and introduced himself. By then the Chinese bidder had left and the auctioneer moved on to the final lots. They'd left the salon and gone looking for a bar. They gave no further thought to 'the suit.' He remembered Bob's shock when told of the death of Alice.

In the intervening time, Bob had kept them up to date on his and Gisèle's visit to Ceccaroli's island and Ricardo's subsequent mystery illness. Ceccaroli was just a name to them and although Hervé and Stephen were interested in the news concerning the new owner of the scissors they were more than preoccupied with their business project and determined that it should prove worthy of Alice's memory. The death of the Chinese collector, Wang Lei seemed to have more serious implications if *Mediascan*'s story proved to be true.

Since their meeting at the cutlery museum Hervé and Stephen had received the proceeds from the sale of the scissors and immediately donated the sum to the poison research centre in Angers. The centre was delighted and wanted to send a local TV news team down to interview them. Hervé and Stephen diplomatically declined their chance of publicity but one of the local papers ran a story under the headline, *'Cadeau d'adieu de femme empoisonné.'* 'Poisoned woman's parting Gift.' They couldn't help but wonder what Alice herself would have made of it all. Could she possibly regret ever meeting Bob? Surely that thought was ascribing too much importance to the scissors. The scissors had always been on the periphery of the action. The major players were people, human beings playing the roles that fate had dealt them. Pure and simple chance, nothing more.

The blame game? Hervé had suspected for some time now that Stephen wanted to find a scapegoat for his mother's death. Bob had been the obvious candidate. It was he who had 'loaned' the scissors to Alice so if Bob and the scissors had never existed his mother would still be alive today – possibly ran Stephen's unspoken argument. Hervé was a pragmatist brought up in the solid French tradition of Cartesian thinking. He believed in what René Descartes himself had said that perception was not dependable and only deduction could arrive at the truth. Deduction told him that Alice was responsible for all her own actions and therefore all subsequent consequences were also down to her. He wondered what Stephen would make of the latest news on Wang Lei.

Stephen arrived back from Narbonne in the early afternoon. Hervé showed him Bob's message.

Stephen shrugged and sighed deeply. 'So, are those damned scissors never going to leave us in peace? It really does seem that they are cursed. What other explanation can there be? Whoever crosses the path of the wretched things ends up in trouble. Just look at the facts, Hervé. Both my parents die with the scissors directly or indirectly implicated. Along comes the Italian industrialist who buys them for his collection and then a few days later falls seriously ill, now Bob is telling us that this Chinese collector is not what he seems and he gets bumped off by the Chinese Communists for warning the world via the French government of an impending catastrophe. Can it get any worse?'

Stephen needed to vent his anger and frustration and Hervé was happy to let the storm blow itself out.

'Not forgetting the history of the scissors before they came into the hands of my mother. Bob tries to play the innocent party in all this but the story always comes back to him. Now he's stirring up the *Mediascan* scandal and to what end? Does he want to pin the blame on someone else so as to expunge his own guilt. The bloody things belonged to his family when all is said and done. Why couldn't they have stayed there for god's sake?'

Hervé had foreseen the argument fermenting in Stephen's mind for several months and he had hoped that eventually reason would take control.

'Look at the whole thing objectively, Stephen. Bob is not trying to stir things up. Be reasonable, think rationally. He promised to keep us up to date with events and that is exactly what he is doing. Wang Lei's connection with the scissors is extremely tenuous. He may have touched them at the auction, that is all. The Italian apparently caught a bug from swimming in the lake and sorry to say but Alice, your mum and my wife died doing what she loved – gathering wild-flowers in the *garrigue*. What else do you cut flowers with other than a pair of scissors?'

Stephen looked hard at Hervé. 'Reason, bloody reason. Is that all you French people can think about. I thought that all you 'Frenchies' were hot blooded Latins. Full of passion and righteous indignation.' Beating his fists on the table he shook his head and stormed off slamming the door behind him.

Seconds later he was back. 'You don't see it do you? She was cutting the flowers with the scissors that belonged to the man she loved.'

Chapter Thirty-One

End of August

The family were in the garden taking afternoon tea their plates piled high with Gisèle's cherry *Clafouti* topped off with a generous helping of *Chantilly* cream. George was playing on the lawn with his box of Disney characters absorbed in some improbable make believe scenario involving Snow White, Bambi and Buzz Lightyear. His parents, Charlie and Jim had flown down the previous Saturday and the three of them would be returning together to the UK from Bergerac the following morning.

The Summer holidays had gone well. Little George had taken his first flight alone and Bob and his wife had picked him up at Orly. They had booked a triple room at Disneyland Paris and planned a couple of days exploring the theme park. An exhausting schedule cramming in as many of the attractions as possible. Bob was a little sceptical about the project. He wasn't a great fan of theme parks but as Gisèle pointed out it was for George not them. It's easy to be a little cynical about theme parks but as Bob and Gisèle found out for themselves, adults end up enjoying it as much as the kids. For George the highlights were having a 'selfie' taken with Darth Vador and watching the afternoon parade of the Disney characters on Main Street.

Charlie and Jim flew down to Bergerac to join the rest of the family for a few days on the lovely Ile de Ré. Great beaches, superb weather and delicious food but George was insistent that he would rather be back at Disneyland.

The summer weather had continued in the same vein, hot sunny days and clammy nights. Now as August was winding down the days were getting shorter and sitting outside in the evening was more pleasant and a light jumper was *de rigueur*.

'More *Clafouti* anyone?' Gisèle's *Clafouti* was unbeatable and there were no refusals as second helpings did the rounds. Jim called to George to come and grab his portion before it had all gone but George was more absorbed in his games of fantasy.

Moments later there was a cry of alarm from somewhere at the bottom end of the garden. Bob and Jim ran to investigate. George was standing with his mouth open, a surprised look in his eyes. 'A snake, I've just seen a snake, a slippery slimy, slivery snake.' He pointed in the direction of the long grass. Bob shuddered at the thought. He knew 'the little buggers' were there somewhere.

'Are you sure? Not your imagination running wild again?' asked his father.

'Yes, certainly,' Bob chipped in somewhat uncertainly. I'm sure there are no snakes here. Just your imagination.'

George was having none of that. 'It was a snake, I tell you. It was sort of black and greeny colour and about this long.'

He held out his arms practically as wide as they would go. It was beautiful!'

'Beautiful?' said his father.

'Beautiful!' repeated Bob. 'I thought you didn't like snakes. When we were in that museum and you saw those scissors with the snake handles and the................' Bob let the sentence hang, now wasn't an appropriate moment to get onto that subject.

George laughed. 'That's funny Pop. I was a little baby then. Now I'm a big boy. Mummy says that I'm a big boy. I am a big boy aren't I mummy?'

'Of course you are my darling.' Charlie replied eyes wide in mock surprise.

'And big boys are not afraid of snakes are they mummy?'

'No, big boys are most definitely not afraid of snakes.'

Bob was speculating on whether the 'gift' of seeing snakes had been passed on to the next generation when Gisèle laughed aloud and unable to resist the opportunity shouted to her husband.

'No, big boys are most certainly not afraid of snakes, are they Pop?'

'Most certainly not! What a thought! Anyone for another cup of tea?'

✂

Early the next morning and George is finishing off his butter croissant and singing between mouthfuls to the tune of 'Three Blind Mice.'

Cut, cut, cut

Cut, cut, cut

Keep your thumbs up!

Keep your thumbs up!

Carry on moving along the line.

Hold on to your paper, you'll be just fine,

Open and shut along with the rhyme and you'll cut, cut cut.

'Wow! What a lovely song. Did you learn that at school?

'Yes, it's called 'The Cutting Song.' We sing that when using the scissors.'

You've got a good voice young man and a good memory for words.' Interrupted Bob. 'Are you going to be a singer when you grow up?'

'No, I want to work in a zoo and look after the crocodiles and snakes. Daddy says I remember too much. Do you remember the scissors Pop? The ones with a 'K' and a 'T' on the handles? I remember them in the museum. Do you think they are still there?'

'Um, that's a very good question. I'm not really sure.'

'But you remember or you don't remember? Mummy says that people lose their memories when they get old. Are you losing yours Pop?'

To Bob's relief the conversation was interrupted by Charlie and Jim.

'C'mon young man. Let's hit the road,' said Jim. 'Give Nan and Pop a big kiss and say, thank-you for a lovely holiday.'

✂

When everyone had gone he was left with a sinking, hollow feeling which he knew would last a couple of days. A sort of melancholia. The house would be so quiet with just the two of them alone again. They had waved until the hire-car had disappeared round the corner at the end of the lane. He squeezed his wife's hand.

'Thanks for all the hard work, *Cherie*. Wonderful cooking as always and thanks for putting up with my family – it can't be easy.'

'No, don't say that. They're my family now, anyway we'll be catching up with what's left of my family at Christmas and you know how much you enjoy that!'

Bob smiled at the thought of the hectic Provençal Christmas, struggling to keep up with the animated conversation of a roomful of Gisèle's family, prattling on about politics in Provençal patois, the relative merits of shellfish and drinking too much pastis, to say nothing about the obligatory eating of each of the thirteen traditional Provençal desserts, from marzipan stuffed dates, figs and chocolate logs to nougat, nuts, candied melon and olive flat bread. By comparison Christmas in England was a walk in the park.

Bob switched on his computer. He had been too busy to check his mails for several days and now was as good a time as any and it would help ease his melancholic mood. As he waited for the machine to boot up he smiled at George's reflections on old age and memory – out of the mouths of babes and sucklings. The wisdom of the young. In Provençe children are expected to name all the thirteen Christmas desserts from memory. If George could remember the scissors then certainly he would remember the desserts. Imagine him remembering his Great, Great Grandparents' initials. Amazing - and why on earth should he ask if the scissors were still in the museum? Bob had not considered it important to explain the present whereabouts of the scissors. Why bother?

A moment or two later and his neurones were re-energised as he opened his e-mails.

Gisèle arrived with a cup of coffee and sat down next to her husband.

'What's new?'

'An e-mail from Clotilde. Just checking her message – bear with me a moment. She's written entirely in French. Can you do the translation, you're quicker than me and understand better the subtleties of your language?'

'Hm, that English *faux charme encore*. Just admit it you're just too lazy.' His wife leaned on his shoulder and read the message.

'She says that she has had some remarkable news that she's just bursting to share with everyone. Apparently, Ricardo Ceccaroli has been in touch with the museum and told them that he wishes to donate unconditionally his entire collection of cutting implements including the scissors. He has instructed his lawyers to draw up the necessary papers and hopes that the transaction can be completed before the end of the year.'

'You're joking!' Bob interjected. 'What on earth has made him arrive at that decision? He's a resolute collector. Those artefacts are worth a fortune, they're the love of his life. They mean everything to him. What will he do without his collection?'

'Just wait a moment. Don't be so impatient. She goes on to say that Ricardo has reached that conclusion due to recent developments. I guess that she's referring to the *Mediascan* investigation. She thinks that he has a superstitious streak and after his recent illness he doesn't want to tempt providence! He has organised a meeting with the museum directors and asked Clotilde to reserve him a room for two nights in a local hotel. She says that she will send us more details after the meeting.'

'Well, is this the closure that we've all been waiting for? The end of the scissor saga. Perhaps it would have been better if Ricardo had thrown them into the depths of Lake Maggiore.'

Bob was beginning to show signs of irritation and frustration at this new turn of events and he too was wondering who was responsible for this sorry state of affairs. He found it difficult to accept his own responsibility in the whole sordid business and he couldn't stop thinking of Alice's role. As much as he hated to admit it he considered that Alice had innocently played a few games with his emotions but was she as innocent as all that? Borrowing the scissors in the first place by none too subtle persuasion and then years later again by none too subtle persuasion persuading Bob to throw the scissors down the well only to retrieve them secretly moments later. Was Alice as innocent as he thought? She always knew that one kiss would have him fairly and squarely under her spell.

'Come off it Bob. You're just feeling a bit down today. If the scissors are going back to the museum then surely that is closure itself. Stop trying to find someone to blame. Call it fate, chance or purely and simply our old friend coincidence. From what I recall hadn't Alice herself said goodbye to the scissors when she had passed them on to a neighbour to eventually sell at a Normandy *brocante*?'

'Yes, and look who found them again and eventually took them back to dear Alice? Bravehearted Bob who would do anything for a kiss from a beautiful woman. Forget coincidence – try damned compliance.'

For a moment Bob wondered why in his life he always remembered the first kiss and not the first sex.

'So, here I am. Your beautiful wife. Kiss me bravehearted husband, kiss me as if it was for the last time.'

Ingrid Bergman's lines from *'Casablanca'* made Bob smile. It was after all their favourite movie. They knew the script backwards. He reached up and kissed Gisèle. 'Here's looking at you kid.'

✂

Several days later and both Bob and his wife were back into their usual routine. Bob had started teaching again and Gisèle was experimenting with some new dessert ideas. Her latest creation was a *Paris Brest* infused with rum soaked raisins. Tonight Bob was going to be the guinea pig for the new creation. He'd picked up a dozen *Oléron* oysters from the *poissonerie* in Sarlat which he was now busy shucking at the garden table, a job he'd once detested until stopping one evening outside a fish restaurant and watching the technique of a sous chef. He could now manage a dozen in five minutes.

He had just finished the last one when his phone rang. It was Hervé in Béziers.

'Hi, Hervé. Lovely surprise! How are you? It's been a long time.'

'I'm fine thanks. Sorry not to have been in touch but life down at the vineyard has been a little crazy recently and there has been no time for any socialising what with the preparation for our first *vendange* and getting the business up and running. Anyway, how is your wife, Gisèle isn't it?'

'She's fine and how about Stephen? Is he well?'

'Hardly ever see him these days. He's very involved with the cooperative and the marketing side of the business plus a new girlfriend from Narbonne. She's called Tilly and believe it or not she has a passion for flowers. Hope he has struck lucky this time – he has been going through a rough time recently what with him still finding it difficult to come to terms with the loss of Alice and the *Mediascan* business.'

'You mean the scissors are still haunting him?'

'Yes, he just feels that the scissors won't go away. He felt that the bequest to the snake venom centre would put the whole business to rest and then with the news of Wang Lei's death it seems to have started over again. A lot of it is in his own mind but nevertheless it is real to him. I hope that if he can start a new life with Tilly and with the development of the business things will change. Let's hope so. I'm quietly dreading the next *Mediascan* report in case things take a further turn for the worse. What do you think, Bob?'

'Difficult to say. What is sure is that once these journalists get their teeth into something they never let go. At least Clotilde has played her cards close to her chest and kept all the 'tin-hat' conspirators at bay and not mentioned the scissors or us for that matter. Let's hope it stays that way.'

'Fingers crossed; I just feel that we're sitting on a 'time bomb' here. The sooner it's diffused the better.'

Agreed. Anyhow what's new at the *Domaine des Tournesols*? Preparing to crack open the first vintage I hope.'

'Well, not exactly but that is the main reason for me calling. The first bottles won't be ready for opening until next year but we are planning a 'Grand Opening' of the wine shop for the beginning of October – exact date not fixed yet - and we're hoping that you and Gisèle will be here to celebrate with us.'

'Wow! That sounds great Hervé. Wouldn't miss that for the world. You bet we will be there. Is there anything we can do to help?'

'Well as a matter of fact there is. You don't suppose that you can persuade your dear wife whom I have yet to meet, to create something special by way of a dessert for the occasion do you? Perhaps a cake? There will be about twenty to thirty guests and I guess they will all have what you English delightfully call 'a sweet tooth.''

'No problem, Hervé. I'm sure she will be delighted. A fanciful French creation with tasteful decoration.'

'No snakes or scissors – promise?'

'Promise. No snakes or scissors.'

✄

'I'll come up with a few ideas, something tasteful yet symbolic,' Gisèle had already begun to think about the cake for Hervé and Stephen's 'Grand Opening.' 'I imagine that most of the guests will be French so none of your English vulgarity, I'm talking about real cream, real 75 percent dark chocolate, none of your milk chocolate muck or over-sweetened icing sugar and heavy-handed dose of alcohol. Anyway, you've eaten all the *Paris Brest* without comment. Not impressed?'

The Oléron oysters had gone down a treat and the bottle of *Pouilly Fumé* was already half-empty. Bob reasoned that Friday night wasn't the time for counting alcohol units. As for the *Paris Brest* Bob always considered himself a dessert man and Gisèle knew that his verdict was worth more than the opinion of half a dozen celebrity *patisserie* chefs.

'The meringue is delicious, just the right consistency and not too sweet but the rum-soaked raisins dominate too much – perhaps a little less rum? Maybe if I try a second helping I can give a better assessment.'

'No chance. It has all gone. Are all Englishmen so greedy?'

'Not greedy. We just know what we like. Now, how about some music. I feel that a little of Mozart's optimism would go down well with a glass of *Armagnac* and a cigar.'

Gisèle switched on her laptop and scrolled down her classical playlists.

'So, let's have a little of Mozart's 37th symphony or should I say Haydn's 25th. You do know that Mozart plagiarised Haydn's work don't you?'

''Good composers borrow, Great ones steal.' Wasn't it Stravinsky who allegedly said that?' Bob was pleased with himself for remembering that. He liked catching out singers and composers who used melodies and themes from other sources. He was convinced that since the end of the 1980's there was nothing new in popular music and that everything was derivative. On classical music, however he secretly bowed to his wife's superior knowledge.

'I thought that it was Picasso. 'Good artists copy, great artists steal.' Anyhow I think that Gore Vidal's 'Plagiarism is creativity by other means' is more succinct don't you?' Gisèle was sure that this would spark off Bob's combativity. She wasn't wrong.

'You know *Cherie*, that is so controversial. Why is it that when someone plagiarises a written document it practically merits the death sentence whilst a musician seems to literally get away with anything on the grounds of 'transformative imitation' – copying something and improving on it. Look at the organ section of Saint-Saën's third symphony, a straight copy from Wagner or Chuck Berry's 'Sweet Little Sixteen and 'Surfin' USA' by The Beach Boys. Not forgetting George Harrison's 'My Sweet Lord.''

Gisèle fought back. 'I seem to remember that in the case of Harrison he went to court and lost. 'My Sweet Lord' was practically an exact copy of an American popular song. I can't recall the title. Do you remember the case?'

'Yes, it was 'The Chiffons' 'He's so Fine.' Well remembered but coincidence,' Bob replied. 'Didn't Harrison argue that the song must have been in his sub-conscious? We hear a song, a piece of music and years later we reproduce it accidently, by chance or dare I say it coincidently?'

'Hm, back to our old friend again. Handel apparently even rifled through his own works and according to one musicologist 'changed pebbles into diamonds'[5]Nice one, no?' smiled Gisèle.

'Like to know what Bob Dylan would make of that. He seems to have spent his whole career making diamonds. I think he would prefer to call it drawing inspiration from traditional sources. One man's plagiarism is another man's light bulb moment. Don't even get me on to John Williams.'

'Guitarist or composer?'

'I'll leave you to guess but listen to 'Star Wars' and Gustave Holst and oh just a final thought jazz musicians do it all the time only they call it improvisation.'

---

[5] A History of Baroque Music. George Buelow. Indiana University Press (2004)

'That reminds me. *Je passe du coq à l'âne.* Discovered something unusual a while ago – might interest you.'

'Wow, how I love that expression. *Passer du coq à l'âne.* A great excuse to change the subject – to pass from the cock to the donkey. So you're bored with my thoughts on plagiarism?'

'No, not at all *Cherie* but I forgot to tell you. Do you remember when we were in Stresa and I said that one day I'd tell you my spoon story?'

'Oh, of course your spoon story. I wondered how long it would be before you got back to that. How could I forget to remind you? Go on fire away.'

'I was in Corina's house back in January; you know the woman who lives with Gunter the cheese maker. Anyway, she'd asked me to give a hand with her *Lasagne,* she was having problems with the *béchamel* sauce. Well, after sorting her sauce out I helped her load up the dishwasher with the dirty pans and plates. I picked up a rather large decorative serving spoon and noticed that on the back of the spoon were the initials 'K' and 'T.' Remembering the initials on the scissors I asked her if she knew anything of the origin of the spoon. Apparently, the spoon was part of a set handed down by her husband's German family and that it was made by a German cutlery firm called *Kohl* and *Thiems* hence the 'K' and 'T.' Fascinating, no? Coincidence?'

'Why are you telling me this?'

'Just to show you that coincidences are happening all the time. It's part of the structure of the world. For some reason or other 'stuff happens' as you English are fond of saying. There is a finite number of ways in which musical notes can be arranged, just as there is a finite number of ways in which initials can be arranged. Eventually, if you wait long enough or search hard enough, you'll find repetition. QED?'

Bob recalled the conversation he had had with Alice in Carcassonne on the same theme a few years ago. Alice, Bob and the scissors finding themselves together again after 60 years.

'Makes you wonder doesn't it? Yes, I guess you're right. I'm off to bed. Are you coming?'

'You have a project?' replied Gisèle throwing a cushion in her husband's face.'

Chapter Thirty-Two

Second Week of September

The latest news from *Mediascan* deepened the mystery and was hardly reassuring. Bob had been eagerly awaiting the new edition but could hardly have predicted the latest steps in the inquiry. The University of Huazhong had still not replied to the journalist's enquiry concerning Wang Lei's research or indeed his death but an anonymous leader of a student dissident group had contacted the journal with what appeared at first sight to be the outrageous claim that Wang Lei had been 'liquidated' for disclosing details of his research to a Western government. A sceptical Jacques le Breton had contacted a trusted Hong Kong journalist and persuaded him to make contact with the dissidents in Huazhong. Much to his surprise the story seems to have been verified by the Hong Kong journalist who had set up a clandestine meeting with a student from the epidemiology department at the Chinese university. The student had given a detailed and apparently expert account of the research programme. According to the report Wang Lei was researching what is known as *'bat virome'* which is the name given to the group of viruses linked to bats. He was trying to establish whether any of the viruses are *'zoonotic'* meaning they could be transferred from animals to humans. His interest seemed to be largely theoretical and academic but when his research was passed on to authorities outside the university it became evident that his work could potentially lead to the production of a viral weapon. Wang had realised for some time that his work could prove to be scientifically and politically sensitive if it fell into the wrong hands. As an active member of his local communist cell he seemingly got wind of his research being hijacked by superiors intent on misusing the findings. For some reason Wang had been called to a special conference in Beijing to discuss his findings and it was after this meeting that the Professor decided that he had a moral and scientific responsibility to guard against the possible misuse of his research.

At this point *Mediascan* are unclear as to what followed but Le Breton has speculated without concrete evidence that Wang had contacted someone at the French embassy in Beijing who set up a meeting with a senior official in Paris. He had used his interest in European cutlery and cutting artefacts as a pretext for travelling to France. Sources seem to be certain that Wang did contact an un-named 'Senior Official' in The Foreign Ministry after attending several meetings with scientific colleagues in The Institute Pasteur. So far a ministry spokesperson has continued to ridicule any suggestions by the press of any conspiracy or 'cover-up' of possible scientific criminality. They claim that 'Mediascan' are 'struggling to make a story without evidence.'

As to the reported death of Wang Lei nothing is conclusive. The dissident student group are pushing their theory of premeditative murder by communist party officials on the grounds that the scientist had betrayed 'The Party' and his country. Another line of argument suggests the possibility that Wang died as a result of his experiments on *zoonotic* viruses although most scientific opinion suggests that anyone working in this field would be aware of the dangers of contamination and take all necessary preventative steps.

Bob having looked at all the evidence increasingly begins to see the plausibility of a Chinese plot against former British colony Hong Kong and an errant Taiwan. So far President Le Pen has avoided any commentary on the subject.

He poured himself another whisky and sat back. He'd never been politically active, considered himself a moderate, centre right voter always putting his cross in the box next to whoever he thought could do the least damage. International politics was a game played by others and he considered that his vote could do little to change events elsewhere in the world whether it be Beijing, Moscow or Valparaiso. As for Europe he was committed to a romantic ideal of borderless frontiers, frictionless movement, common currency, free-trade and cultural exchange for all. BREXIT had put paid to those dreams in the country of his birth. A cultural, political and economic catastrophe brought about by corrupt, power-seeking popularist politicians plying their lies through a 'tame,' largely right-wing tabloid press feeding the prejudices of a largely badly educated and unthinking populous. Somewhat cruelly he called them 'The Great Unwashed' but it was the nearest expression that encapsulated the anger he felt. The words Turkey and Christmas sprung to mind! He'd taken French nationality to put himself back in the game, reclaim his right to vote and go through the European gate at the airport but he knew in his heart that he would always be English.

'So, what's new?' Gisèle came and sat on the arm of his chair. 'Not still obsessing about those darned scissors?'

Bob explained the latest news from *Mediascan*.

'So you're still feeling guilty about your role with the scissors, is that it? A diplomatic spat invented by an investigative journalist wanting to make a name for himself with unproven theories implicating an unpopular French government and a detested foreign regime and somehow you feel responsible. When is my darling husband going to see that his cursed embroidery scissors have absolutely nothing to do with this story or so-called investigation? It's all coincidence, Bob, don't you see? What do you really imagine is going to come out of all this? China declaring war on France?'

'No, possibly worse than that.'

'C'mon, what could be worse than war?'

'I don't know but no good is going to come out of all this. I'm sure.'

'For goodness sake, Bob, stop being so dismal. You're always criticising the French for being so miserable and now you're doing a passable impression of my compatriots. Where is that famous English phlegm and stiff upper lip? Always look on the right side of life.'

'Bright.'

'Pardon.'

'Always look on the bright side of life. It's a song. Monty Python. 'Life of Brian.''

Gisèle chose to ignore her husband's correction and decided to take another route. 'Haven't you checked out the BBC or CNN to see if they've picked up on the story. Surely if the implications are as serious as 'Mediascan' are suggesting then the mainstream media would be on to it?'

'BBC Radio 4 was down this morning. Suspect someone pulled the plug because they'd gone more than half an hour without mentioning 'climate,' 'gender identity, 'harassment' or 'slavery.' The inquisition starts here. Are you, or have you ever been a member of The Benny Hill Fan Club?'

'Oh yes, I remember him. Very funny man, always chasing the girls and slapping that little bald man on the head. Extremely popular in France.'

'Right on, *Cherie*. He finished his life on the *Côte d'Azur* – didn't dare go back to *Blighty* for fear of being lynched.'

'You Anglo-Saxons are really a strange lot. What ever happened to your famed sense of humour?'

'Good question. Probably buried alongside Sid James and Les Dawson.'

'Who?'

'Oh, just a couple of very funny comedians from way back. Benny Hill crossed the cultural channel because he was essentially visual like Chaplin, Marcel Marceau, Jacques

Tati or more recently Mr. Bean. Sid and Les would have got lost in translation.'

'Hm, whatever.' Gisèle thought for a moment recollecting with a chuckle the image of bowler hatted 'Charlo' disappearing into the horizon twirling his cane. Suddenly she remembered that she had forgotten to tell her husband about the invitation.

'Oh, nearly forgot. Something to cheer you up. Look what came in the post this morning. *Une très jolie carte d'invitation.* Hervé's and Stephen's official invitation.' Gisèle picked an envelope from the bookshelf and passed it to her husband. Bob smiled in recognition at the glorious photo.

'A field of radiant sunflowers can only mean one thing.' Bob opened the card with anticipation. As expected it was the invitation to the opening of Hervé's and Stephen's new venture in Béziers. He read aloud,

'Domaine des Tournesols' Grand Ouverture. Stephen and Hervé have the pleasure of inviting Gisèle and Bob Martin to a ' Toujours debout' evening on Saturday 15th October.

'Toujours debout.' Gisèle frowned at her husband. 'I hope that doesn't mean we'll be expected to drink a lot. My capacity is very limited you know.'

Bob looked puzzled for a moment and then it came to him. 'No, nothing like that *Cherie*. Translated into English it means 'still on my feet.' I think it's an obtuse reference to one of Alice's favourite songs, *'A Case of You'* by Joni Mitchell.'

'I could drink a case of you darling, and I would still be on my feet.' For a moment Bob was by the side of the fountain back in Carcassonne.

'How very romantic,' Interrupted Gisèle. 'Yes, I remember some of that song in French.'

'Oh, tu es dans mon sang comme du vin sacré,

Tu as un goût si amer et si doux,

Oh, je pourrais boire une caisse de toi, chérie

Et je serais toujours debout.'

'Bravo! Beautiful song. I'm not so sure that I don't prefer the French words. Did you know that it was written for Graham Nash or maybe Leonard Cohen? Probably a lovers' tiff. Come to think of it I'm not really sure but it's still a great song. The bitter-sweet taste of love. She must have sung it to Stephen or Hervé. *'Toujours debout.'* I guess she would have liked that.'

'A good excuse for a new outfit.' Gisèle enthused. 'Something flowery or vinicultural – it will still be quite warm in Béziers by the middle of October. Do you think we will know any of the others? Didn't Hervé say there would be about twenty guests?'

'Um, not sure. I presume they have a lot of new friends in the cooperative, neighbours and so on. I guess Clotilde will have been invited and certainly some of Stephen's colleagues from the business school but apart from that I've really no idea. I'm sure it will be a big surprise. Have you had any ideas for the cake by the way?'

'Well, one or two but I'm keeping them secret for the moment. I want it to be a surprise.'

'I will wait with bated breath or salivating chops. Take your pick. In the mean-time I must get in touch with Clotilde and see what she thinks about the latest developments in the Professor Wang business.'

Chapter Thirty-Three

Second Week of October

The spokeswoman for '*Meteo France*' had promised 'a golden October' and as Bob and Gisèle travelled along the pretty country lanes of the Dordogne department it was evident that the forecast had been accurate. Most of the grapes had been picked and now the farmers were busy harvesting the fields of golden maize.

They'd decided to avoid the autoroute. The journey to Béziers would only take about 4 hours and they had all day ahead of them to enjoy the Autumn sunshine. As usual Bob was thinking of his stomach.

'How about stopping for lunch at that pretty restaurant in Millau. You know the one with the lovely terrace overlooking the river Tarn and that fantastic viaduct? Seem to remember they did a superb *Roquefort Quiche* and what was the name of that delicious potato purée that I couldn't get enough of?'

'You must mean the *Aligot*. A purée made from potatoes and *Tome* cheese. Don't forget we'll need to have an appetite for this evening and I don't want you falling asleep at the wheel and destroying my *pièce de résistance* dessert. I hope you secured it carefully in the back, a lot of work has gone into that.'

'So, your cake now takes precedence over your darling husband. Don't worry it's carefully wedged between our suitcases and the spare wheel. Perhaps you're right and we'd better forsake the *Aligot* for a 'Big Mac.''

'You have to be joking, of course. From the sublime to the ridiculous. I'll compromise and settle for the quiche with just ONE glass of white wine – how does that suit you? By the way did you manage to talk to Clotilde? You said you were going to give her a call?'

'No, I spoke to her assistant at the museum and she said that Clotilde was taking a few days leave. I assume she'll be there tonight but it's strange that she hasn't been in touch. Obviously a woman not to be underestimated, hidden depths!'

'What on earth are you suggesting, Bob?'

'She just seems like a woman who usually gets what she wants. Determined, independent, intelligent and beautiful. Never married I wonder why?'

'Obviously not found the right man and won't settle for anything but the best! I'm guessing of course having never met her but from what you've told me you were certainly impressed. I'm sure my darling husband wouldn't say no to a *cinq-à-sept* with *Mademoiselle* Clotilde.'

'What on earth are you suggesting *Cherie*. I'm a happily married man and anyway I don't finish work until seven. How about some music? What about some Ravel?'

'There you go changing the subject again. No harm in admitting that you find her attractive. Anyway, you don't have to restrict yourself to that time of the day – *cinq-à-sept* is just an expression for what you English like to crudely call 'a bit on the side'............. Yes, Ravel but only if it's his waltz but first can we listen to the latest news on *France Inter*?'

Bob swiped the radio channel selector to '*France Inter*' feeling slightly guilty that he'd ever given the impression of 'fancying' Clotilde Estampe. Privately he had to admit that he'd always had a penchant for women with ponytails and glasses.

They both listened intently to the latest news, an eclectic mixture of the best and worst of French culture with a bit of world news tacked on to the end before the weather forecast. Street demos in Paris, drug busts in Marseille, defeat for PSG in the French Cup, new novel from Michel Houellebecq, retrospective rock album from Johnny Hallyday.

'What is it about you French and street demonstrations? You're always at it. What's wrong with a Saturday afternoon down the pub and an evening feet up in front of the television? For goodness sake you're a democracy. You elect a president; you elect a government and as soon as they're in power you take to the streets to complain. What is it with you people?'

Gisèle chose to ignore her husband's rant, she'd heard it all before. She was listening intently to the end of the news. 'Shut up for a moment Bob. Did you hear that last item of news?'

Bob turned up the sound but the news reader was already on to the weather forecast. 'No, didn't catch it, something interesting?'

'Well, didn't catch it all but it seems that there's been several unexplained sudden deaths at a Chinese University research Lab and a group of similar but as yet unrelated deaths in the Taiwanese capital of Taipei. Wouldn't it be a weird coincidence if ....'

Bob cut his wife off in mid-sentence. 'Don't even go there *Cherie*. It's me who normally has the 'coincidence bug.' Lie back and think of Ravel.' He swiped to Ravel's waltz on the console and upped the volume.

Lunch in Millau was a disappointment. The Quiche was no longer on the menu and the *Aligot* was cold. Gisèle sent it back to be re-heated but the flavour was still insipid. The glass of chilled *Côtes de Millau* and the *Créme Caramel* could only partly redeem the meal.

'Doesn't it always happen?' remarked Bob after paying the bill. 'Second visits to restaurants that impressed first time round are invariably disappointing. We never seem to learn our lesson.'

'Not always true,' replied his wife. I can think of several restaurants that we've visited on more than one occasion and never been disappointed. Think of that place in Bergerac with the delicious sole. Always good. I suspect that sometimes our memory exaggerates first impressions so that we build up our expectations for a second visit.'

'At least the viaduct was still there. The view of the bridge and the River Tarn was spectacular and I suppose that makes the restaurant worth a visit. Have seen the viaduct several times from all directions and never tire of it. Bet you didn't know that it was designed by an English architect, and is reputedly the tallest bridge in the world? One of the great engineering feats of the early 21st Century.'

'Do stop it Bob! Everyone in France knows the architect was Englishman Norman Foster and the structure has become one of our National Treasures. One of the most beautiful bridges in the world in one of the most beautiful regions of one of the most beautiful countries in the world. If you want one more stunning fact you may or may not like to know that my ex, Raymond crossed the two middle towers over the River Tarn on a slack line just before the bridge opened in 2004.'

'I can't follow that. Were you there?' It wasn't often that Gisèle spoke of her husband and Bob was always keen to garner some more information on his illustrious predecessor.'

'No, in fact. I didn't know he was doing it. Many of his feats were illegal and only known to a small group of colleagues. I only knew afterwards when he telephoned. Sometimes I only learned from the newspaper or a TV report and sometimes he never told me anything.'

'So, presumably you learned to live with it?'

'You might say that. It's all in the past now. More music?' Gisèle scrolled through her playlist until she found what she was looking for. A tinkling piano, a lyrical French voice accompanied by subdued strings. Gisèle started humming the tune and then broke into the words,

'C'est en septembre,

Quand les voiliers sont dévoilés

Et que la plage tremble

Sous l'ombre.........'

Bob picked up the melody and smiling with recognition joined in,

'September morn,

We danced until the night became a brand-new day,

Two lovers playing scenes from some romantic play.'

'Gilbert Bécaud,' shouted Gisèle.

'Neil Diamond,' retorted Bob. They both laughed and in unison added the final couplet in English.

'September mornings always make me feel that way.'

'I assume that my darling husband has booked a hotel.' It was late afternoon by the time that they arrived in Béziers. Gisèle always left that side of things to Bob. She knew full well that he liked to be in control or at least wanted to give the impression of being in control. They pulled up in front of a modern charmless chain hotel.

'Is The Pope a Catholic!' Bob retorted with his usual air of English male superiority. Bob had this theory that to be successful in life you had to be able to control your environment. In practice this meant to be well-organised, conscious of possible pitfalls, 'the best laid plans of mice and men', and all that, to misquote Robert Burns. Always plan with the worst scenario in mind and then you won't be thrown off course when the worst does happen.' For Bob living in a foreign country epitomised this theory. Learn the language, understand the culture and get to know the people. What could go wrong?

'I'll go and check in while you find a parking space.' She returned moments later with a sour look on her face. 'The receptionist says that she has no record of our booking. Are you sure you booked for tonight? You have the printout of the confirmation I suppose?'

Bob delved into his jacket pocket without success and then realised that he'd probably put it into his brief case alongside his bedside reading.. 'I'm certain that I'd booked in at 'L'Auberge du Moulin.'' He slammed the car door and rummaged around in the boot eventually finding the reservation tucked into a side pocket of his briefcase.

'Do be careful of the cake box. It's very delicate. They're expecting a cake not a trifle.' Gisèle shouted knowing full well that Bob probably wasn't listening.

'Here it is. Found it!' Bob unfolded the paper and stabbing the date with his forefinger announced with indignation, 'There you go – Saturday 15th – *'Le Moulin.'* Double room, breakfast included. The receptionist must be a trainee or maybe a foreigner.'

Gisèle took the paper from Bob and scrutinised the letter heading. 'You're right, correct date, wrong hotel. We're booked in at *'Le Moulin Vert.'* This one is the *'L'Auberge du Moulin.'* The one we want is the other side of town. The receptionist said that visitors to the town often get confused by the names, particularly the English she said.'

'Don't believe you. How would she know that your husband was English?'

'I told her, of course. I said that she must excuse the mistake because my husband is an English teacher and can't read French.'

Bob glowered and stuck the car into reverse. He shot out into the road narrowly avoiding a collision with a bus. Gisèle smiled at him indulgently. 'Calm down *Cherie.* Just a little bit of French humour. You see we do have a sense of humour contrary to what you Brits think. Now do remind me again of your advice to foreigners travelling in France. Something about being in control wasn't it?'

✂

Bob flopped down on the bed. 'I think I need a siesta after all that. How was I to know that there are two hotels with *'Moulin'* in their name. After all a windmill is a windmill isn't it?'

'Only when it says it's a green one. Admit it you were wrong.'

Bob huffed and puffed for a moment before reluctantly conceding defeat.

'Anyway, was the cake box still in one piece?'

'Yes, yes. For goodness sake stop worrying. It will be fine. We're only a few kilometres from Hervé's place so as long as there are no unexpected potholes the cake should be just fine. About a ten-minute drive by my reckoning.'

'Well, I'll go and take a shower Why not check out France 24 or CNN and see if there's any more on those deaths in the Chinese laboratory?'

Bob flicked through the channels not sure what he was looking for. Whatever happened to those glorious days when you only had two channels to choose from he wondered and when the only satellite in the sky was called 'Sputnik?' How could anyone make sense of 500 channels?

He checked the list of news channels on the bedside table. CNN was into its Global Financial Report so ignoring that he went across to Sky News. Normally he had no truck with the Murdoch media but he just happened to catch the hourly news round up. Nothing new here, the usual mix of British political and Royal Family scandals, a two-minute slot of 'International News' covering an earthquake in Turkey and an Icelandic volcanic eruption followed by Spanish League football results and transfer news. Over to BBC World News where an anorak cladded journalist was walking along a wind-swept beach attempting to unravel the science of rising sea levels, coastal erosion and what the media love to call 'extreme weather events.' Climate change! Bob silently speculated why it was no longer 'man-made climate change.' Back in the studio an earnest-looking journalist was banging on about 'diversity' or was it lack of it in that Great British sport of Crown Green Bowling whilst his female colleague was wondering about the increasing incidence of sexual harassment at the supermarket check-out by the over 70-year-olds and could there be a connection?

Bob decided he didn't need a siesta after all. All this news was just too stimulating for his brain. He flicked across to French channel BFMTV always to be relied on to broadcast stories that other channels wouldn't touch either because they were too boring or too intellectually challenging for the average viewer. The 'usual suspects' were gathered around the table, the male philosopher, writer and academic, the female journalist from 'Paris Match' and the male ex-Presidential Advisor to Jacques Chirac. The French studio director was good on close-ups, warts and all and seemingly a 'technical interest' for periodic under the table shots of the female journalist's thighs.

Something on the scrolling news ticker at the foot of the screen caught Bob's eye. *'Ensuite – Mediascan révélations.'* Bob sat up on the bed his curiosity aroused by the up-coming item on the latest *Mediascan* investigation. He watched impatiently as the publicity and weather dominated the screen. A few moments later and the face of investigative journalist, Le Breton appeared. Bob opted for English sub-titles. The news anchor gave a brief background to the story explaining how *Mediascan* had unearthed information that a Chinese academic professor specialising in animal epidemiology had allegedly had secret talks with the French Government concerning the Chinese use of a virus as a possible weapon of mass destruction. The virus, it was claimed was a result of research into animal-human cross over viral transmission, the very speciality that the Professor was working on. The news anchor-man concluded his introduction by saying that the French government had denied any knowledge of such a meeting but now some more serious and very worrying news had come *Mediascan's* way. He turned to Le Breton for further explanation. In the background a picture of a lab-coated researcher was flashed up. Even without his grey suit his identity was known to Bob.

'Yes, we have known for some time that the researcher in question is Professor Yong Wang Lei and our latest information indicates that he is now dead. Only yesterday we received some new information emanating from a dissident student group loosely attached to the University of Huazhong. They claim that they have positive evidence that Yong Wang was 'liquidated' by Party agents from Beijing after having received information that he had been meeting with the French Foreign Ministry in Paris. At present we have no way of confirming this information and as you said earlier in your introduction despite frequent requests to the Foreign Ministry they have refuted and rubbished all of our allegations. This morning the offices of *Mediascan* noted press agency reports of the death of several people in the Taiwanese capital of Taipei. It is being reported that Taiwanese medical sources are expressing serious concern over the possible emergence of a new and deadly virus. In view of our earlier speculation over the possible use of a laboratory virus as a weapon against Hong Kong or Taiwan it would be wise to follow up possible links between the late Professor's work and the outbreak in Taipei. We are urging the French government yet again to confirm or deny Wang Lei's meeting with the Foreign Ministry. The University of Huazhong has not replied to any of our requests for further confirmation concerning the death of Wang Lei. However, a Taiwanese government official has confirmed the mystery deaths and we are keeping channels open for further information in the next few hours.'

The anchor thanked Le Breton and assured viewers that BFMTV would be keeping a close watch on the situation. Bob muted the channel as Gisèle stuck her towelled head around the bathroom door. 'What's the latest news, Cherie?'

Bob feigned indifference and stretching out across the bed muttering, 'nothing special, the usual madness.' He decided to keep quiet for the moment, there would be plenty of time to give Gisèle the details later.

'How about this new dress you've been keeping a secret? Do I get a private fashion parade?'

'Il faut que tu sois patient. Let me finish drying my hair.'

Ten minutes later and Gisèle made her grand entrance.

'Wow! Exclaimed Bob. Where on earth did you find that?' Gisèle did a quick twirl. 'That must have cost a fortune. Stunning, absolutely stunning.'

The dress was a deep burgundy red, buttoned up the front with small white buttons with wine glass insignia. A high-necked white collar and delicately shaded pink sleeves rounded off the ensemble.

'You like it? It's a non-too subtle nod to the great French wine industry don't you think? Red rosé and white. Saw something similar in an internet video clip publicising a wine fair in Lyon and persuaded Corina of *bechamel* sauce fame to run me up something similar. Her dress making skills put her *bechamel* in the shade. You don't think it too extravagant do you?'

'Absolutely perfect. You'll be the star of the show. Now come and give me a big kiss and tell me which tie I should wear.'

'Bob, no tie! How many times do I have to tell you to stop being so English? As for the kiss I'll take a rain check as the Americans like to say. Hurry or we'll be late.'

✂

Bob and Gisèle had taken the rough track leading from the D37 across *Le canal du Midi* and River Libron following the signs to *Domaine des Tournesols*. The pot-holed lane had Gisèle pleading with Bob to remember the cake and threatening him with the direst of consequences if anything should damage her creation.

As the sun began to sink over the mountains to the west they arrived in a small dusty carpark where several vehicles were already parked including Herve's familiar grey DS. On one side was the entrance to the vineyard, on the other a large u-shaped *mas* or farmhouse, the ochre stonework reflecting red in the setting sun. The area was surrounded by a mature bamboo plantation giving protection from the wind. By the door to the *mas* a vintage Ferguson tractor was parked with a large sign in black letters on a yellow background propped against the windscreen stating *'Bienvenue – Toujours Debout'* underneath was a large Roman *amphora* containing a single sunflower.

'Well, it looks as though we've found the right place.' Bob sounded somewhat relieved. The satnav had made too many errors in the past for him to have much confidence in the technology. He had grim memories of being lost in a Spanish mountain town at two in the morning surrounded by drunken youths. Tonight he had preferred to follow Hervé's directions. Sometimes good old-fashioned map reading skills were more dependable than a box of magic tricks on the car's dashboard.

'I guess you want me to carry the cake box.'

'You've guessed right, *Cherie*. Do be careful.'

Pushing open the heavy wooden door they entered a sombre chapel-like room with dozens of candles throwing sinister shadows against the wooden walls. There was a heady odour, a mix of ageing oak barrels and musty wine. The walls of the *cave* were lined with wine barrels and two enormous stainless-steel vats. In one corner was a high tower of crated empty bottles and industrial pallets. The walls were covered in old French advertising signs extolling the virtues of *'Ricard,' 'Dubonnet' 'Absinthe' and 'French 75.'* Ahead of them Bob and Gisèle could see brighter lights and the sound of lively French chatter. They pushed a half-opened door to be greeted by the warm smell of barbecued sausage and chicken. The room was festooned with streamers and balloons and at the far side a DJ was warming up with a 'Daft Punk' track.

Hervé was the first to see them. He came darting across the room looking like the devil incarnate in his red chef's apron and barbecue fork in hand.

'Welcome, welcome! How good it is to see you again, Bob. Do I assume that the beautiful lady hanging on to your arm is your charming wife? Delighted to meet you Madame,' He took Gisèle's hand and brushed it against his lips.

'Yes, Hervé may I present you my wife Gisèle. Gisèle, Hervé. I should explain, *Cherie*, that Hervé is well known for his expertise in flowers and wine not forgetting that he makes the meanest brandy cocktail south of the Loire.'

'You exaggerate Bob. An appreciation of the good things in life is a pre-requisite of being French. All real French people have it in their DNA. And you Madame Martin your reputation as a fine pastry cook precedes you and I can't begin to praise your exquisite dress. Wonderful and so appropriate.' Gisèle did a mock curtsey. Hervé smiled broadly at Bob. 'What a lucky man you are Bob and now I assume that the contents of the box that you are carrying will, how you say, cement your wife's reputation.'

'Please call me Gisèle. How I hate the French love of formalities. As for cementing my reputation I trust that the icing on the cake is a little softer. Perhaps you can show me where to put the cake before my dear husband drops it.'

'Yes, yes, of course. Over here on the table and then you must come and meet Stephen. He's busy making the punch.' Hervé turned to Bob and lowering his voice to a whisper said, 'he's with his new girlfriend. I think you may be impressed.'

Whilst Bob was carefully placing the cake box on a table Hervé had taken Gisèle's arm and was guiding her across the room to where Stephen was busy uncorking a wine bottle. Hervé clearly in control was chatting to Gisèle in French as if he had known her all his life. Bob shrugged. He'd grown used to the French camaraderie and instant complicity. Put two French people together and before you can say Jean-Jacques Rousseau. they'll be rattling on about politics and philosophy. Bob's French was good but he couldn't compete at that level. He beat them to where Stephen was standing and shook his hand and patted his back vigorously.

'Stephen great to see you again. How are you? What a pleasure!' Bob was mindful of Stephen's ambivalence towards him when they'd first met and the feeling that somehow Bob was responsible for the tragic death of his mother perhaps still lingered. Stephen, however, seemed genuinely pleased to see him or was it a case of English hypocrisy raising its ugly head? Bob wasn't sure.

'Bob good to see you too. Delighted that you've made it to our open evening. Here let me get you an aperitif. What do you fancy? Pastis, whiskey, port or a great glass of punch prepared by the fair hand of Tilly here.'

A petite woman probably in her 30's was busy slicing up oranges and nectarines, her long chestnut hair falling over her face. For a brief moment Bob imagined he saw a young version of Alice. She looked up, brushed her hair back over her ears and smiled at Bob.

'Tilly let me introduce you to Bob. Bob is an old friend of my Mum's. They grew up together in the North of England.'

Tilly wiped her hand on her apron and shook Bob's hand. 'Delighted to meet you. Stephen has often spoken of you.'

Her English was practically perfect and Bob couldn't resist asking. 'Congratulations on your English Tilly. Where did you learn to speak so well?'

Tilly smiled and looked at Stephen. 'Well Stephen has been a great teacher but in reality I spent a year in the UK on an *Erasmus* programme and then later I qualified as a teacher of English as a foreign language and now I work in the local Business School.'

'Good old *Erasmus* programme eh,' reflected Bob. ''*Auberge Espanol*' and all that. Sadly no more thanks to my country leaving the European Union. What an opportunity lost. Cultural and language exchanges thrown to the dogs and all to satisfy the whims of power grabbing, thieving, lying politicians. But enough of that. I would love to taste a glass of your delectable punch.'

Tilly passed Bob the glass as Gisèle and Hervé joined them at the improvised bar and. introductions were renewed. 'Is my husband boring you with his tales of English doom and gloom?' Gisèle asked Tilly with a withering sideways glance towards her husband.

'No, not at all,' she replied. 'In fact it's a pleasure to hear someone speaking their mind about the wretched business.' She passed glasses of punch to the others and then Stephen raised his glass. 'I propose a toast to Europe and here's to the day when common sense will prevail once more.'

A rousing 'Here, here! Tchin Tchin! Bravo!' from Bob and Hervé and hoots of laughter from the others who were always ready to laugh at the English and their eccentricities.

'So, if you don't mind me asking a personal question.' Gisèle turned to Tilly. 'Why are you called 'Tilly' – not a very French name?'

'Nothing very interesting I'm afraid to say. I was baptised 'Tiffany' which I always hated but my dad always called me 'Tilly' and eventually it stuck. Tiffany always sounded like someone from a Wodehouse novel or something that you might eat. So what about you, Gisèle? I understand that you are running a cookery school – sounds fascinating – tell me more.'

The room was gradually filling as others began to arrive. Gisèle and Tilly chatted away enthusiastically whilst Stephen and Hervé greeted newcomers. Bob took the opportunity to look around the room. He remembered that it had been Alice's idea to set up the farm shop. Display cases and shelving around the walls were stocked with a fascinating array of bottled olives, preserves and honey. A selection of cased wines leaning against straw bales together with bottles of various shapes and sizes filled with colourful fruit liquors - apricot and peach, raspberry and strawberry. All the produce was stamped with the ubiquitous Alice sunflower trademark. On the walls hung baskets of dried herbs and flowers, Provençal prints, a large watercolour of Carcassonne, prints of Van Gogh's sunflowers, Monet's water lilies, flowers from Klimt and Warhol. One picture that caught Bob's eye was Matisse's 'The Fall of Icarus.' Presumably Alice had seen the symbolism in this work. Icarus flying too near the sun but had Alice known that this piece of art represented the beginning of a new phase in the artist's life? For the first time he had used a pair of scissors to create art. Bob smiled wryly to himself and hoped that she had recognised the irony or perhaps the coincidence.

In the spaces between the pictures and shelving Alice's love of literature manifested itself with succinct quotes from some of her favourite writers. Hugo, Shakespeare, Stendhal, Austen, Balzac. One in particular stood out bearing what Bob considered to be the hallmark of Alice's sensuality and sensibility. It really encapsulated everything he wanted to remember her by.

Every kiss provokes another. Oh, in those earliest days of love how naturally the kisses spring to life! So closely, in their profusion, do they crowd together that lovers would find it as hard to count the kisses exchanged in an hour as to count the flowers in a meadow in May.

Marcel Proust

Bob was still lost in his thoughts when he heard a familiar voice. 'Bob, what are you doing hiding away in a corner?'

He turned to see what on first appearances was an unfamiliar figure but paradoxically recognisable. Practically unrecognisable. Gone was the signature ponytail and glasses, no cardigan and pearls today. Her hair hung loose and she was wearing a low-cut white blouse and a pair of Levis which accentuated her figure in a way that Bob had never noticed before.

'Clotilde! How wonderful! I thought you'd disappeared off the face of the earth, what on earth have you been doing? When I rang the museum your secretary told me that you'd taken a short holiday. Somewhere exotic no doubt.'

'Well, you might say that. Two weeks in The Maldives in fact – absolutely wonderful. Best of all it was, how do you say my *'lune de miel?'*"

'You were on honeymoon! Fantastic, congratulations!' Bob warmly kissed her on both cheeks. 'And who is the lucky man?'

Gisèle came across the room beaming, followed none other by Ricardo Ceccaroli. 'Bob, you'll never believe this.

You've just been talking to the new Signora Ceccaroli. Ricardo and Clotilde are now as you English like to say, 'an item.''

Ricardo overwhelmed emotionally as only an Italian can clutched Bob in the most expansive and generous of hugs before replicating the gesture with Gisèle.

'Bob and Gisèle, I never thought we would meet again. How can I possibly express my pleasure after all that has happened since we last met? This is like a dream come true for me, no amount of money could buy me this pleasure, The Milan stock market doesn't trade in happiness shares. You like that Bob? You see I have a good memory for what you taught me.' He laughed with full throated vigour, clutching Clotilde, Bob and Gisèle in something resembling a sporting huddle.

Bob shook his head in disbelief and taking Ricardo and his new wife by the hand called over to Tilly to bring over some drinks. 'Your best champagne please Tilly or perhaps I should say your best *Prosecco* for our Italian friend.' He was curious to know how they had got together but that would have to wait.

Stephen and Hervé came across eager to meet Ricardo for the first time and shake his hand. The other invited guests, the cooperative workers, neighbouring *vignerons*, a couple of dignitaries from the local Town Hall and a provincial journalist were crowding around eager to find out what was going on. Gisèle decided that it was time she made herself useful and present her *piéce de resistance*. She slipped a message to the DJ.

The cake was splendid they all agreed. Gisèle had done her homework with intricate icing reliefs depicting Cezanne's Mont Victoire, the Chateau of Carcassonne and striking through the middle a bright yellow sunflower. Emblems that she knew would resonate with Stephen and Hervé. The DJ played Chakia Bleu's *'Sunflower of my dreams.'* As the music faded a round of applause rippled through the gathering as Stephen called for quiet and took a microphone from the DJ.

'Thanks, I'm going to be extremely brief otherwise I will embarrass myself. First of all, thanks Gisèle for this wonderful cake. For someone who never met my mother you've certainly depicted the symbolism and symbiotic relationship between her and the sunflower. The sunflower certainly encapsulated everything about mum both spiritually and materially expressing happiness, vitality, love, beauty and freedom. Alice was always seeking out the light just as the sunflower itself turns its head to follow the sun. What you see around you is not her memorial it's her creation, a creation that will evolve and expand helped by the love and friendship of those gathered here who knew her well. Thanks to all of you for your presence here tonight and now I know Hervé would like to say a few words.'

Hervé took the micro somewhat tentatively. 'Some of you in this room tonight have known Alice for far longer than I. I know Bob will not need me to remind him that he knew Alice when she was just a teenage girl and is perhaps one of the few people who knows her full story in all its shades of light and dark.' He paused for a moment. ' *'Toujours Debout.'* Those delightful words from one of Alice's favourite songs. Alice had a song for every occasion but this was the one that she sang most particularly when she was working with her flower arrangements. You'll forgive me if I recite the words. I have never aspired to being an Aznavour or Trenet.' He cleared his throat and launched into Joni Mitchel's lyrics.

'I remember that time you told me
You said, "Love is touching souls"
Surely you touched mine
'Cause part of you pours out of me
In these lines from time to time

Oh, you're in my blood like holy wine
You taste so bitter and so sweet
Oh, I could drink a case of you, darling
And I would still be on my feet
Oh, I would still be on my feet.'

Hervé paused gathering his emotions. The room fell silent.

'She once told me half-jokingly that she had started singing the song to relieve the monotony of standing up for several hours when she worked on a Normandy market. It was then that she adopted the sunflower as a sort of personal trademark. The flower was always tucked into the top of her green gardener's apron.' He continued in French.

'Oh, je pourrais boire une caisse de toi, chérie
Et je serais toujours debout
Oh, je serais toujours debout.'

Hervé raised his glass. 'A toast to Alice. *'Toujours debout.''*
'Toujours debout ! Toujours debout!' The words rang out
across the room.

✂

'So, how you say – I traded my collection for a wife. The
collection now belongs to the museum.' Ricardo was holding
the floor as the others intrigued by Clotilde's marriage
announcement listened eagerly. Clotilde herself looked a
little sheepish and was doubtless hoping that her new
husband wouldn't say anything too indiscrete. 'You know,'
he continued, 'tonight is the first time that I have the pleasure
of meeting some of you. I know we are here tonight to
celebrate Alice, a woman I never had the pleasure of
meeting. Without doubt she was extraordinary. I am not
important. I am just an interloper on this occasion but if I
may say so my beautiful wife and I found each other because
of a pair of scissors. A pair of scissors which as some of you
know have a very unfortunate history but it was the best
business deal I ever made.'

Stephen was the first to react. 'Maybe this now marks the
end of the unfortunate history of the scissors. Perhaps now
they can do no more damage. A museum is the best place for

them. Hopefully future generations of visitors will stay ignorant of their colourful history and just appreciate them for what they are. A fine piece of Italian craftsmanship.'

Clotilde looked across at Bob and Ricardo saying, 'Without Bob and my husband's distant families none of this would have been possible. If I may be so bold as to say that in my opinion no one here should feel any sense of guilt over the saga. What has happened has happened. Call it chance, superstition or coincidence. There are some things in life which can never be explained and perhaps never should be. Clearly there are some loved ones who should be here tonight but paradoxically without the scissors none of us would be here.'

'A real *conte de fée.*' Said Gisèle. I hope that like all fairy stories this one has a happy ending. To Clotilde and Ricardo, a long and happy marriage.'

The toast echoed around the room. The DJ managed to come up with a couple of Puccini arias. Ricardo jumped up and began singing *'Nessun Dorma'* whilst doing a passable Pavarotti impression of wiping his brow with a silk handkerchief. The other guests good naturedly groaned and shouted for something in French. 'Piaf, Piaf, Piaf,' several demanded as Clotilde, Gisèle and Tilly launched into an impromptu rendering of *'No, je ne regrette rien.'*

The evening passed agreeably. Bob found himself in deep discussion with a couple of the cooperative workers on the future of wine production in the Languedoc region. For some years Bob had found the local red wines to his liking. Never too expensive and invariably suited to his taste. Bob wondered why the regional wines had not made a bigger impact on the international market. Apparently much of it, he was told was down to marketing. The French traditionally hadn't marketed their wines as aggressively as say the Australians or the Americans but now that was changing as on-line advertising enabled *vignerons* to reach new markets. Simple things like the design of the label or even the name made such a difference and very importantly, not too cheap. The market in many Western countries is maturing. Gone are the days when people would rush to buy a *'Vin de Table'* for a few centimes. People like to feel that if they spend a few euros extra they're getting quality. Not forgetting the Chinese who can't get enough of the stuff. They're even buying up whole Bordelais vineyards. As for the Anglo-Saxons they like to buy their everyday drinking wine by grape variety. A bottle of *Merlot, Shiraz* or a case of *Chardonnay* was easier on the tongue than some small appellation tucked away in the middle of rural France. From what they were saying it seemed that the local cooperative was expecting great things from the new *'Domaine des Tournesols'* with the wine due to come on to the market next year. Stephen and Hervé had made a good impression on the long-established vignerons in the area and with their hard work and commitment to quality had somewhat shaken up their potential competitors.

The local mayor, Tricolour sash draped around his shoulder just to remind people who he was came and joined in the conversation. *'Ah les Chinois. Pas de scrupules et pas de goût, sauf pour l'argent. Regardez ce qui s'est passé aujourd'hui. Plusieurs morts à cause d'un virus échappé. Vous verrez qu'ils deviendront les maîtres du monde.'*

The others nodded sagely leaving Bob wondering what really was going on in China. The earlier report of deaths in Taipei had unsettled him and he was eager to get the latest from *Mediascan.*'

Clotilde was busy tasting Gisèle's 'sunflower cake.'

'How on earth do you get the sponge so light? My cakes invariably fall through the bottom of the oven!'

'You know, Clotilde there is no secret. It's just that I can't explain. It's sort of intuitive. Put it down to experience or maybe it's a gift I don't know.........but enough of my cake tell me about your romance with Ricardo. How on earth did you become Madame Ceccaroli? Was that intuition or a simple twist of fate?'

'Like your cake recipe it's hard to explain. It just happened. We had exchanged e-mails several times before the auction in Troyes. He wanted to know more about the scissors and even suggested that I might visit him in Stresa. I've been working in the museum for 20 years and got used to the flattery and charms of our visitors but I began to feel that with Ricardo it was different. Unfortunately, I always had the impression that he was wedded to his collection and his relationship with me was purely professional. Then shortly after I discovered he had been taken ill I spoke to Bob. Bob told me of your trip to visit Ricardo and of you discovering later that he was seriously ill in a Milanese hospital. I remember speculating with Bob on the phone that Ricardo's illness might somehow be related to the death of the Chinese Professor Wang Lei. It was a couple of weeks later I learned that Ricardo was recovering. I thought little more of it but the story of the scissors increasingly fascinated me. Then suddenly I had a call from Ricardo. He was back home but planning to visit the museum with a professional proposition. We'd booked him in at a local hotel for a couple of nights. The day he arrived we met at the museum together with Monsieur Roulot the founder of the museum. Ricardo came straight to the point. He wanted to donate his whole collection of cutlery including the scissors to the museum. He had brought a portfolio with him containing photographs and details of his collection of some 300 objects. The value was inestimable. He suggested we dined together the same evening to go over the details.' Clotilde smiled in fond recollection before disclosing in a whisper, 'and you can guess the rest.'

'So, why had Ricardo reached this momentous life changing decision?' Gisèle had failed to notice Ricardo and Bob had come over to join them.

Ricardo kissed his wife on the cheek proclaiming, 'feminine complicity don't you see Bob. Now we have no more secrets. The rabbit is out of the bag.'

'Perhaps it would be better to let the cat out of the bag, Ricardo.'

'*Alora!* Cats, dogs, rabbits whatever! I have made the biggest and best decision of my entire life. After my time in the hospital, it was difficult, not sure whether I was going to live or die. I talked to many friends some good some bad. You never know who your real friends are but when I arrived back home I made the decision myself. What good could my collection do if I was dead huh? Give the collection away, retire from the company and marry a beautiful woman. There is no happier man in the whole of Italy today.'

'What about Rosa?' asked Bob. 'What does she think of it all?'

'Ah, Rosa, God bless her. She has wanted me to get rid of the collection for years. When I bought the scissors she was sure it was a bad sign. Italian women of a certain age can be very superstitious you know. She is very happy for me and Clotilde. At present she is back on the island with my faithful Winston preparing the house for our return.'

'So, Clotilde, are you giving up your work at the museum,' asked a slightly concerned Gisèle always conscious of her role as a self-proclaimed protector of female freedoms.

'Certainly not.' Replied Clotilde with exaggerated astonishment. 'The museum will need me to organise the additions to our collection. Ricardo and I have discussed the situation in detail. We plan to buy a house near to the museum where we will live for several months of the year and the museum trustees have agreed that Ricardo will become an unpaid consultant and unofficial guide. His expertise in the cutlery business is perhaps second only to

Jean-Marie Roulot and it will be a great step forward in putting the museum on the map.'

'And the house on the Borromean Island? You're not going to leave Rosa all alone in that mansion?'

Ricardo slapped his thigh and laughing turned to his wife. 'What about Rosa *mio amore*? Surprise our friends with her little secret.'

Clotilde hesitated obviously wanting to choose her words carefully. 'Rosa and Tommaso, *Il postino,* the postman, have been very close for some time and it seems that she may be taking in a *locataire.* Ricardo has known about her little trips across the water to Stresa for some time so we thought why not make it official and solve several problems at the same time?'

'Rosa taking the postman in as a lodger! Well, that is a surprise. You seem to have really fallen on your feet.' Laughed Bob.

'Fallen on the feet! What is this strange English expression, Bob? I hope that is something good.'

'Well, think of a cat Ricardo. When a cat falls from a height it always lands ....'

'In a bag? Let the cat out of the bag?' Ricardo proposed.

'No,on his feet,' cried Clotilde and Gisèle in unison.

'I fall on my feet. That's good Bob, very good.' For additional effect he turned to his wife and repeated, 'we have fallen on our feet *mio amore*. I think we must employ Bob as our permanent English teacher what do you think Bob?'

Bob laughed and picking up his glass wandered over to where Stephen and Tilly were serving drinks.

'What will it be this time Bob? Another glass of our delicious punch or something stronger. Got a nice little *Armagnac* we picked up in Marciac last year when we were visiting the jazz festival.'

'Sounds great. So, you manage to get over to the Marciac festival then. It's an ambition of mine but never seem to get round to making reservations.'

Tilly passed Bob a generous measure of Armagnac 'Honestly I wouldn't bother if I were you. Used to be good when it started small thirty or so years ago but now it's gone the way of all these cult festivals. Booked for Stacey Kent and Carlos Santana. Stacey Kent is a talented artist in a small venue but put her in a large arena and she's very ordinary, all you do is watch the large video screens. You Tube is cheaper!. Santana is a legend but when you're surrounded by ten thousand alcohol or drug crazed fans shouting and screaming you wonder what you paid your money for.'

'Atmosphere, honey, atmosphere,' interrupted Stephen, 'and being able to say that you've seen one of the legends of rock music.'

Bob sipped his drink and agreed that it was an excellent *Armagnac*. Momentarily he thought it might be an appropriate moment to mention the latest news from China. Aware of Stephen's sensitivity towards him and the scissors he thought better of it. However, Stephen seemed to have an agenda of his own and excusing himself from Tilly's company suggested that he and Bob have a brief private conversation.

Bob was a little wary of where this conversation might lead particularly as both had consumed a moderate amount of alcohol. He wasn't in the mood for any arguments.

He needn't have worried. Stephen had a surprising proposition. Bob's first reaction was disbelief but when Stephen finished and said, 'both Hervé and I think that you're the right person. You were especially important to Alice.' He felt he had little choice but to accept.

'So, tomorrow morning about 10 here at the *mas*?'

Bob nodded in agreement but still unsure as to whether he really was the best person for the task that Stephen and Hervé had in mind.

✂

By the time the evening was winding down, Bob was feeling a little worse for the wear. After his discussion with Stephen he'd had another large *Armagnac* and Ricardo insisted they finish off the evening with a round of dry martinis and several toasts to whoever happened to be in close proximity.

They parted with much back slapping, kissing and *ciao ciaoing*. Ricardo invited everyone to the island 'the next time you're near to Lake Maggiore' whilst Clotilde in a more sober state reminded everyone to get over to Nogent for the opening of the new cutlery collection sometime next year. Stephen and Hervé thanked everyone and hoped that they'd all be back next year for the first tasting of the *Domaine des Tournesols*.

'Don't forget tomorrow at 10.' Hervé shouted to Bob as they made their way back to the car.

'I think you'd better do the driving *Cherie.'* Slurred Bob as he passed the keys to Gisèle. It's all been a little too much for me.'

'You'll never learn. Why can't the English hold their alcohol? How often have I told you that mixing drinks is a route to disaster? Punch, champagne, *Armagnac*, dry martini. Really Bob! I despair. And what are you arranging for tomorrow morning? You'll be fit for nothing. Don't forget that you promised to take me to see the Cathedral of St Nazaire and lunch by the canal to see the *Fonseranes* locks.'

Bob tried his best to clearly explain Stephen and Herve's proposition. Gisèle remained impassive but hoped that the gesture might finally see the closure of the scissor saga.

Back at the hotel Bob kissed his wife before collapsing on the bed muttering 'darling you were wonderful tonight! The dress, the cake, everything. Thank-you. *Je t'aime.'*

Chapter Thirty-Four

The Next Day

'So, how's the head this morning?' Gisèle asked.

'Oh, it's fine thanks,' Bob lied. They'd slept a little longer than planned, skipped breakfast and made do with an instant coffee in the hotel room. Bob felt dehydrated but a couple of coffees and a large glass of water to wash down a paracetamol and he was feeling nearly back on track.

They arrived at the *mas* to find Stephen, Tilly and Hervé already waiting in Stephen's 1980's long wheel-based Land Rover.

'Not using the DS then Hervé?' shouted Bob. I would have thought the occasion merited a little old-fashioned French luxury.'

'Morning Bob,' replied Hervé. 'On form this morning?' He didn't wait for an answer. 'The *vieille dame* wouldn't be able to handle the rough tracks so it's back to good old British engineering. Up in the back with me and we'll leave Stephen and the ladies up front.' He opened the rear doors and in they climbed.

'So, I guess you've heard the news this morning?'

'No, what's happened? Didn't have time to switch on the TV. Slept late.'

''France Inter' had an interview with *Mediascan's* Jacques Le Breton. Seems that there's been another 20 deaths in Taipei and a report of several people from the University of Huazhong being taken seriously ill.'

'Isn't that the university where Wang Lei worked?'

'Exactly, it may be a coincidence of course. The report from the Taiwan capital seems to be reliable but there's no way of confirming the accuracy of the report from Huazhong.'

Gisèle turned her head and gave Bob an anxious glance. Neither spoke. It was Stephen negotiating the bumpy track and clutching the wheel who broke the silence.

'*Mediascan* is ramping up the pressure on the government. They must make a statement soon. The story has now been picked up by many of the other 24/7 channels and although I haven't had time to read the morning paper it seems that *Figaro* are running it on their front page and an editorial demanding a response from the Foreign Ministry.'

Bob looked out at the passing *garrigue*. It was a perfect windless Autumn morning. A thin mist still clung to the valleys and over to the east the morning sun reflected brightly over the sea. The few remaining straggly vines were turning yellow and what remained of the unpicked grapes were rapidly withering on the branches. Stephen brought the Land Rover to a halt.

'Well, here we are – everyone out.'

They stood in a circle on a bare patch of ground surrounded by sun scorched scrub. The thyme and lavender giving off that irrepressible smell that always evokes Mediterranean France.

Hervé reached under the seat and brought out a cardboard box. He opened the lid and took out a green urn. He passed it to Stephen who gently laid a kiss on the printed label before placing it in the centre of the circle.

'It's what she would have wanted Bob. I know that I've been guilty of putting the blame on your shoulders but now that I know the full story I realise how wrong I was. Mum often spoke of you with respect and affection. She once told me that it was you who created the rite of passage between Alice the child and Alice the woman and the seeds of courage that she needed for the rest of her life had been sown by you.'

They formed a circle around a clump of wild asparagus and straggly vines. Tilly took Stephen's and Hervé's hands whilst Stephen reached for the hand of Bob and Gisèle completed the circle by taking Hervé's hand. After several moments of silence Stephen looked across to Bob. Bob picked up the urn and carefully unscrewing the top let the ashes fall to the ground. Out of the morning calm a light zephyr breeze sprung up swirling the ashes towards the edge of the *garrigue*. Bob shook the urn empty and replaced the lid. He read the inscription on the side of the urn:

Alice Tara Clopé (Woods)

30 novembre 1949 – 4 mai 2019

'The Sunflower Girl'

Chapter Thirty-Five

Later the same Day

'What do you suppose will happen to them all now?' They were walking along the towpath of the *canal du midi*. Before Bob could answer, Gisèle pointed to a group of white flowers on the embankment. 'Look, *Cherie*, white *Asphodel*. What an unfortunate coincidence.' She bent down to pick one in full bloom. 'Do you think that they've finally drawn a line under all this terrible scissor business?'

Bob winced at the sight of the flower. 'I hope so, Stephen seems to have found his soul mate in Tilly and Hervé seems to have found a new lease of life with the wine business and farm shop. They're both very conscious of Alice's legacy and for the time being at least they're determined to make it work. Of course in the long run who knows. Life is never a *long fleuve tranquil* as you French are fond of saying. We can hardly describe our own lives as having been a long peaceful river and let's face it would we have wanted it any other way?'

Gisèle twisted the *asphodel* between her fingers. 'The flower of death. What a sad description of such a lovely flower. I remember you first telling me of Alice's death and how she was clutching a bunch of them when her body was found. Such a shock to think of the flower's association with the underworld and its supposed powers against snake bite. Too much to conclude it a coincidence unfortunate or not.'

She passed the flower to her husband who hesitated before taking it and pushing it down the front of his unbuttoned shirt. He stuck his hands casually in his pockets and turned to face the water as a red and white narrowboat negotiated the lock basin.

'But in his lapel, discreetly, he wore a sprig of *asphodel.*' Bob recited. A poem by Leonard Cohen. 'Do you know it? 'Satan in Westmount.' It was from a book of poetry called 'Let us compare Mythologies.''

'Never read his poetry.' Gisèle replied. 'Have listened to some of his songs but a bit too melancholic for my liking.'

✂

They continued walking until they reached the site of the 9 locks of *Fonseranes.* Gisèle had wanted to take advantage of their short stay in Béziers by visiting the World Heritage Site and had dutifully done her homework. She was curious to know what Bob's initial reaction might be.

'Wow! Amazing! What a feat of engineering. C'mon then you're obviously dying to play the tourist guide. Tell me all about it.'

Bob's sudden rush of enthusiasm visibly lightened the hitherto sombre mood of the morning.

'Well, I guess you know why it was built – a direct route connecting the Atlantic with the Med. An easier way of doing business with the Spanish without the perils of crossing the Pyrenees or fighting off pirates in the Straits of Gibraltar. It was the idea of Pierre Paul Riquet a rich local businessman and in 1666 King Louis XIV gave his approval for the plan.'

'1666?' interrupted Bob. 'A memorable year for many reasons. The bubonic Plague came to an end and The Fire of London started. No problems for the French who were more concerned with digging a canal. Sorry to interrupt *Cherie* just trying to put it all into historical perspective.'

'Thank-you teacher. May I continue? There are 8 locks but only 6 of them actually work,' continued Gisèle. 'In 1858 an aqueduct was built to cross the River Orb which resulted in the redundancy of the 2 locks. An inclined plane was also built to help boats too big for the locks to bypass them but this proved too technically difficult. Quite a project don't you think?'

Gisèle was interrupted by the ringtone from Bob's cell phone. It was Stephen. Gisèle shrugged in frustration and walked over to read a tourist information board by the lock gates.

Stephen spoke with some urgency and a discernible anxiety in his voice. 'Just been checking out '*The Figaro*' article I mentioned to you this morning. The headline runs '*La Peste*

Chinoise,' the Chinese Plague. *'Figaro'* reckons that the number of infected people has been underestimated by the Chinese. I turned up the *Mediascan* report as well. Won't bore you with the details but take a look at their website when you have a minute. There are some reports coming in that the President will make a statement later today.'

Bob thanked Stephen for the call and caught up with his wife still boning up on the canal's history.

'Bet you didn't know that Riquet sub-contracted a lot of the work to some people called the Medailhes brothers who were both illiterate. Imagine that! Also, it says here that many of the workers on the construction were women.'

'Sorry to interrupt *Cherie* but this is important. That was Stephen. Unwelcome news from the Chinese front. Apparently, *'Figaro'* are saying that the situation in Taiwan and mainland China is worse than first supposed. They're talking about a Chinese plague! *Madame La President* is due to speak later.

'Sounds a bit like a typical media exaggeration, panic headlines and unverified reports. You mentioned a short time ago the bubonic plague in London. How many died?

'Nobody's really sure, there were reports of seventy thousand deaths in London alone, fifteen percent of the population but in reality the figure could have been nearer one hundred thousand. Data collection was hardly dependable in the 17th century.'

'And the Spanish influenza epidemic in 1918?'

'Um, the one in which Ricardo's grandparents died you mean? About 50 million world-wide.'

Gisèle thought for a moment. 'The last outbreak of the bubonic plague in Europe was in Marseille in 1720. One hundred thousand deaths. The media is getting excited over less than 50 deaths on the other side of the world in the 21st century where medical science has all but eradicated *la peste*. Pure journalistic hyperbole.'

'Look there's a snack bar at the top of the locks by the information centre,' Bob pointed to the sign at the side of the path. 'Let's go and have a couple of beers, I need to sit down. All this learning is giving me a thirst. You can finish your history lesson in comfort.'

✂

'English man, *anglais*?' Replied the waiter in response to Bob ordering 2 beers. Before Bob could reply the waiter wiping the table with a rather dubious looking dishcloth continued somewhat breathlessly, 'President Le Pen! Madame la President on the radio. She says all borders must close from 6 this evening. All foreigners to report to local gendarmerie. All Chinese residents to be repatriated. *La peste, la peste!*'

Bob looked over to his wife. 'What on earth is he going on about?' Gisèle spoke to the waiter in French whilst Bob scrolled down to the latest breaking news on his i-phone. The phone simultaneously began to ring. It was Stephen again.

'Bob? It's me again. Are you keeping up to date? Le Pen's saying that national security is under threat because of the events in Taiwan. She's suspended French membership of the EU, says that France must act as a sovereign nation. Borders closed, repatriation of foreigners and mobilised the army. She's taken control of the media outlets and *Mediascan's* Paris office has been occupied by the police. Rumours that others might be implicated.'

'You must be joking. Too much pastis last night. Another social media conspiracy?'

'No, this is serious Bob. Le Pen has just been on the tele. Apparently some researcher at The Institute Pasteur has poured his heart out after revealing having met with our late friend 'The Suit.' He's now under arrest and there are rumours of him having assisted a foreign government in endangering the security and integrity of the French Republic. Plus, and this bit is even more worrying, Clotilde rang to say that she and Ricardo have been held by border police on the Italian frontier – no explanations. Ricardo apparently making a big fuss and demanding that his friends Berlusconi and the Cardinal Abramo of Milan intervene.

'But that's ridiculous. It's an affront to all French democratic values. Where's the proof and for goodness sake how are a few deaths in Taiwan going to impact on France and what the hell has Ricardo done?'

'Local reports from Italy are suggesting that Ricardo had a connection with the Chinese 'Suit'! Stephen paused and took a deep breath. 'There are also unconfirmed reports of several deaths on a Taiwanese owned vineyard in the Bordeaux region. Seems that the proprietor and his family have just returned from Taipei. Health authorities are already looking into the possibility that there might be a link. Le Pen's having a field day. It's the opportunity that she's been waiting for to impose her brand of right-wing authoritarianism on the country. All that election rhetoric about immigration is no longer just blah blah, loss of sovereignty to the EU, France for the French and all that. Happily the likes of you and I have our dual nationality which might give us some protection but would we want to stay here under what amounts to a fascist regime?'

Bob had to concede that Stephen had a point. It was a scenario that many French had been dreading for the last 20 years as inner-city tensions, so called 'culture wars' and attacks on republican values took hold. A small minority 'lunatic' fringe party growing into a populist dictatorship. A nightmare becoming reality. Bob could hardly believe that the French could be so gullible but he only had to reflect on Trump's America and Johnson's and Farage's treachery in the UK to see that it was all too plausible.

'Deliberate strategy by the Chinese?' asked Gisèle as they stood up from the table, 'or just a very careless accident?'

'Who knows? My pessimistic sides suggests that a new dark age is on its way. If all this is true I fear the worse. Not for us. We're past caring or to put it in other words too old to care. It's been on the cards for some considerable time.

Democracy has become banal, taken for granted, why bother voting – it changes nothing, politicians are all corrupt. The French fall for financial scams, the Brits for the sex. Good on you Boris! Get in there whoa! Tell them how it is Donald, we know you're lying but then don't we all!'

'No, it's our kids and grandchildren I feel sorry for. We're the last of the 'never had it so good' generation, free health care, half-decent free education, triple locked pensions, home-owners – well many of us and perhaps controversially security from any more global wars. Now look what we've got – 3 of the most powerful countries in the world being ruled by idiots and arguably the future's most powerful country ready to unleash a killer virus to gain world domination.'

Gisèle remained silent for a moment weathering Bob's storm. Eventually she reached across and took the white *asphodel* from the front of her husband's shirt.

'So you think that it's all a deliberate ploy by the Chinese?' She twisted the flower around her fingers until the sap formed a sticky patch on her hand. 'And what is our role in all this? Just innocent by-standers?' Bob didn't reply. He was still brooding on the possible motives for Ricardo's arrest.

Another thought suddenly came to Bob's mind. 'By the way, did you notice Alice's full married name on the urn? Alice Tara Clopé – any good at anagrams?'

Gisèle looked puzzled for a moment, her mind struggling to do the permutation of letters. She could make no sense of it all. She looked to Bob for help.

'Forget her first name. Concentrate on her middle and married name.'

Gisèle pronounced the letters carefully like a child learning to read an unfamiliar word. 'T.A.R.A.C.L.O.P.E. She screwed up her eyes and nose in thought for a moment before realisation hit home, '*Mon Dieu*, it's obvious. Stupid me, why didn't I see it earlier?'

'Why should you. Neither of us knew her middle name until we saw the urn. Even as teenagers I never knew. It wasn't something we ever discussed. Perhaps her parents were fans of '*Gone with the Wind.*' Remember the plantation house was called '*Tara.*''

Gisèle smiled in recognition. It was one of her favourite films but her mind suddenly changed tack as another memory came into her consciousness.

'I don't know if I have ever told you but a few years ago I briefly dabbled in Buddhism. It was when I was with Raymond. He was interested in the whole idea of contemplative meditation and focussing his mind before attempting a crossing. Seem to remember that Tara was connected with a goddess called *Janguli*. I'd have to check that out but I've got a vague idea that Tara was a sort of liberator from ignorance and more to the point famous for granting protection from poisons. Follow my thinking? Poisons – snakes – asps - viper family and of course that famous Egyptian Queen.'

Bob gave her a long, hard look. He walked a few paces towards the lock gate before speaking. 'You're not suggesting that Alice and Cleopatra are somehow connected? That would be too ridiculous for words. It's just chance, coincidence or maybe wishful thinking. You'll be telling me next that there was a Buddhist deity of scissors or a patron saint of forceps.'

'Funny you should say that. Have you ever heard about Saint Agatha of Sicily? Supposedly mutilated by a pair of scissors. *Cherie?*'

Bob was no longer listening. He had stopped to look at an information panel that explained in several languages how it was the *canal du Rhone* that completed the final link to the Mediterranean at the old fishing port of Sète. The English version described this as 'the final cut' of the undertaking. A 'cut' being a short section of canal. Bob smiled to himself muttering under his breath 'bloody coincidences.'

✄

They silently watched a pleasure cruiser negotiating the last lock and as the gates began to close Gisèle threw the *asphodel* into the churned-up waters. She wiped her hand nervously on her jeans as the flower was chopped in two by the closing gates and sucked under by the mirky maelstrom of water. Moments later on the opposite bank a convoy of military vehicles arrived. After coming to a halt a detachment of armed soldiers climbed down and headed their way.

Printed in Great Britain
by Amazon